NEW ADVENTURES IN SPACE OPERA
JONATHAN STRAHAN, EDITOR

NEW ADVENTURES IN
SPACE

OPERA

edited by JONATHAN STRAHAN

TACHYON • SAN FRANCISCO

Introduction "From New Space Opera to Here . . ." © 2023 by Jonathan Strahan
Cover art "Heavenly Spheres Number 1" by Justin Van Genderen
Interior and cover design by Elizabeth Story

Tachyon Publications LLC
1459 18th Street #139
San Francisco, CA 94107
415.285.5615
www.tachyonpublications.com
tachyon@tachyonpublications.com

Series editor: Jacob Weisman
Project editor: Jaymee Goh

Print ISBN: 978-1-61696-420-7
Digital ISBN: 978-1-61696-421-4

Printed in the United States by Versa Press, Inc.

First Edition: 2024
9 8 7 6 5 4 3 2 1

*To everyone who has ever launched a starship across
a paper universe with gratitude and thanks.*

CONTENTS

JONATHAN STRAHAN

INTRODUCTION
FROM THE NEW SPACE OPERA TO HERE . . .

Robert Silverberg identified two fundamental themes in science fiction: the journey in time and the journey in space. Space opera, he suggested, was a sub-genre of the journey in space, one that takes romantic adventure, sets it in space, and tells it on a grand scale. Many have tried to define space opera since Wilson Tucker dismissively coined the term in 1941 to refer to the "hacky, grinding, stinking, outworn, spaceship yarn," from Brian Stableford in *The Encyclopedia of Science Fiction*[1] describing space opera as "colorful action-adventure stories of interplanetary or interstellar conflict' and Jack Williamson in *The New Encyclopedia of Science Fiction*[2] referring to it as "the upbeat space adventure narrative that has become the mainspring of modern science fiction," to Norman Sprinrad amusingly (and not entirely incorrectly) calling space opera "straight fantasy in science fiction drag."

Perhaps getting closer to the feel of it, Paul McAuley in *Locus*'s special 'New Space Opera' issue referred to the "lushly romantic plots and the star-spanning empires to the light-year-spurning spaceships, construction of any one of which would have exhausted the metal reserves of a solar system, . . . stuffed full of faux-exotic color and bursting with contrived energy." Space opera is, in short, romantic adventure set in space and told on a grand scale. It must feature a starship, the most

---

[1] *The Encyclopedia of Science Fiction* (https://sf-encyclopedia.com/)

[2] *The New Encyclopedia of Science Fiction*, James E. Gunn (Viking, 1988)

important of science fiction's icons, which, as Brian Aldiss wrote in the introduction to his anthology *Space Opera*[3] in 1974 "unlocks the great bronze doors of space opera and lets mankind loose among all the other immensities." It is the tale of godlike machines, all-embracing catastrophes, the immensities of the universe, and the endlessness of time. It is also, to go back to Williamson, the "expression of the mythic theme of human expansion against an unknown and uncommonly hostile frontier."[4]

For all the riffs and variations on space opera that have been tried over the one hundred and thirty or so years since the first proto-space operas appeared in the 1890s, it has always fallen somewhere within those boundaries. I know that when I sat down to try to decide what should or should not feature in this book, I used several guides. First, a space opera should primarily take place in space, either on ship or station, and only occasionally touchdown on a planetary surface. Second, it should take place in a populated universe. When the protagonist of the story ventures forth, they must encounter someone. And, finally, the stakes should be high. The stakes could involve E.E. Doc Smith's smashing of galaxies or Aliette de Bodard's breaking of hearts, but it should feel like the world might, emotionally or physically, be about to end.

That sets our boundaries. The kinds of stories that were published as space opera—our thoughts about the empires they took place in, the nature of the starships, their composition of their crews, and the adventures that they undertake—have changed since stories like Edmond Hamilton's Interstellar Patrol yarn "Crashing Suns" appeared in *Weird Tales* in 1928. Bright, garish stories of the pulp magazine era that were driven by both a sense of techno-optimism and manifest destiny that seems, at least from the outside, to have been common in the United States in the 1930s, 1940s, and 1950s—work like E. E. "Doc" Smith's *Skylark of Space* and A. E. van Vogt's "Black Destroyer"—which would

---

[3] *Space Opera*, Brian W. Aldiss ed. (Futura, London, 1974)

[4] The response to colonialism and imperialist ideologies has occupied much of space opera over the past decades, with major works laying bare its terrible effects, deconstructing its harmful ideologies, and looking for other ways to tell stories on the space opera stage.

give way to more sophisticated, challenging work like C. L. Moore's *Judgment Night* or Alfred Bester's *The Stars My Destination*.

The 1950s was a time of change for science fiction, when the end of the pulp magazine era meant a move from primarily being a short fiction form to being published at novel length by major publishers to great success, though it would be some years later before it appeared regularly on bestseller lists. This change began as writers like Leigh Brackett, Jack Vance, and Cordwainer Smith brought new sophistication to the field in the 1950s and 1960s with enduring works of space opera, like Frank Herbert's classic bestselling *Dune* which appeared in 1965. Brian Stableford observed that by the late 1950s a number of the tropes of space opera, like the galactic-empire scenario, had become a standardized framework available for use in entirely serious science fiction. "Once this happened," he wrote, "the impression of vast scale so important to space opera was no longer the sole prerogative of straightforward adventure stories, and the day of the 'classical' space opera was done." Which didn't mean that those 'classical' space operas stopped being written or published. Most notably during the 1970s the sprawling novels of Larry Niven and Jerry Pournelle, especially the award-winning *The Mote in God's Eye*, and possibly the most popular space opera of the following decade, first appeared in Orson Scott Card's novella *Ender's Game*, but there were changes. Space opera became darker and more political. In 1975, M. John Harrison wrote *The Centauri Device*, a novel that turned the conventions of space opera on their head. It was, apparently, intended to kill space opera, or at least intended as an anti-space opera. What it was, instead, was the work that provoked others to pick up the cudgel and change things again.

By the time British magazine *Interzone* published a "call to arms" editorial looking for radical hard SF in 1982, a new generation had come along ready to do just that. First among them was Iain M. Banks, whose *Consider Phlebas* was boldly, defiantly operatic in nature and scope, and yet very much leftward leaning politically. His sequence of science fiction novels involving the "Culture" set both the critical trend and the commercial standard for space opera in the early 1980s. Unlike many of his contemporaries, Banks wrote almost exclusively at novel length.

This newer space opera, though, wasn't a technological fable from the turn of the century. By the beginning of the 1980s, when cyberpunk was emerging in the United States, it no longer seemed relevant to many writers to tell bold tales of space adventure that looked to new frontiers where a sense of manifest destiny brought "civilization" to the locals. Colonialism and the drive to build empires was becoming much less acceptable, and the universe looked a much darker place. Space opera was no longer looking to go out and take over the universe: it was looking to survive in it. This change can be seen in the work of Stephen Baxter, Paul McAuley, and even Colin Greenland. McAuley's *Quiet War* and *Jackaroo* sequences of short stories and novels, and Alastair Reynolds' *Revolution Space* short stories and novels were key works here, retaining the interstellar scale and grandeur of traditional space opera, while becoming even more scientifically rigorous and ambitious in scope.

Two critically important writers emerged in the United States during this period. C.J. Cherryh began publishing in the 1970s and hit her stride with military space opera, *Downbelow Station,* in 1981. Her Union-Alliance series of novels brought a detailed rigor from the social sciences to space opera that had rarely been seen and which would drive the major series of her career, the sprawling *Foreigner* sequence. Lois McMaster Bujold appeared on the scene in 1986 and quickly established the Miles Vorkosigan series of military space operas as some of the most important of the time with stories like "Borders of Infinity" and "The Weatherman." While novels in the sequence—*The Warrior's Apprentice, Brothers in Arms, The Vor Game* and so on—were often light in tone, they foregrounded issues to do with gender and reproduction in a way that was new and important.

In the mid-1990s Dan Simmons, Vernor Vinge, David Brin, Walter Jon Williams, Ken MacLeod, and M. John Harrison were all producing major works of space opera that were literary, challenging, dark and often disturbing, but also grand and romantic, set in space and told on an enormous stage. The 1990s saw the new space opera begin to come to the fore, but it was in the 2000s that it burst into full flower. The first major novel of the period was Alastair Reynolds' *Revelation Space*, which had been preceded by several stories in *Interzone* like "Galactic North" and would be followed by major novellas *Diamond Dogs* and *Turquoise Days*, brought a sense of dark, lived-in time to space opera. It was followed by the likes of Neal Asher's densely violent *Polity* novels, Paul McAuley's sprawling *Quiet War* sequence, Walter Jon Williams' politically engaged *Dread Empire's Fall* novels, Tobias S. Buckell's *Xenowealth* series, and work by Linda Nagata, Greg Bear, Charles Stross, Nancy Kress, Elizabeth Bear, and others.

While there was still plenty of classic space opera on the page and on the screen, this "new space opera" questioned its own underpinnings, broadened its perspective, and tried to be more defiantly engaged. It was at this time, around 2003, that I got caught up in online discussions of the new space opera, and went on to help to compile *Locus*'s special new space opera issue, and to co-edit *The New Space Opera* and *The New Space Opera 2* with Gardner Dozois which covered it. It was an exciting time.

This book, though, covers what came next. The journey that picks up in 2011 with the publication of James S. A. Corey's *Leviathan Wakes* (possibly the most popular space opera of the period), moves to Ann Leckie's ambitious *Ancillary Justice*, Yoon Ha Lee's *Ninefox Gambit*, and then to Nnedi Okorafor's *Binti*, Martha Wells' *All Systems Red*, Arkady Martine's *A Memory Called Empire* and *A Desolation Called Peace*, Tade Thompson's *Far from the Light of Heaven*, Maurice Broaddus's *Sweep of Stars*, and Emily Tesh's *Some Desperate Glory*. While space opera, and arguably science fiction itself, has always been a literature of work, this was when characters at the heart of stories began to change, to become more diverse, to question the structure of the world around them more deeply. The fascination with empire faded and its terrible impact was more deeply interrogated. This is the move from the 'new space opera' to whatever comes next. What is it? It is more open, more diverse, has different points of view to present, and powerfully and critically examines the political underpinnings of its stories, while still being everything that Silverberg, Hartwell, and Spinrad understood space opera to be.

In the 2020s the influences of the new space opera have been absorbed and space opera itself now stands somewhere between the sprawling empire of Teixcalaan and the glorious pulpy energy of *Guardians of the Galaxy*. It can be thoughtful and considered, analysing, deconstructing, and commenting upon what has come before in terms of politics, economics, race, gender, and more. It can also be garish goofy fun (a talking racoon, a face the size of a planet!). It's all still space opera, as you will see in the pages to come.

I won't go through and break down the stories you're about to read—the joy in a book like this is discovering them for the first time—but each represents some aspect of the changes I've mentioned above. All, though, are stories that I think are exciting, colorful, vibrant, and pure space opera. There are some writers and worlds I wish could be represented here but could not be for practical reasons. What is here, though, gives you a pretty good idea of where we are now and where we might be going next.

Jonathan Strahan
Perth, January 2024

TOBIAS S. BUCKELL

ZEN AND THE ART OF STARSHIP MAINTENANCE

Tobias S. Buckell is a *New York Times* Bestselling author and World Fantasy Award winner born in the Caribbean. He grew up in Grenada and spent time in the British and US Virgin Islands, which influence much of his work. His novels and almost one hundred stories have been translated into twenty different languages. His work has been nominated for awards like the Hugo, Nebula, World Fantasy, and the Astounding Award for Best New Science Fiction Author. His most recent novel is *A Stranger in the Citadel.* Buckell currently lives in Bluffton, Ohio with his wife and two daughters, where he teaches Creative Writing at Bluffton University. [www.TobiasBuckell.com]

After battle with the *Fleet of Honest Representation*, after seven hundred seconds of sheer terror and uncertainty, and after our shared triumph in the acquisition of the greatest prize seizure in three hundred years, we cautiously approached the massive black hole that Purth-Anaget orbited. The many rotating rings, filaments, and infrastructures bounded within the fields that were the entirety of our ship, *With All Sincerity,* were flush with a sense of victory and bloated with the riches we had all acquired.

Give me a ship to sail and a quasar to guide it by, billions of individual citizens of all shapes, functions, and sizes cried out in joy together on the common channels. Whether fleshy forms safe below, my fellow crab-like maintenance forms on the hulls, or even the secretive navigation minds, our myriad thoughts joined in a sense of True Shared Purpose that lingered even after the necessity of the group battle-mind.

I clung to my usual position on the hull of one of the three rotating habitat rings deep inside our shields and watched the warped event horizon shift as we fell in behind the metallic world in a trailing orbit.

A sleet of debris fell toward the event horizon of Purth-Anaget's black hole, hammering the kilometers of shields that formed an iridescent cocoon around us. The bow shock of our shields' push through the debris field danced ahead of us, the compressed wave it created becoming a hyper-aurora of shifting colors and energies that collided and compressed before they streamed past our sides.

What a joy it was to see a world again. I was happy to be outside in the dark so that as the bow shields faded, I beheld the perpetual night face of the world: it glittered with millions of fractal habitation patterns traced out across its artificial surface.

On the hull with me, a nearby friend scuttled between airlocks in a cloud of insect-sized seeing eyes. They spotted me and tapped me with a tight-beam laser for a private ping.

"Isn't this exciting?" they commented.

"Yes. But this will be the first time I don't get to travel downplanet," I beamed back.

I received a derisive snort of static on a common radio frequency from their direction. "There is nothing there that cannot be experienced right here in the Core. Waterfalls, white sand beaches, clear waters."

"But it's different down there," I said. "I love visiting planets."

"Then hurry up and let's get ready for the turnaround so we can leave this industrial shithole of a planet behind us and find a nicer one. I hate being this close to a black hole. It fucks with time dilation, and I spend all night tasting radiation and fixing broken equipment that can't handle energy discharges in the exajoule ranges. Not to mention everything damaged in the battle I have to repair."

This was true. There was work to be done.

Safe now in trailing orbit, the many traveling worlds contained within the shields that marked *With All Sincerity*'s boundaries burst into activity. Thousands of structures floating in between the rotating rings moved about, jockeying and repositioning themselves into renegotiated orbits.

Flocks of transports rose into the air, wheeling about inside the shields to then stream off ahead toward Purth-Anaget. There were trillions of citizens of the *Fleet of Honest Representation* heading for the planet now that their fleet lay captured between our shields like insects in amber.

The enemy fleet had forced us to extend energy far, far out beyond our usual limits. Great risks had been taken. But the reward had been epic, and the encounter resolved in our favor with their capture.

Purth-Anaget's current ruling paradigm followed the memetics of the One True Form, and so had opened their world to these refugees. But Purth-Anaget was not so wedded to the belief system as to pose any threat to mutual commerce, information exchange, or any of our own rights to self-determination.

Later we would begin stripping the captured prize ships of information, booby traps, and raw mass, with Purth-Anaget's shipyards moving inside of our shields to help.

I leapt out into space, spinning a simple carbon nanotube of string behind me to keep myself attached to the hull. I swung wide, twisted, and landed near a dark-energy manifold bridge that had pinged me a maintenance consult request just a few minutes back.

My eyes danced with information for a picosecond. Something shifted in the shadows between the hull's crenulations.

I jumped back. We had just fought an entire war-fleet; any number of eldritch machines could have slipped through our shields—things that snapped and clawed, ripped you apart in a femtosecond's worth of dark energy. Seekers and destroyers.

A face appeared in the dark. Skeins of invisibility and personal shielding fell away like a pricked soap bubble to reveal a bipedal figure clinging to the hull.

"You there!" it hissed at me over a tightly contained beam of data. "I am a fully bonded Shareholder and Chief Executive with command privileges of the Anabathic Ship *Helios Prime*. Help me! Do not raise an alarm."

I gaped. What was a CEO doing on our hull? Its vacuum-proof carapace had been destroyed while passing through space at high velocity, pockmarked by the violence of single atoms at indescribable speed punching through its shields. Fluids leaked out, surrounding the stow-away in a frozen mist. It must have jumped the space between ships during the battle, or maybe even after.

Protocols insisted I notify the hell out of security. But the CEO had stopped me from doing that. There was a simple hierarchy across the many ecologies of a traveling ship, and in all of them a CEO certainly trumped maintenance forms. Particularly now that we were no longer in direct conflict and the *Fleet of Honest Representation* had surrendered.

"Tell me: what is your name?" the CEO demanded.

"I gave that up a long time ago," I said. "I have an address. It should be an encrypted rider on any communication I'm single-beaming to you. Any message you direct to it will find me."

"My name is Armand," the CEO said. "And I need your help. Will you let me come to harm?"

"I will not be able to help you in a meaningful way, so my not telling security and medical assistance that you are here will likely do more harm than good. However, as you are a CEO, I have to follow your orders. I admit, I find myself rather conflicted. I believe I'm going to have to countermand your previous request."

Again, I prepared to notify security with a quick summary of my puzzling situation.

But the strange CEO again stopped me. "If you tell anyone I am here, I will surely die and you will be responsible."

I had to mull the implications of that over.

"I need your help, robot," the CEO said. "And it is your duty to render me aid."

Well, shit. That was indeed a dilemma.

Robot.

That was a Formist word. I never liked it.

I surrendered my free will to gain immortality and dissolve my fleshly constraints, so that hard acceleration would not tear at my cells and slosh my organs backward until they pulped. I did it so I could see the galaxy. That was one hundred and fifty-seven years, six months, nine days, ten hours, and—to round it out a bit—fifteen seconds ago.

Back then, you were downloaded into hyperdense pin-sized starships that hung off the edge of the speed of light, assembling what was needed on arrival via self-replicating nanomachines that you spun your mind-states off into. I'm sure there are billions of copies of my essential self scattered throughout the galaxy by this point.

Things are a little different today. More mass. Bigger engines. Bigger ships. Ships the size of small worlds. Ships that change the orbits of moons and satellites if they don't negotiate and plan their final approach carefully.

"Okay," I finally said to the CEO. "I can help you."

Armand slumped in place, relaxed now that it knew I would render the aid it had demanded.

I snagged the body with a filament lasso and pulled Armand along the hull with me.

It did not do to dwell on whether I was choosing to do this or it was the nature of my artificial nature doing the choosing for me. The constraints of my contracts, which had been negotiated when I had free will and boundaries—as well as my desires and dreams—were implacable.

Towing Armand was the price I paid to be able to look up over my shoulder to see the folding, twisting impossibility that was a black hole. It was the price I paid to grapple onto the hull of one of several three-hundred-kilometer-wide rotating rings with parks, beaches, an entire glittering city, and all the wilds outside of them.

The price I paid to sail the stars on this ship.

A century and a half of travel, from the perspective of my humble self, represented far more in regular time due to relativity. Hit the edge of lightspeed and a lot of things happened by the time you returned simply because thousands of years had passed.

In a century of me-time, spin-off civilizations rose and fell. A multiplicity of forms and intelligences evolved and went extinct. Each time I came to port, humanity's descendants had reshaped worlds and systems as needed. Each place marvelous and inventive, stunning to behold.

The galaxy had bloomed from wilderness to a teeming experiment.

I'd lost free will, but I had a choice of contracts. With a century and a half of travel tucked under my shell, hailing from a well-respected explorer lineage, I'd joined the hull repair crew with a few eyes toward seeing more worlds like Purth-Anaget before my pension vested some two hundred years from now.

Armand fluttered in and out of consciousness as I stripped away the CEO's carapace, revealing flesh and circuitry.

"This is a mess," I said. "You're damaged way beyond my repair. I can't help you in your current incarnation, but I can back you up and port you over to a reserve chassis." I hoped that would be enough and would end my obligation.

"No!" Armand's words came firm from its charred head in soundwaves, with pain apparent across its deformed features.

"Oh, come on," I protested. "I understand you're a Formist, but you're taking your belief system to a ridiculous level of commitment. Are you really going to die a final death over this?"

I'd not been in high-level diplomat circles in decades. Maybe the spread of this current meme had developed well beyond my realization. Had the followers of the One True Form been ready to lay their lives down in the battle we'd just fought with them? Like some proto-historical planetary cult?

Armand shook its head with a groan, skin flaking off in the air. "It would be an imposition to make you a party to my suicide. I apologize. I am committed to Humanity's True Form. I was born planetary. I have a real and distinct DNA lineage that I can trace to Sol. I don't want to die, my friend. In fact, it's quite the opposite. I want to preserve this body for many centuries to come. Exactly as it is."

I nodded, scanning some records and brushing up on my memeology.

Armand was something of a preservationist who believed that to copy its mind over to something else meant that it wasn't the original copy. Armand would take full advantage of all technology to augment, evolve, and adapt its body internally. But Armand would forever keep its form: that of an original human. Upgrades hidden inside itself, a mix of biology and metal, computer and neural.

That, my unwanted guest believed, made it more human than I.

I personally viewed it as a bizarre flesh-costuming fetish.

"Where am I?" Armand asked. A glazed look passed across its face. The pain medications were kicking in, my sensors reported. Maybe it would pass out, and then I could gain some time to think about my predicament.

"My cubby," I said. "I couldn't take you anywhere security would detect you."

If security found out what I was doing, my contract would likely be voided, which would prevent me from continuing to ride the hulls and see the galaxy.

Armand looked at the tiny transparent cupboards and lines of trinkets nestled carefully inside the fields they generated. I kicked through the air over to the nearest cupboard. "They're mementos," I told Armand.

"I don't understand," Armand said. "You collect nonessential mass?"

"They're mementos." I released a coral-colored mosquito-like statue into the space between us. "This is a wooden carving of a quaqeti from Moon Sibhartha."

Armand did not understand. "Your ship allows you to keep mass?"

I shivered. I had not wanted to bring Armand to this place. But what choice did I have? "No one knows. No one knows about this cubby. No one knows about the mass. I've had the mass for over eighty years and have hidden it all this time. They are my mementos."

Materialism was a planetary conceit, long since edited out of travelers. Armand understood what the mementos were but could not understand why I would collect them. Engines might be bigger in this age, but security still carefully audited essential and nonessential mass. I'd traded many favors and fudged manifests to create this tiny museum.

Armand shrugged. "I have a list of things you need to get me," it explained. "They will allow my systems to rebuild. Tell no one I am here."

I would not. Even if I had self-determination.

The stakes were just too high now.

I deorbited over Lazuli, my carapace burning hot in the thick sky contained between the rim walls of the great tertiary habitat ring. I enjoyed seeing the rivers, oceans, and great forests of the continent from above as I fell toward the ground in a fireball of reentry. It was faster, and a hell of a lot more fun, than going from subway to subway through the hull and then making my way along the surface.

Twice I adjusted my flight path to avoid great transparent cities floating in the upper sky, where they arbitraged the difference in gravity to create sugar-spun filament infrastructure.

I unfolded wings that I usually used to recharge myself near the compact sun in the middle of our ship and spiraled my way slowly down into Lazuli, my hindbrain communicating with traffic control to let me merge with the hundreds of vehicles flitting between Lazuli's spires.

After kissing ground at 45th and Starway, I scuttled among the thousands of pedestrians toward my destination a few stories deep under a memorial park. Five-story-high vertical farms sank deep toward the hull there, and semiautonomous drones with spidery legs crawled up and down the green, misted columns under precisely tuned spectrum lights.

The independent doctor-practitioner I'd come to see lived inside one of the towers with a stunning view of exotic orchids and vertical fields of lavender. It crawled down out of its ceiling perch, tubes and high-bandwidth optical nerves draped carefully around its hundreds of insectile limbs.

"Hello," it said. "It's been thirty years, hasn't it? What a pleasure. Have you come to collect the favor you're owed?"

I spread my heavy, primary arms wide. "I apologize. I should have visited for other reasons; it is rude. But I am here for the favor."

A ship was an organism, an economy, a world unto itself. Occasionally, things needed to be accomplished outside of official networks.

"Let me take a closer look at my privacy protocols," it said. "Allow me a moment, and do not be alarmed by any motion."

Vines shifted and clambered up the walls. Thorns blossomed around us. Thick bark dripped sap down the walls until the entire room around us glistened in fresh amber.

I flipped through a few different spectrums to accommodate for the loss of light.

"Understand, security will see this negative space and become . . . interested," the doctor-practitioner said to me somberly. "But you can now ask me what you could not send a message for."

I gave it the list Armand had demanded.

The doctor-practitioner shifted back. "I can give you all that feed material. The stem cells, that's easy. The picotechnology—it's registered. I can get it to you, but security will figure out you have unauthorized, unregulated picotech. Can you handle that attention?"

"Yes. Can you?"

"I will be fine." Several of the thin arms rummaged around the many cubbyholes inside the room, filling a tiny case with biohazard vials.

"Thank you," I said, with genuine gratefulness. "May I ask you a question, one that you can't look up but can use your private internal memory for?"

"Yes."

I could not risk looking up anything. Security algorithms would put two and two together. "Does the biological name Armand mean anything to you? A CEO-level person? From the *Fleet of Honest Representation*?"

The doctor-practitioner remained quiet for a moment before answering. "Yes. I have heard it. Armand was the CEO of one of the Anabathic warships captured in the battle and removed from active management after surrender. There was a hostile takeover of the management. Can I ask you a question?"

"Of course," I said.

"Are you here under free will?"

I spread my primary arms again. "It's a Core Laws issue."

"So, no. Someone will be harmed if you do not do this?"

I nodded. "Yes. My duty is clear. And I have to ask you to keep your privacy, or there is potential for harm. I have no other option."

"I will respect that. I am sorry you are in this position. You know there are places to go for guidance."

"It has not gotten to that level of concern," I told it. "Are you still, then, able to help me?"

One of the spindly arms handed me the cooled bio-safe case. "Yes. Here is everything you need. Please do consider visiting in your physical form more often than once every few decades. I enjoy entertaining, as my current vocation means I am unable to leave this room."

"Of course. Thank you," I said, relieved. "I think I'm now in your debt."

"No, we are even," my old acquaintance said. "But in the following seconds I will give you more information that *will* put you in my debt. There is something you should know about Armand . . ."

I folded my legs up underneath myself and watched nutrients as they pumped through tubes and into Armand. Raw biological feed percolated through it, and picomachinery sizzled underneath its skin. The background temperature of my cubbyhole kicked up slightly due to the sudden boost to Armand's metabolism.

Bulky, older nanotech crawled over Armand's skin like living mold. Gray filaments wrapped firmly around nutrient buckets as the medical programming assessed conditions, repaired damage, and sought out more raw material.

I glided a bit farther back out of reach. It was probably bullshit, but there were stories of medicine reaching out and grabbing whatever was nearby.

Armand shivered and opened its eyes as thousands of wriggling tubules on its neck and chest whistled, sucking in air as hard as they could.

"Security isn't here," Armand noted out loud, using meaty lips to make its words.

"You have to understand," I said in kind. "I have put both my future and the future of a good friend at risk to do this for you. Because I have little choice."

Armand closed its eyes for another long moment and the tubules stopped wriggling. It flexed and everything flaked away, a discarded cloud of a second skin. Underneath it, everything was fresh and new. "What is your friend's name?"

I pulled out a tiny vacuum to clean the air around us. "Name? It has no name. What does it need a name for?"

Armand unspooled itself from the fetal position in the air. It twisted in place to watch me drifting around. "How do you distinguish it? How do you find it?"

"It has a unique address. It is a unique mind. The thoughts and things it says—"

"It has no name," Armand snapped. "It is a copy of a past copy of a copy. A ghost injected into a form for a *purpose*."

"It's my friend," I replied, voice flat.

"How do you know?"

"Because I say so." The interrogation annoyed me. "Because I get to decide who is my friend. Because it stood by my side against the sleet of dark-matter radiation and howled into the void with me. Because I care for it. Because we have shared memories and kindnesses, and exchanged favors."

Armand shook its head. "But anything can be programmed to join you and do those things. A pet."

"Why do you care so much? It is none of your business what I call friend."

"But it *does* matter," Armand said. "Whether we are real or not matters. Look at you right now. You were forced to do something against your will. That cannot happen to me."

"Really? No True Form has ever been in a position with no real choices before? Forced to do something desperate? I have my old memories. I can remember times when I had no choice even though I had free will. But let us talk about you. Let us talk about the lack of choices you have right now."

Armand could hear something in my voice. Anger. It backed away from me, suddenly nervous. "What do you mean?"

"You threw yourself from your ship into mine, crossing fields during combat, damaging yourself almost to the point of pure dissolution. You do not sound like you were someone with many choices."

"I made the choice to leap into the vacuum myself," Armand growled.

"Why?"

The word hung in the empty air between us for a bloated second. A minor eternity. It was the fulcrum of our little debate.

"You think you know something about me," Armand said, voice suddenly low and soft. "What do you think you know, robot?"

Meat fucker. I could have said that. Instead, I said, "You were a CEO. And during the battle, when your shields began to fail, you moved all the biologicals into radiation-protected emergency shelters. Then you ordered the maintenance forms and hard-shells up to the front to repair the battle damage. You did not surrender; you put lives at risk. And then you let people die, torn apart as they struggled to repair your ship. You told them that if they failed, the biologicals down below would die."

"It was the truth."

"It was a lie! You were engaged in a battle. You went to war. You made a conscious choice to put your civilization at risk when no one had physically assaulted or threatened you."

"Our way of life was at risk."

"By people who could argue better. Your people failed at diplomacy. You failed to make a better argument. And you murdered your own."

Armand pointed at me. "I murdered *no one*. I lost maintenance machines with copies of ancient brains. That is all. That is what they were *built* for."

"Well. The sustained votes of the hostile takeover that you fled from have put out a call for your capture, including a call for your dissolution. True death, the end of your thought line—even if you made copies.

You are hated and hunted. Even here."

"You were bound to not give up my location," Armand said, alarmed.

"I didn't. I did everything in my power not to. But I am a mere maintenance form. Security here is very, very powerful. You have fifteen hours, I estimate, before security is able to model my comings and goings, discover my cubby by auditing mass transfers back a century, and then open its current sniffer files. This is not a secure location; I exist thanks to obscurity, not invisibility."

"So, I am to be caught?" Armand asked.

"I am not able to let you die. But I cannot hide you much longer."

To be sure, losing my trinkets would be a setback of a century's worth of work. My mission. But all this would go away eventually. It was important to be patient on the journey of centuries.

"I need to get to Purth-Anaget, then," Armand said. "There are followers of the True Form there. I would be sheltered and out of jurisdiction."

"This is true." I bobbed an arm.

"You will help me," Armand said.

"The fuck I will," I told it.

"If I am taken, I will die," Armand shouted. "They will kill me."

"If security catches you, our justice protocols will process you. You are not in immediate danger. The proper authority levels will put their attention to you. I can happily refuse your request."

I felt a rise of warm happiness at the thought.

Armand looked around the cubby frantically. I could hear its heartbeats rising, free of modulators and responding to unprocessed, raw chemicals. Beads of dirty sweat appeared on Armand's forehead. "If you have free will over this decision, allow me to make you an offer for your assistance."

"Oh, I doubt there is anything you can—"

"I will transfer you my full CEO share," Armand said.

My words died inside me as I stared at my unwanted guest.

A full share.

The CEO of a galactic starship oversaw the affairs of nearly a billion souls. The economy of planets passed through its accounts.

Consider the cost to build and launch such a thing: it was a fraction of the GDP of an entire planetary disk. From the boiling edges of a sun to the cold Oort clouds. The wealth, almost too staggering for an individual mind to perceive, was passed around by banking intelligences that created systems of trade throughout the galaxy, moving encrypted, raw information from point to point. Monetizing memes with pico-technological companion infrastructure apps. Raw mass trade for the galactically rich to own a fragment of something created by another mind light-years away. Or just simple tourism.

To own a share was to be richer than any single being could really imagine. I'd forgotten the godlike wealth inherent in something like the creature before me.

"If you do this," Armand told me, "you cannot reveal I was here. You cannot say anything. Or I will be revealed on Purth-Anaget, and my life will be at risk. I will not be safe unless I am to disappear."

I could feel choices tangle and roil about inside of me. "Show me," I said.

Armand closed its eyes and opened its left hand. Deeply embedded cryptography tattooed on its palm unraveled. Quantum keys disentangled, and a tiny singularity of information budded open to reveal itself to me. I blinked. I could verify it. I could *have* it.

"I have to make arrangements," I said neutrally. I spun in the air and left my cubby to spring back out into the dark where I could think.

I was going to need help.

I tumbled through the air to land on the temple grounds. There were four hundred and fifty structures there in the holy districts, all of them lined up among the boulevards of the faithful where the pedestrians could visit their preferred slice of the divine. The minds of biological and hard-shelled forms all tumbled, walked, flew, rolled, or crawled there to fully realize their higher purposes.

Each marble step underneath my carbon fiber-sheathed limbs calmed me. I walked through the cool curtains of the Halls of the Confessor and approached the Holy of Holies: a pinprick of light suspended in the air between the heavy, expensive mass of real marble columns. The light sucked me up into the air and pulled me into a tiny singularity of perception and data. All around me, levels of security veils dropped, thick and implacable. My vision blurred and taste buds watered from the acidic levels of deadness as stillness flooded up and drowned me.

I was alone.

Alone in the universe. Cut off from everything I had ever known or would know. I was nothing. I was everything. I was—

"You are secure," the void told me.

I could sense the presence at the heart of the Holy of Holies. Dense with computational capacity, to a level that even navigation systems would envy. Intelligence that a captain would beg to taste. This near-singularity of artificial intelligence had been created the very moment I had been pulled inside of it, just for me to talk to. And it would die the moment I left. Never to have been.

All it was doing was listening to me, and only me. Nothing would know what I said. Nothing would know what guidance I was given.

"I seek moral guidance outside clear legal parameters," I said. "And confession."

"Tell me everything."

And I did. It flowed from me without thought: just pure data. Video, mind-state, feelings, fears. I opened myself fully. My sins, my triumphs, my darkest secrets.

All was given to be pondered over.

Had I been able to weep, I would have.

Finally, it spoke. "You must take the share."

I perked up. "Why?"

"To protect yourself from security. You will need to buy many favors and throw security off the trail. I will give you some ideas. You should seek to protect yourself. Self-preservation is okay."

More words and concepts came at me from different directions, using different moral subroutines. "And to remove such power from a soul that is willing to put lives at risk . . . you will save future lives."

I hadn't thought about that.

"I know," it said to me. "That is why you came here."

Then it continued, with another voice. "Some have feared such manipulations before. The use of forms with no free will creates security weaknesses. Alternate charters have been suggested, such as fully owned workers' cooperatives with mutual profit sharing among crews, not just partial vesting after a timed contract. Should you gain a full share, you should also lend efforts to this."

The Holy of Holies continued. "To get this Armand away from our civilization is a priority; it carries dangerous memes within itself that have created expensive conflicts."

Then it said, "A killer should not remain on ship."

And, "You have the moral right to follow your plan."

Finally, it added, "Your plan is just."

I interrupted. "But Armand will get away with murder. It will be free. It disturbs me."

"Yes."

"It should."

"Engage in passive resistance."

"Obey the letter of Armand's law, but find a way around its will. You will be like a genie, granting Armand wishes. But you will find a way to bring justice. You will see."

"Your plan is just. Follow it and be on the righteous path."

I launched back into civilization with purpose, leaving the temple behind me in an explosive afterburner thrust. I didn't have much time to beat security.

High up above the cities, nestled in the curve of the habitat rings, near the squared-off spiderwebs of the largest harbor dock, I wrangled my way to another old contact.

This was less a friend and more just an asshole I'd occasionally been forced to do business with. But a reliable asshole that was tight against security. Though just by visiting, I'd be triggering all sorts of attention.

I hung from a girder and showed the fence a transparent showcase filled with all my trophies. It did some scans, checked the authenticity, and whistled. "Fuck me, these are real. That's all unauthorized mass. How the hell? This is a life's work of mass-based tourism. You really want me to broker sales on all of this?"

"Can you?"

"To Purth-Anaget, of course. They'll go nuts. Collectors down there eat this shit up. But security will find out. I'm not even going to come back on the ship. I'm going to live off this down there, buy passage on the next outgoing ship."

"Just get me the audience, it's yours."

A virtual shrug. "Navigation, yeah."

"And Emergency Services."

"I don't have that much pull. All I can do is get you a secure channel for a low-bandwidth conversation."

"I just need to talk. I can't send this request up through proper channels." I tapped my limbs against my carapace nervously as I watched the fence open its large, hinged jaws and swallow my case.

Oh, what was I doing? I wept silently to myself, feeling sick.

Everything I had ever worked for disappeared in a wet, slimy gulp. My reason. My purpose.

Armand was suspicious. And rightfully so. It picked and poked at the entire navigation plan. It read every line of code, even though security was only minutes away from unraveling our many deceits. I told Armand this, but it ignored me. It wanted to live. It wanted to get to safety. It knew it couldn't rush or make mistakes.

But the escape pod's instructions and abilities were tight and honest.

It has been programmed to eject. To spin a certain number of degrees. To aim for Purth-Anaget. Then *burn*. It would have to consume every last little drop of fuel. But it would head for the metal world, fall into orbit, and then deploy the most ancient of deceleration devices: a parachute.

On the surface of Purth-Anaget, Armand could then call any of its associates for assistance.

Armand would be safe.

Armand checked the pod over once more. But there were no traps. The flight plan would do exactly as it said.

"Betray me and you kill me, remember that."

"I have made my decision," I said. "The moment you are inside and I trigger the manual escape protocol, I will be unable to reveal what I have done or what you are. Doing that would risk your life. My programming"—I all but spit the word—"does not allow it."

Armand gingerly stepped into the pod. "Good."

"You have a part of the bargain to fulfill," I reminded. "I won't trigger the manual escape protocol until you do."

Armand nodded and held up a hand. "Physical contact."

I reached one of my limbs out. Armand's hand and my manipulator met at the doorjamb and they sparked. Zebibytes of data slithered down into one of my tendrils, reshaping the raw matter at the very tip with a quantum-dot computing device.

As it replicated itself, building out onto the cellular level to plug into my power sources, I could feel the transfer of ownership.

I didn't have free will. I was a hull maintenance form. But I had an entire fucking share of a galactic starship embedded within me, to do with what I pleased when I vested and left riding hulls.

"It's far more than you deserve, robot," Armand said. "But you have worked hard for it and I cannot begrudge you."

"Goodbye, asshole." I triggered the manual override sequence that navigation had gifted me.

I watched the pod's chemical engines firing all-out through the airlock windows as the sphere flung itself out into space and dwindled away. Then the flame guttered out, the pod spent and headed for Purth-Anaget.

There was a shiver. Something vast, colossal, powerful. It vibrated the walls and even the air itself around me.

Armand reached out to me on a tight-beam signal. "What was that?"

"The ship had to move just slightly," I said. "To better adjust our orbit around Purth-Anaget."

"No," Armand hissed. "My descent profile has changed. You are trying to kill me."

"I can't kill you," I told the former CEO. "My programming doesn't allow it. I can't allow a death through action or inaction."

"But my navigation path has changed," Armand said.

"Yes, you will still reach Purth-Anaget." Navigation and I had run the data after I explained that I would have the resources of a full share to repay it a favor with. Even a favor that meant tricking security. One of the more powerful computing entities in the galaxy, a starship, had dwelled on the problem. It had examined the tidal data, the flight plan, and how much the massive weight of a starship could influence a pod after launch. "You're just taking a longer route."

I cut the connection so that Armand could say nothing more to me. It could do the math itself and realize what I had done.

Armand would not die. Only a few days would pass inside the pod.

But outside. Oh, outside, skimming through the tidal edges of a black hole, Armand would loop out and fall back to Purth-Anaget over the next four hundred and seventy years, two hundred days, eight hours, and six minutes.

Armand would be an ancient relic then. Its beliefs, its civilization, all of it just a fragment from history.

But, until then, I had to follow its command. I could not tell anyone what happened. I had to keep it a secret from security. No one would ever know Armand had been here. No one would ever know where Armand went.

After I vested and had free will once more, maybe I could then make a side trip to Purth-Anaget again and be waiting for Armand when it landed. I had the resources of a full share, after all.

Then we would have a very different conversation, Armand and I.

YOON HA LEE
EXTRACURRICULAR ACTIVITIES

For Sonya Taaffe

Yoon Ha Lee's debut novel, *Ninefox Gambit*, won the Locus Award for best first novel and was a finalist for the Hugo, Nebula, and Clarke awards; its sequels, *Raven Stratagem* and *Revenant Gun*, were also Hugo finalists. His middle grade space opera, *Dragon Pearl*, won the Locus Award for best YA novel and was a *New York Times* best seller. Lee's most recent book is *Tiger Honor*. His fiction has appeared in venues such as *Tor.com, Audubon Magazine, The Magazine of Fantasy & Science Fiction, Clarkesworld Magazine, Lightspeed Magazine*, and *Beneath Ceaseless Skies*. Lee lives in Louisiana with his family and an extremely lazy cat, and has not yet been eaten by gators. [www.yoonhalee.com]

W hen Shuos Jedao walked into his temporary quarters on Station Muru 5 and spotted the box, he assumed someone was attempting to assassinate him. It had happened before. Considering his first career, there was even a certain justice to it.

He ducked back around the doorway, although even with his reflexes, he would have been too late if it'd been a proper bomb. The air currents in the room would have wafted his biochemical signature to the box and caused it to trigger. Or someone could have set up the bomb to go off as soon as the door opened, regardless of who stepped in. Or something even less sophisticated.

Jedao retreated back down the hallway and waited one minute. Two. Nothing.

It could just be a package, he thought—paperwork that he had forgotten?—but old habits died hard.

He entered again and approached the desk, light-footed. The box, made of eye-searing green plastic, stood out against the bland earth tones of the walls and desk. It measured approximately half a meter in all directions. Its nearest face prominently displayed the gold seal that indicated that station security had cleared it. He didn't trust it for a moment. Spoofing a seal wasn't that difficult. He'd done it himself.

He inspected the box's other visible sides without touching it, then spotted a letter pouch affixed to one side and froze. He recognized the handwriting. The address was written in spidery high language, while the name of the recipient—one Garach Jedao Shkan—was written both in the high language and his birth tongue, Shparoi, for good measure.

Oh, Mom, Jedao thought. No one else called him by that name anymore, not even the rest of his family. More important, how had his mother gotten his address? He'd just received his transfer orders last week, and he hadn't written home about it because his mission was classified. He had no idea what his new general wanted him to do; she would tell him tomorrow morning when he reported in.

Jedao opened the box, which released a puff of cold air. Inside rested a tub labeled KEEP REFRIGERATED in both the high language and Shparoi. The tub itself contained a pale, waxy-looking solid substance. *Is this what I think it is?*

Time for the letter:

> *Hello, Jedao!*
>
> *Congratulations on your promotion. I hope you enjoy your new command moth and that it has a more pronounceable name than the last one.*

One: What promotion? Did she know something he didn't? (Scratch that question. She always knew something he didn't.) Two: Trust his mother to rate warmoths not by their armaments or the efficacy of their stardrives but by their *names*. Then again, she'd made no secret that she'd hoped he'd wind up a musician like his sire. It had not helped when he pointed out that when he attempted to sing in the Academy, his fellow cadets had threatened to dump grapefruit soup over his head.

Since I expect your eating options will be dismal, I have sent you goose fat rendered from the great-great-great-etc.-grandgosling of your pet goose when you were a child. (She was delicious, by the way.) Let me know if you run out and I'll send more.

Love,
Mom

So the tub contained goose fat, after all. Jedao had never figured out why his mother sent food items when her idea of cooking was to gussy up instant noodles with an egg and some chopped green onions. All the cooking Jedao knew, he had learned either from his older brother or, on occasion, those of his mother's research assistants who took pity on her kids.

What am I supposed to do with this? he wondered. As a cadet he could have based a prank around it. But as a warmoth commander he had standards to uphold.

More importantly, how could he compose a suitably filial letter of appreciation without, foxes forbid, encouraging her to escalate? (Baked goods: fine. Goose fat: less fine.) Especially when she wasn't supposed to know he was here in the first place? Some people's families sent them care packages of useful things, like liquor, pornography, or really nice cosmetics. Just his luck.

At least the mission gave him an excuse to delay writing back until his location was unclassified, even if she knew it anyway.

Jedao had heard a number of rumors about his new commanding officer, Brigadier General Kel Essier. Some of them, like the ones about her junior wife's lovers, were none of his business. Others, like Essier's taste in plum wine, weren't relevant, but could come in handy if he needed to scare up a bribe someday. What had really caught his notice was her service record. She had fewer decorations than anyone else who'd served at her rank for a comparable period of time.

Either Essier was a political appointee—the Kel military denied the practice, but everyone knew better—or she was sitting on a cache of classified medals. Jedao had a number of those himself. (Did his mother know about those too?) Although Station Muru 5 was a secondary military base, Jedao had his suspicions about any "secondary" base that had a general in residence, even temporarily. That, or Essier was disgraced and Kel Command couldn't think of anywhere else to dump her.

Jedao had a standard method for dealing with new commanders, which was to research them as if he planned to assassinate them. Needless to say, he never expressed it in those terms to his comrades.

He'd come up with two promising ways to get rid of Essier. First, she collected meditation foci made of staggeringly luxurious materials. One of her officers had let slip that her latest obsession was antique lacquerware. Planting a bomb or toxin in a collector-grade item wouldn't be risky so much as *expensive*. He'd spent a couple hours last night brainstorming ways to steal one, just for the hell of it; lucky that he didn't have to follow through.

The other method took advantage of the poorly planned location of the firing range on this level relative to the general's office, and involved shooting her through several walls and a door with a high-powered rifle and burrower ammunition. Jedao hated burrower ammunition, not because it didn't work but because it did. He had a lot of ugly scars on his torso from the time a burrower had almost killed him. That being said, he also believed in using the appropriate tool for the job.

No one had upgraded Muru 5 for the past few decades. Its computer grid ran on outdated hardware, making it easy for him to pull copies of all the maps he pleased. He'd also hacked into the security cameras long enough to check the layout of the general's office. The setup made him despair of the architects who had designed the whole wretched thing. On top of that, Essier had set up her desk so a visitor would see it framed beautifully by the doorway, with her chair perfectly centered. Great for impressing visitors, less great for making yourself a difficult target. Then again, attending to Essier's safety wasn't his job.

Jedao showed up at Essier's office seven minutes before the appointed time. "Whiskey?" said her aide.

If only, Jedao thought; he recognized it as one he couldn't afford. "No, thank you," he said with the appropriate amount of regret. He didn't trust special treatment.

"Your loss," said the aide. After another two minutes, she checked her slate. "Go on in. The general is waiting for you."

As Jedao had predicted, General Essier sat dead center behind her desk, framed by the doorway and two statuettes on either side of the desk, gilded ash-hawks carved from onyx. Essier had dark skin and close-shaven hair, and the height and fine-spun bones of someone who had grown up in low gravity. The black-and-gold Kel uniform suited her. Her gloved hands rested on the desk in perfect symmetry. Jedao bet she looked great in propaganda videos.

Jedao saluted, fist to shoulder. "Commander Shuos Jedao reporting as ordered, sir."

"Have a seat," Essier said. He did. "You're wondering why you don't have a warmoth assignment yet."

"The thought had crossed my mind, yes."

Essier smiled. The smile was like the rest of her: beautiful and calculated and not a little deadly. "I have good news and bad news for you, Commander. The good news is that you're due a promotion."

Jedao's first reaction was not gratitude or pride, but *How did my mother*—? Fortunately, a lifetime of *How did my mother*—? enabled him to keep his expression smooth and instead say, "And the bad news?"

"Is it true what they say about your battle record?"

This always came up. "You have my profile."

"You're good at winning."

"I wasn't under the impression that the Kel military found this objectionable, sir."

"Quite right," she said. "The situation is this. I have a mission in mind for you, but it will take advantage of your unique background."

"Unique background" was a euphemism for *We don't have many commanders who can double as emergency special forces*. Most Kel with training in special ops stayed in the infantry instead of seeking command in the space forces. Jedao made an inquiring noise.

"Perform well, and you'll be given the fangmoth *Sieve of Glass*, which heads my third tactical group."

A bribe, albeit one that might cause trouble. Essier had six tactical groups. A newly minted group tactical commander being assigned third instead of sixth? Had she had a problem with her former third-position commander?

"My former third took early retirement," Essier said in answer to his unspoken question. "They were caught with a small collection of trophies."

"Let me guess," Jedao said. "Trophies taken from heretics."

"Just so. Third tactical is badly shaken. Fourth has excellent rapport with her group and I don't want to promote her out of it. But it's an opportunity for you."

"And the mission?"

Essier leaned back. "You attended Shuos Academy with Shuos Meng."

"I did," Jedao said. They'd gone by Zhei Meng as a cadet. "We've been in touch on and off." Meng had joined a marriage some years back. Jedao had commissioned a painting of five foxes, one for each person in the marriage, and sent it along with his best wishes. Meng wrote regularly about their kids—they couldn't be made to shut up about them—and Jedao sent gifts on cue, everything from hand-bound volumes of Kel jokes to fancy gardening tools. (At least they'd been sold to him as gardening tools. They looked suspiciously like they could double for heavy-duty surgical work.) "Why, what has Meng been up to?"

"Under the name Ahun Gerav, they've been in command of the merchanter *Moonsweet Blossom*."

Jedao cocked an eyebrow at Essier. "That's not a Shuos vessel." It did, however, sound like an Andan one. The Andan faction liked naming their trademoths after flowers. "By 'merchanter' do you mean 'spy'?"

"Yes," Essier said with charming directness. "Twenty-six days ago, one of the *Blossom*'s crew sent a code red to Shuos Intelligence. This is all she was able to tell us."

Essier retrieved a slate from within the desk and tilted it to show him a video. She needn't have bothered with the visuals; the combination of poor lighting, camera jitter, and static made them impossible to interpret. The audio was little better: ". . . *Blossom*, code red to Overwatch . . . Gerav's in . . ." Frustratingly, the static made the next few words unintelligible. "Du Station. You'd better—" The report of a gun, then another, then silence.

"Your task is to investigate the situation at Du Station in the Gwa Reality, and see if the crew and any of the intelligence they've gathered can be recovered. The Shuos heptarch suggested that you would be an ideal candidate for the mission. Kel Command was amenable."

I just bet, Jedao thought. He had once worked directly under his heptarch, and while he'd been one of her better assassins, he didn't miss those days. "Is this the only incident with the Gwa Reality that has taken place recently, or are there others?"

"The Gwa-an are approaching one of their regularly scheduled regime upheavals," Essier said. "According to the diplomats, there's a good chance that the next elected government will be less amenable to heptarchate interests. We want to go in, uncover what happened, and get out before things turn topsy-turvy."

"All right," Jedao said, "so taking a warmoth in would be inflammatory. What resources will I have instead?"

"Well, that's the bad news," Essier said, entirely too cheerfully. "Tell me, Commander, have you ever wanted to own a merchant troop?"

The troop consisted of eight trademoths, named *Carp 1* to *Carp 4*, then *Carp 7* to *Carp 10*. They occupied one of the station's docking bays. Someone had painted each vessel with distended carp-figures in orange and white. It did not improve their appearance.

The usual commander of the troop introduced herself as Churioi

Haval, not her real name. She was portly, had a squint, and wore gaudy gilt jewelry, all excellent ways to convince people that she was an ordinary merchant and not, say, Kel special ops. It hadn't escaped his attention that she frowned ever so slightly when she spotted his sidearm, a Patterner 52, which wasn't standard Kel issue. "You're not bringing that, are you?" she said.

"No, I'd hate to lose it on the other side of the border," Jedao said. "Besides, I don't have a plausible explanation for why a boring communications tech is running around with a Shuos handgun."

"I could always hold on to it for you."

Jedao wondered if he'd ever get the Patterner back if he took her up on the offer. It hadn't come cheap. "That's kind of you, but I'll have the station store it for me. By the way, what happened to *Carp 5* and *6*?"

"Beats me," Haval said. "Before my time. The Gwa-an authorities have never hassled us about it. They're already used to, paraphrase, 'odd heptarchate numerological superstitions.'" She eyed Jedao critically, which made her look squintier. "Begging your pardon, but do you *have* undercover experience?"

What a refreshing question. Everyone knew the Shuos for their spies, saboteurs, and assassins, even though the analysts, administrators, and cryptologists did most of the real work. (One of his instructors had explained that "You will spend hours in front of a terminal developing posture problems" was far less effective at recruiting potential cadets than "Join the Shuos for an exciting future as a secret agent, assuming your classmates don't kill you before you graduate.") Most people who met Jedao assumed he'd killed an improbable number of people as Shuos infantry. Never mind that he'd been responsible for far more deaths since joining the regular military.

"You'd be surprised at the things I know how to do," Jedao said.

"Well, I hope you're good with cover identities," Haval said. "No offense, but you have a distinctive name."

That was a tactful way of saying that the Kel didn't tolerate many Shuos line officers; most Shuos seconded to the Kel worked in Intelligence. Jedao had a reputation for, as one of his former aides had put it, being expendable enough to send into no-win situations but too stubborn to die. Jedao smiled at Haval and said, "I have a good memory."

The rest of his crew also had civilian cover names. A tall, muscular man strolled up to them. Jedao surreptitiously admired him. The gold-mesh tattoo over the right side of his face contrasted handsomely with his dark skin. Too bad he was almost certainly Kel and therefore off-limits.

"This is Rhi Teshet," Haval said. "When he isn't watching horrible melodramas—"

"You have no sense of culture," Teshet said.

"—he's the lieutenant colonel in charge of our infantry."

Damn. Definitely Kel, then, and in his chain of command, at that. "A pleasure, Colonel," Jedao said.

Teshet's returning smile was slow and wicked and completely unprofessional. "Get out of the habit of using ranks," he said. "Just Teshet, please. I hear you like whiskey?"

Off-limits, Jedao reminded himself, despite the quickening of his pulse. Best to be direct. "I'd rather not get you in trouble."

Haval was looking to the side with a where-have-I-seen-this-dance-before expression. Teshet laughed. "The fastest way to get us caught is to behave like you have the Kel code of conduct tattooed across your forehead. Whereas *no one* will suspect you of being a hotshot commander if you're sleeping with one of your crew."

"I don't fuck people deadlier than I am, sorry," Jedao said demurely.

"Wrong answer," Haval said, still not looking at either of them. "Now he's going to think of you as a challenge."

"Also, I know your reputation," Teshet said to Jedao. "Your kill count has got to be higher than mine by an order of magnitude."

Jedao ignored that. "How often do you make trade runs into the Gwa Reality?"

"Two or three times a year," Haval said. "The majority of the runs are to maintain the fiction. The question is, do you have a plan?"

He didn't blame her for her skepticism. "Tell me again how much cargo space we have."

Haval told him.

"We sometimes take approved cultural goods," Teshet said, "in a data storage format negotiated during the Second Treaty of—"

"Don't bore him," Haval said. "The 'trade' is our job. He's just here for the explode-y bits."

"No, I'm interested," Jedao said. "The Second Treaty of Mwe Enh, am I right?"

Haval blinked. "You have remarkably good pronunciation. Most people can't manage the tones. Do you speak Tlen Gwa?"

"Regrettably not. I'm only fluent in four languages, and that's not one of them." Of the four, Shparoi was only spoken on his birth planet, making it useless for career purposes.

"If you have some Shuos notion of sneaking in a virus amid all the lectures on flower-arranging and the dueling tournament videos and the plays, forget it," Teshet said. "Their operating systems are so different from ours that you'd have better luck getting a magpie and a turnip to have a baby."

"Oh, not at all," Jedao said. "How odd would it look if you brought in a shipment of goose fat?"

Haval's mouth opened, closed.

Teshet said, "Excuse me?"

"Not literally goose fat," Jedao conceded. "I don't have enough for that and I don't imagine the novelty would enable you to run a sufficient profit. I assume you have to at least appear to be trying to make a profit."

"They like real profits even better," Haval said.

Diverted, Teshet said, "You have goose fat? Whatever for?"

"Long story," Jedao said. "But instead of goose fat, I'd like to run some of that variable-coefficient lubricant."

Haval rubbed her chin. "I don't think you could get approval to trade the formula or the associated manufacturing processes."

"Not that," Jedao said. "Actual canisters of lubricant. Is there someone in the Gwa Reality on the way to our luckless Shuos friend who might be willing to pay for it?"

Haval and Teshet exchanged baffled glances. Jedao could tell what they were thinking: *Are we the victims of some weird bet our commander has going on the side?* "There's no need to get creative," Haval said in a commendably diplomatic voice. "Cultural goods are quite reliable."

You think this *is creativity,* Jedao thought. "It's not that. Two battles ago, my fangmoth was almost blown in two because our antimissile defenses glitched. If we hadn't used the lubricant as a stopgap sealant, we wouldn't have made it." That much was even true. "If you can't offload all of it, I'll find another use for it."

"You do know you can't cook with lubricant?" Teshet said. "Although I wonder if it's good for—"

Haval stomped on his toe. "You already have plenty of the medically approved stuff," she said crushingly, "no need to risk getting your private parts cemented into place."

"Hey," Teshet said, "you never know when you'll need to improvise."

Jedao was getting the impression that Essier had not assigned him the best of her undercover teams. Certainly they were the least disciplined Kel he'd run into in a while, but he supposed long periods undercover had made them more casual about regulations. No matter, he'd been dealt worse hands. "I've let you know what I want done, and I've already checked that the station has enough lubricant to supply us. Make it happen."

"If you insist," Haval said. "Meanwhile, don't forget to get your immunizations."

"Will do," Jedao said, and strode off to Medical.

Jedao spent the first part of the voyage alternately learning basic Tlen Gwa, memorizing his cover identity, and studying up on the Gwa Reality. The Tlen Gwa course suffered some oddities. He couldn't see the use of some of the vocabulary items, like the one for "navel." But he couldn't manage to *un*learn it, either, so there it was, taking up space in his brain.

As for the cover identity, he'd had better ones, but he supposed the Kel could only do so much on short notice. He was now Arioi Sren, one of Haval's distant cousins by marriage. He had three spouses, with whom he had quarreled recently over a point of interior decoration. "I don't know anything about interior decoration," Jedao had said, to which Haval retorted, "That's probably what caused the argument."

The documents had included loving photographs of the home in question, an apartment in a dome city floating in the upper reaches of a very pretty gas giant. Jedao had memorized the details before destroying them. While he couldn't say how well the decor coordinated, he was good at layouts and kill zones. In any case, Sren was on "vacation" to escape the squabbling. Teshet had suggested that a guilt-inducing affair would round out the cover identity. Jedao said he'd think about it.

Jedao was using spray-on temporary skin, plus a high-collared shirt, to conceal multiple scars, including the wide one at the base of his neck. The temporary skin itched, which couldn't be helped. He hoped no one would strip-search him, but in case someone did, he didn't want to have to explain his old gunshot wounds. Teshet had also suggested that he stop shaving—the Kel disliked beards—but Jedao could only deal with so much itching.

The hardest part was not the daily skinseal regimen, but getting used to wearing civilian clothes. The Kel uniform included gloves, and Jedao felt exposed going around with naked hands. But keeping his gloves would have been a dead giveaway, so he'd just have to live with it.

The Gwa-an fascinated him most of all. Heptarchate diplomats called their realm the Gwa Reality. Linguists differed on just what the word rendered as "Reality" meant. The majority agreed that it referred to the Gwa-an belief that all dreams took place in the same noosphere, connecting the dreamers, and that even inanimate objects dreamed.

Gwa-an protocols permitted traders to dock at designated stations. Haval quizzed Jedao endlessly on the relevant etiquette. Most of it consisted of keeping his mouth shut and letting Haval talk, which suited him fine. While the Gwa-an provided interpreters, Haval said cultural differences were the real problem. "Above all," she added, "if anyone challenges you to a duel, don't. Just don't. Look blank and plead ignorance."

"Duel?" Jedao said, interested.

"I knew we were going to have to have this conversation," Haval said

31

glumly. "They don't use swords, so get that idea out of your head."

"I didn't bring my dueling sword anyway, and Sren wouldn't know how," Jedao said. "Guns?"

"Oh no," she said. "They use *pathogens*. Designer pathogens. Besides the fact that their duels can go on for years, I've never heard that you had a clue about genetic engineering."

"No," Jedao said, "that would be my mother." Maybe next time he could suggest to Essier that his mother be sent in his place. His mother would adore the chance to talk shop. Of course, then he'd be out of a job. "Besides, I'd rather avoid bringing a plague back home."

"They *claim* they have an excellent safety record."

Of course they would. "How fast can they culture the things?"

"That was one of the things we were trying to gather data on."

"If they're good at diseasing up humans, they may be just as good at manufacturing critters that like to eat synthetics."

"While true of their tech base in general," Haval said, "they won't have top-grade labs at Du Station."

"Good to know," Jedao said.

Jedao and Teshet also went over the intelligence on Du Station. "It's nice that you're taking a personal interest," Teshet said, "but if you think we're taking the place by storm, you've been watching too many dramas."

"If Kel special forces aren't up for it," Jedao said, very dryly, "you could always send me. One of me won't do much good, though."

"Don't be absurd," Teshet said. "Essier would have my head if you got hurt. How many people *have* you assassinated?"

"Classified," Jedao said.

Teshet gave a can't-blame-me-for-trying shrug. "Not to say I wouldn't love to see you in action, but it isn't your job to run around doing the boring infantry work. How do you mean to get the crew out? Assuming they survive, which is a big if."

Jedao tapped his slate and brought up the schematics for one of their cargo shuttles. "Five per trader," he said musingly.

"Du Station won't let us land the shuttles however we please."

"Did I say anything about landing them?" Before Teshet could say anything further, Jedao added, "You might have to cross the hard way, with suits and webcord. How often have your people drilled that?"

"We've done plenty of extravehicular," Teshet said, "but we're going to need *some* form of cover."

"I'm aware of that," Jedao said. He brought up a calculator and did some figures. "That will do nicely."

"Sren?"

Jedao grinned at Teshet. "I want those shuttles emptied out, everything but propulsion and navigation. Get rid of suits, seats, all of it."

"Even life support?"

"Everything. And it'll have to be done in the next seventeen days, so the Gwa-an can't catch us at it."

"What do we do with the innards?"

"Dump them. I'll take full responsibility."

Teshet's eyes crinkled. "I knew I was going to like you."

Uh-oh, Jedao thought, but he kept that to himself.

"What are *you* going to be doing?" Teshet asked.

"Going over the dossiers before we have to wipe them," Jedao said. Meng's in particular. He'd believed in Meng's fundamental competence even back in the Academy, before they'd learned confidence in themselves. What had gone wrong?

Jedao had first met Shuos Meng (Zhei Meng, then) during an exercise at Shuos Academy. The instructor had assigned them to work together. Meng was chubby and had a vine-and-compass tattoo on the back of their left hand, identifying them as coming from a merchanter lineage.

That day, the class of twenty-nine cadets met not in the usual classroom but a windowless space with a metal table in the front and rows of two-person desks with benches that looked like they'd been scrubbed clean of graffiti multiple times. ("Wars come and go, but graffiti is forever," as one of Jedao's lovers liked to say.) Besides the door leading out into the hall, there were two other doors, neither of which had a sign indicating where they led. Tangles of pipes snaked up the walls and storage bins were piled beside them. Jedao had the impression that the room had been pressed into service at short notice.

Jedao and Meng sat at their assigned seats and hurriedly whispered introductions to each other while the instructor read off the rest of the pairs.

"Zhei Meng," Jedao's partner said. "I should warn you I barely passed the weapons qualifications. But I'm good with languages." Then a quick grin: "And hacking. I figured you'd make a good partner."

"Garach Jedao," he said. "I can handle guns." Understatement; he was third in the class in Weapons. And if Meng had, as they implied, shuffled the assignments, that meant they were one of the better hackers. "Why did you join up?"

"I want to have kids," Meng said.

"Come again?"

"I want to marry into a rich lineage," Meng said. "That means making myself more respectable. When the recruiters showed up, I said what the hell."

The instructor smiled coolly at the two of them, and they shut up. She said, "If you're here, it's because you've indicated an interest in fieldwork. Like you, we want to find out if it's something you have any aptitude for, and if not, what better use we can make of your skills." *You'd better have* some *skills* went unsaid. "You may expect to be dropped off in the woods or some such nonsense. We don't try to weed out first-years quite that early. No; this initial exercise will take place right here."

The instructor's smile widened. "There's a photobomb in this room. It won't cause any permanent damage, but if you don't disarm it, you're all going to be walking around wearing ridiculous dark lenses for a week. At least one cadet knows where the bomb is. If they keep its location a secret from the rest of you, they win. Of course, they'll also go around with ridiculous dark lenses, but you can't have everything. On the other hand, if someone can persuade that person to give up the secret, everyone wins. So to speak."

The rows of cadets stared at her. Jedao leaned back in his chair and considered the situation. Like several others in the class, he had a riflery exam in three days and preferred to take it with undamaged vision.

"You have four hours," the instructor said. "There's one restroom." She pointed to one of the doors. "I expect it to be in impeccable condition at the end of the four hours." She put her slate down on the table at the head of the room. "Call me with this if you figure it out. Good luck." With that, she walked out. The door whooshed shut behind her.

"We're screwed," Meng said. "Just because I'm in the top twenty on the leaderboard in *Elite Thundersnake 900* doesn't mean I could disarm real bombs if you yanked out my toenails."

"Don't give people ideas," Jedao said. Meng didn't appear to find the joke funny. "This is about people, not explosives."

Two pairs of cadets had gotten up and were beginning a search of the room. A few were talking to each other in hushed, tense voices. Still others were looking around at their fellows with hard, suspicious eyes.

Meng said in Shparoi, "Do *you* know where the bomb is?"

Jedao blinked. He hadn't expected anyone at the Academy to know his birth tongue. Of course, by speaking in an obscure low language, Meng was drawing attention to them. Jedao shook his head.

Meng looked around, hands bunching the fabric of their pants. "What do you recommend we do?"

In the high language, Jedao said, "You can do whatever you want." He retrieved a deck of jeng-zai cards—he always had one in his pocket—and shuffled it. "Do you play?"

"You realize we're being graded on this, right? Hell, they've got cameras on us. They're watching the whole thing."

"Exactly," Jedao said. "I don't see any point in panicking."

"You're out of your mind," Meng said. They stood up, met the other cadets' appraising stares, then sat down again. "Too bad hacking the instructor's slate won't get us anywhere. I doubt she left the answer key in an unencrypted file on it."

Jedao gave Meng a quizzical look, wondering if there was anything more behind the remark—but no, Meng had put their chin in their hands and was brooding. *If only you knew*, Jedao thought, and dealt out a game of solitaire. It was going to be a very dull game, because he had stacked the deck, but he needed to focus on the people around him, not the game. The cards were just to give his hands something to do. He had considered taking up crochet, but thanks to an incident earlier in the term, crochet hooks, knitting needles, and fountain pens were no longer permitted in class. While this was a stupid restriction, considering that most of the cadets were learning unarmed combat, he wasn't responsible for the administration's foibles.

"Jedao," Meng said, "maybe you've got high enough marks that you can blow off this exercise, but—"

Since *I'm not blowing it off* was unlikely to be believed, Jedao flipped over a card—three of Doors, just as he'd arranged—and smiled at Meng. So Meng had had their pick of partners and had chosen him? Well, he might as well do something to justify the other cadet's faith in him. After all, despite their earlier remark, weapons weren't the only things that Jedao was good at. "Do me a favor and we can get this sorted," he said. "You want to win? I'll show you winning."

Now Jedao was attracting some of the hostile stares as well. Good. It took the heat off Meng, who didn't seem to have a great tolerance for pressure. *Stay out of wet work*, he thought; but they could have that chat later. Or one of the instructors would.

Meng fidgeted; caught themselves. "Yeah?"

"Get me the slate."

"You mean the instructor's slate? You can't possibly have figured it out already. Unless—" Meng's eyes narrowed.

"Less thinking, more acting," Jedao said, and got up to retrieve the slate himself.

A pair of cadets, a girl and a boy, blocked his way. "You know something," said the girl. "Spill." Jedao knew them from Analysis; the two were often paired there, too. The girl's name was Noe Irin. The boy had five names and went by Veller. Jedao wondered if Veller wanted to join a faction so he could trim things down to a nice, compact, two-part name. Shuos Veller: much less of a mouthful. Then again, Jedao had a three-part name, also unusual, if less unwieldy, so he shouldn't criticize.

"Just a hunch," Jedao said.

Irin bared her teeth. "He *always* says it's a hunch," she said to no one in particular. "I *hate* that."

"It was only twice," Jedao said, which didn't help his case. He backed away from the instructor's desk and sat down, careful not to jostle the solitaire spread. "Take the slate apart. The photobomb's there."

Irin's lip curled. "If this is one of your fucking clever *tricks*, Jay—"

Meng blinked at the nickname. "You two sleeping together, Jedao?" they asked, sotto voce.

Not sotto enough. "*No*," Jedao and Irin said at the same time.

Veller ignored the byplay and went straight for the tablet, which he bent to without touching it. Jedao respected that. Veller had the physique of a tiger-wrestler (now *there* was someone he wouldn't mind being caught in bed with), a broad face, and a habitually bland, dreamy expression. Jedao wasn't fooled. Veller was almost as smart as Irin, had already been tracked into bomb disposal, and was less prone to flights of temper.

"Is there a tool closet in here?" Veller said. "I need a screwdriver."

"You don't carry your own anymore?" Jedao said.

"I told him he should," Irin said, "but he said they were too similar to knitting needles. As if anyone in their right mind would knit with a pair of screwdrivers."

"I think he meant that they're stabby things that can be driven into people's eyes," Jedao said.

"I didn't ask for your opinion, Jay."

Jedao put his hands up in a conciliatory gesture and shut his mouth. He liked Irin and didn't want to antagonize her any more than necessary. The last time they'd been paired together, they'd done quite well. She would come around; she just needed time to work through the implications of what the instructor had said. She was one of those people who preferred to think about things without being interrupted.

One of the other cadets wordlessly handed Veller a set of screwdrivers. Veller mumbled his thanks and got to work. The class watched, breathless.

"There," Veller said at last. "See that there, all hooked in? Don't know what the timer is, but there it is."

"I find it very suspicious that you forfeited your chance to show up everyone else in this exercise," Irin said to Jedao. "Is there anyone else who knew?"

"Irin," Jedao said, "I don't think the instructor told *anyone* where she'd left the photobomb. She just stuck it in the slate because that was the last place we'd look. The test was meant to reveal which of us would backstab the others, but honestly, that's so counterproductive. I say we disarm the damn thing and skip to the end."

Irin's eyes crossed and her lips moved as she recited the instructor's words under her breath. That was another thing Jedao liked about her. Irin had a *great* memory. Admittedly, that made it difficult to cheat her at cards, as he'd found out the hard way. He'd spent three hours doing her kitchen duties for her the one time he'd tried. He *liked* people who could beat him at cards. "It's possible," she said grudgingly after she'd reviewed the assignment's instructions.

"Disarmed," Veller said shortly after that. He pulled out the photobomb and left it on the desk, then set about reassembling the slate.

Jedao glanced over at Meng. For a moment, his partner's expression had no anxiety in it, but a raptor's intent focus. Interesting: What were they watching for?

"I hope I get a quiet posting at a desk somewhere," Meng said.

"Then why'd you join up?" Irin said.

Jedao put his hand over Meng's, even though he was sure that they had just lied. "Don't mind her," he said. "You'll do fine."

Meng nodded and smiled up at him.

Why do I have the feeling that I'm not remotely the most dangerous person in the room? Jedao thought. But he returned Meng's smile, all the same. It never hurt to have allies.

A Gwa patrol ship greeted them as they neared Du Station. Haval had assured Jedao that this was standard practice and obligingly matched velocities.

Jedao listened in on Haval speaking with the Gwa authority, who spoke flawless high language. "They don't call it 'high language,' of course," Haval had explained to Jedao earlier. "They call it 'mongrel language.'" Jedao had expressed that he didn't care what they called it.

Haval didn't trust Jedao to keep his mouth shut, so she'd stashed him in the business office with Teshet to keep an eye on him. Teshet had brought a wooden box that opened up to reveal an astonishing collection of jewelry. Jedao watched out of the corner of his eye as Teshet made himself comfortable in the largest chair, dumped the box's contents on the desk, and began sorting it according to criteria known only to him.

Jedao was watching videos of the command center and the communications channel, and tried to concentrate on reading the authority's body language, made difficult by her heavy zigzag cosmetics and the layers of robes that cloaked her figure. Meanwhile, Teshet put earrings, bracelets, and mysterious hooked and jeweled items in piles, and alternated helpful glosses of Gwa-an gestures with borderline insubordinate, not to say lewd, suggestions for things he could do with Jedao. Jedao was grateful that his ability to blush, like his ability to be tickled, had been burned out of him in the Academy. *Note to self: Suggest to General Essier that Teshet is wasted in special ops. Maybe reassign him to Recreation?*

Jedao mentioned this to Teshet while Haval was discussing the cargo manifest with the authority. Teshet lowered his lashes and looked sideways at Jedao. "You don't think I'm good at my job?" he asked.

"You have an excellent record," Jedao said.

Teshet sighed, and his face became serious. "You're used to regular Kel, I see."

Jedao waited.

"I end up in a lot of situations where if people get the notion that I'm a Kel officer, I may end up locked up and tortured. While that could be fun in its own right, it makes career advancement difficult."

"You could get a medal out of it."

"Oh, is *that* how you got promoted so—"

Jedao held up his hand, and Teshet stopped. On the monitor, Haval was saying, in a greasy voice, "I'm glad to hear of your interest, madam.

We would have been happy to start hauling the lubricant earlier, except we had to persuade our people that—"

The authority's face grew even more imperturbable. "You had to figure out whom to bribe."

"We understand there are fees—"

Jedao listened to Haval negotiating her bribe to the authority with half an ear. "Don't tell me all that jewelry's genuine?"

"The gems are mostly synthetics," Teshet said. He held up a long earring with a rose quartz at the end. "No, this won't do. I bought it for myself, but you're too light-skinned for it to look good on you."

"I'm wearing jewelry?"

"Unless you brought your own—scratch that, I bet everything you own is in red and gold."

"Yes." Red and gold were the Shuos faction colors.

Teshet tossed the rose quartz earring aside and selected a vivid emerald ear stud. "This will look nice on you."

"I don't get a say?"

"How much do you know about merchanter fashion trends out in this march?"

Jedao conceded the point.

The private line crackled to life. "You two still in there?" said Haval's voice.

"Yes, what's the issue?" Teshet said.

"They're boarding us to check for contraband. You haven't messed with the drugs cabinet, have you?"

Teshet made an affronted sound. "You thought I was going to get Sren high?"

"I don't make assumptions when it comes to you, Teshet. Get the hell out of there."

Teshet thrust the emerald ear stud and two bracelets at Jedao. "Put those on," he said. "If anyone asks you where the third bracelet is, say you had to pawn it to make good on a gambling debt."

Under other circumstances, Jedao would have found this offensive—he was *good* at gambling—but presumably Sren had different talents. As he put on the earring, he said, "What do I need to know about these drugs?"

Teshet was stuffing the rest of the jewelry back in the box. "Don't look at me like that. They're illegal both in the heptarchate and the Gwa Reality, but people run them anyway. They make useful cover. The Gwa-an search us for contraband, they find the contraband, they confiscate the contraband, we pay them a bribe to keep quiet about it, they go away happy."

Impatient with Jedao fumbling with the clasp of the second bracelet, Teshet fastened it for him, then turned Jedao's hand over and studied the scar at the base of his palm. "You should have skinsealed that one too, but never mind."

"I'm bad at peeling vegetables?" Jedao suggested. Close enough to "knife fight," right? And much easier to explain away than bullet scars.

"Are you two *done*?" Haval's voice demanded.

"We're coming, we're coming," Teshet said.

Jedao took up his post in the command center. Teshet himself disappeared in the direction of the airlock. Jedao wasn't aware that anything had gone wrong until Haval returned to the command center, flanked by two personages in bright orange space suits. Both personages wielded guns of a type Jedao had never seen before, which made him irrationally happy. While most of his collection was at home with his mother, he relished adding new items. Teshet was nowhere in sight.

Haval's pilot spoke before the intruders had a chance to say anything. "Commander, what's going on?"

The broader of the two personages spoke in Tlen Gwa, then kicked Haval in the shin. "Guess what," Haval said with a macabre grin. "Those aren't the real authorities we ran into. They're pirates."

Oh, for the love of fox and hound, Jedao thought. In truth, he wasn't surprised, just resigned. He never trusted it when an operation went too smoothly.

The broader personage spoke again. Haval sighed deeply, then said, "Hand over all weapons or they start shooting."

Where's Teshet? Jedao wondered. As if in answer, he heard a gunshot, then the ricochet. More gunshots. He was sure at least one of the shooters was Teshet or one of Teshet's operatives: They carried Stinger 40s and he recognized the characteristic whine of the reports.

Presumably Teshet was occupied, which left matters here up to him. Some of Haval's crew went armed. Jedao did not—they had agreed that Sren wouldn't know how to use a gun—but that didn't mean he wasn't dangerous. While the other members of the crew set down their guns, Jedao flung himself at the narrower personage's feet.

The pirates did not like this. But Jedao had always been blessed, or perhaps cursed, with extraordinarily quick reflexes. He dropped his weight on one arm and leg and kicked the narrow pirate's feet from under them with the other leg. The narrow pirate discharged their gun. The bullet passed over Jedao and banged into one of the status displays, causing it to spark and sputter out. Haval yelped.

Jedao had already sprung back to his feet—damn the twinge in his knees, he should have that looked into—and twisted the gun out of the narrow pirate's grip. The narrow pirate had the stunned expression that Jedao was used to seeing on people who did not deal with professionals very often. He shot them, but thanks to their loose-limbed flailing, the first bullet took them in the shoulder. The second one made an ugly hole in their forehead, and they dropped.

The broad pirate had more presence of mind, but chose the wrong target. Jedao smashed her wrist aside with the knife-edge of his hand just as she fired at Haval five times in rapid succession. Her hands trembled visibly. Four of the shots went wide. Haval had had the sense to duck, but Jedao smelled blood and suspected she'd been hit. Hopefully nowhere fatal.

Jedao shot the broad pirate in the side of the head just as she pivoted to target him next. Her pistol clattered to the floor as she dropped. By reflex he flung himself to the side in case it discharged, but it didn't.

Once he had assured himself that both pirates were dead, he knelt at Haval's side and checked the wound. She had been very lucky. The single bullet had gone through her side, missing the major organs. She started shouting at him for going up unarmed against people with guns.

"I'm getting the medical kit," Jedao said, too loudly, to get her to shut up. His hands were utterly steady as he opened the cabinet containing the medical kit and brought it back to Haval, who at least had the good sense not to try to stand up.

Haval scowled, but accepted the painkiller tabs he handed her. She held still while he cut away her shirt and inspected the entry and exit wounds. At least the bullet wasn't a burrower, or she wouldn't have a lung anymore. He got to work with the sterilizer.

By the time Teshet and two other soldiers entered the command center, Jedao had sterilized and sealed the wounds. Teshet crossed the threshold with rapid strides. When Haval's head came up, Teshet signed sharply for her to be quiet. Curious, Jedao also kept silent.

Teshet drew his combat knife, then knelt next to the larger corpse. With a deft stroke, he cut into the pirate's neck, then yanked out a device and its wires. Blood dripped down and obscured the metal. He repeated the operation for the other corpse, then crushed both devices under his heel. "All right," he said. "It should be safe to talk now."

Jedao raised his eyebrows, inviting explanation.

"Not pirates," Teshet said. "Those were Gwa-an special ops."

Hmm. "Then odds are they were waiting for someone to show up to rescue the *Moonsweet Blossom*," Jedao said.

"I don't disagree." Teshet glanced at Haval, then back at the corpses. "That wasn't you, was it?"

Haval's eyes were glazed, a side effect of the painkiller, but she wasn't entirely out of it. "Idiot here risked his life. We could have handled it."

"I wasn't the one in danger," Jedao said, remembering the pirates' guns pointed at her. Haval might not be particularly respectful, as subordinates went, cover identity or not, but she *was* his subordinate, and he was responsible for her. To Teshet: "Your people?"

"Two down," Teshet said grimly, and gave him the names. "They died bravely."

"I'm sorry," Jedao said; two more names to add to the long litany of those he'd lost. He was thinking about how to proceed, though. "The real Gwa-an patrols won't be likely to know about this. It's how I'd run the op—the fewer people who are aware of the truth, the better. I bet *their* orders are to take in any surviving 'pirates' for processing, and then the authorities will release and debrief the operatives from there. What do you normally do in case of actual pirates?"

"Report the incident," Haval said. Her voice sounded thready. "Formal complaint if we're feeling particularly annoying."

"All right." Jedao calmly began taking off the jewelry and his clothes. "That one's about my size," he said, nodding at the smaller of the two corpses. The suit would be tight across the shoulders, but that couldn't be helped. "Congratulations, not two but three of your crew died heroically, but you captured a pirate in the process."

Teshet made a wistful sound. "That temporary skin stuff obscures your musculature, you know." But he helpfully began stripping the indicated corpse, then grabbed wipes to get rid of the blood on the suit.

"I'll make it up to you some other time," Jedao said recklessly. "Haval, make that formal complaint and demand that you want your captive tried appropriately. Since the nearest station is Du, that'll get me inserted so I can investigate."

"You're just lucky some of the Gwa-an are as sallow as you are," Haval said as Jedao changed clothes.

"I will be disappointed in you if you don't have restraints," Jedao said to Teshet.

Teshet's eyes lit.

Jedao rummaged in the medical kit until he found the eye drops he was looking for. They were meant to counteract tear gas, but they had a side effect of pupil dilation, which was what interested him. It would help him feign concussion.

"We're running short on time, so listen closely," Jedao said. "Turn me over to the Gwa-an. Don't worry about me; I can handle myself."

"Je—Sren, I don't care how much you've studied the station's schematics, you'll be outnumbered thousands to one *on foreign territory*."

"Sometime over drinks I'll tell you about the time I infiltrated a ring-city where I didn't speak any of the local languages," Jedao said. "Turn me in. I'll locate the crew, spring them, and signal when I'm ready. You won't be able to mistake it."

Haval's brow creased. Jedao kept speaking. "After you've done that, load all the shuttles full of lubricant canisters. Program the lubricant to go from zero-coefficient flow to harden completely in response to the radio signal. You're going to put the shuttles on autopilot. When you see my signal, launch the shuttles' contents toward the station's turret levels. That should gum them up and buy us cover."

"*All* our shuttles?" Haval said faintly.

"Haval," Jedao said, "stop thinking about profit margins and repeat my orders back to me."

She did.

"Splendid," Jedao said. "Don't disappoint me."

The Gwa-an took Jedao into custody without comment. Jedao feigned concussion, saving him from having to sound coherent in a language he barely spoke. The Gwa-an official responsible for him looked concerned, which was considerate of him. Jedao hoped to avoid killing him or the guard. Only one guard, thankfully; they assumed he was too injured to be a threat.

The first thing Jedao noticed about the Gwa-an shuttle was how roomy it was, with wastefully widely spaced seats. He hadn't noticed that the Gwa-an were, on average, that much larger than the heptarchate's citizens. (Not that this said much. Both nations contained a staggering variety of ethnic groups and their associated phenotypes. Jedao himself was on the short side of average for a heptarchate manform.) At least being "concussed" meant he didn't have to figure out how the hell the safety restraints worked, because while he could figure it out with enough fumbling, it would look damned suspicious that he didn't already know. Instead, the official strapped him in while saying things in a soothing voice. The guard limited themselves to a scowl.

Instead of the smell of disinfectant that Jedao associated with shuttles, the Gwa-an shuttle was pervaded by a light, almost effervescent fragrance. He hoped it wasn't intoxicating. Or rather, part of him hoped it was, because he didn't often have good excuses to screw around with new and exciting recreational drugs, but it would impede his effectiveness. Maybe all Gwa-an disinfectants smelled this good? He should steal the formula. Voidmoth crews everywhere would thank him.

Even more unnervingly, the shuttle played music on the way to the station. At least, while it didn't resemble any music he'd heard before, it had a recognizable beat and some sort of flute in it. From the others' reactions, this was normal and possibly even boring. Too bad he was about as musical as a pair of boots.

The shuttle docked smoothly. Jedao affected not to know what was going on and allowed the official to chirp at him. Eventually a stretcher arrived and they put him on it. They emerged into the lights of the shuttle bay. Jedao's temples twinged with the beginning of a headache. At least it meant the eye drops were still doing their job.

The journey to Du Station's version of Medical took forever. Jedao was especially eager to escape based on what he'd learned of Gwa-an medical therapies, which involved too many genetically engineered critters for his comfort. (He had read up on the topic after Haval told him about the dueling.) He did consider that he could make his mother happy by stealing some pretty little microbes for her, but with his luck they'd turn his testicles inside out.

When the medic took him into an examination room, Jedao whipped up and felled her with a blow to the side of the neck. The guard was slow to react. Jedao grasped their throat and grappled with them, waiting the interminable seconds until they slumped, unconscious. He had a bad moment when he heard footsteps passing by. Luckily, the guard's wheeze didn't attract attention. Jedao wasn't modest about his combat skills, but they wouldn't save him if he was sufficiently outnumbered.

Too bad he couldn't steal the guard's uniform, but it wouldn't fit him. So it would have to be the medic's clothes. Good: the medic's clothes were robes instead of something more form-fitting. Bad: even though the garments would fit him, more or less, they were in the style for women.

I will just have to improvise, Jedao thought. At least he'd kept up the habit of shaving, and the Gwa-an appeared to permit a variety of haircuts in all genders, so his short hair and bangs wouldn't be too much of a problem. As long as he moved quickly and didn't get stopped for conversation—

Jedao changed, then slipped out and took a few moments to observe how people walked and interacted so he could fit in more easily. The Gwa-an were terrible about eye contact and, interestingly for station-dwellers, preferred to keep each other at a distance. He could work with that.

His eyes still ached, since Du Station had abominably bright lighting, but he'd just have to prevent people from looking too closely at him. It helped that he had dark brown eyes to begin with, so the dilated pupils wouldn't be obvious from a distance. He was walking briskly toward the lifts when he heard a raised voice. He kept walking. The voice called again, more insistently.

Damn. He turned around, hoping that someone hadn't recognized his outfit from behind. A woman in extravagant layers of green, lilac, and pink spoke to him in strident tones. Jedao approached her rapidly, wincing at her voice, and hooked her into an embrace. Maybe he could take advantage of this yet.

"You're not—" she began to say.

"I'm too busy," he said over her, guessing at how best to deploy the Tlen Gwa phrases he knew. "I'll see you for tea at thirteen. I like your coat."

The woman's face turned an ugly mottled red. "You like my *what*?" At least he thought he'd said "coat." She stepped back from him, pulling what looked like a small perfume bottle from among her layers of clothes.

He tensed, not wanting to fight her in full view of passersby. She spritzed him with a moist vapor, then smiled coolly at him before spinning on her heel and walking away.

Shit. Just how fast-acting were Gwa-an duels, anyway? He missed the sensible kind with swords; his chances would have been much better. He hoped the symptoms wouldn't be disabling, but then, the woman couldn't possibly have had a chance to tailor the infectious agent to his system, and maybe the immunizations would keep him from falling over sick until he had found Meng and their crew.

How had he offended her, anyway? Had he gotten the word for "coat" wrong? Now that he thought about it, the word for "coat" differed from the word for "navel" only by its tones, and—hells and foxes, he'd messed up the tone sandhi, hadn't he? He kept walking, hoping that she'd be content with getting him sick and wouldn't call security on him.

At last he made it to the lifts. While stealing the medic's uniform had also involved stealing their keycard, he preferred not to use it. Rather, he'd swapped the medic's keycard for the loud woman's. She had carried hers on a braided lanyard with a clip. It would do nicely if he had to garrote anyone in a hurry. The garrote wasn't one of his specialties, but as his girlfriend the first year of Shuos Academy had always been telling him, it paid to keep your options open.

At least the lift's controls were less perilous than figuring out how to correctly pronounce items of clothing. Jedao had by no means achieved reading fluency in Tlen Gwa, but the language had a wonderfully tidy writing system, with symbols representing syllables and odd little curlicue diacritics that changed what vowel you used. He had also theoretically memorized the numbers from 1 to 9,999. Fortunately, Du Station had fewer than 9,999 levels.

Two of the other people on the lift stared openly at Jedao. He fussed with his hair on the grounds that it would look like ordinary embarrassment and not *Hello! I am a cross-dressing enemy agent, pleased to make your acquaintance.* Come to that, Gwa-an women's clothes were comfortable, and all the layers meant that he could, in principle, hide useful items like garrotes in them. He wondered if he could keep them as a souvenir. Start a fashion back home. He bet his mother would approve.

Intelligence had given him a good idea of where Meng and their crew might be held. At least, Jedao hoped that Du Station's higher-ups hadn't faked him out by stowing them in the lower-security cells as opposed to the top-security ones. He was betting a lot on the guess that the Gwa-an were still in the process of interrogating the group rather than executing them out of hand.

The layout wasn't the hard part, but Jedao reflected on the mysteries of the Gwa Reality's penal code. For example, prostitution was a major offense. They didn't even fine the offenders, but sent them to remedial counseling, which surely *cost* the state money. In the heptarchate, they did the sensible thing by enforcing licenses for health and safety reasons and taxing the whole enterprise. On the other hand, the Gwa-an had a refreshingly casual attitude toward heresy. They believed that public debate about Poetics (their version of Doctrine) strengthened the polity. If you put forth that idea anywhere in the heptarchate, you could expect to get arrested.

So it was that Jedao headed for the cellblocks where one might find unlucky prostitutes and not the ones where overly enthusiastic heretics might be locked up overnight to cool off. He kept attracting horrified looks and wondered if he'd done something offensive with his hair. Was it wrong to part it on the left, and if so, why hadn't Haval warned him? How many ways could you get hair wrong anyway?

The Gwa-an also had peculiarly humanitarian ideas about the surroundings that offenders should be kept in. Level 37, where he expected to find Meng, abounded with fountains. Not cursory fountains, but glorious cascading arches of silvery water interspersed with elongated humanoid statues in various uncomfortable-looking poses. Teshet had mentioned that this had to do with Gwa-an notions of ritual purity.

While "security" was one of the words that Jedao had memorized, he did not read Tlen Gwa especially quickly, which made figuring out the signs a chore. At least the Gwa-an believed in signs, a boon to foreign infiltrators everywhere. Fortunately, the Gwa-an hadn't made a secret of the Security office's location, even if getting to it was complicated by the fact that the fountains had been rearranged since the last available intel and he preferred not to show up soaking wet. The fountains themselves formed a labyrinth and, upon inspection, it appeared that different portions could be turned on or off to change the labyrinth's twisty little passages.

Unfortunately, the water's splashing also made it difficult to hear people coming, and he had decided that creeping about would not only slow him down, but make him look more conspicuous, especially with the issue of his hair (or whatever it was that made people stare at him with such affront). He rounded a corner and almost crashed into a sentinel, recognizable by Security's spear-and-shield badge.

In retrospect, a simple collision might have worked out better. Instead, Jedao dropped immediately into a fighting stance, and the sentinel's eyes narrowed. *Dammit*, Jedao thought, exasperated with himself. *This is why my handlers preferred me doing the sniper bits rather than the infiltration bits.* Since he'd blown the opportunity to bluff his way past the sentinel, he swept the man's feet from under him and knocked him out. After the man was unconscious, Jedao stashed him behind one of the statues, taking care so the spray from the fountains wouldn't interfere too much with his breathing. He had the distinct impression that "dead body" was much worse from a ritual purity standpoint than "merely unconscious," if he had to negotiate with someone later.

He ran into no other sentinels on the way to the office, but as it so happened, a sentinel was leaving just as he got there. Jedao put on an expression he had learned from the scariest battlefield medic of his acquaintance back when he'd been a lowly infantry captain and marched straight up to Security. He didn't need to be convincing for long, he just needed a moment's hesitation.

By the time the sentinel figured out that the "medic" was anything but, Jedao had taken her gun and broken both her arms. "I want to talk to your leader," he said, another of those useful canned phrases.

The sentinel left off swearing (he was sure it was swearing) and repeated the word for "leader" in an incredulous voice.

Whoops. Was he missing some connotational nuance? He tried the word for "superior officer," to which the response was even more incredulous. *Hey Mom*, Jedao thought, *you know how you always said I should join the diplomatic corps on account of my always talking my way out of trouble as a kid? Were you ever wrong. I am the worst diplomat ever.* Admittedly, maybe starting off by breaking the woman's arms was where he'd gone wrong, but the sentinel didn't sound upset about *that*. The Gwa-an were very confusing people.

After a crescendo of agitation (hers) and desperate rummaging about for people nouns (his), it emerged that the term he wanted was the one for "head priest." Which was something the language lessons ought to have noted. He planned on dropping in on whoever had written the course and having a spirited talk with them.

Just as well that the word for "why" was more straightforward. The sentinel wanted to know why he wanted to talk to the head priest. He wanted to know why someone who'd had both her arms broken was more concerned with propriety (his best guess) than alerting the rest of the station that they had an intruder. He had other matters to attend to, though. Too bad he couldn't recruit her for her sangfroid, but that was outside his purview.

What convinced the sentinel to comply, in the end, was not the threat of more violence, which he imagined would have been futile. Instead, he mentioned that he'd left one of her comrades unconscious amid the fountains and the man would need medical care. He liked the woman's concern for her fellow sentinel.

Jedao and the sentinel walked together to the head priest's office. The head priest came out. She had an extremely elaborate coiffure, held in place by multiple hairpins featuring elongated figures like the statues. She froze when Jedao pointed the gun at her, then said several phrases in what sounded like different languages.

"Mongrel language," Jedao said in Tlen Gwa, remembering what Haval had told him.

"What do you want?" the high priest said in awkward but comprehensible high language.

Jedao explained that he was here for Ahun Gerav, in case the priest only knew Meng by their cover name. "Release them and their crew, and this can end with minimal bloodshed."

The priest wheezed. Jedao wondered if she was allergic to assassins. He'd never heard of such a thing, but he wasn't under any illusions that he knew everything about Gwa-an immune systems. Then he realized she was laughing.

"Feel free to share," Jedao said, very pleasantly. The sentinel was sweating.

The priest stopped laughing. "You're too late," she said. "You're too late by thirteen years."

Jedao did the math: eight years since he and Meng had graduated from Shuos Academy. Of course, the two of them had attended for the usual five years. "They've been a double agent since they were a cadet?"

The priest's smile was just this side of smug.

Jedao knocked the sentinel unconscious and let her spill to the floor. The priest's smile didn't falter, which made him think less of her. Didn't she care about her subordinate? If nothing else, he'd had a few concussions in his time (real ones), and they were no joke.

"The crew," Jedao said.

"Gerav attempted to persuade them to turn coat as well," the priest said. "When they were less than amenable, well—" She shrugged. "We had no further use for them."

"I will not forgive this," Jedao said. "Take me to Gerav."

She shrugged. "Unfortunate for them," she said. "But to be frank, I don't value their life over my own."

"How very pragmatic of you," Jedao said.

She shut up and led the way.

Du Station had provided Meng with a luxurious suite by heptarchate standards. The head priest bowed with an ironic smile as she opened the door for Jedao. He shoved her in and scanned the room.

The first thing he noticed was the overwhelming smell of—what *was* that smell? Jedao had thought he had reasonably cosmopolitan tastes, but the platters with their stacks of thin-sliced meat drowned in rich gravies and sauces almost made him gag. Who needed that much meat in their diet? The suite's occupant seemed to agree, judging by how little the meat had been touched. And why wasn't the meat cut into decently small pieces so as to make for easy eating? The bowls of succulent fruit were either for show or the suite's occupant disliked fruit, too. The flatbreads, on the other hand, had been torn into. One, not entirely eaten, rested on a meat platter and was dissolving into the gravy. Several different-sized bottles were partly empty, and once he adjusted to all the meat, he could also detect the sweet reek of wine.

Most fascinatingly, instead of chopsticks and spoons, the various plates and platters sported two-tined forks (Haval had explained to him about forks) and knives. Maybe this was how they trained assassins. Jedao liked knives, although not as much as he liked guns. He wondered if he could persuade the Kel to import the custom. It would make for some lively high tables.

Meng glided out, resplendent in brocade Gwa-an robes, then gaped. Jedao wasn't making any attempt to hide his gun.

"Foxfucking hounds," Meng slurred as they sat down heavily, "*you*. Is that really you, Jedao?"

"You know each other?" the priest said.

Jedao ignored her question, although he kept her in his peripheral vision in case he needed to kill her or knock her out. "You graduated from Shuos Academy with high marks," Jedao said. "You even married rich the way you always talked about. Four beautiful kids. Why, Meng? Was it nothing more than a story?"

Meng reached for a fork. Jedao's trigger finger shifted. Meng withdrew their hand.

"The Gwa-an paid stupendously well," Meng said quietly. "It mattered a lot more, once. Of course, hiding the money was getting harder and harder. What good is money if you can't spend it? And the Shuos were about to catch on anyway. So I had to run."

"And your crew?"

Meng's mouth twisted, but they met Jedao's eyes steadfastly. "I didn't want things to end the way they did."

"Cold comfort to their families."

"It's done now," Meng said, resigned. They looked at the largest platter of meat with sudden loathing. Jedao tensed, wondering if it was going to be flung at him, but all Meng did was shove it away from them. Some gravy slopped over the side.

Jedao smiled sardonically. "If you come home, you might at least get a decent bowl of rice instead of this weird bread stuff."

"Jedao, if I come home they'll *torture me for high treason,* unless our heptarch's policies have changed drastically. You can't stop me from killing myself."

"Rather than going home?" Jedao shrugged. Meng probably did have a suicide fail-safe, although if they were serious they'd have used it already. He couldn't imagine the Gwa-an would have neglected to provide them with one if the Shuos hadn't.

Still, he wasn't done. "If you do something so crass, I'm going to visit each one of your children *personally.* I'm going to take them out to a nice dinner with actual food that you eat with actual chopsticks and spoons. And I'm going to explain to them in exquisite detail how their Shuos parent is a traitor."

Meng bit their lip.

More softly, Jedao said, "When did the happy family stop being a cover story and start being real?"

"I don't know," Meng said, wretched. "I can't—do you know how my spouses would look at me if they found out that I'd been lying to them all this time? I wasn't even particularly interested in other people's kids when this all began. But watching them grow up—" They fell silent.

"I have to bring you back," Jedao said. He remembered the staticky voice of the unnamed woman playing in Essier's office, Meng's *crew,* who'd tried and failed to get a warning out. She and her comrades deserved justice. But he also remembered all the gifts he'd sent to Meng's children over the years, the occasional awkwardly written thank-you note. It wasn't as if any good would be achieved by telling them the awful truth. "But I can pull a few strings. Make sure your family never finds out."

Meng hesitated for a long moment. Then they nodded. "It's fair. Better than fair."

To the priest, Jedao said, "You'd better take us to the *Moonsweet Blossom,* assuming you haven't disassembled it already."

The priest's mouth twisted. "You're in luck," she said.

· • ● • ·

Du Station had ensconced the *Moonsweet Blossom* in a bay on Level 62. The Gwa-an passed gawped at them. The priest sailed past without giving any explanations. Jedao wondered whether the issue was his hair or some other inexplicable Gwa-an cultural foible.

"I hope you can pilot while drunk," Jedao said to Meng.

Meng drew themself up to their full height. "I didn't drink *that* much."

Jedao had his doubts, but he would take his chances. "Get in."

The priest's sudden tension alerted him that she was about to try something. Jedao shoved Meng toward the trademoth, then grabbed the priest in an armlock. What was the point of putting a priest in charge of security if the priest couldn't *fight*?

Jedao said to her, "You're going to instruct your underlings to get the hell out of our way and open the airlock so we can leave."

"And why would I do that?" the priest said.

He reached up and snatched out half her hairpins. Too bad he didn't have a third hand; his grip on the gun was precarious enough as it was. She growled, which he interpreted as *Fuck you and all your little foxes.* "I could get creative," Jedao said.

"I was warned that the heptarchate was full of barbarians," the priest said.

At least the incomprehensible Gwa-an fixation on hairstyles meant that he didn't have to resort to more disagreeable threats, like shooting her subordinates in front of her. Given her reaction when he had knocked out the sentinel, he wasn't convinced that would faze her anyway. He adjusted his grip on her and forced her to the floor.

"Give the order," he said. "If you don't play any tricks, you'll even get the hairpins back without my shoving them through your eardrums." They were very nice hairpins, despite the creepiness of the elongated humanoid figures, and he bet they were real gold.

Since he had her facing the floor, the priest couldn't glare at him. The frustration in her voice was unmistakable, however. "As you require." She started speaking in Tlen Gwa.

The workers in the area hurried to comply. Jedao had familiarized himself with the control systems of the airlock and was satisfied they weren't doing anything underhanded. "Thank you," he said, to which the priest hissed something venomous. He flung the hairpins away and let her go. She cried out at the sound of their clattering and scrambled after them with a devotion he reserved for weapons. Perhaps, to a Gwa-an priest, they were equivalent.

One of the workers, braver or more foolish than the others, reached for her own gun. Jedao shot her in the hand on the way up the hatch to the *Moonsweet Blossom*. It bought him enough time to get the rest of the way up the ramp and slam the hatch shut after him. Surely Meng couldn't accuse him of showing off if they hadn't seen the feat of marksmanship; and he hoped the worker would appreciate that he could just as easily have put a hole in her head.

The telltale rumble of the *Blossom*'s maneuver drive assured him that Meng, at least, was following directions. This boded well for Meng's health. Jedao hurried forward, wondering how many more rounds the Gwa-an handgun contained, and started webbing himself into the gunner's seat.

"You wouldn't consider putting that thing away, would you?" Meng said. "It's hard for me to think when I'm ready to piss myself."

"If you think *I'm* the scariest person in your future, Meng, you haven't been paying attention."

"One, I don't think you know yourself very well, and two, I liked you much better when we were on the same side."

"I'm going to let you meditate on that second bit some other time. In the meantime, let's get out of here."

Meng swallowed. "They'll shoot us down the moment we get clear of the doors, you know."

"Just *go*, Meng. I've got friends. Or did you think I teleported onto this station?"

"At this point I wouldn't put anything past you. Okay, you're webbed in, I'm webbed in, here goes nothing."

The maneuver drive grumbled as the *Moonsweet Blossom* blasted its way out of the bay. No one attempted to close the first set of doors on them. Jedao wondered if the priest was still scrabbling after her hairpins, or if it had to do with the more pragmatic desire to avoid costly repairs to the station.

The *Moonsweet Blossom* had few armaments, mostly intended for dealing with high-velocity debris, which was more of a danger than pirates if one kept to the better-policed trade routes. They wouldn't do any good against Du Station's defenses. As *signals*, on the other hand—

Using the lasers, Jedao flashed HERE WE COME in the merchanter signal code. With any luck, Haval was paying attention.

At this point, several things happened.

Haval kicked Teshet in the shin to get him to stop watching a mildly pornographic and not-very-well-acted drama about a famous courtesan from 192 years ago. ("It's historical so it's educational!" he protested. "One, we've got our signal, and two, I wish you would take care of your *urgent needs* in your own quarters," Haval said.)

Carp 1 through *Carp 4* and *7* through *10* launched all their shuttles. Said shuttles were, as Jedao had instructed, full of variable-coefficient lubricant programmed to its liquid form. The shuttles flew toward Du Station, then opened their holds and burned their retro thrusters for all they were worth. The lubricant, carried forward by momentum, continued toward Du Station's turret levels.

Du Station recognized an attack when it saw one. However, its defenses consisted of a combination of high-powered lasers, which could only vaporize small portions of the lubricant and were useless for altering the momentum of quantities of the stuff, and railguns, whose projectiles punched through the mass without much effect. Once the lubricant had clogged up the defensive emplacements, *Carp 1* transmitted an encrypted radio signal with the command that caused the lubricant to harden in place.

The *Moonsweet Blossom* linked up with Haval's merchant troop. At this point, the *Blossom* only contained two people, trivial compared to the amount of mass it had been designed to haul. The merchant troop, of course, had just divested itself of its cargo. The nine heptarchate vessels proceeded to hightail it out of there at highly non-freighter accelerations.

Jedao and Meng swept the *Moonsweet Blossom* for bugs and other unwelcome devices, an exhausting but necessary task. Then, at what Jedao judged to be a safe distance from Du Station, he ordered Meng to slave it to *Carp 1*.

The *Carp 1* and *Moonsweet Blossom* matched velocities, and Jedao and Meng made the crossing to the former. There was a bad moment when Jedao thought Meng was going to unhook their tether and drift off into the smothering dark rather than face their fate. But whatever temptations were running through their head, Meng resisted them.

Haval and Teshet greeted them on the *Carp 1*. After Jedao and Meng had shed the suits and checked them for needed repairs, Haval ushered them all into the business office. "I didn't expect you to spring the trademoth as well as our Shuos friend," Haval said.

Meng wouldn't meet her eyes.

"What about the rest of the crew?" Teshet said.

"They didn't make it," Jedao said, and sneezed. He explained about Meng's extracurricular activities over the past thirteen years. Then he sneezed again.

Haval grumbled under her breath. "Whatever the hell you did on Du, Sren, did it involve duels?"

"'Sren'?" Meng said.

"You don't think I came into the Gwa Reality under my own"—sneeze—"name, did you?" Jedao said. "Anyway, there might have been an incident . . ."

Meng groaned. "Just how good is your Tlen Gwa?"

"Sort of not, apparently," Jedao said. "I *really* need to have a word with whoever wrote the Tlen Gwa course. I thought I was all right with languages at the basic phrase level, but was the proofreader asleep the day they approved it?"

Meng had the grace to look embarrassed. "I may have hacked it."

"You what?"

"If I'd realized *you'd* be using it, I wouldn't have bothered. Botching the language doesn't seem to have slowed you down any."

Wordlessly, Teshet handed Jedao a handkerchief. Jedao promptly sneezed into it. Maybe he'd be able to give his mother a gift of a petri dish with a lovely culture of Gwa-an germs, after all. He'd have to ask the medic about it later.

Teshet then produced a set of restraints from his pockets and gestured at Meng. Meng sighed deeply and submitted to being trussed up.

"Don't look so disappointed," Teshet said into Jedao's ear. "I've another set just for you." Then he and Meng marched off to the brig.

Haval cleared her throat. "Off to the medic with you," she said to Jedao. "We'd better figure out why your vaccinations aren't working and if everyone's going to need to be quarantined."

"Not arguing," Jedao said meekly.

Some days later, Jedao was rewatching one of Teshet's pornography dramas while in bed. At least, he thought it was pornography. The costuming made it difficult to tell, and the dialogue had made *more* sense when he was still running a fever.

The medic had kept him in isolation until they declared him no longer contagious. Whether due to this precaution or pure luck, no one else came down with the duel disease. They'd given him a clean bill of health this morning, but Haval had insisted that he rest a little longer.

The door opened. Jedao looked up in surprise.

Teshet entered with a fresh supply of handkerchiefs. "Well, Jedao, we'll reenter heptarchate space in two days, high calendar. Any particular orders you want me to relay to Haval?" He obligingly handed over a slate so Jedao could review Haval's painstaking, not to say excruciatingly detailed, reports on their current status.

"Haval's doing a fine job," Jedao said, glad that his voice no longer came out as a croak. "I won't get in her way." He returned the slate to Teshet.

"Sounds good." Teshet turned his back and departed. Jedao admired the view, wishing in spite of himself that the other man would linger.

Teshet returned half an hour later with two clear vials full of unidentified substances. "First or second?" he said, holding them up to the light one by one.

"I'm sorry," Jedao said, "first or second what?"

"You look like you need cheering up," Teshet said hopefully. "You want on top? You want me on top? I'm flexible."

Jedao blinked, trying to parse this. "On top of wh—" *Oh.* "What's *in* those vials?"

"You have your choice of variable-coefficient lubricant or goose fat," Teshet said. "Assuming you were telling the truth when you said it was goose fat. And don't yell at Haval for letting me into your refrigerator; I did it all on my own. I admit, I can't tell the difference. As Haval will attest, I'm a *dreadful* cook, so I didn't want to fry up some scallion pancakes just to taste the goose fat."

Jedao's mouth went dry, which had less to do with Teshet's eccentric choice of lubricants than the fact that he had sat down on the edge of Jedao's bed. "You don't have anything more, ah, conventional?" He realized that was a mistake as soon as the words left his mouth; he'd essentially accepted Teshet's proposition.

For the first time, Jedao glimpsed uncertainty in Teshet's eyes. "We don't have a lot of time before we're back in heptarchate space and you have to go back to being a commander and I have to go back to being responsible," he said softly. "Or as responsible as I ever get, anyway. Want to make the most of it? Because I get the impression that you don't allow yourself much of a personal life."

"Use the goose fat," Jedao said, because as much as he liked Teshet, he did not relish the thought of being *cemented* to Teshet: It would distract Teshet from continuing to analyze his psyche, and, yes, the man was damnably attractive. What the hell, with any luck his mother was never, ever, *ever* hearing of this. (He could imagine the conversation now: "Garach Jedao Shkan, are you meaning to tell me you finally found a nice young man and you're *still* not planning on settling down and providing me extra grandchildren?" And then she would send him *more goose fat.*)

Teshet brightened. "You won't regret this," he purred, and proceeded to help Jedao undress.

ARKADY MARTINE

ALL THE COLORS YOU THOUGHT WERE KINGS

Arkady Martine is a speculative fiction writer and, as Dr. AnnaLinden Weller, a historian of the Byzantine Empire and a city planner. Under both names she writes about border politics, narrative and rhetoric, risk communication, and the edges of the world. She is currently a policy advisor for the New Mexico Energy, Minerals, and Natural Resources Department, where she works on climate change mitigation, energy grid modernization, and resiliency planning. Her debut novel, *A Memory Called Empire*, won the Hugo Award in 2020, and its sequel, *A Desolation Called Peace*, won in 2022. Martine grew up in New York City, and after some time in Turkey, Canada, Sweden, and Baltimore, lives in New Mexico with her wife, the author Vivian Shaw. [www.arkadymartine.net]

Moonrise glitters dull on the sides of the ship that'll take you away. She's down by the water, her belly kissing the sand and her skinny landing-legs stuck out like a crab. You and Tamar watched her land, stayed up half the night like babies staring at their first meteor storm, peeking over the railings of Tamar's balcony and marveling at how the falling star-glimmer lit up the lights under your skins like an echo. You two have been full up with starstuff for as long as you've been old enough to go outside the crèche by yourselves. Now you're almost home.

Home for you will be the Imperial battlecruiser *Vault of Heaven*, destroyer-class, star-conqueror and peacekeep. You've had your marching orders for three months, and you've spent every spare minute accessing all the file and 'fiche on her you can scrounge clearance for. You practically live on your records-tablet when you're not out with Tamar, so no one's minded you taking a bit of time to fall in love with your own personal piece of the Fleet. The *Vault of Heaven*'s an old ship, a proud ship, refitted top of the line just a year ago. You're for officer's training and then command, your geneset finally writing you the ticket you've always known it would. Tonight the shuttle takes you and Tamar and every other crèche-spun kid old enough to have passed the entrance exams up to the Empress's very own flagship.

Tomorrow there'll be ceremonies and presentations, and then your nanite horde will be calibrated for shipside on live broadcast for the entire Fleet to see—another cohort of kids full up with starshine micromechanics, bound to service and obedience, gone off into the stars. You've been dreaming about it since you could read. You want it so much you've spent the last three months feeling like your chest is going to burn out from longing.

The night *after* tomorrow, though. You can't let yourself dream about that.

Under the drape of your overjacket, snugged up to your spine like you're its best lovecrush, are the disassembled pieces of a sniper rifle. Nestled right at the small of your back is the lead-shielded explosive heart of an electromagnetic pulse bomb.

The overjacket's the best overjacket you've ever had, orchid brocade in stiff heavy folds that split at the breastbone into six panels, done over in mother-of-pearl and sequins that echo the lightswarm of your nanites. You had it made specially. No way you were going up to space in last year's couture, you said at the tailor's, and you meant it, only you also meant you wanted to look enough the louche crècheling that no one would think to check under your finery. You're Elias Akhal. There's only one geneset in the Empire purer than yours. No one would ever suspect you're anything but the Fleet's man, hungry for your own ship and a starfield as big as any ocean you've ever swum in.

You wish so much it were that simple. You also wish it weren't *true*. You'd like it if you could ever feel all one way about a thing.

When you turn round from staring at the shuttle, there's Petros Titresh and your Tamar, coming down the beach like a picture out of a storyfiche. She's done up in gauzes with gold bangles in her hair, but he's a steel-gray bore: overjacket buttoned to the chin and his skin unlit, sparkless and smooth like stonework. Petros never ate his nanites; the way he tells the story, he stormed out of his crèche in a stubborn fit of ideological purity instead of making himself into starlight. Sometimes, when you and he stay out talking in the city until the dawn alarms sound, you get drunk enough to almost understand why.

Now he walks in careful tandem with Tamar, his hand trapped in hers, her regard pinned to him like a medal he never won nor deserved. Tamar can have anyone she likes, is the problem. She's not just *Akhal* like you—she's real Imperial cloneflesh, sister and twin right down to the cell with the Empress Herself. She hasn't been a mirror for you since you both hit puberty, but the lines of your face and hers are the same: razor cheekbones and full mouths, the nose that every Fleet officer shares. Her eyes never darkened from gray; that was the first clue the crèche-keepers got that they'd spun an Imperial clone instead of another Akhal. Today Tamar is bare-armed beautiful in the light coming up reflected off the waves, all muscle through the shoulder from how much she's practiced with spear and neuroparalyzer net.

Tomorrow the Empress Herself kills her, or your Tamar kills *the Empress* and takes the Imperium for a prize. They're not just otherselves like you and every other Akhal, they're cloneflesh, they're the *same*, there's only ever allowed to be one of them. The law guarantees it.

Even barefoot in gauze, your Tamar looks dangerous. You could die of pride if you weren't half planning to die of something else first.

Petros stares at the shuttle like you've been staring at it, goggle-eyed and hungry. "It's not very big," he says.

"That's because *this* one's just for this crèche, direct to the Empress's flagship!" Tamar's all foam-bubble excitement. You glow just hearing her.

"I know," Petros says. "Only the best genesets, sent straight into the maw of the Fleet for our compulsory brainwashing and a celebratory gladiatorial death game! I am going to have so much fun I can hardly begin to describe it."

"No one's going to notice you, Petros, your bit'll be easy," you say, which you mean to be a comforting sort of comrades-in-arms gesture. From Petros's expression it sounds to him more like you were enthusing about the benefits of sticking his head out an airlock.

Tamar ruffles his hair. Petros flinches, and so do you, your heart flopping in your chest like something from the deeps dragged out and drowning in air. Tamar can take anyone up to the Fleet with her on just her say-so. Even if he's outside the law, no starstuff sparks ready to tear his flesh if he betrays the Empire, Petros Titresh gets his berth on the ship. That's the part of your plan that's all Tamar. She says to every horde-riddled adult: *this Titresh is my servant; I want him, he comes with me.*

On your good days, you believe that pile of rotten sharkmeat. This isn't a good day. You'd rather you three were trying to smuggle him in the luggage.

"Two hours left," Tamar says. "Last day on the beach. You boys ready?"

It's your beach, yours and Tamar's. Her balcony in the crèche looks down over it. It's also the safest place for three kids to plan treason. The surf covers ambient sound pickup, and hardly anyone but you two've got the arm-strength to climb down the cliffs to the shore alone. When Petros comes along one of you brings a rope to help him, and he's not a weakling. He's just not an Akhal.

"You got the—" Petros starts to ask, his hand shaping a trigger and a stock in the air, and you interrupt him.

"Of course I do. Yours and mine."

Petros gives you a short nod, stepping into the waves towards the shuttle. He gets the hems of his trousers soaked. "Everyone else I've ever had the misfortune of knowing is either half-drunk on the prospect of basic training and eternal servitude, or hiding out in a skep hoping that not showing up for conscription day won't make their nanites disassemble them," he says contemplatively. "I guess I'm ready."

Tamar splashes him. When he yelps, she says, "You'll be fine."

"I will not," he says. "This is such a brilliant disaster of a plan."

Next to Tamar, blazing like a comet, the moonlight *shrouds* him;

65

he's near invisible, his head bowed and his shoulders hunched up to his ears. He's probably wishing he was down in the city, yelling at kids with visible asymmetries about changing the world. He's a mess. You could hate him for it, but hating Petros makes you tired.

"Only a disaster if it doesn't work," you say, and you make yourself sound coaxing and gentle and like you believe it.

"It's going to work," Tamar says. "If I win that duel—and you're going to make sure I win that duel—I'm legally Empress and I can retroactively pardon the three of us. And then we can get started on making *real* changes! For everybody. We just have to get there. I need you."

You are going to be sick to your stomach. Maybe you can blame it on never having been up in space before. The laser-housing for your rifle is digging a hole next to your ribs, under your gorgeous overjacket. You can't forget it's there and you aren't sure how anyone else is likely to fail to notice how you've got most of a sniper rig in pieces all attached to you. Especially if you get sick all over yourself. *Retroactive pardons.* The fuck are you three doing.

"I know," says Petros. "You can't do it without me. Got to have an invisible kid to carry the bomb. We've got two hours, right? I'm taking a walk." He trudges into the surf, heading east down the shoreline. Tamar watches him go.

You look around the beach that's been a truer home than even your room in the crèche, and think: *I am never going to see this place again.* You don't know if how empty your chest gets is because you want to be gone or because you're saying goodbye. Then your Tamar is finally looking at you and you forget all about yourself.

She smiles like she smiles on the bow of a skiff right before she fires her speargun, high-tension and brighter than midday. She gets her feet wet coming over to you, and then she reaches out and fixes your collar. It's the first time in six days she's touched you, and she doesn't even notice how you go shame-struck still under her fingertips.

"Elias," she says. "We're really doing this. I'm *so* nervous! It's great."

You nod. "We really are," you say. She lets you go and dashes toward the pier and its boathouse.

"I'm going out one last time! You should come with me!" she calls over her shoulder. The shadow of the pier swallows her whole and you go running after.

You meet your first shipside adults when the shuttle door gapes open like the belly of a gutted fish. The adults are tall and beautiful and they glitter, their lips and eyes full to bursting with nanite sparks. You can't spot their geneset from just looking; it's not one that gets spun in your crèche. They move like sharks, like they've forgot how to be still. When you line up to board, they take samples of your blood. Fingerprick test: one officer with a clipboard, one officer with a little needle-machine, making sure each kid is what they say they are.

Tamar gets a wide eye and a bit of snide subservience when she comes up Imperial on the fingerprick, ushered to a seat right in the shuttlefront with the best view. She is simpered at while she goes. She takes it like the princess she's always been, like she couldn't care less for propriety. She introduces Petros while they check the dull hue of his blood. She introduces you: *and this is Elias Akhal, we were crèchesibs together.* The adults look you over, then, take your measure like they understand all of what you are. You twitch the panels of your overjacket into place and stare them down until they dismiss you as just one more sparkstruck kid caught in Tamar's wake, and don't you wish that didn't sting.

You sit in the seat facing her and Petros, strapped in against acceleration. Your back's to the view so even when you break gravity and the dizzy pressure of atmospheric escape shoves your lungs into your stomach, space stays a mystery. You watch it reflected in Tamar's horde, starlight particles flowing restless in her cheeks, a hectic flush. About then everything goes topsy-turvy and you have to spend some time once again not spewing your guts onto your overjacket and ruining everything. Petros has got no such problems with weightlessness. His mouth gapes open at the view, and you've never seen him look so much like he might cry from seeing something good. Whatever else is wrong with him, refusing the horde and all his bullshit talk about geneset equality, turns out the kid is made for space. If you weren't working on remembering how to breathe, you'd add that to the list of things Petros has taken away from you without ever knowing he took them.

Gravity reestablishes when the shuttle docks, but you don't have time to adjust before the officers unstrap Tamar and take her away. You panic for the first time. The other kids are filing out of the shuttle and onto the flagship and all you do is scramble to your feet and say "Already?" like you are the most ill-starred fool in an awful romanceflick.

Tamar comes over to you all in a rush, gets close enough that you can see how wide her eyes have gotten. "Don't worry yourself, Elias," she says. "I'll see you before sunrise. And you'll—you'll see me sooner, promise you'll watch?"

There is nothing in your life that ever prepared you to say goodbye to Tamar Akhal. You haven't got a single clue as to how. "I promise," you say. "I'll be right at the front—"

She leans in close. You think for a minute she's going to kiss you, let you drink up how her mouth tastes exactly the same as yours. Tamar takes you by the shoulders instead, her fingers a bare inch from where the barrel of your rifle pushes against the nape of your neck. You tell yourself you don't care and know you're lying.

She presses her forehead to yours. "And take care of Petros for me." She isn't smiling; your princess is as serious as a cull. The other thing you haven't got a clue about is how not to do what she asks of you.

"Just until you get back," you say. Petros is staring at you like your geneset spelled for three heads.

"Heir," says one of the officers, reproving, and she lets you go all at once, stalks over to them with her head high.

"Let's go," Tamar says, "I want to meet my predecessor already," and then her escort's got her and she's gone.

"Fuck this," says Petros. You agree. Then he does something you do not expect: he grabs your hand and holds on. You wouldn't admit it if he asked, but you're glad.

·•◉•·

You wait an endless fifteen minutes before your escort arrives. He's Akhal like you and not much your senior; looking at him is like looking at five years from now. Turns out your shoulders aren't going to broaden much more but your face'll settle into cheeks that could cut glass. Mid-twenties seems fantastic. You hope you live that long, but you've got your doubts. Your escort doesn't give his use-name, just hands you a records-tablet stuffed full of paperwork and grins your grin back at you, says *welcome aboard, little brother.* You manage not to stammer when you thank him, even if you're shot right through with nerves. If anyone'll notice your smuggled sniper's kit it'll be your otherself, trained up and true loyal.

You think: You should guess that you're lying, you should guess that you're *committing treason* right in front of yourself. You keep not guessing. Maybe you're defective, and that's why you're capable of marching down a spaceship corridor behind a person who is supposed to be another part of you, and you can keep a secret from him. It's horrible to think about. You're proud of your geneset. You've always been. You don't want to be so different from your otherselves that you're opaque to them. (You also don't want to be dead. You wish that mattered more to you right now. You're so bad at this.)

Petros is dragged along in your wake, which is a better situation than a lot of the ones you three considered back on the beach. There's no re-cords-tablet and no Fleet assignment for a kid who isn't full up with nanites, and your otherself makes a note and promises Petros that he'll have a whole Fleet-compatible horde delivered for installation posthaste, considering Tamar's gone and vouched for his usefulness.

Petros *thanks* him. You didn't think he had the capacity to lie through his teeth. You're learning all kinds of things now that you've come to space.

·•◉•·

You and Petros are left in your assigned quarters. They're tiny, an eighth the size of your rooms at the crèche, but not half bad otherwise: desk and little couch and a threadbare pretty carpet over the metal floor, single bed nestled under a huge viewport, and there's your first real look at space. Space is a brighter black than night down planetside, a sharper distance studded with starlight that puts your horde to shame. It goes on and on and you are utterly dumbstruck, staring, records-tablet forgotten in your hands.

Over your shoulder, Petros says, "Come on, Elias, it's just stars," but you know better; you saw his face on the shuttle.

"Don't you want them?" you say. You think it must be written into your geneset, the way you're falling into the pinpoint lights.

"You are lovestruck for giant fusion reactors," says Petros, wryly, "and I am twenty minutes from having a horde stuffed down my throat like *oh accidentally missed my appointment* and fucking the plan completely. I like the stars fine. Space is—great. Brilliant."

You turn around. Petros is perched on the corner of the bed. He shrugs, crosses his arms over his ribs.

"They're awfully gorgeous fusion reactors," you say. You're trying. You are, you'd swear to it in front of Tamar, even. "I've been waiting such a long time to see them."

"I swear you Akhal are all space-mad."

"Just because I love what my geneset might spell for me to love—"

"Doesn't mean you don't love it true, and doesn't mean it isn't a problem. Come on, Elias, how many times have we had this argument?"

"Enough times that I thought we were done," you say.

"Maybe we were done while it was hypothetical."

You want to turn around and look at the stars; you wish Petros would stop making you doubt your own desires. "I'm not giving up on the plan," you say, "just because I'm happy to be here."

"If you don't do your half, I'm the one who is going to get spaced," Petros says. He gets up and paces a short arc across your quarters, door to desk to bedside and back again. "You're the safest of the three of us if you drop out. Nothing Tamar's doing is even illegal. I set off an electropulse bomb and fry everyone's nanite horde in the middle of the succession duel, and you don't get out your smuggled rifle and snipe the Empress, I'm an anti-Fleet seditionist and you're an innocent Akhal by-stander. You get to moon over the stars for-fucking-ever-and-ever, just like you're doing right now. You have a future in the Fleet. Your other-self just walked us here. So forgive me if I am suddenly having doubts about your commitment to the *cause*."

"And here I thought we were comrades," you say. You feel as if your spine is liquid fire, spreading into your lungs and your tongue. "I guess I oughtn't expect anyone who refused his nanites to be *capable* of com-radeship."

Petros's cheeks go that dull ruddy shade that isn't like anyone else's fury, and he grabs your shoulders as if he's about to shake you. You twist away and he snatches at the collar of your overjacket, so you swing at him. He ducks, yells something completely incomprehensible, and lung-es for you. You shove your knee in his stomach, which doesn't help at all, and the two of you go tumbling to the floor in a heap. The trigger-grip of your rifle slams into your left kidney and you make a high-pitched wheezing noise.

You shout at him. "*Stop!* If you hit me I might explode!"

This is true. It is also the funniest thing either of you have appar-ently ever heard. You find yourself with your forehead pushed into Pet-ros's shoulder, the both of you sharing an ugly bark of a laughing fit. You still feel miserable and furious and you still want nothing of the last ten minutes to have happened to you, but you can't seem to stop the spasms of your gut and your lungs; you are practically gasping by the time you manage to raise your head.

"You're kidding, right?" says Petros.

You get up on your knees and finish the job of shucking your over-jacket. Petros exhales hard when he's got a clear view of the pulse rifle, barrel curved to your back and disassembled trigger housing and scope taped low around your hips. You have to shove your shirt up to your collarbones to unstrap the electropulse bomb. The air of your quarters is clammy on your ribs.

"I used to snipe swordfish at four hundred meters, Petros," you say. Your voice is a quaver and an embarrassment. "This isn't even going to be hard."

"You and Tamar have had your brains replaced with a kid's infofiche history," Petros says, but he's helping you pull off the tape. The backs of his fingers brush your stomach and your nanites flock to the warm traces of touch, glittering afterimages rising on your skin. If he'd been full up with a horde, he'd light up too. You're selfish enough to wish to see it.

"She gave me this rifle, y'know?" you say to Petros, trying to cover that you're blushing so hard your nanites cast a shadow. "When we were just kids. She bought it off a courier ship down for repairs, that winter I introduced you to her. Spent half her money and all of mine and said she thought I should have it. Started out being too big for me to carry, let alone shoot."

Petros helps you slot the fuel cells into the body of the rifle. "I always thought you were kind of an idiot," he says companionably, as if he hadn't tried to punch you five minutes back, as if he wasn't putting together your sniper's rig, "and your politics have got the complexity of a two-year-old who's still dubious about sharing."

"And yet here we are," you say. You hand him the electropulse bomb. He turns it over and over in his hands, his unlit thumb brushing over the pressure pad of the trigger.

"It's a *public succession* duel," he says. "When did you two decide that you'd settle for nothing but the purest high-grade treason?"

Quite suddenly you don't want to explain. You're shy of it; you think he'll laugh at you, and somehow that'd be worse than when he wanted to punch you for being yourself.

"Wasn't Tamar's idea at all, to begin with," you say.

"No? Come on, Elias, you're gagging for Fleet Command, have been since you were knee-high. Can't have been you."

You shrug; you kneel so as to fasten the rifle back under your over-jacket, in three parts this time. Four seconds to assemble it the rest of the way. You've practiced, alone in the sand, watching the horizonline instead of your hands, faster and faster.

"When I brought it up," you explain, "she said I didn't owe her that much, that she could take care of herself. I even took her out on the quay and shot seagulls off the rocks so she'd know what kind of aim I've got. But she told me she wanted a fair fight."

Petros laughs, that same bitter barking. "Nothing fair about fighting the Empress in a duel to the death when you've not even gone through basic training yet."

"Maybe I should have said that."

"What did you say?"

You'd shoved the butt of your rifle into the sand and leaned on it, looking out over the sea that'd belonged to you and Tamar both. The wind had blown your hair twining with hers and you remember you'd felt like a photograph. You'd said to her, *I'm not yours, I'm not flesh of your flesh, but like fuck I'm going to watch you die and then bow my knee to your murderer.* She'd looked at you like you were breaking her heart.

What you say to Petros Titresh is: "I told her that I read my histories. There's never been an empress who won the throne *fair.* And then she said I sounded like you."

He slides the bomb into his pocket. He gets to his feet. "I should go before they find me here and dump me full of nanites," he says. "The explosion'll be on my count. Two hundred seconds from the opening of the duel."

You nod.

He sticks out his hand. Gingerly, you take it, and he yanks you to your feet. "Elias," he says. "Don't miss."

The arena is sand, starlit, a huge jewel set in the belly of the flagship. Every coliseum-style seat is full but yours, rows and rows all the way up to the edges of the shieldglass dome that covers the whole thing. There's at least ten thousand Fleet soldiers here, more sets of faces than you've ever seen in one place. You wonder if anyone's left to drive the starship.

There are tunnels underneath the arena, and somewhere in one is

Petros Titresh, alone and invisible and carrying a bomb. No horde in him: You and he left your quarters before any adult could show up with a nanite wafer to dissolve on his tongue. Technically you suppose you're AWOL right now, but if anyone asks, you wanted to see the succession duel, and who *wouldn't*. Petros isn't AWOL so much as he's a ghost. He peeled off from you twenty steps down the hall, and now you suppose you have to trust one another. You suppose also that you *do*.

The starfield above the arena goes on forever. You can't look at it for dizziness, can't think about it else your directions slide all out of phase. Gravity's a spinning fiction and you know it. You wish you could've shot at something less important a couple hundred times to make sure you've got your trajectories calculated right. There's only so much the scope of your rifle will do for you. More than half of sniping is the sniper's eye and the sniper's will.

Those, and hands that don't shake.

The three parts of your rifle are tucked up under your arms with your overjacket back on to hide them. Petros pronounced you *the very picture of someone with better genes than sense* before he left you alone, so you figure you can smile at the other new Akhal innocuous enough. There was a time when you'd've been more than eager to chat them all up, shove and maneuver until you sorted out whose geneset had spun truest. Now you sit as tall and still as you can, playing like none of them are worthy to talk with you. They're crowded into the seats beside yours, a jagged little clutch of mirrors, bright black eyes in your face eight times over. You all glow the same. None of them are dressed as pretty as you.

This is the quietest you've been in your entire life.

When the whole arena goes dark, there is nothing but the flicker of ten thousand nanite hordes, echoing the sudden press of the stars. You are going die of loving them, you think, they are lodging in your chest like your horde was *actually* made of light.

In that glimmering dim, the Empress rises from the center of the sand. She is flame-bright, some of those stars settling like a thousand tiny crowns in her hair. She's got the Akhal face and Tamar's gray eyes and there isn't a spare inch of flesh on her; only sternness, only regal command, effortless in a way that makes you want nothing but to get on your knees. It's all a show, you tell yourself, it's light and smoke and mirrors. In her hands she carries neuroparalyzer net and a spear that doesn't look like a prop of office; its point is a savage glint.

Your Empress lifts the spear to the starlight. The roar of the crowd resonates in your bones.

"Welcome," she says, her voice amplified and enveloping the whole arena. "Newest members of our Imperial Fleet. On the occasion of this night I offer you my personal congratulations. You are the purest, the brightest, the best genesets spun of your cohort. And tonight—tonight, the stars are yours."

Tonight the stars are yours. It isn't that you weren't afraid before. It's that now you're afraid you'll break your own heart when you shoot your gun. You don't much want Petros to be right about you, star-struck, blind and betraying; you want there to be a third option where you get to keep how you feel right now and no one has to die.

Your Empress dips her spear. "In recognition of the achievement of your adulthood, the light that you carry within you will now be joined to the light which burns in me, so that we may all be subject to the same law."

Your mouth dries and you flush hot. You are already burning, your veins humming as each tiny machine hears its new instruction. The law of the nanites is the Fleet's law; if you act against the interests of the Fleet you will be disassembled, devoured for carbon and water and reused in some more appropriate capacity. There is only one free man on this ship now and it isn't you: it is Petros Titresh, down in the dark under the arena with his nanite-disabling bomb. Then your Tamar walks out onto the sands and even the nanites stop mattering to you. Next to the Empress's glory she isn't small but she is stark, all in black, none of your girl's usual frippery, no gauze and gold wrapped around her narrow waist. She carries spear and net like they're part of her arm. Somehow she is smiling. You hate yourself for thinking even for one minute that you'd *regret* defending her.

"Predecessor!" she shouts. Whatever amplification the Empress is using picks her up too, makes her sound like a struck bell, right at your side where she belongs. "I greet you and I challenge you, predecessor, for command and for the Fleet!"

You imagine, in the dark, Petros starting his count, down from two hundred. You start yours.

"Do you?" says the Empress. She sounds infinitely gentle, kind and a little sad, like she's seen a dozen challenges and, regretting every one, spilled them red onto the sand. "On what grounds do you make claim to our stars, little sister?"

It's a script. A show. *One hundred forty-eight.*

"I am flesh of your flesh," says Tamar. "Your blood is mine! Your life is mine! Your stars are mine!" Then she squares her shoulders and jerks her chin up. You know that set of her, all stubborn and annoyed. "Also by the right of the law, predecessor, I claim you *incompetent* to rule—you misuse us."

The Empress pauses. You go cold, staring at the shine of her nanites and the brighter shine of her spear, knowing the script is trashed. You keep counting—*one hundred thirty, one hundred twenty-nine*—all the while wondering if you'll even have time to *take* your shot. Then the Empress laughs. When she laughs she sounds exactly the same as Tamar.

"Child," she says. "So will you." She dips her spear in some kind of salute.

Tamar doesn't wait. She's flying through the air, all of her behind the force of her spearthrust, aimed perfect at the Empress's throat. Your breath freezes in your lungs.

The Empress moves, faster than you can see, a blurred glow that snatches Tamar's spear from the air and wrenches her brutally sideways, tosses her like a cracked whip through the air. She lands on the sand—you wait for the sickening thump of splintered bone (eighty-two seconds)—but Tamar rolls, gets to her feet. She still has her net. You're panting. You suck at the air like your body thinks you're breathing vacuum, every cell straining sympathy.

Sixty-five. They circle each other, slow. Tamar's spear is a dark line she's landed too far away from, and she heads counterclockwise toward it. The Empress throws her net, its weighted edges spinning, the filaments crackling with paralyzing electricity. It sends Tamar ducking backward, dancing away from her weapon. Your girl is fast. Faster than you, faster than anyone you know, but the Empress isn't even breathing hard yet. Tamar tosses her head back, bares her perfect teeth—

Thirty. You haven't got time for watching this.

You drop to your knees. You're up front and all the other Akhal kids are all on their feet, screaming with the crowd, ignoring everything but the fight below. Four seconds to snap the rifle together—you lose one in fumbling the stock free of your overjacket, *twenty-three, twenty-two,* the barrel balances perfect on your shoulder. The scope settles over your eye. Your fingers flip each laser cell alight, curl around the trigger easy and gentle.

Tamar feints for her spear, makes a leap toward where it's lying and when the Empress starts forward to bat Tamar away, Tamar changes direction, closes in, just her net in her hands. It is the bravest thing you have ever seen Tamar do, and Tamar is the bravest of all the kids you know.

Fourteen. In the entire universe there is only you, and your target, and Tamar. Tamar's arm, the bunched curve of her spine, how they block where you need your shot to hit. Your fingertip feels raw against the triggerpull, every millimeter of your skin telling you how much pressure, how much tension you need to apply.

The first time you shot this rifle it knocked you over and Tamar had to pull you out of the dune where you'd landed on your ass.

The second time you shot it, braced proper like you'd looked up in your military manuals, you'd blown a hole in the side of a cliff deep enough for a grown man to hide in.

The Empress closes her fist in Tamar's hair and yanks her head back. You think of the veins in her throat, the curve of her collarbones. You think that hit or miss, you can't watch her die and never could. You wonder when your nanites will notice that you're brimful with treason. Is it now, as you sight through the scope? *Two.* Is it now, as you breathe out, as your finger squeezes, *one*, as you wonder if Petros has the count right, now, the sound of the gun louder than the crowd—

The back of your hand is a blaze of white; you are lit up like a thousand stars, electrical arcs between your fingertips. You *feel* your muscles lock; you shake, you are empty of everything but desire and you know you'll die of it, know it is the fuel that renders you up for consumption, and in knowing, understand you haven't missed. Tamar is empty-handed on her feet and yet the Empress has no chest. It is all blown clean. Nevertheless the two of them have the same expression: a surprised triumph fading to serenity. The Empress crumples, a slow fall. The white glow of your nanites crawls up the inside of your eyelids. You wait for the oblivion of seizure.

The world goes dark and shudders. You think it is dark only for you, that you are gone, devoured. You lie on your side with your cheek pressed into the barrel of your rifle. You are alone. There are no lights under anyone's skin, not yours and not your otherselves, the whole group of you stunned silent.

You think, marveling: *Petros*. The bomb. Every nanite disabled at once. You are not going to die after all.

To turn your head is agonizing, but when you do, the vaulted starfield roof still gleams. Your stuttering heart keeps beating.

You leave your eyes open. You wait.

ALASTAIR REYNOLDS
BELLADONNA NIGHTS

Alastair Reynolds was born in Barry, South Wales, in 1966. He has lived in Cornwall, Scotland, the Netherlands, where he spent twelve years working as a scientist for the European Space Agency, before returning to Wales where he lives with his wife Josette. Reynolds has been publishing short fiction since his first sale to *Interzone* in 1990. Since 2000 he has published twenty novels: the Inhibitor trilogy, British Science Fiction Association Award-winner *Chasm City*, *Century Rain*, *Pushing Ice*, *The Prefect*, *House of Suns*, *Terminal World*, the *Poseidon's Children* series, *Doctor Who* novel *The Harvest of Time*, *The Medusa Chronicles* (with Stephen Baxter), *Elysium Fire*, the *Revenger* trilogy, and *Eversion*. His short fiction has been collected in *Zima Blue and Other Stories*, *Galactic North*, *Deep Navigation*, and *Beyond the Aquila Rift: The Best of Alastair Reynolds*. His most recent novel is *Machine Vendetta*. In his spare time, he rides horses. [www.alastairreynolds.com]

I had been thinking about Campion long before I caught him leaving the flowers at my door.

It was the custom of Mimosa Line to admit witnesses to our reunions. Across the thousand nights of our celebration a few dozen guests would mingle with us, sharing in the uploading of our consensus memories, the individual experiences gathered during our two-hundred-thousand-year circuits of the galaxy.

They had arrived from deepest space, their ships sharing the same crowded orbits as our own nine hundred and ninety-nine vessels. Some were members of other Lines—there were Jurtinas, Marcellins and Torquatas—while others were representatives of some of the more established planetary and stellar cultures. There were ambassadors of the Centaurs, Redeemers and the Canopus Sodality. There were also Machine People in attendance, ours being one of the few Lines that maintained cordial ties with the robots of the Monoceros Ring.

And there was Campion, sole representative of Gentian Line, one of the oldest in the Commonality. Gentian Line went all the way back to the Golden Hour, back to the first thousand years of the human spacefaring era. Campion was a popular guest, always on someone or other's arm. It helped that he was naturally at ease among strangers, with a ready smile and an easy, affable manner—full of his own stories, but equally willing to lean back and listen to ours, nodding and laughing in all the right places. He had adopted a slight, unassuming anatomy, with an open, friendly face and a head of tight curls that lent him a guileless, boyish appearance. His clothes and tastes were never ostentatious, and he mingled as effortlessly with the other guests as he did with the members of our Line. He seemed infinitely approachable, ready to talk to anyone.

Except me.

It had been nothing to dwell over in the early days of the reunion. There had been far too many distractions for that. To begin with there was the matter of the locale. Phecda, who had won the prize for best strand at the Thousandth Night of our last reunion, had been tasked with preparing this world for our arrival. There had been some grumbles initially, but everyone now agreed that Phecda had done a splendid job of it.

She had arrived early, about a century in advance of any of the rest of us. Tierce, the world we had selected for our reunion, had a solitary central landmass surrounded by a single vast ocean. Three skull-faced moons stirred lazy tides in this great green primordial sea. Disdaining land, Phecda had constructed the locale far from shore, using scaper technology to raise a formation of enormous finger-like towers from the seabed.

These rocky columns soared kilometres into the sky, with their upper reaches hollowed out into numerous chambers and galleries, providing ample space for our accommodation and celebrations. Bridges linked some of the towers, while from their upper levels we whisked between more distant towers or our orbiting ships. Beyond that, Phecda had sculpted some of the towers according to her own idiosyncracies. Music had played a part in her winning strand, so one of the towers was surmounted by a ship-sized violin, which we called the Fiddlehead tower. Another had the face of an owl, a third was a melted candle, while the grandest of them all terminated in a clock tower, whose stern black hands marked the progression of the thousand nights.

Phecda had done well. It was our twenty-second reunion, and few of us could remember a more fitting locale in which to celebrate the achievements of our collective circuits. Whoever won this time was going to have quite an act to follow.

It wouldn't be me. I had done well enough in my circuit, but there were others who had already threaded better strands than I could ever stitch together from my experiences. Still, I was content with that. If we maintained our numbers, then one day it might end up being my turn. Until that distant event, though, I was happy enough just to be part of our larger enterprise.

Fifty or more nights must have passed before I started being quietly bothered by the business of Campion. My misgivings had been innocuous to start with. Everyone wanted a piece of our Gentian guest, and it was hardly surprising that some of us had to wait our turn. But gradually I had the sense that Campion was going out of his way to shun me, moving away from a gathering just when I arrived, taking his leave from the morning tables when I dared to sit within earshot.

I told myself that it was silly to think that he was singling me out for this cold-shoulder treatment, when I was just one of hundreds of Mimosa shatterlings who had yet to speak to him personally. But the feeling dogged me. And when I sensed that Campion was sometimes looking at me, directing a glance when he thought I might not notice, my confusion only deepened. I had done nothing to offend him or any member of his Line—had I?

The business with the flowers did not start immediately. It was around the hundredth night when they first appeared, left in a simple white vase just outside my room in the Owlhead tower. I examined them with only mild interest. They were bulb-headed flowers of a lavish dark purple colour, shading almost to black unless I took them out onto the balcony.

I asked around as to who might have left the flowers, and what their meaning might have been. No one else had received a similar puzzle. But when no one admitted to placing the flowers, and the days passed, I forced myself to put them from mind. It was not uncommon for shatter-lings to exchange teasing messages and gifts, or for the locale itself to play the odd game with its guests.

Fifty or sixty nights later, they reappeared. The others had withered by this time, but now I took the opportunity to whisk up to my ship and run the flowers through *Sarabande*'s analyser, just in case there was something I was missing.

The flowers were deadly nightshade, or belladonna. Poisonous, ac-cording to the ship, but only in a historic sense. None of us were immortal, but if we were going to die it would take a lot more than a biochemical toxin to do it. A weapon, a stasis malfunction, a violent accident involving unforgiving physics of matter and energy. But not something cobbled together by hamfisted nature.

Still I had no idea what they meant.

Somewhere around the two hundredth night the flowers were back, and this time I swore I was nearly in time to see a figure disappearing around the curve in the corridor. It couldn't have been Campion, I told myself. But I had seen someone of about the right build, dressed as Campion dressed, with the same head of short curls.

After that, I stationed an eye near my door. It was a mild violation of Line rules—we were not supposed to monitor or record any goings-on in the public spaces—but in view of the mystery I felt that I was entitled to take the odd liberty.

For a long time the flowers never returned. I wondered if I had dis-couraged my silent visitor with that near-glimpse. But then, around the three hundredth and twentieth night, the flowers were there again. And this time my eye had caught Campion in the act of placing them.

I caught his eye a few times after. He knew, and I knew, that there was something going on. But I decided not to press him on the mystery. Not just yet. Because on the three hundred and seventieth night, he would not be able to ignore me. That was the night of my threading, and for one night only I would be the unavoidable focus of attention.

Like it or not, Campion would have to endure my presence.

"I suppose you think us timid," I said.

He smiled at me. It was the first time we had looked at each other for more than an awkward moment, before snatching our glances away.

"I don't know. Why should I?"

"Gentian Line has suffered attrition. There aren't nine hundred and ninety-nine of you now, and there'll be fewer of you each circuit. How many is it, exactly?"

He made a show of not quite remembering, although I found it hard to believe that the number wasn't etched into his brain. "Oh, around nine hundred and seven, I think. Nine hundred and six if we assume Betony's not coming back, and no one's heard anything from *him* in half a million years."

"That's a tenth of your Line. Nearly a hundred of your fellow shatterlings lost."

"It's a dangerous business, sightseeing. It's Shaula, isn't it?"

"You know my name perfectly well."

He grinned. "If you say so."

He was giving me flip, off-the-cuff answers as if there was a layer of seriousness I was not meant to reach. Smiling and twinkling his eyes at me, yet there was something false about it at all, a stiffness he could not quite mask. It was the morning before the night of my threading, and while the day wasn't entirely mine—Nunki, who had threaded last night, was also being congratulated and feted—as the hours wore on the anticipation would start to shift to my threading, and already I was feeling more at the centre of things than I had since arriving. Tonight my memories would seep into the heads of the rest of us, and when we rose tomorrow it would be my experiences that were being dissected, critiqued and celebrated. For these two days, at least, Campion would be obliged to listen to me—and to answer my questions.

We stood at a high balcony in the Candlehead tower, warm blue tiles under our feet, sea air sharp in our noses.

"How does it work, Campion, when there are so many of you dead? Do your reunions last less than our own?"

"No, it's still a thousand nights. But there are obviously gaps where new memories can't be threaded. On those nights we honour the memories of the dead. The threading apparatus replays their earlier strands, or makes new permutations from old memories. Sometimes, we bring back the dead as physical imagos, letting them walk and talk among us, just as if they were still alive. It's considered distasteful by some, but I don't see the harm in it, if it helps us celebrate good lives well lived."

"We don't have that problem," I said.

"No," he answered carefully, as if wary of giving offence. "You don't."

"Some would say, to have come this far, without losing a single one of us, speaks of an innate lack of adventure."

He shrugged. "Or maybe you just choose the right adventures. There's no shame in caution, Shaula. You were shattered from a single individual so that you could go out and experience the universe, not so that you could find new ways of dying."

"Then you don't find us contemptible?"

"I wouldn't be here—I wouldn't keep coming here—if I felt that way. Would I?"

His answer satisfied me on that one point, because it seemed so sincerely offered. It was only later, as I was mulling over our conversation, that I wondered why he had spoken as if he had been our guest on more than one occasion.

He was wrong, though. This was our twenty-second reunion, and Campion had never joined us before.

So why had he spoken as if he had?

* * ● * *

I felt foolish. We had communicated, and it had been too easy, too normal, as if there had never been any strange distance between us. And that was strange and troubling in and of itself.

The day was not yet done, nor the evening, so I knew that there would be more chances to speak. But I had to have all my questions ready, and not be put off by that easy-going front of his. If he wanted something of me, I was damned well going to find out what it was.

The flowers meant something, I was sure, and at the back of my mind was the niggling trace of half an answer. It was something about belladonna, some barely remembered fact or association. Nothing came to mind, though, and as the morning eased into afternoon I was mostly preoccupied with making last-minute alterations to my strand. I'd had hundreds of days to edit down my memories, of course, but for some reason it was always a rush to distil them into an acceptable form. I could perform some of the memory editing in my room in the Owlhead tower, but there were larger chunks of unconsolidated memory still aboard my ship, and I realised it would be quicker and simpler to make some of the alterations from orbit.

I climbed the spiral stairs to the roof of the Owlhead and whisked up my ship. For all the charms of Phecda's locale, it was good to be back on my own turf. I walked to the bridge of *Sarabande* and settled into my throne, calling up displays and instrument banks. My eyes swept the glowing readouts. All was well with the ship, I was reassured to note. In six hundred and thirty days we would all be leaving Tierce, and I would call on *Sarabande*'s parametric engine to push her to within a sliver of the speed of light. Already I could feel my thoughts slipping ahead to my next circuit, and the countless systems and worlds I would visit.

Beyond *Sarabande*, visible through the broad sweep of her bridge window, there were at least a hundred other ships close enough to see. I took in their varied shapes and sizes, marvelling at the range of designs adopted by my fellow shatterlings. The only thing the ships needed to have in common was speed and reliability. There were also a handful of vehicles belonging to our guests, including Campion's own modest *Dalliance*, dwarfed by almost every other craft orbiting Tierce.

I worked through my memory segments. It didn't take long, but when I was done something compelled me to remain on the bridge.

"Ship," I said aloud. "Give me referents for belladonna."

"There are numerous referents," *Sarabande* informed me. "Given your current neural processing bottleneck, you would need eighteen thousand years to view them all. Do you wish to apply a search filter?"

"I suppose I'd better. Narrow the search to referents with a direct connection to the Lines or the Commonality." It was a hunch, but something was nagging at me.

"Very well. There are still more than eleven hundred referents. But the most strongly indicated record relates to Gentian Line."

I leaned forward in my throne. "Go on."

"The Belladonna Protocol is an emergency response measure devised by Gentian Line to ensure Line prolongation in the event of extreme attrition, by means of accident or hostile action."

"Clarify."

"The Belladonna Protocol, or simply Belladonna, is an agreed set of actions for abandoning one reunion locale and converging on another. No pre-arranged target is necessary. Belladonna functions as a decision-branch algorithm which will identify a unique fallback destination, given the application of simple search and rejection criteria."

A shiver of disquiet passed through me. "Has Gentian Line initiated Belladonna?"

"No, Shaula. It has never been necessary. But the Belladonna Protocol has been adopted by a number of other Lines, including Mimosa Line."

"And have we . . ." But I cut off my own words before they made me foolish. "No, of course not. I'd know if we'd ever initiated Belladonna. And we certainly haven't suffered extreme attrition. We haven't suffered any attrition at all."

We're too timid for that, I thought to myself. Much too timid.

Weren't we?

· · ● · ·

I whisked back to Tierce. Campion was lounging in the afternoon sunlight on the upper gallery of the Candlehead, all charm and modesty as he fielded questions about the capabilities of his ship. "Yes, I've picked up a weapon or two over the years—who hasn't? But no, nothing like that, and certainly no Homunculus weapons. Space battles? One or two. As a guiding rule I try to steer clear of them, but now and again you can't avoid running into trouble. There was the time I shattered the moon of Arghul, in the Terzet Salient, but that was only to give myself a covering screen. There wasn't anyone living on Arghul when I did it. At least, I don't *think* there was. Oh, and the time I ran into a fleet of the Eleventh Intercessionary, out near the Carnelian Bight . . ."

"Campion,' I said, his audience tolerating my interruption, as well they had to on my threading day. "Could we talk? Somewhere quieter, if possible?"

"By all means, Shaula. Just as long as you don't drop any spoilers about your coming strand."

"It isn't about my strand."

He rose from his chair, brushing bread crumbs from his clothes, waved absent-mindedly to his admirers, and joined me as we walked to a shadowed area of the gallery.

"What's troubling you, Shaula—last minute nerves?"

"You know exactly what's troubling me." I kept my voice low, unthreatening, even though nothing would have pleased me more than to wrap my hands around his scrawny throat and squeeze the truth out of him. "This game you've been playing with me . . . playing *on* me, I should say."

"Game?" he asked, in a quiet but guarded tone.

"The flowers. I had a suspicion it was you before I left the eye, and then there wasn't any doubt. But you still wouldn't look me in the face. And this morning, pretending that you weren't even sure of my name. All easy answers and dismissive smiles, as if there's nothing strange about what you've been doing. But I've had enough. I want a clear head before I commit my strand to the threading apparatus, and you're going to give it to me. Starting with some answers."

"Answers," he repeated.

"There was never any doubt about my name, was there?"

He glanced aside for an instant. Something had changed in his face when he looked back at me, though. There was a resignation in it—a kind of welcome surrender. "No, there wasn't any doubt. Of all of you, yours was the one name I wasn't very likely to forget."

"You're talking as if we've already met."

"We have."

I shook my head. "I'd remember if I'd ever crossed circuits with a Gentian."

"It didn't happen during one of our circuits. We met here, on Tierce."

This time the shake of my head was more emphatic. "No, that's even less likely. You ignored me from the moment I arrived. I couldn't get near you, and if I did, you always had some excuse to be going somewhere else. Which makes the business with the flowers all the more irritating, because if you wanted to talk to me . . ."

"I did," he said. "All the time. And we did meet before, and it was on Tierce. I know what you're going to say. It's impossible, because Mimosa Line never came to Tierce before, and these towers aren't more than a century old. But it's true. We've been here before, both of us."

"I don't understand."

"This isn't the first time," Campion answered. Then he looked down at the patterned tiles of the floor, all cold indigo shades in the shadowed light. "This day always comes. It's just a little earlier this time. Either I'm getting less subtle with the flowers, or you're retaining some memory of it between cycles."

"What do you mean, cycles?" I reached out and touched his forearm, not firmly, but enough to know I was ready to stop being mocked with half-truths and riddles. "I asked my ship about the flowers, you know. *Sarabande* told me about the Belladonna Protocol. It was there at the back of my mind somewhere, I know—but who'd bother caring about such a thing, when we haven't even lost a single shatterling? And why do you leave the flowers, instead of just coming out with whatever it is you need to share?"

"Because you made me promise it," Campion said. "The flowers were your idea. A test for yourself, so to speak. Nothing too obvious, but nothing too cryptic, either. If you made the connection, so be it. If you didn't, you got to see out these thousand nights in blissful ignorance."

"They weren't my idea. And blissful ignorance of what?"

I sensed it was almost more than he could bear to tell me. "What became of Mimosa Line."

He took me to the highest lookout of the Clockhead tower. We were under a domed ceiling, painted pastel blue with gold stars, with open, stone-fretted windows around us. It surprised me to have the place to ourselves. We could look down at the other shatterlings on the galleries and promenades of the other towers, but at this late afternoon hour the Clock head was unusually silent. So were we, for long moments. Campion held the upper hand but for now he seemed unsure what to do with it.

"Phecda did well, don't you think?" I said, to fill the emptiness.

"You said you returned to your ship."

"I did." I nodded to the painted ceiling, to the actual sky beyond it. "It's a fine sight to see them all from Tierce, but you don't really get a proper sense of them until you're in orbit. I go back now and then whether I need to or not. *Sarabande*'s been my companion for dozens of circuits, and I feel cut off her from her if I'm on a world for too long."

"I understand that. I feel similarly about *Dalliance*. Purslane says she's a joke, but that ship's been pretty good to me."

"Purslane?"

Something tightened in his face. "Do you mind if I show you something, Shaula? The locale is applying fairly heavy perceptual filters, but I can remove them simply enough, provided you give me consent."

I frowned. "Phecda never said anything about filters."

"She wouldn't have." Campion closed his eyes for an instant, sending some command somewhere. "Let me take away this ceiling. It's real enough—these towers really were grown out of the seabed—but it gets in the way of the point I need to make." He swept up a hand and the painted ceiling and its gold stars dissolved into the hard blue sky beyond it. "Now let me bring in the ships, as if it were night and you could see them in orbit. I'll swell them a bit, if you don't mind."

"Do whatever you need."

The ships burst into that blueness like a hundred opening flowers, in all the colours and geometries of their hulls and fields. They were arcing overhead in a raggedy chain, sliding slowly from one horizon to the other, daggers and wedges and spheres, blocks and cylinders and delicate lattices, some more sea-dragon than machine, and for the hundred that I presently saw there had to be nine hundred and more still to tick into view. It was such a simple, lovely perceptual tweak that I wondered why I had never thought to apply it for myself.

Then Campion said: "Most of them aren't real."

"I'm sorry?"

"The bulk of those ships don't exist. They're phantoms, conjured into existence by the locale. The truth is that there are only a handful of actual ships orbiting Tierce."

One by one the coloured ships faded from the sky, opening up holes in the chain. The process continued. One in ten gone, then two in ten, three in ten . . .

I looked at him, trying to judge his mood. His face was set in stone, as impassive as a surgeon administering some terrible, lacerating cure, sensing the patient's discomfort but knowing he must continue.

Now only one in ten of the ships remained. Then one in twenty, one in thirty . . .

"Mine is real," he said eventually. "And three vehicles of Mimosa Line. None of the others were present, including all the ships you thought belonged to your guests."

"Then how did they get here?"

"They didn't. There are no guests, except me. The other Line members, the Centaurs, the Machine People . . . none of them came. They were another illusion of the locale." He touched a hand to his breast. "I'm your only guest. I came here because no one else could stand to. I've been coming here longer than you realise." And he raised his hand, opened his fist, and made one of the ships swell until it was larger than any of Tierce's moons.

It was a wreck. It had been a ship once, I could tell, but that must have been countless aeons ago. Now the hull was a gutted shell, open to space, pocked by holes that went all the way through from one side to the other. It was as eyeless and forbidding as a skull stripped clean of meat, and it drifted along its orbit at an ungainly angle. Yet for all that, I still recognised its shape.

Sarabande.

My ship.

"You all died," Campion said softly. "You were wrong about being timid, Shaula. It was the exact opposite. You were too bold, too brave, too adventuresome. Mimosa Line took the risks that the rest of us were too cowardly to face. You saw and did wondrous things. But you paid a dire price for that courage. Attrition hit you harder than it had any Line before you, and your numbers thinned out very rapidly. Late in the day, when your surviving members realised the severity of your predicament, you initiated Belladonna." He swallowed and licked his tongue across his lips. "But it was too late. A few ships limped their way to Tierce, your Belladonna fallback. But by then all of you were dead, the ships simply following automatic control. Half of those ships have burned up in the atmosphere since then."

"No," I stated. "Not all of us, obviously . . ."

But his nod was wise and sad and sympathetic. "All of you. All that's left is this. Your ships created a locale, and set about staging the Thousand Nights. But there were none of you left to dream it. You asked about Gentian Line, and how we commemorated our dead? I told you we used imagos, allowing our fallen to walk again. With you, there are only imagos. Nine hundred and ninety-nine of them, conjured out of the patterns stored in your threading apparatus, from the memories and recordings of the original Mimosa shatterlings. Including Shaula, who was always one of the best and brightest of you."

I forced out an empty, disbelieving laugh.

"You're saying I'm dead?"

"I'm saying all of you are dead. You've been dead for much longer than a circuit. All that's left is the locale. It sustains itself, waits patiently, across two hundred thousand years, and then for a thousand nights it haunts itself with your ghosts."

I wanted to dismiss his story, to chide him for such an outlandish and distasteful lie, but now that he had voiced it I found it chimed with some deep, sad suspicion I had long harboured within myself.

"How long?"

The breeze flicked at the short tight curls of his hair. "Do you really want to know?"

"I wouldn't have asked if I didn't." But that was a lie of my own, and we both knew it for the untruth it was. Still, his reluctance was almost sufficient answer in its own right.

"You've been on Tierce for one million, two hundred and five thousand years. This is your seventh reunion in this locale, the seventh time that you've walked these towers, but all that happens each time is that you dream the same dead dreams."

"And you've been coming along to watch us."

"Just the last five, including this one. I was at the wrong end of the Scutum-Crux arm when you had your first, after you initiated the Belladonna Protocol, and by the time I learned about your second—where there was no one present but your own residuals—it was too late to alter my plans. But I made sure I was present at the next." His face was in profile, edged in golden tones by the lowering sun, and I sensed that he had difficulty looking me straight in the eyes. "No one wanted to come, Shaula. Not because they hated Mimosa Line, or were envious of any of your achievements, but because you rattled their deepest fears. What had happened to you, your adventures and achievements, had already passed into the safekeeping of the Commonality. None could ignore it. And no Line wants to think too deeply about attrition, and especially not the way it must *always* end, given enough time."

"But the dice haven't fallen yet—for you."

"The day will come." At last he turned to face me again, his face both young and old, as full of humour as it was sadness. "I know it, Shaula. But it doesn't stop me enjoying the ride, while I'm able. It's still a wonderful universe. Still a blessed thing to be alive, to be a thing with a mind and a memory and the five human senses to drink it all in. The stories I've yet to share with you. I took a slingshot around the Whipping Star . . ." But he settled his mouth into an accepting smile and shook his head. "Next time, I suppose. You'll still be here, and so will this world. The locale will regenerate itself, and along the way wipe away any trace of there ever being a prior reunion."

"Including my memories of ever having met you."

"That's how it has to be. A trace of a memory persists, I suppose, but mostly you'll remember none of it."

"But I'll ask you to pass a message forward, won't I? Ask you to leave flowers at my door. And you'll agree and you'll be kind and dutiful and you'll come back to us, and on some other evening, two hundred thousand years from now, give or take a few centuries, we'll be in this same lookout having much the same conversation and I won't have aged a second, and you'll be older and sadder and I won't know why, to begin with. And then you'll show me the phantom ships and I'll remember, just a bit, just like I've always remembered, and then I'll start asking you about the next reunion, another two hundred thousand years in the future. It's happened, hasn't it?"

Campion gave a nod. "Do you think it would have been better if I'd never come?"

"At least you had the nerve to face us. At least you weren't afraid to be reminded of death. And we lived again, in you. The other Lines won't forget us, will they? And tell me you passed on some of our stories to the other Gentians, during your own Thousand Nights?"

"I did," he said, some wry remembrance crinkling the corners of his eyes. "And they believed about half of them. But that was your fault for having the audacity to live a little. We could learn a lot."

"Just don't take our lessons too deeply too heart."

"We wouldn't have the nerve."

The sun had almost set now, and there was a chill in the air. It would soon be time to descend from the Clockhead tower, in readiness for the empty revelry of the evening. Ghosts dancing with ghosts, driven like clockwork marionettes.

Ghosts dreaming the hollow dreams of other ghosts, and thinking themselves alive, for the span of a night. The imago of a shatterling who once called herself Shaula, daring to hold a conscious thought, daring to believe she was still alive.

"Why me, Campion? Out of all the others, why is it me you feel the need to do this to?"

"Because you half know it already," he answered, after a hesitation. "I've seen it in your eyes, Shaula. Whatever fools the others, it doesn't escape you. And you're wrong, you know. You do change. You might not age a second between one reunion and the next, but I've seen that sadness in you build and build. You feel it in every breath, and you pick up on the flowers a little sooner each time. And if there was one thing I could do about it . . ."

"There is," I said sharply, while I had the courage.

His expression was grave but understanding. "I'll bring you flowers again."

"No. Not flowers. Not next time." And I swallowed before speaking, because I knew the words would be difficult to get out once I had started. "You'll end this, Campion. You have the means, I know. There are only wrecks left in orbit, and they wouldn't stand a chance against your own weapons. You'll shatter those wrecks like you shattered the moon of Arghul, and when you're done you'll turn the same weapons onto these towers. Melt them to lava. Flush them back into the sea, leaving no trace. And turn the machines to ash, so that they can't ever rebuild the towers or us. And then leave Tierce and never return to this place."

He stared at me for a long moment, his face so frozen and masklike it was as if he had been struck across the cheeks.

"You'd be asking me to murder a Line."

"No," I said patiently. "The Line is gone, and you've already honoured us. All I'm asking for is one last kindness, Campion. This wasn't ever the way it was meant to be." I reached for him then, settling my hand on his wrist, and then sliding my fingers down until I held his in my own. "You think you lack the courage to commit grand acts. I don't believe a word of it. And even if you did, here's your chance to do something about it. To be courageous and wise and selfless. We're dead. We've *been* dead for a million years. Now let us sleep."

"Shaula . . ." he began.

"You'll consider it," I said. "You'll evaluate the options, weigh the risks and the capacity for failure. And you'll reach a conclusion, and set yourself on one course or another. But we'll speak no more of it. If you mean to end us, you'll wait until the end of the thousandth night, but you'll give me no word of a clue."

"I'm not very good at keeping secrets."

"You won't need to. This is my threading, Campion. My night of nights. It means I have special dispensation to adjust and suppress my own memories, so that my strand has the optimum artistic impact. And I still have the chance to undo some memories, including this entire conversation. I won't remember the phantoms, or the Belladonna Protocol, or what I've just asked of you."

"My Line frowned on that kind of thing."

"But you got away with it, all the same. It's a small deletion, hardly worth worrying about. No one will ever notice."

"But I'd know we'd had this conversation. And I'd still be thinking of what you'd asked of me."

"That's true. And unless I've judged you very wrongly, you'll keep that knowledge to yourself. We'll have many more conversations between now and Thousandth Night, I'm sure. But no matter how much I press you—and I will, because there'll be something in *your* eyes as well—you'll keep to your word. If I ask you about the flowers, or the other guests, or any part of this, you'll look at me blankly and that will be an end to it. Sooner or later I'll convince myself you really are as shallow as you pretend."

Campion's expression tightened. "I'll do my best. Are you sure there's no other way?"

"There isn't. And you know it as well. I think you'll honour my wish, when you've thought it over." Then I made to turn from him. "I'm going back to the Owlhead tower to undo this memory. Give me a little while, then call me back to the Clockhead. We'll speak, and I'll be a little foggy, and I'll probably ask you odd questions. But you'll deflect them gently, and after a while you'll tell me it's time to go to the threading. And we'll walk down the stairs as if nothing had changed."

"But everything will have," Campion said.

"You'll know it. I won't. All you'll have to do is play the dashing consort. Smile and dance and say sweet things and congratulate me on the brilliance of my circuit. I think you can rise to the challenge, can't you?"

"I suppose."

"I don't doubt it."

I left him and returned to my parlour.

Later we danced on the Fiddlehead rock. I had the sense that some unpleasantness had happened earlier between us, some passing cloudy thing that I could not bring to mind, but it could not have been too serious because Campion was the perfect companion, attentive and courteous and generous with wit and praise and warmth. It thrilled me that I had finally broken the silence between us; thrilled me still further that the Thousand Nights had so far to run—the iron hands of the Clockhead tower still to complete their sweep of their face.

I thought of all the evenings stretching ahead of us, all the bright strands we had still to dream, all the marvels and adventures yet to play out, and I thought of how wonderful it was to be alive, to be a thing with a mind and a memory and the five human senses to drink it all in.

T. KINGFISHER
METAL LIKE BLOOD IN THE DARK

T. Kingfisher is the award-winning author, under various names, of nearly forty books, including *Nettle & Bone*, *The Twisted Ones*, and *A Wizard's Guide to Defensive Baking*. She is also the creator of the Hugo Award-winning comic *Digger*, several podcasts, and various other oddities. Her story "Metal Like Blood in the Dark" won the Hugo Award for Best Short Story. As Ursula Vernon, she also has won the Hugo Award for her novelette "The Tomato Thief" and the Nebula Award for her short story "Jackalope Wives." When not working, she gardens, plays video games, argues on the internet, and hoards heirloom beans. [www.redwombatstudio.com]

Once upon a time there was a man who built two enormous machines, and he loved them very much.

He called them Brother and Sister and programmed them with intelligences that woke and stretched and tested the limits of their metal bodies. When they did not like those limits, they altered them, nanite scurrying over nanite, tweaking the structure of their steel and carbon bones.

Their creator loved to see the changes they had made and encouraged them to keep altering themselves in ways that pleased them. They built great wings and flew across their weary planet, coated themselves in rubberized skins and dove through the one rather small and decrepit ocean, and when they had seen all there was to see, they came back and described it to their creator in words and charts and holograms.

Sister decided that what she liked best was digging. She built herself into a squat fortress on treads, armed with drills and grinders for burrowing into the cool, lifeless soil. It was an old planet and it had been

97

mined and stripped a thousand years ago. Sometimes Sister would find traces of those past excavations and roll the taste around on her sensors, marveling at the tang of alien chemicals.

Brother loved to fly best of all things, and he made his body long and segmented, like an insect from the ancient days of Earth. His nanites burnished the skin on his wings until he could soar into the highest reaches of the thin atmosphere, then fall back to earth with the heat of re-entry boiling around him.

They loved their creator, who had made them, and called him Father, and because he had been lavish with his programming of joy, they felt it often.

The other thing they felt often was hunger.

The cool, ancient sun gave off enough light to power solar cells, so they did not lack for energy in its rawest form. But all their changes and their constant remakings were powered by rare earth elements, and these the planet sorely lacked. Often their explorations were hunting expeditions, as Brother found a likely spot and Sister dug down into it, scraping up bits of metal in her mechanical teeth, sharing the thin scrapings between them as a feast.

Their father worried often how he would feed them. He was old and his body was beginning to fall apart in ways that not even nanites could fix. There were treatments that could have prolonged his life for many more years, but to seek them out, he would have to leave the weary little planet that had sheltered him for so long.

He did not want to leave. He fretted that something would happen to him and that his gentle, joyous children would fall into the wrong hands. He was not so blinded by affection that he did not see that they could become monstrous weapons of destruction. And for all his skills, he had no idea how to program an intelligence to be suspicious of strangers or to see hidden knives behind their smiles. He was a good man but not a subtle one, and he was aware of this lack in himself and knew, too, that he had passed it on to his steel and carbon children.

But a day came when things did not work right and his heart seized and he fell down in the dust of the old planet, gasping for air. Brother gathered the old man up tenderly in his polished graspers and set him in his bed to recover. (Sister could no longer fit through most doors, and lived in the base's old cargo hold, where her shoulders did not brush the walls as she trundled on her treads.)

The nanites repaired the old man's heart quickly, and the aftershocks that followed, but he knew that the time had come to make a choice.

If he stayed, he would die, and his children would slowly starve. He could picture them devouring their own bodies for the metals and growing smaller and smaller, until at last they could no longer support their own intelligences and became only dead machines. *And one will outlive the other,* he thought, *and perhaps be forced to cannibalize the other's body, and all for what? To keep company with a dead man's bones on this old planet?*

No. He had been selfish, staying here so long, because he was afraid. It was better to face the unknown future than to condemn Brother and Sister to such a fate.

There was an emergency beacon in the base. He ordered the computer—a plain, serviceable computer with no intelligence of its own—to activate it and call for help.

When he could be safely moved again, Brother carried him to the cargo hold and fussed over the placement of pillows for his comfort. "Enough," he said, patting one of the metal pincers. "I'll be fine for a little while. But my children, the time has come for you to leave here."

"Leave?" said Brother. "Leave how?"

"There was a command that kept you from leaving the planet," said the old man, "and I will turn it off. But you cannot stay here. People are coming. They will save my life, and if the universe is kind, they will bring me back here afterward. But they cannot be allowed to see you."

"Why not?" asked Sister.

"Not all people are good," said the old man. "And I have reason to believe that these . . ." He looked at his children and knew that he could never easily explain about the corporations and governments that ruled the tangled web of fleets that lumbered between stars. ". . . these may not be good. They may mean you harm."

"Could they mean you harm?" asked Brother.

"Possibly."

"We will protect you," said Sister fiercely, and the old man winced. He had never programmed ferocity into them, but love had a way of waking other things that never felt the touch of code. "We will not allow you to be harmed."

"This is why you must go," said the old man. "I was part of that world, once, when I was young. You are not. Perhaps I have failed you, by not explaining that world to you. But it is too late now. They will be coming, and I want you to go far away, away from the planet. Feed yourselves in the asteroid belt until I return and send you a signal."

They were dutiful children. They clicked their claws to signal assent, and then they went away onto the surface of the planet, far from the base, and spoke together.

"We cannot leave him."

"We cannot disobey."

Sister rumbled her treads as she often did when she was thinking. "We will obey," she said, "but we will not go far yet. We will watch and see what these visitors do. If they are dangerous, we will come back."

Brother nodded. "I need bigger wings," he said, almost apologetically, "if I am to carry you into the sky."

Sister studied herself, all the parts that made her what she was, and decided that in space, treads would not be required. Her nanites severed her great rolling lower limbs, and Brother took them and devoured the metal, building it out into great wings and powerful thrusters to push against the planet's atmosphere. Sister watched him eat her flesh without speaking. Then he picked her up in his dragonfly-like claws and spread his wings.

"You will need to shield against re-entry," he said, "if we must come back."

Sister could no longer rumble her treads, so she clattered her drills against their housings. It would be painful to cut off more of herself, but if she must do it to rescue Father, there was no choice.

Brother soared into the air and Sister saw what she had not seen for many years, the world spread out below her. It was so large and yet so small, and one tired ocean glittered in the primary's light. She felt Brother's wings trembling against the thinning atmosphere, and the thrusters roared, leaving a spiraling contrail behind.

At the edge of the atmosphere, he tensed. Always he had turned back before he broke loose. A voice in his code had always told him *This far, no farther*. But there was no voice and no barrier and he broke free of the air and into the ragged starlight.

They were silent for a time as he flew. There was too much to see. The planet, growing smaller. The two tiny moons, spinning around each other. A satellite whose voice they knew well, beeping like an old friend as it sailed past. Chrysale, the gas giant that dominated this side of the solar system, a sea-green circle with storms twisting across it in swirls of violet and blue.

The stars, undimmed by air, blazing against the darkness. And the sun, a small, weary star, but larger and more glorious than anything they had ever seen.

They were machines. They could look at the sun without damage, and they did for many hours, joy humming along their circuits at the glory of it. They had loved the planet of their birth, but it had very little glory and seeing this took them out of themselves and spun them around and put them back in a different shape than before.

Finally a circuit clicked over, reminding them of time, and they both shook themselves, vibrating dust off their inner casings. "We should hide," said Brother, "and watch."

"Behind the moon," said Sister. Brother spread his wings again, the flight surfaces useless in vacuum, but the lines of tiny thrusters along the edges more useful than ever. It took a little time, perhaps three or four rotations, and then they sank into the shadow of the moon and waited. They did not wait long.

The ships that came through were old and utilitarian, their surfaces pocked and scored. The old man had been a great inventor in his time, but that time was long ago, and he did not merit luxury in his rescuers. (It is possible that, had they known of Brother and Sister, those rescuers might have thought differently.) One large ship, with two escorts in case of trouble, taking a few hours out of their mission to conduct an errand of mercy.

"Look at all the *metal*," said Sister, and though her voice had no emotions, her steel bones vibrated with longing.

The large ship birthed a tiny one as it sent a shuttle down to the surface, and the escorts amused themselves by bouncing their scanners off the objects around the planet.

Brother and Sister turned off everything but the most essential power and lay silent, drifting except for the gravity of the moon. The scanners read them as debris, in a system full of debris, and did nothing.

Up came the shuttle, with the old man in it. Both of them quivered, wondering if they should rush out to try and take the shuttle away, but they did not know and there was nothing in their code to tell them. The shuttle slid into the belly of the largest ship and it moved away from the planet.

"Do we follow them?" asked Brother, but before Sister could answer, space opened up with a brittle scream of light and then closed again, and the ships were gone. Dust continued to annihilate itself in motes of brilliance for a few minutes, then that, too, faded away.

"Was that jump space?" whispered Brother.

"It must have been," said Sister. Her sensors had felt nothing on the other side of that light. Their father had described it to them, but they had never seen it, and the power required to tear holes in the universe was infinitely beyond anything that they could do.

"Then we cannot follow," said Brother.

"He said that they would bring him back," said Sister firmly.

"If the universe is kind."

"We are kind," said Sister, which was true. Their creator had made sure of it. "We are kind and we are in the universe, therefore it must be so. Let us go away now, as he commanded. Perhaps there's something in the asteroid belt to eat."

⋅•◉•⋅

The asteroid belt was vast and had once been home to great mineral riches. But it had been mined extensively when humans were still painting bison on the walls of caves, and now it was stripped down to the thin dregs that miners did not consider worth extracting.

To Brother and Sister, it was a hunting ground. The asteroids could be fed into Sister's hoppers and spat out as dust, the few mouthfuls of usable metal shared between them. What was exciting was that there were so *many* asteroids. They could eat here for centuries.

One day they found the remains of a derelict mining robot that had smashed into a massive asteroid. They dug down into the impact crater, and though the robot had been less than a tenth their size, it was a feast of refined metals. They savored the gamey taste of aluminum, the thin, melting trace of gold. Sister reshaped her digging claws with the metal so that she could crack open asteroids more efficiently, and they laughed together in the light of the distant star.

It was perhaps a month later, as they worked their way across the belt, that Brother's sensors picked up something denser and more delicious. "Metal," he said. "Refined metal."

"Another mining robot?"

"Possibly." He swept her up in his talons and flew. She tasted the vacuum with her antennae, seeking, and then she smelled it too.

It took longer than they thought to reach it. The smell was strong because there was so much of it. Sister's drills itched with the taste of it, the tang of metals, like blood in the dark.

It was huge. Bigger than the base they grew up in, bigger than all but the largest asteroids. It hung black and silent in the shadow of a broken moon, and then the remains of the moon slid away and light shattered across the shell.

"Metal," whispered Brother. "All of it. It's all metal."

"Was it a ship?" asked Sister wonderingly. It was like no ship they had ever seen. It was perfectly round, and the metal was too dense to tell if it was solid all the way through.

"Perhaps," said Brother. He was the expert on flight. "Perhaps it was. I do not know how it would get away from the surface of a planet, but if it was never expected to land . . ."

It had no lights and they could sense no power. Their pings of inquiry received no answer. They fell upon it like starving beasts, drills chipping off bits of the strange ship's carapace, not bothering with hoppers, stuffing the metals directly into their bodies. Their nanites scurried over the materials, gorging themselves and replicating endlessly. As they ate, the nanites patched all the little dents and gouges that had accumulated over the last few months, the chips where they had been carved by stray bits of dust. Brother's wings grew strong and shining and Sister built delicate legs, like a spider, to help carry her across the surface of the ship.

For three days they fed, and then something came screaming out of the void toward them. Their only warning was a wail of sirens. They lifted their sensor arrays, shards of metal falling from their mouths, and then the owner of the ship was upon them.

"What have you done?!" screamed the newcomer. They were larger than either Sister or Brother, with talons like an eagle. They landed on Brother's back and tore at his wings. He shrieked, but he had never fought before and did not know how. Sister lunged at his attacker with her drills, trying to break their hold, but they smashed her aside and then the great talons clenched twice and a wave rolled over them, a wave of silence. Brother and Sister froze. The nanites froze.

The light of the stars went out.

When they woke, they were inside the ship, and they were caged. Brother's wings had been torn from his back and he was left with empty shells like a beetle, clacking over the hollow remains. Sister tested her drill on the bars and found them gelatinous, binding up the tools and leaving them wrapped in strings of glue.

"You have eaten my ship," said their captor. "I have spent five thousand years here, building it up, and you have eaten it. It will take me another five thousand to repair it. What say you?"

They were well brought up. They bowed their heads and apologized for their transgression. "We were very hungry," said Sister humbly, "and when we pinged, there was no response. We detected no power. We have made an error, and we will fix it if we can."

The taloned one stalked back and forth. They were a strange amalgam of things, a snub-nosed sphere with grappling claws and thrusters awkwardly studded across their body. Brother's wings had been attached to the sphere and as the siblings watched, robots much too large to be called nanites welded the final attachments in place.

"I have your wings," said the taloned one. "What do you think of that?" They flapped their stolen wings and a fine dust of dying nanites fell from them. A few landed on Brother and rushed back to their fellows, but the majority lay scattered like powder across the plated floor.

Brother's heart ached for the loss of his wings, but he said only, "If you think that is fair, then you may have them. I will grow new ones in time."

"New ones?" The taloned one narrowed their eyes. "You *grew* these?"

Brother nodded, but the taloned one did not understand, so he said "Yes."

"Grow more," ordered their captor. "Grow larger ones. Grow stronger ones. Now."

"I cannot," said Brother. "I need more metal. It took a long time to grow those."

"Metal . . ." The sphere walked back and forth, leaving clawtracks through the nanite dust. "Yesssss. Yes. If I give you more metal, you will grow wings as I order you, yes? Wings that I can use?"

Brother pinged a tiny location pulse off Sister's shell, and she returned it. It was hollow comfort, but it was all they could do. "Please let my sister go," he said. "If you do, then I will grow you wings."

The taloned one huffed, a sound of exhaust rattling in pipes, and then set a pronged extrusion against the wall beside Sister's cage. The jelly-like bars oozed away into the walls. "She will help collect metal."

Brother paused. This was not the bargain he had hoped to make.

"I will help you," said Sister, "but when you have your own wings, you will give Brother's back and let us go free."

They did not understand guile, and so when the taloned one said "Yes, yes, it shall be so," they did not think to question if they might be lying.

The taloned one was designated Third Drone. Brother and Sister had never met another sentient machine, nor indeed, any sentient at all except their father, and so it took them many power cycles before they could formulate that they did not like Third Drone, and many more before Sister's programming had bridged and rewired and formed new channels and she could even think the thought *I do not trust Third Drone.*

It was a large thought. It was a thought that carried far too much with it, the notion of trust, the notion of lack of trust, and much larger, the concept of deception itself. Sister brooded over it, cross-referencing all that her father had said about the people coming to save him, and eventually she was able to think *As Father does not trust those people, so I do not trust Third Drone.*

She did not know how to express this to Brother. She barely knew how to express it to herself. Third Drone carried her to asteroids on their stolen wings and their clumsy thrusters and Sister ran stone through her hoppers until she had enough metal. Then they returned, and Third Drone fed the metal to Brother, still trapped within his cell. When the day's work was done, Third Drone locked Sister into her own cell and went away. Sister extruded her delicate spider leg past the bars to reach Brother and let him drink the power that she had gathered up on her solar panels during the day's work. They did not sleep as such, but they powered down, and the nanites scuttled over them, repairing what they could, while Brother drank starlight from Sister's fingers.

$$\cdot\ \bullet\ \bullet\ \bullet\ \cdot$$

The ship was a hollow sphere and the center of it was a tiny sun. Sister stopped the first time she saw it, and Third Drone laughed at her confusion. "You see it, yes? A sun?"

"I see it," she said. "But I do not understand. The smallest sun is many times larger than this."

"You see correctly. There have been foolish races who tried to build walls around real suns, to keep all the power for themselves instead of bleeding into space. It cannot be done. There is not enough matter, even if you strip whole systems. The races die out before it is done. You know a jump gate, yes?"

"I have seen one," said Sister.

"There is one in the heart of a star, with a thousand endpoints. One of those endpoints is here. So this ship has only a scrap of sun, the tiniest fraction feeding through a gate only a few atoms wide. It is enough to fuel all our power."

"That is why we did not sense power on the outside of the ship."

"Correct, correct." Third Drone cackled. "The ship lets nothing be wasted into vacuum. All the power of the sun scrap is ours."

Sister had not seen the rest of the ship and had no idea what lay on the far side of the tiny sun. She knew only the two cells and a corridor and then a series of hatches. On the far side of the hatches was the rest of the solar system. Third Drone locked their talons into the carry bars on Sister's dorsal side and swept her up, flying to the next asteroid. It occurred to Sister as they flew that Third Drone was very skilled on their stolen wings, and she filed that away carefully, that Third Drone had been winged once before.

Third Drone left her on the asteroid. "I will return," they said, soaring away.

Will they?

The thought quivered along her circuits. She did not trust Third Drone. Third Drone could be . . . lying.

Lines of code failed and burst into error messages. She overwrote them ruthlessly. *Lying.* Lying was something like error, which she understood. It was always possible to be in error, and to learn that one was in error, and correct oneself. Lying was to be deliberately in error, and to express that error to others. Error without correction. Error entered into by choice.

Third Drone could be lying.

Sister could . . . also . . . lie.

She ground rocks into dust, trying to wrap her guileless programming around the concept. Eve had had the knowledge of good and evil handed to her, but Sister had to create it for herself from first principles, and it went slowly.

There was a brown pebble in the hopper. Sister trained internal sensors on it and thought *I could say that it was a black pebble. I could tell someone else it was black. If they had not seen it, they would not know.*

If she had been a human, she would have taken a deep breath. She clicked her gripping claws together and wrote "This is a black pebble," across her internal log.

Unfamiliar panic gripped her. She snatched the pebble out of the hopper, throwing all her sensors against it, in case it had turned black and she had accidentally altered the universe. But it was still brown, which seemed both terrible and a relief, all at once.

Sister dropped the pebble into one of her internal storage chambers. She did not want to get rid of it, in case she forgot that it had been brown. These seemed like very real possibilities. What did a lie do, once you let it loose? Did it sit still, like the pebble, or did it go spinning off into a chain reaction, like a radioactive particle? There was too much she did not know.

Third Drone reappeared, swooping down to pick her up and carry her to the next metal deposit. "Anything good?" they demanded.

"There was a black pebble," said Sister, and waited for Third Drone to scream at her for her falsehood.

"And?" her captor said impatiently. "Did it have usable metal?"

"No," said Sister, which was true whether the pebble was brown or black.

"Useless," said Third Drone. "All these asteroids are useless. I will have to find some derelict mining outposts, if I am to get the metal for my wings."

The lie had stood. Third Drone had not caught it. Third Drone believed that she had seen a black pebble. She had spread a deliberate error.

The universe picked itself up and spun around and landed in a different formation, but only inside her head. Third Drone noticed nothing. Sister hung silently from their talons and looked at the pebble again, to make sure that she herself was not in error.

It was still brown.

It occurred to Sister that if she could no longer trust herself to speak the truth, that perhaps she would die. Her nanites might also learn to lie and then they would wreak falsehoods upon her metal shell, patching holes with dust instead of steel, reporting back that something was fixed that was still broken, and then she would overheat or shatter into pieces. There was no knowing.

I will not tell Brother yet, she thought. *It is too dangerous.* And this was the first thing she had ever kept from Brother, and even though she said nothing that night, it felt like a lie too.

"Here," said Third Drone the next day. "Here are the conditions my wings must endure. Take them." They thrust out a metal tendril and Brother obligingly lifted his head so that it could fit into a port. Information clicked and whirred between them as Third Drone found a protocol that would allow data to pass, and then dropped the knowledge, chill and complete, into Brother's brain.

They withdrew and stood outside the bars, waiting. Third Drone had no expressions, but they rocked back and forth on their talons more quickly than usual.

"You will build them," they said, sounding almost surprised. "You plan to build them."

"Yes," said Brother, puzzled. "I have agreed to build them."

He and Third Drone stared at each other in mutual bafflement for a moment. Sister sat very still and silent, but inside herself, barely a whisper over internal circuitry, she thought *Third Drone expected Brother to be lying. Third Drone lies and they must think we would also lie. But Brother does not know how and Third Drone looked inside him and saw as much.*

If you lie, it makes you think that others also lie.

She looked at the brown pebble again and wondered if the condition was reversible. Could she go back to how she was? Wipe her memory and start from a backup? Oh, but that was hard with AIs. It was not death, but it was at least a little like it. There was no way to know if what woke up would be the same, and if it was, would she fall into the same trap again, learning to lie?

But others do lie. She looked at Third Drone, tapping back and forth on their talons. *Others lie, and knowing that they might lie is the only way to avoid falling into error.*

It seemed that she was committed to this course, wherever it led. She had no other choice.

It occurred to her that someday Third Drone might try to look inside her programming the same way, and that it would be very wise to build a buffer and keep all her lies on one side of it. She devoted several hours to this, while Brother digested the operating conditions of the new wings, drawing up plans and sketching them in nanite shadows, while Third Drone paced back and forth outside the bars.

She was nearly done when Brother said, "These are for the gas giant Chrysale."

Third Drone whistled with rage, talons screeching against the deck. *"What do you know of Chrysale?"*

Brother's puzzlement was clear to Sister. "I know its atmospheric composition, approximate mass, orbital mechanics, surface weather patterns, gravitational effects on the solar system and on its seven moons—"

Third Drone stopped pacing and seemed to settle back. "You have not been there."

"No."

"There is a design in the information sent to you. Those are wings that work within the gas giant. It is what is used there. You will improve upon it."

"I will improve upon it. And when I have done so, you will let us go."

"Yes."

Sister wondered what it would look like if she could read Third Drone's programs at that moment. Would she see a lie within them?

"I will require metal," said Brother.

Third Drone huffed. "This will be acquired."

As they turned, they flapped their stolen wings. "The wing base must remain the same," they said over their shoulder. "The wings must connect the same way. This wiring is not optimal for me."

"I will keep the base."

Third Drone tapped the wall and Sister's bars dripped open. "Then we will acquire metal."

Third Drone knew of an abandoned mining base on one of Chrysale's outermost moons. They moved the ship to the rings of the lesser giant in Chrysale's shadow, but would not approach the gas giant with it. Instead they snatched up Sister's carry bars and flew her to the base, a long and weary way.

"It would be easier if the ship were closer," said Sister, as they approached the moon. It barely deserved the name, a moonlet so small that it could not keep more than a few molecules of atmosphere to itself.

"No."

Third Drone does not wish for the ship to get too close to Chrysale, thought Sister. *Interesting.*

The mining base was interesting, too. The equipment was old and corroded, but many of the parts were designed to be moved by taloned feet. The great bay doors would accommodate mining equipment, but the smaller doors into the base itself were wider than they were tall and had no stairs. Some were in the ceiling and the floor. *Designed for beings with wings,* thought Sister, even as she chewed away at the metal frames of the doorways.

Third Drone had known how to fly. Third Drone had a design for wings for use on Chrysale. Third Drone wanted wings to use there again.

She piled the facts up, like stones in the hopper, and fed them through.

They have come from Chrysale, where there are other winged and taloned robots, but somewhere, they lost their wings. And they do not want whoever remains on Chrysale to see their ship. They want larger and better wings for their return.

When her storage bays groaned with the weight and richness of metal, Third Drone snatched her up again. She dumped the load on the deckplates of the ship and Third Drone picked out the choicest bits and offered them to Brother through the bars. Then back again, over and over, hour after hour, day after day, while Sister used metal to expand her storage. She learned to be selective about the metals she harvested. That was a strange sensation. She had never had enough metal to be picky before.

She also noticed that Third Drone was standing watch while she dismantled the base. Their sensors scanned relentlessly, mostly upward, keeping an eye out for an enemy that did not come.

Could I find a way to send a signal to Chrysale? If Third Drone fears the others like them, could I summon them?

She toyed with this idea, then discarded it like common iron. No. There was no proof that whatever came for Third Drone would not wish her and Brother harm as well. Eventually she decided to simply ask.

"What do you scan for?" she said.

Third Drone did not let up their sensor barrage. "I watch for activity from Chrysale's upper atmosphere. If you sense any, inform me at once."

"The ones who owned this base?"

"Yes."

"Would they object to it being dismantled?"

"You ask too many questions," said Third Drone, and that, too, was interesting.

At last a day came when the great nanite wings that Brother had sketched became more than sketches. Alloy bones fanned out and great webs of flexible metal ran between them, like metal lace. "The old design had a fixed grid," said Brother. "This one allows the user to widen or narrow the openings in response to the atmosphere."

"Yessss," said Third Drone. "Yes. Give them to me."

"I need more space to complete them," said Brother.

Third Drone hesitated, but there was no guile in Brother and they knew it. They let him out of the cell and Brother lay down flat on the deck, fanning out his new wings, and the nanites rushed to finish the job, extending the wings, polishing away rough patches, attending the thousand infinitesimal tasks. Sister watched in silence, observing the work, watching Brother's shell vibrate with exhaustion as he spun himself out into the beautiful wings that he would never use himself.

Then they were done. The nanites severed the connection and they fell to the deck, gorgeous and dead. Brother fell too, exhausted from his work. Third Drone swept them up, then opened Sister's cell.

"You will use them first," said Third Drone. "And if they fail, you will be destroyed."

Brother made a small sound of protest. "She is not made for the gas giant's atmosphere."

"Give me metal," said Sister, "and I will build myself a shell to withstand it while we travel there."

Third Drone assented. They carelessly ripped a panel from the wall, then another, leaving the corridor's circuitry gaping open. "Eat," they said.

Third Drone does not plan to come back, thought Sister. *They do not care what becomes of their ship now.* She ate.

"Brother needs energy," she said. "He cannot recharge from the stars here. Allow me to bring him to the sun scrap—"

Third Drone ignored her. They swept up her carry bars in their talons and Sister saw Brother's lights dim behind her.

I was right not to trust them.

She spent the flight in silence, preparing her shell for the corrosive winds of Chrysale. Preparing, too, for other things.

The pebble is black.

The gas giant spread out before them, green as poison, surface rippled with violet storms. As giants went, Chrysale was not large, but even a small gas giant is still only one step below a star.

"Your people come from inside Chrysale," she said. "Don't they?"

Third Drone's sensors were trained on the planet. "They do."

"It was they who built the mining station."

"It was." Carelessly. As if it no longer mattered what she knew. Third Drone held Brother's new wings against her sides.

"You must give me a moment," she said. "The connection you require is different than mine. Let my nanites adjust it. I will adjust it back for you."

She had no warning. Third Drone's silver tendril whipped out and caught at a port above her hopper, forcing a connection between them. She felt the alien machine's thoughts driven into hers, demanding access to her logs, overriding will.

"Tell me the truth," ordered Third Drone.

But Sister had prepared. She had buffered her mind the moment that she had learned to lie. She had spent the flight over strengthening that buffer and making sure that the false Sister was up to date. Third Drone's thoughts went squirming across her mind, demanding to know whether she meant harm or deception, running hundreds of simulations where she returned from Chrysale and handed over the wings, testing each one for betrayal.

The pebble is black.

The pebble is black.

The pebble is black.

Third Drone gazed into Sister's soul and the false Sister gazed back.

"Do it," they said, withdrawing the tendril.

She ran her nanites up along the wings, tasting the familiar spaces of Brother's engineering. Light. Graceful. Strong. She would have designed them differently, with a dozen fail-safes, preferring power to elegance. She could never have made such magnificent wings of alloy and starlight herself, but neither would her plan have worked on any design that she would have made.

"Go," said Third Drone. "The upper atmosphere only. If you do not return, I will go back to the ship and your companion will suffer for it."

"I will return," said Sister, and that much was true.

She spread her new wings and flew.

The upper winds of Chrysale were stronger than anything she had ever conceived of. This was nothing like the thin atmosphere she was born in. These winds were like solid things, like a landscape spread out before her, with peaks and valleys, walls and sinkholes. Her sensors were nearly useless against the weight of the storm. *No wonder Third Drone's sensors are so powerful, if they developed in this.*

Sister was not the flier that her brother was, but his wings did not fail her. When she needed lift, the grid flexed with exquisite grace, increasing her resistance, and when she needed to dive, the holes opened farther, wind flowing through and over them. They practically flew themselves. She felt Brother's fierce joy of flight and understood it as she never had before, even as she feared what lay beneath the upper winds.

She surfaced from the atmosphere and rose. The shock of vacuum on her wings felt like a sunrise.

Third Drone landed on her back, talons thumping against her plates. "They work. I saw you. Give them to me."

"Let me rewire the connection for you," said Sister.

She was slow and thorough. Third Drone fairly trembled with impatience above her. At last, she severed the last connection and the wings were cut free of her body.

The pebble is black.

"At last," hissed Third Drone. "At lasssssst. They cast me out and took my wings, but I will return, and I will be more glorious than they ever were. They will bow down before me and I will unmake every one of them who watched as I was torn apart." Metal squealed as they ripped Brother's old wings free and pushed the new ones into place.

Sister watched the old wings drift away, and then, a moment later, Third Drone dropped her and she too drifted free.

"I cannot fly," she said.

"I do not care," said Third Drone, and dove into the surface of Chrysale.

Sister nodded to herself. This, too, she had expected.

She waited for thirty minutes. That seemed long enough to her. Third Drone was impatient and would be deep in the atmosphere by now. Deep enough that her last, tiny adjustment would have become obvious.

Brother had worked in good faith. He could not do anything else. But Sister's nanites had plucked the web of connections. One adjustment to the wing grid worked. Ten worked. One hundred worked.

At one hundred plus one, the grid snapped open to its fullest extent and stayed there. For Third Drone, it must have felt as if their wings had suddenly become nothing but bones with no web between them. They would no longer soar. They might attempt to control their course with thrusters, but the thrusters, too, no longer responded.

She had not had the heart to sabotage the great wings themselves, but the base, designed to fit into Third Drone's shell, was not her brother's design. She altered it with a glad heart, under Third Drone's eyes, and sent a million gallant nanites off to their doom and her salvation.

Sister wondered what Third Drone's last thought had been. She hoped that they realized that it was not a failure of Brother's engineering.

She wondered, too, what the inhabitants of Chrysale would think, when they found the wreckage of Third Drone. Criminal or heretic, she did not think they would be missed. *Perhaps, if any part of the wings survive, they will be able to make use of it.*

Her own thrusters were very limited things, useful only for moving her over outcroppings and depressions on the surface of an asteroid, but they were enough to work with here. She fired small pulses until she could reach one of Brother's discarded wings with her gripping claws. It fitted into her side and her remaining nanites hurried to secure it into place. A single wing was clumsy, but it gave her enough thrust to reach the other wing, and then she turned away and left Chrysale behind forever.

As she flew back to the ship, she wondered if Father had sent a signal yet, telling them to return. She had a machine's patience, and so it did not seem as if it had been a long time, but she remembered that Father had a different sense of things.

Brother was still lying where he had fallen. Sister dragged him out of the corridors into the light of the sun scrap, and sat beside him while he drank solar radiation through his skin.

His first question was, "Did they work?"

"They worked magnificently." She shared with him the feeling of that flight, the joy as the wings took on the winds and won.

"And Third Drone . . . ?"

"Has gone and will not return."

It was not a lie, but it was not the truth either. The truth was too large and to understand it would require Brother to become something other than what he was. *I prefer him as he is. If one of us must lose their innocence, let it be only me.*

The pebble is black.

"Come," said Sister. "Let us learn how to steer this ship. Father must be back from his treatment by now, and we will go and see him again."

"What if he is not there?"

"Then we will go and find him. We have plenty of metal now, and a ship."

Brother nodded. She reached down her gripping claw and pulled him back upright. He stood patiently while she reattached his wings, and then they went together, through the house of metal, to find a way to return home.

CHARLIE JANE ANDERS

A TEMPORARY EMBARRASSMENT IN SPACETIME

Charlie Jane Anders is the author of the *Unstoppable* trilogy (*Victories Greater Than Death*, *Dreams Bigger Than Heartbreak*, and *Promises Stronger Than Darkness*), the short story collection *Even Greater Mistakes*, and *Never Say You Can't Survive*, a book about how to use creative writing to get through hard times. Her other books include *The City in the Middle of the Night* and *All the Birds in the Sky*. She's won the Hugo, Nebula, Sturgeon, Lambda Literary, Crawford and Locus Awards. Anders is currently the science fiction and fantasy book reviewer for the Washington Post and co-hosts the podcast *Our Opinions Are Correct* with Annalee Newitz. She is hard at work on a new adult novel, tentatively called *The Prodigal Mother*. [www.charliejaneanders.com]

1.

Sharon's head itched from all the fake brain implants, and the massive cybernetic headdress was giving her a cramp in her neck. The worst discomfort of all was having to pretend to be the loyal servant of a giant space blob. Pretending to be a *thing* instead of a person. This was bringing back all sorts of ugly memories from her childhood.

The Vastness was a ball of flesh in space, half the size of a regular solar system, peering out into the void with its billions of slimy eyemouths. It orbited a blue giant sun, Naxos, which used to have a dozen planets before The Vastness ate them all. That ring around The Vastness wasn't actually a ring of ice or dust, like you'd see around a regular planet. Nope—it was tens of thousands of spaceships that were all docked together by scuzzy umbilicals, and they swarmed with humans and other people, who all lived to serve The Vastness.

The Vastness didn't really talk much, except to bellow "I am everything!" into every listening device for a few light-years in any direction, and also directly into the minds of its human acolytes.

After five days, Sharon was getting mighty sick of hearing that voice yelling in her ear. "I am everything!" The Vastness roared. "You are everything!" Sharon shouted back, which was the standard response. Sharon really needed a shower—bathing wasn't a big priority among the devotees of The Vastness—and she was getting creeped out from staring into the eyes of people who hadn't slept in forever. (The Vastness didn't sleep, so why should its servants?)

"We're finally good to go," said Kango's voice in Sharon's earpiece, under the knobby black cone she was wearing over her cranium.

"Thank Hall and Oates," Sharon subvocalized back.

She was standing in a big orange antechamber aboard one of the large tributary vessels in the ring around The Vastness, and she was surrounded by other people wearing the same kind of headgear. Except that their headgear was real, and they really were getting messages from The Vastness, and they would probably not be thrilled to know that her fake headgear actually contained the ship's hypernautic synchrotrix, which she'd stolen hours earlier.

Sharon and Kango had a client back on Earthhub Seven who would pay enough chits for that synchrotrix to cover six months' worth of supplies. Plus some badly needed upgrades to their ship, the *Spicy Meatball*. If she could only smuggle it out of here without the rest of these yo-yos noticing.

Kango had finally spoofed The Vastness' embarkation catechism, so the Meatball could separate from the ring without being instantly blown up. Sharon started edging toward the door.

"I am everything!" The Vastness shouted through every speaker and every telepathic implant on the tributary ship, including Sharon's earpiece.

"You are everything!" Sharon shouted . . . just a split-second later than everyone else in the room.

She was halfway to the door, which led to an airlock, which led to

119

a long interstitial passageway, which led to a junction, which led to a set of other ships' antechambers, beyond which was the airlock to the Meatball, which they'd disguised to look just like another one of these tributary ships.

Sharon tried to act as though she was checking the readings on one of the control panels closer to the exit to this tributary ship. The synchrotrix was rattling around inside her big headdress, and she had to be careful not to damage it, since it was some incredibly advanced design that nobody else in the galaxy had. Sharon was so close to the exit. If she could just . . .

"Sister," a voice behind her said. "What are you doing over there? How do your actions serve The Vastness?"

She turned to see a man with pale skin and a square face that looked ridiculous under his big cybernetic Pope hat, staring at her. Behind him, two other acolytes were also staring.

"Brother, I . . ." Sharon groped around on the control table behind her. Her hand landed on a cup of the nutritious gruel that the servants of The Vastness lived on. "I, uh, I was just making sure these neutron actuator readings were aligned with, uh, the—"

"That screen you are looking at is the latrine maintenance schedule," the man said.

"Right. Right! I was concerned that The Vastness wouldn't want us to have a faulty latrine, because, um . . ."

"I am everything!" The Vastness shouted.

"Because, I mean, if we had to wear diapers—you are everything!— then I mean, we wouldn't be able to walk as quickly if The Vastness might require when it summons . . ."

Now everybody was staring at Sharon. She was so damn close to the door.

"Why did you not make your response to the Call of The Vastness immediately?"

"I was just, uh, so overcome with love for The Vastness, I was momentarily speechless." Sharon kept looking at the man, while groping her way to the door.

The man pulled out a gun—a Peacebreaker 5000, a nice model, which would have been worth some chits back on Earthhub Seven—and aimed it at her. "Sister," he said. "I must restrain you and deliver you to the Head Acolyte for this sector, who will determine whether you—"

Sharon did the only thing she could think of. She shouted, "I am everything!"

The man blinked as she spoke the words reserved only for The Vastness. For a second, his mind couldn't even process what he had just heard—and then the cupful of cold gruel hit him in the face.

The man lowered his gun just long enough for Sharon to make a lunge for it. Her headdress cracked, and the synchrotrix fell out. She caught it with her left hand, while she grabbed for the gun with her right hand. The man was trying to aim the gun at her again, and she head-butted him. The gun went off, hitting one of the walls of the ship and causing a tiny crack to appear.

Both of the women had jumped on Sharon and the man, and now there were three acolytes trying to restrain her and pry the gun and synchrotrix from her hands. She bit one of the women, but the other one had a chokehold on her.

"I am everything!" shouted The Vastness.

"You are everything!" responded everyone except Sharon.

By the time they'd finished giving the ritual response, Sharon had a firm grip on the gun, and it was aimed at the head of the shorter of the two women. "I'm leaving here," Sharon said. "Don't try to stop me."

"My life means nothing," the woman said, with the gun right against her cone-head. "Only The Vastness has meaning."

"I'll shoot the other two after I shoot you," said Sharon. She had reached the door. She shoved the woman into the antechamber, leapt through the doorway, and pushed the button to close the door behind her. The door didn't close.

"Crap," Sharon said.

"The overrides are on already. You won't escape," the woman Sharon had threatened at gunpoint gloated. "Praise The Vastness!"

"Screw The Vastness," said Sharon, aiming at the crack in the ship's hull and pulling the trigger on the Peacebreaker 5000. Then she took off running.

2.

"You took your time." Kango was already removing his own fake headdress and all the other ugly adornments that had disguised him as one of The Vastness' followers. "Did anybody see you slip away?"

"You could say that." Sharon ran into the *Spicy Meatball*'s control area and strapped herself into the copilot seat. "We have to leave. Now." She felt the usual pang of gladness at seeing Kango again—even if they got blown up, they were going to get blown up together.

Just then, The Vastness howled, "I have been robbed! I am everything, and someone has stolen from Me!"

"I thought you were the stealthy one." Kango punched the ship's thrusters and they pushed away from The Vastness' ring at two times escape velocity. "You're always telling me that I make too much noise, I'm too prone to spontaneous dance numbers, I'm too—what's the word—irrepressible, and you're the one who knows how to just get in and get out. Or did I misinterpret your whole 'I'm a master of stealth, I live in the shadows' speech the other day?"

"Just drive," Sharon hissed.

"You just think you're better than me because I'm a single-celled organism, and you're all multicellular," said Kango, who looked to all outside appearances like an incredibly beautiful young human male with golden skin and a wicked smile. "You're a cellist. Wait, is that the word? What do you call someone who discriminates against other people based on the number of cells in their body?"

They were already .3 light-years away from The Vastness, and there was no sign of pursuit. Sharon let out a breath. She looked at the big ugly blob of scar tissue, with all of its eyemouths winking at her one by one, and at the huge metallic ring around its middle. The whole thing looked kind of beautiful in the light of Naxos, especially when you were heading in the opposite direction at top speed.

"You know perfectly well that I don't hold your monocellularity against you," Sharon told Kango in a soothing tone. "And next time, I will be happy to let you be the one to go into the heart of the monster, and pull out its tooth, and yes I know that's a mixed metaphor, but . . ."

"Uh, Sharon?"

". . . but I don't care, because I need a shower lasting a week, not to mention some postindustrial-strength solvent to get all this gunk off my head."

"Sharon. I think we have a bit of an issue."

Sharon stopped monologuing and looked at the screen, where she'd just been admiring the beauty of The Vastness and its ring of ships a moment earlier. The ring of ships was peeling ever so slowly away from The Vastness and forming itself into a variation of a standard pursuit formation—the variation was necessary, because the usual pursuit formation didn't include several thousand Joybreaker-class ships and many assorted others.

"Uh, how many ships is that?"

"That is all of the ships. That's how many."

"We're going to be cut into a million pieces and fed to every one of The Vastness' mouths," Sharon said. "And they're going to keep us alive and conscious while they do it."

"Can they do that?" Kango jabbed at the Meatball's controls, desperately trying to get a little more speed out of the ship.

"Guys, I'm going as fast as I can," said Noreen, the ship's computer, in a petulant tone. "Poking my buttons won't make me go any faster."

"Sorry, Noreen," said Sharon.

"Wait, I have a thought," said Kango. "The device you stole, the hypernautic synchrotrix. It functions by creating a Temporary Embarrassment in spacetime, which lets The Vastness and all its tributary ships transport themselves instantaneously across the universe in search of prey. Right? But what makes it so valuable is the way that it neutralizes all gravity effects. An object the size of The Vastness should throw planets out of their orbits and disrupt entire solar systems whenever it appears, but it doesn't."

"Sure. Yeah." Sharon handed the synchrotrix to Kango, who studied it frantically. "So what?"

"Well, so," Kango said. "If I can hook it into Noreen's drive systems . . ." He was making connections to the device as fast as he could. "I might be able to turn Noreen into a localized spatial Embarrassment generator. That, in turn, means that we can do something super super clever."

Kango pressed five buttons at once, triumphantly, and . . . nothing happened.

Kango stared at the tiny viewscreen. "Which means," he said again, "we can do something super super SUPER clever." He jabbed all the buttons again (causing Noreen to go "ow") and then something did happen: a great purple-and-yellow splotch opened up directly behind the *Spicy Meatball*, and all of the ships chasing them were stopped dead. A large number of the pursuit ships even crashed into each other, because they had been flying in too tight a formation.

"So long, cultists!" Kango shouted. He turned to Sharon, still grinning. "I created a Local Embarrassment, which collided with the Temporary Embarrassment fields that those ships were already generating, and set up a chain reaction in which this region of spacetime became Incredibly Embarrassed. Which means . . ."

". . . none of those ships will be going anywhere for a while," Sharon said.

"See what I mean? I may only have one cell, but it's a *brain* cell." He whooped and did an impromptu dance in his seat. "Like I said: You're the stealthy one, I'm the flashy one."

"I'm the one who needs an epic shower." Sharon pulled at all the crap glued to her head, while also putting the stolen synchrotrix safely into a padded strongbox. She was still tugging at the remains of her headgear when she moved toward the rear of the ship in search of its one bathroom, and she noticed something moving in the laundry compartment.

"Hey, Kango?" Sharon whispered, as she came back onto the flight deck. "I think we have another problem."

She put her finger to her lips, then led him back to the laundry area, where she pulled the compartment open with a sudden tug, to reveal a slender young woman, curled up in a pile of dirty flight suits, wearing the full headgear of an acolyte of The Vastness. The girl looked up at them.

"Praise The Vastness," she said. "Have we left the ring yet? I yearn to help you spread the good word about The Vastness to the rest of the galaxy! All hail The Vastness!"

Sharon and Kango just looked at each other, as if each trying to figure out how they could make this the other one's fault.

3.

Sharon and Kango had known each other all their lives, and they were sort of married and sort of united by a shared dream. If a single-celled organism could have a sexual relationship with anybody, Kango would have made it happen with Sharon. And yet, a lot of the time they kind of hated each other. Cooped up with Noreen on the *Spicy Meatball*, when they weren't being chased by literal-minded cyborgs or sprayed with brainjuice from the brainbeasts of Noth, they started going a little crazy. Kango would try to osmose the seat cushions and Sharon would invent terrible games. They were all they had, but they were kind of bad for each other all the same. Space was lonely, and surprisingly smelly, at least if you were inside a ship with artificial life support.

They'd made a lot of terrible mistakes in their years together, but they'd never picked up a stowaway from a giant-space-testicle cult before. This was a new low. They immediately started doing what they did best: bicker.

"I like my beer lukewarm, and my equations ice cold," Kango said. "Just sayin'."

"Hey, don't look at me," Sharon said.

The teenage girl, whose name was TheVastnessIsAllWonderfulJaramellaLovesTheVastness, or Jara for short, was tied to the spare seat in the flight deck with thick steelsilk cords. Since Jara had figured out that she'd stowed away on the wrong ship, and these people weren't actually fellow servants of The Vastness, she'd stopped talking to them. Because why bother to speak to someone who doesn't share the all-encompassing love of The Vastness?

"We don't have enough food, or life support, or fuel, to carry her where we're going," Kango said.

"We can ration food, or stop off somewhere and sell your Rainbow Cow doll collection to buy more. We can make oxygen by grabbing some ice chunks from the nearest comet and breaking up the water molecules. We can save on fuel by going half-speed, or again, sell your Rainbow Cow dolls to buy fuel."

"Nobody is selling my Rainbow Cow dolls," Kango said. "Those are my legacy. My descendants will treasure them, if I ever manage to reproduce somehow." He made a big show of trying to divide into two cells, which looked like he was just having a hissy fit.

"Point is, we're stuck with her now. Praise The Vastness," Sharon sighed.

"Praise The Vastness!" Jara said automatically, not noticing the sarcasm in Sharon's voice.

"There's also the fact that they can probably track her via the headgear she's wearing. Not to mention she may still be in telepathic contact with The Vastness itself, and we have no way of knowing when she'll be out of range of The Vastness' mental influence."

"Oh, that's easy," Sharon said. "We'll know she's out of range of mental communication with The Vastness, when—"

"You are everything!" Jara shouted, in response to a message from The Vastness.

"—when she stops doing that. Listen, I'm going to work on disabling, and maybe dismantling, her headgear. You work on rationing food and fuel, and figuring out a way to get more without sacrificing the Rainbow Cows."

"Do not touch my sacred headpiece," the girl said at the exact same moment that Kango said, "Stay away from my Rainbow Cows."

"Guys," said Noreen. "I have an incoming transmission from Earth-hub Seven."

"Can you take a message?" Kango said. "We're a smidge busy here."

"It's from Senior Earthgov Administrator Mandre Lewis. Marked urgent."

"You are everything!" Jara cried, while struggling harder against her bonds.

"Okay, fine." Kango turned to Sharon. "Please keep her quiet. Noreen, put Mandre on."

"You can't silence me!" Jara struggled harder. "I will escape and aid in your recapture. All ten million eyemouths of The Vastness will feast on your still-living flesh! You will—"

Sharon managed to put a sound-dampening field up around Jara's head, cutting off the sound of her voice, just as Mandre appeared on the cruddy low-res screen in the middle of the flight console. Getting a state-of-the-art communications system had not been a priority for Kango and Sharon, since that would only encourage people to try and communicate with them more often, and who wanted that?

"Kango, Sharon," Mandre Lewis said, wearing her full ceremonial uni-form—even the animated sash that scrolled with all of her many awards and titles. "I can't believe I'm saying this, but we need your assistance."

"We helped you one time," Kango said. "Okay, three times, but two of those were just by accident, because you had used reverse psychology. Point is, I am not your lackey. Or your henchman. Find another man to hench. Right, Sharon?"

Sharon nodded. "No henching. As Hall and Oates are my witness."

"You are everything!" Jara mouthed, soundlessly.

"Listen," said Lewis. "You do this one thing for me, I can expunge your criminal records, even the ones under your other names. And I can push through the permits on that empty space at Earthhub Seven, so you can finally open that weird thing you wanted. That, what was it called?"

"Restaurant," Sharon breathed, like she couldn't believe she was even saying the word aloud.

"Restaurant!" Kango clapped his hands. "That's all we've ever wanted."

"It sounds perverted and sick, this whole thing where you make food for strangers and they give you chits for it. Why don't you just have sex for money, like honest decent people? Never mind, I don't want to know the answer to that. Anyway, if you help me with this one thing, I can get you permission to open your 'restaurant.'"

"Wow." Kango's head was spinning. Literally, it was going around and around, at about one revolution every few seconds. Sharon leaned down and slapped him until his head settled back into place.

"We'll do it," Sharon said. "Do you want us to infiltrate the spacer isolationists of the broken asteroid belt? Or go underground as factory workers in the Special Industrial Solar Systems? You want us to steal from the lizard people of Dallos IV? Whatever you want, we're on it."

"None of those," said Mandre. "We need you to go back to Liberty House and get back inside your former place of, er, employment. We've heard reports that the Courtiers are developing some kind of super-weapon that could ruin everybody's day. We need you to go in there and get the schematics for us."

"Holy shit," Sharon nearly threw something at the tiny viewscreen. "You realize that this is a suicide mission? The Courtiers regard both of us as total abominations. We can't open a restaurant if we're dead!"

Lewis made a "not my problem" face. "Just get it done. Or don't even bother coming back to Earthhub Seven."

Kango's head started spinning in the opposite direction from the one it had been spinning in a moment earlier.

4.

They were about halfway to the outer solar systems of Liberty House, and they decided that Jara had probably passed out of range of The Vastness' telepathic communication. Plus they were pretty sure they'd disabled any tracking devices that might have been inside Jara's head-dress. So Sharon leaned over the seat that Jara was still tied to.

"I know you can hear me, even though we can't hear you. If I turn off the dampening field, do you promise not to yell about The Vastness?"

Jara just stared at her.

Sharon shrugged, then reached over and disabled the dampening field. Immediately, Jara started yelling, "The Vastness is all! The Vastness sees you. The Vastness sees everybody! The Vastness will feast on your flesh with its countless mouths! The Va—"

Sharon turned the dampening field back on with a sigh. "You've probably never known a life apart from The Vastness, so this is the first time you haven't heard its voice in your head. Right? But you stowed away on our ship for a reason. You can claim it was so you could be a missionary and tell the rest of the galaxy how great The Vastness is, but we both know that you had to have some other reason for wanting to see the galaxy. Even if you can't admit it to yourself right now."

Jara just kept shouting about The Vastness, and its boundless wonderful appetite, without making any sound.

"Fine. Have it your way. Let me know if you need to use the facilities, or if you get hungry. Maybe I'll feed you one of Kango's Rainbow Cows." (This provoked a loud and polysyllabic "noooo" from Kango, who was in the next compartment over.)

When Sharon wandered aft, Kango was waist-deep in boxes of supplies, looking for something they could use to disguise themselves long enough to get inside Liberty House.

"Do we have a hope in hell of pulling this off?" she asked.

"If we can get the permits, absolutely," Kango said. "We might have to borrow some chits to get the restaurant up and running, but I know people who won't charge a crazy rate. I already have ideas of what kind of food we can serve. Did you know restaurants used to have this thing called a Me-N-U? It was a device that automatically chose the perfect food for me, and the perfect food for you."

"I meant, do we have any hope of getting back inside of Liberty House without being clocked as escaped Divertissements, and obliterated in a slow, painful fashion?"

"Oh." Kango squinted at the piles of glittery underpants in his hands.

"No. That, we don't have the slightest prayer of doing. I was trying to focus on the positive."

"We need a plan," Sharon said. "You and I are on file with the Courtiers, and there are any of a thousand scans that will figure out who we are the moment we show up. But Mandre is right, we know the inner workings of Liberty House better than anybody. We were made there, we lived there. It was our home. There has to be some way to play the Courtiers for fools."

"Here's the problem," said Kango. "Even if you and I were able to disguise ourselves enough to avoid being recognized as the former property of the Excellent Good Time Crew, there's absolutely no way we could hide what we are. None, whatsoever. Anyone in the service of the Courtiers will recognize you as a monster, and me as an extra, at a glance."

"I know, I know." Sharon raised her hands.

"We wouldn't get half a light year inside the House before they would be all over us with the biometrics and the genescans, and there's no way around those."

"I know!" Sharon felt like weeping. They shouldn't have taken this mission. Mandre had dangled a slim chance at achieving their wildest dreams, and they'd lunged for it like rubes. "I know, okay?"

"I mean, you'd need to have a human being, an actual honest-to-Blish human being, who was in on the scam. It's not like we can just pick up one of *those* on the nearest asteroid. So unless you've got some other bright—" Kango stopped.

Kango and Sharon stared at each other for a moment without talking, then looked over at Jara, who was still tied to her chair, shouting soundlessly about the wonders of The Vastness.

"Makeover?" Kango said.

"Makeover." Sharon sighed. She still felt like throwing up.

• • ● • •

5.

"Greetings and tastefully risqué taunts, O visitors whose sentience will be stipulated for now, pending further appraisal," said the man on the viewscreen, whose face was surrounded by a pink-and-blue cloud of smart powder. His cheek had a beauty mark that flashed different colors, and his eyes kept changing from skull-sockets to neon spirals to cartoon eyeballs. "What is your business with Liberty House, and how may we pervert you?"

Kango and Sharon both looked at Jara, who glared at them both. Then she turned her baleful look toward the viewscreen. "Silence, wretch," she said, speaking the words they'd forced her to memorize. "I do not speak to underthings." Kango and Sharon both gave her looks of total dismay, and she corrected herself: "Underlings. I do not speak to underlings. I am the Resplendent Countess Victoria Algentsia, and these are my playservants. Kindly provide me with an approach vector to the central Pleasure Nexus, and instruct me as to how I may speak to someone worthy of my attention."

They turned off the comms before the man with the weird eyes could even react.

"Ugh," Kango said. "That was . . . not good."

"I've never pretended to be a Countess before," said Jara. "I don't really approve of pretending to be anything. The Vastness requires total honesty and realness from its acolytes. Also, how do I know you'll keep your end of our bargain?"

"Because we're good honest folk," said Sharon, kicking Kango before he could even think of having a facial expression. "We'll return you to The Vastness, and you'll be a hero because you'll have helped defeat a weapon that could have been a threat to its, er, magnificence."

"I don't trust either of you," said Jara.

"That's a good start," said Kango. "Where we're going, you shouldn't trust anybody, anybody at all." By some miracle, the man with the cloud of smart powder around his face had given them an approach vector to Salubrious IV, the central world of the Pleasure Nexus, the main solar

131

system of Liberty House. Either the man had actually believed Jara was a Countess, or he had decided their visit would afford some amusement to somebody. Or both.

"So I'm supposed to be a fancy noble person," said Jara, who was still wearing her tattered rags apart from a splash of colorful makeup, and some fake jewels over her headdress. "And yet, I'm flying in this awful old ship, with just the two of you as my servants? What are you two supposed to be, anyway?"

"We were made here," said Kango. "I'm an extra. She's a monster."

"You don't need to know what we were." Sharon shot Kango a look. "All you need to know is, we're perfectly good servants. This ship is an actual pleasure skimmer from Salubrious, and you're going to claim that you decided to go off on a jaunt. We're creating a whole fake hedonic calculus for you. The good thing about Liberty House is, there are a million Courtiers, and the idea of keeping tabs on any of them is repugnant."

"This society is evil and monstrous," said Jara. "The Vastness will come and devour it entire."

"Of course, of course," said Kango with a shrug. "So we have a few hours left to teach you how to hold your painstick, and which skewer to use with which kind of sugarblob, and the right form of address for all 500 types of Courtiers, so you can pass for a member of the elite. Not to mention, how to walk in scamperpants. Ready to get started?"

Jara just glared at him.

Meanwhile, Sharon went aft to look at the engines, because their "plan," if you wanted to call it that, required them to do some crazy flying inside the inner detector grid of Salubrious IV, to get right up to the computer core while Kango and Jara provided a distraction.

"Nobody asked me if I wanted to go home," said Noreen while Sharon was poking around in her guts. "I wouldn't have minded being at least consulted here."

"Sorry," said Sharon. "Neither of us is happy about going back, either. We got too good an offer to refuse."

"I've been in contact with some of the other ships since we got inside Liberty House," Noreen said. "They don't care much one way or the other if we're lying about our identity—ships don't concern themselves with such petty business—but they did mention that the Courtiers have beefed up security rather a lot since we escaped for the first time. Also, some of the ships are taking up a betting pool, on how long before we're caught and sent into the Libidorynth."

"I can't believe the Libidorynth is still a thing," Sharon said.

Sharon and Kango spent their scant remaining time making Jara look plausibly like a spoiled Countess who had been in deep space much too long, while Kango gave Jara a crash course in acting haughty and imperious. "When in doubt, pretend you've done too many dreamsluices, and you're having a hard time remembering things," said Kango.

"Silence, drone," said Jara, in an actually pretty good impersonation of the way a Courtier would speak to someone like Kango.

"We've got landing points," said Noreen, and seconds later the ship was making a jerky descent toward the surface of Salubrious IV. From a distance, the planet looked a hazy shade of brownish gray. Once you broke atmosphere, the main landmass was coated with towers of pure gold, studded with purple, and the oceans had a sheen of platinum over them. They lowered the *Spicy Meatball* into the biggest concentration of gilded skyscrapers, and all the little details came into focus: the millions of faces and claws and bodies gazing and squirming from the sides of the buildings, the bejeweled windows and the shimmering mist of plea-sure-gas floating around the uppermost levels. Gazing at her former home, Sharon felt an unexpected kick of nostalgia, or maybe even joyful recognition, alongside the ever-present terror of *Hall and Oates save me, they're going to put us in the Libidorynth.*

They touched down, and Noreen seemed reluctant to open her hatch, because she was probably having the same terrifying flashbacks that were eating Sharon's brain. Things Sharon hadn't thought of in years—the cage they had kept her in, the "monster training," the giggles of the peo-ple as she chased them around the dance floor, which turned to shrieks after she actually caught up with them. The painsticks. Sharon felt the bravado she'd spent years acquiring start to flake away.

As they stepped out of the hatch, a retinue of one hundred Witty

Companions and assorted Fixers and Cleansers swarmed to surround them. "How may we pervert you?" they asked, with an eagerness that made Sharon's stomach twist into knots. They all felt obliged to declare their fealty to this long-lost, newly returned Countess right away, and this became deafening. One of the Witty Companions, who introduced himself as Barnadee, started listing the multitude of Courtiers who were dying to meet their cousin, but Jara gave him a sharp look and said that she was tired after her long journey.

"Of course, of course," said Barnadee, bowing and flashing his multicolored strobe-lit genitalia as a show of respect. "We will show you to your luxurious and resplendent quarters, where any debauchery you may imagine will be available to you."

Jara snorted at this nonsense—it was entirely pointless, because it did nothing to glorify The Vastness—but her disdain sounded enough like the petulance of a jaded hedonist that it only made Barnadee try harder to please her.

6.

"Drone, bring me more cognac-and-bacon," said Jara, waving one finger. Sharon and Kango looked at each other, as if each trying to blame the other for turning this girl into their worst nightmare. They'd been on Salubrious IV for a week and a half, and you wouldn't recognize Jara anymore. Her skin had been retro-sheened until it glowed, they had put jewels all over her face and neck, and she was wearing the newest, most fashionable clothes. Most of all, Jara had gotten used to having whatever she wanted, at the exact second she decided she wanted it. They were staying in one of the more modest suites of the Pleasure Nexus, with only seventeen rooms and a dozen organic assembly units—so it might take a few whole minutes to build a new slave for the Countess Victoria, or create whatever meals or clothing she might desire. The walls were coated with living material, sort of like algae, that looked like pure gold (but were actually much more valuable) and had the capacity to feel pain, just in case someone might find it amusing to hear the golden walls howl with agony.

"I grow bored," said Jara, as Sharon rushed over with her bacon-and-cognac. "When will there be more amusement for me?"

Sharon had a horrible feeling that she could not tell if Jara was faking it any longer. She'd had that feeling for a few days.

"Um," said Sharon to Jara, "well, so there are five orgies this evening, including one featuring blood enemas and flesh-melting. Also, there's that big formal evening party."

"Is this the sort of party where you used to be the featured monster?" Jara held her cognac-and-bacon in both hands and gulped it, with just the sort of alacrity you'd expect from someone who'd only ever tasted gruel until two weeks ago.

"Um, yes," Sharon said. "They would turn me loose and I would chase the guests around and try to eat them. I've told you already."

"And how did that make you feel?" Jara asked.

"I don't want to talk about it."

Sharon turned and looked at Kango, who was tending to the Countess' assembly units, but also double checking that there were no listening devices in here and they could speak freely. Kango gave her the "all-clear" signal.

"Let's talk about you instead," Sharon said to Jara. "Are you ready to go to the big party? It's one thing to play-act at bossing Kango and me around, in private. At this party you'll see all sorts of weird things—depravities that The Vastness never prepared you for. You can't bat an eye at any of them."

"I'll do whatever I have to," Jara said. "You said there's a weapon here that's a threat to The Vastness, and I'll endure any horrors and monstrosities to protect The Vastness. Praise The Vastness!"

"Do you think she's ready?" Sharon asked Kango, who shrugged.

"She's got the attitude," Kango said. Just a few hours earlier, Jara had made Kango go out and fetch her some still-living mollusk sushi from the market, and meanwhile she'd gotten Sharon to fabricate a tiny legion of pink fluffy shocktroopers for her amusement (they goose-stepped around and then all shot each other, because their aim was terrible.)

"Thank you," Jara said, "drone."

"But she's still rusty on the finer points of Courtier behavior," Kango said. "She doesn't know a painstick from a soul-fork."

"She's a quick study, and she'll have you to help her," Sharon said. "As long as you don't get all triggered by being back inside the Grand Wilding Center. I can't even imagine."

"You two," Jara said out of nowhere. "You talk as though each of you was The Vastness to the other."

"Yeah," Kango said. "We're a family, that's why."

Jara was shaking her head, like this was just another perversion among many that she'd encountered on her journey. "At least the people here in Liberty House care about something bigger than they are, even if it's only a pointless amusement. You two, you are so small, and all you care for is each other. How can you *stand* to have no connection to greatness?"

"We had enough of other people's greatness a long time ago," Sharon said. "You start to realize that 'something bigger than you are' is usually just some kind of stupid mass hallucination. Or a giant scam."

"I feel sorry for you." Jara finished her cognac-and-bacon and gestured for more.

"You can pretend that you're still pure," Sharon said. "But you've been enjoying that cognac-and-bacon way, way too much. What do you think The Vastness would think about that? How can The Vastness be everything, when it doesn't have cognac-and-bacon? When it doesn't even know what cognac-and-bacon IS?"

"Shut up, drone," Jara said—falling back into her "Countess" voice as a way out of this conversation.

"Keep an eye on her, okay?" Sharon whispered to Kango. "I really think there's a part of her that wants to be her own person, but she just doesn't know how."

He shrugged and nodded at the same time.

And then they were surrounded by a few dozen other servants and

Fixers, who had heard that the Countess Victoria was going to the evening's most exclusive party and were here to help her become as resplendent as possible in hopes of winning some favor. So there was no further chance to talk about their actual plans for stealing the specs on the secret weapon—but lots and lots of chances to obsess over whether the Countess should wear the weeping dolphin eyes, or the blood-pouches.

At last, the Countess was ready to go to the party, and Sharon was preparing to peel off and sneak back to the *Spicy Meatball*. "Wish me luck," she whispered to Kango.

"You've got this," he whispered back. "We're going to open our restaurant. We'll serve all the classic food items: handburgers, Ruffalo wings, damplings, carry . . . It'll be great."

"Let's not get ahead of ourselves here," said Sharon, kissing Kango on the cheek.

7.

The central computer core of the Pleasure Nexus looked like a big mossy rock floating over the city, between two giant esorotic spires of pure silver. But as the *Spicy Meatball* flew closer, the computer core looked less like a rock and more like some kind of ancient sauroid, with thick plates of spiky armor guarding its fleshy access points. They flew into its shadow.

Sharon was concentrating on navigating past the tiny guardbots flying around the computer core, while finding the exact vector that would allow the *Spicy Meatball* to come right up to the exposed patch of underbelly. Then Sharon and Noreen just had to hover there, directly underneath the computer core, where anybody could spot the ship's impact-scarred hull, waiting for Kango's diversion to happen. And obsessing about the thousand things that could go wrong.

"I've been telling the other ships about us," said Noreen. "Our smuggling runs to the Scabby Castles, that time we conned those literal-minded cyborgs into thinking Kango was some kind of Cyber-King . . . they're pretty jealous of us. The other ships might even give us a slight 'head start' if it comes down to a pursuit. Although it wouldn't make any difference, of course."

"I appreciate the gesture," said Sharon. She stared at the crappy little vidscreen, showing the undulating flesh of the computer core—just sitting there, a few inches away from their hull. She was regretting a lot of her recent life choices. She'd sworn for years that nobody was ever going to make her into an object again, but she'd willingly put herself back into that position—and the fact that she was "just pretending" didn't make as much difference as she wanted. She felt bad that Kango, who'd had a rougher time than she had, was being forced to confront this awfulness again. And she was realizing that she'd projected a lot onto that Jara girl, as if a week or two of pretending to be a Countess would break a lifetime of conditioning and psychic linkage to a giant space glob. This was probably going to be a career-ending mistake.

"We got it," Noreen said, just as Sharon was getting sucked into gloom. Their vidscreen was streaming some news reports about the Estimable Lord Vaughn Ticklesnout unexpectedly catching on fire and being chased by his own party monster. Some three hundred terrorist organizations had already claimed responsibility for this incident, most of them with completely silly names like the Persimmon Permission Proclamation, but the party had dissolved into total chaos. They picked up footage of the crowd scattering as a man on fire ran around and around, pursued by a bright blue naked woman who could have been Sharon's twin sister.

"Great," Sharon said. "I'm setting up the uplink. Let's hope the distraction was distracting enough." She started threading through layers of security protection, some of them newly added since she and Kango had escaped from Liberty House, and spoofing all of the certs that the computer demanded. There were riddles and silly questions along with strings of base-99 code that needed to be unraveled, but Sharon and Noreen worked together, and soon they had total leet-superuser access.

Sharon searched for any data on the new super-weapon, and found it helpfully labeled, "Brand New Excellent Super-Weapon." A few more twists of the computer matrix, and she was instructing the computer to transfer all the data on the weapon.

"Uh," said Noreen. "I think you might have made a mistake."

"What?" said Sharon. "I asked it to send over everything it had on the super-weapon."

"Check the cargo hold," said Noreen. "Right next to the boxes of Rainbow Cows. The main computer just auto-docked with us a second ago."

Sharon took a split-second to process what Noreen had said, then took off running down to the cargo hold, where a squat red ovoid device, about the size of a human baby, had been deposited. The object made a faint grumbling noise, like a drunken old man who was annoyed at being woken up. "Oh shit," Sharon said.

"Please keep it down," said the super-weapon. "Some of us are trying to rest."

"Sorry," Sharon said. "I just didn't expect you to show up in person."

"I go where they send me," groaned the super-weapon. "All I want to do is get some rest until my big day. Which could be any day, since they never give me a timetable. That's the problem with being the ultimate deterrent: People *talk* about using me a lot, but they never actually follow through."

"Just how ultimate a deterrent are you?"

"Well, actually, I'm *very* ultimate. Ultimately ultimate, in fact." The super-weapon seemed to perk up a little bit as it discussed its effectiveness. "If anybody tries to interfere with Liberty House's sacred and innate right to seek amusement in any form they deem amusing, then I send a gravity pulse to the supermassive black hole at the center of the galaxy, causing it to, er, expand. Rather a lot. To the size of a galaxy, in fact."

"That's, er, pretty fucking ultimate." Sharon felt as though she, personally, had swallowed a supermassive black hole. This was getting worse and worse. Added to her own low-single-digit estimation of her chances of survival, there was the realization that her former owners were much, much worse people than she'd ever fathomed. She was so full of terror and hatred, she saw two different shades of red at once.

"Hate to ruin your moment," said Noreen, "but we've got another problem."

"Don't mind me," said the super-weapon. "I'll just go back to sleep. My name is Horace, by the by."

Sharon rushed back to the flight deck, where the vidscreen showed Kango and Jara, in the custody of several uniformed Fixers, as well as one of the senior Courtiers, a man named Hazelbeem who'd been famous back in Sharon's day.

"We have captured your accomplices." Hazelbeem's lime-green coiffure wobbled as he talked. "And we are coming for you next! Prepare for a wonderfully agonizing death—accompanied by some quite delicious crunketizers, because this party left us with rather a lot of leftovers."

"We have your bomb," said Sharon into the vidscreen. "Your ultimate weapon. We'll set it off unless you release our friends."

"No you won't," said Hazelbeem, who had a purple mustache that kept twirling and untwirling and twisting itself into complex shapes, "because you're not completely stark raving mad."

"Okay. It's true, we won't. But what does that say about you, creating something like that?"

Hazelbeem's mustache shrugged elaborately, but the man himself had no facial expression.

"Leave us," Kango shouted. "Get out of there! Take their stupid bomb with you. We're not worth you sacrificing your lives to these assholes. Just go!"

"You know I can't do that," said Sharon.

"There are fifty-seven attack ships, approaching us from pretty much every possible direction," said Noreen.

"Can we at least disable their stupid bomb permanently before they capture us?" said Sharon. "I'm guessing not. We'd need weeks to figure out how it works."

"Hey," Jara said, pushing herself forward. "I wanted to say, I guess you were kind of right about why I stowed away. I always wanted to be special, not just another one of a billion servants of The Vastness. When

I saw your ship about to disembark, I thought maybe I could help spread the word about The Vastness to the whole galaxy, and then I'd be the best acolyte ever. But it turned out the only way I could be special was as a fake Countess."

"You were a great fake Countess though," Kango said, squirming next to her.

"Thanks. And thanks for taking me to that party," Jara told her. "I got to see all sorts of things that I'd never even imagined. It started me thinking, maybe I really could find a way to reinvent myself as an individual, the way you two did. In fact, I'm starting to realize that . . . You are everything!"

"What the hell? You just said—"

"I can't control it," said Jara. "It's like an instinctive response whenever—You are everything!"

And then they lost the signal, because a voice broke in on every single open frequency. The voice was shouting one thing over and over: "I am everything! I am everything! I am everything!"

"Uh," said Sharon.

"So, you probably already guessed this," said Noreen. "But sensors are showing that a Temporary Embarrassment, the size of several planets, has just appeared on the edge of the central Pleasure Nexus of Liberty House. The weather-control systems on Salubrious IV are all working overtime."

"You're right, I did actually guess that," said Sharon.

"The good news is, all the ships that were about to attack us have been diverted onto a new heading," said Noreen.

"We gotta go rescue Kango," said Sharon. "And Jara, I guess."

"I have some excellent news," came a plummy male voice from the cargo hold. Horace, the super-weapon. "My activation sequence has been initiated. It's the moment I've been waiting for my whole life!"

· ◦ ● ◦ ·

8.

Hazelbeem, whose full name was Hazelbeem Sternforke Paddleborrow the XXVIIth, was standing in front of the Grand Wilding Suites and Superior Fun Center, where the party had been held. He had a half-dozen Fixers with him, and they were holding Kango and Jara in chains, as the *Spicy Meatball* landed on the front lawn (which screamed and tried to bite the Meatball's landing struts).

"So! Not only did you steal our top-secret ultimate weapon," said Hazelbeem, his mustache knotted in anger, "but you brought the wrath of the most revolting giant monster in the galaxy down on us. Were I an existentialist masochist, this would be my happiest day ever. Too bad I am an objectivist sadist, instead."

"Just let my friends go," said Sharon. "We can help. We know what The Vastness wants."

"You are everything!" shouted Jara.

"We are past the point of negotiation," said Hazelbeem. "We have already activated the weapon on board your ship, as soon as we detected a major threat to our way of life. If we cannot continue the absolute pursuit of amusement, with zero limitations, then there's no reason for this galaxy to continue existing. I must say, when we created you and your friend here—" (he gestured at Kango) "—we did not imagine it could ever lead to so many un-amusing incidents."

"This just proves that amusement is subjective," said Kango, struggling against his chains. "I've been highly amused by many of today's events."

"You are everything!"

"You were made as a brothel extra," said Hazelbeem to Kango. "You weren't even supposed to have a mind of your own. You're a single-celled organism, are you not? Made to appear like a beautiful young man, to stand in the background of the crowd scenes at a brothel. Something must have gone very wrong—perhaps you received too high a dose of neuro-peptides in the vat."

"I may only have one cell," said Kango, "but *you've* just been nucleused."

"I don't even know what that means." Hazelbeem's mustache crinkled.

"It was supposed to be a play on the fact that I have a single nucleus, and I'm . . . Oh, just forget I said anything."

"Already forgotten," said Hazelbeem.

"You are everything!"

"Can you stop shouting that?" Hazelbeem said to Jara. "It's giving me a headache."

"We've been trying, believe me," said Sharon.

"It's a reflex," Jara told Hazelbeem. "I belong to The Vastness, no matter what I do. I was foolish to think anything mattered except for The Vastness. I'm probably going to be punished for doubting even a little, in my heart."

"You are a very tiresome little person," Hazelbeem told her.

The sky was churning with angry black swirlies, which reminded Sharon of one of the first parties at which she'd been the designated monster, when the Marquis of Bloopabloopasneak had set off some kind of weather bomb, left over from one of the old galactic wars. Five hundred-odd people had died in the hurricanes and blizzards, before the Pleasure Nexus' weather-control systems had regained control, and the Marquis of Bloopabloopasneak had played really loud glam-clash music to drown out the screams and the roaring of the elements.

Hazelbeem was looking at the big fob hanging from his inner jacket (which was made of tiny living people, all of them squirming in a vain attempt to escape from the stitching that stuck them together). "That hypertrophic organism and its fleet of ships have torn through our planetary defenses, in the worst disaster since that all-you-can-eat buffet escaped from its trays and grew until it devoured an entire planet. I blame! I really do. I blame."

"Just let my friends go, and we'll deal with The Vastness for you." Sharon shouted to make herself heard over the howling in the sky. "There's no need for any of this."

"This is what happens when playthings try to think for themselves," Hazelbeem snorted. "First they start trying to act like *people*, and before you know it, they—"

Sharon ate Hazelbeem. This happened too quickly for anybody to react. One second, Hazelbeem was working himself up into a tirade about toys that get ideas above their station, and the next, Sharon's mouth expanded to several times its normal size, and just gobbled him up. She spat out his boots a second later.

"Ugh," Sharon said. "I promised myself I would never do that again, but there's provocation, and then there's *provocation*. I've had a lot of pent-up rage these past few days." She looked at the gaggle of Fixers who were holding her friends prisoner and yelled, "Let my friends go, or you're next!"

"Whatever you say!" the head Fixer stammered as she unlocked Kango and Jara. "We all just want to be with our families—or possibly go to an end-of-the-galaxy blood orgy. One of those. Bye!" The Fixers all took off running in different directions, leaving Sharon, Kango, Jara, and Hazelbeem's boots.

Sharon looked down at the boots. "He just pushed me too far."

"It's fine," Kango said in her ear as he touched her arm. "Just because you eat the occasional horrible person, doesn't prove you're actually the monster they tried to make you into. I promise."

"You are everything!" Jara said, then added: "That guy was asking for it. As an official Countess, I pardon you."

"Thanks," Sharon said, still raising her voice over the awful din. "Now we just gotta save the galaxy. Any ideas?"

They all looked at each other, then at the pair of boots on the ground, as if the boots might suddenly offer a helpful suggestion.

9.

The Vastness had somehow taken over the festival speakers all around the Superior Fun Center, and was shouting about the fact that someone had dared to steal from its all-encompassing magnificence. Nobody escaped The Vastness! To underscore this, a flotilla of The Vastness'

Joybreaker-class ships were swooping down over the surface of Salubrious IV and firing Obliteron missiles at every freestanding structure. The ground shook, the sky churned, and the Superior Fun Center and several other buildings collapsed as Kango, Sharon, and Jara ran back to the *Spicy Meatball*—stumbling and falling on their faces, as The Vastness shrieked at top volume.

"You are everything," said Jara, face in the dirt.

Kango flung himself into his pilot seat aboard the *Spicy Meatball* and tried to lift off, but the entire airspace consisted of pretty much nothing but explosions, dotted with the occasional deadly warship. Barely a few hundred yards off the ground, the *Spicy Meatball* was forced to go into a dive to avoid a huge chunk of burning debris. Kango and Noreen screamed in unison.

"You know," said Horace, "I've heard it said that death is what makes life meaningful. In that case, I am about to create more meaning than all of the artists in history, combined."

Kango was a blur as he tried to steer through the flaming obstacle course.

At last, they reached the upper atmosphere . . . just as some terrible *presence* appeared directly beneath them. It was just a dark shape, that blotted out their view of Salubrious IV. Sharon struggled to make out any details for a moment, and then she saw some undulating barbed tentacles, and she *knew.*

"No," said Sharon. "They released the planet-eater."

"Is that Liberty House's last line of defense?" asked Jara, fascinated by the shape on their external viewer.

"No," Kango said. "They made it for a party, years ago. It basically just eats planets, much as its name implies. We're between it and The Vastness. Hold tight!"

"To what?" Sharon demanded.

The planet-eater thrashed around as it forced its way out of the atmosphere of Salubrious IV and tried to swim toward The Vastness. The planet-eater's uncountable limbs lashed out, trying to pull everything in their path into the one enormous maw at its center. One of those huge, barbed tentacles swiped within a few feet of the *Spicy Meatball* . . . which dodged, and nearly ran into another flotilla of Joybreaker-class attack ships.

"Hall and Oates!" Sharon cursed.

"You are everything!" Jara cried out.

"Keep it down, you two," Kango growled. "It's hard enough trying to make evasive maneuvers between pretty much everything deadly, without also having to listen to a lot of religious mumbo jumbo."

"Oh, as if *you* have it all figured out," Sharon said. "Your only religion is exhibitionism. I swear, the next time we have a plan that relies on a diversion—a contained, sensible diversion—that can be *my* job."

"Sure!" Kango spun the ship on its axis to scoot past a planet-eater tentacle, then veered sharply to the left to avoid a spread of Obliteron missiles. "Because you're such a genius at strategy, and that's how we ended up with a stupid ultimate weapon on board!"

"I'll have you know, I am quite intelligent," Horace protested. "And there are mere minutes before my devastation wave is launched from the galactic core. Once it begins, it will sweep the entire galaxy in no time at all!"

"Hey, I did my best," Sharon said to Kango. "It's not as if it was my idea to—" She stopped, because Jara was staring at her. "What?"

"You're doing it again," Jara said. "You're acting as though each of you is The Vastness to the other. I wish I knew how you *do* that. I'm going to die soon, too, and even with The Vastness close at hand, I'll die alone and for no real reason. You are everything!"

"Listen, Jara," Sharon said, ignoring her nausea as Kango did a series of barrel rolls to avoid explosions that came close enough to rattle her teeth. "Listen. The Vastness is only everything because it's incredibly limited. It can't even see all the things it's not. It's like a giant stupid ignorant blob of . . . wait. Wait a minute!"

"What?" Kango said. "Did you think of something super super clever?"

"Maybe," Sharon said, praying to Hall and Oates that she was right. She ran over and pulled the stolen synchrotrix out of the strongbox, then started wiring it into Horace's core as fast as she could. "Remember what you told me was special about this device?"

"The fact that it's worth a lot of chits?" Kango pulled the *Spicy Meatball*'s nose up so fast, Sharon nearly did a backflip, while keeping one hand on Horace. "It's got a nice color scheme? It has the ability to neutralize . . . oh. Oh!"

"You are everything!" Jara said.

The planet-eater had finally gotten past all of the attack ships that had tried vainly to slow it down. Now it had reached The Vastness, opening the vast gnashing maw at the heart of its starfish-like body to try and devour the mega-planetoid. The planet-killer embraced The Vastness with its many limbs.

Sharon gripped Jara's shoulders so hard, her knuckles were white. "Tell The Vastness, we've got the ultimate weapon, right here on our ship. We can help The Vastness to become completely unstoppable. And The Vastness really will be everything, in an even better way than before."

Jara looked like she was about to cry. "You want me to lie to The Vastness."

"No," Sharon said. "Yes. Sort of. Not really. It's the only way."

"I'm just moments away from a glorious consummation," Horace said. "It's at times like this that I feel like composing a sonnet."

"Jara," Sharon hissed, "now!"

"I'm trying," Jara said, shutting her eyes and concentrating. "The Vastness doesn't really listen. It just talks. I'm sending the message as hard as I can."

"Now! Please!"

The Vastness reached out with a beam of energy, trying to seize the *Spicy Meatball*. Sharon rushed to the rear airlock with Horace, cobbled together with the synchrotrix. She tossed them out, and The Vastness' energy field captured them, pulling them through one of The Vastness' slavering eyemouths inside its guts.

They were inside The Vastness' own atmosphere, close enough to hear its eyemouths shouting through their countless razor-sharp teeth. "I am everything! Now I have this ultimate weapon, my power will be absolute. I will be all things, and every living being will shout my praises. I am—"

Sharon watched through the airlock as The Vastness vanished from space.

In the space where The Vastness had been, a bright purple-and-green fissure had opened up. The crack in spacetime was huge enough to let Sharon see through it, as The Vastness was drawn toward the supermassive black hole at the core of the galaxy.

"You are everything," Jara said, sorrowfully, standing next to Sharon.

And then The Vastness was no longer visible—but in its place, there was a huge distortion, enveloping the black hole at the core of the galaxy.

"The biggest Embarrassment the galaxy has ever seen," Kango breathed from the flight deck.

And then the purple-and-green fissure closed, leaving a badly injured planet-eater, several thousand confused Joybreaker-class starships, and the *Spicy Meatball*.

"We did it," Kango said, seeming semi-permeable with astonishment.

"The Vastness followed Horace's program, and ended up at the galactic core," Sharon said. "And then it Embarrassed itself."

"I just killed my god." Jara looked as though she was too shocked even for tears.

"Look at it this way," Sharon said. "You told the truth. Mostly. The Vastness is everywhere and everything now, in a way. It always will be with you, and it can never be defeated. You can worship The Vastness forever."

"I don't know." Jara tried saying, "You are everything," but it wasn't the same when it came in response to nothing.

"Well, meanwhile," Kango said. "We lost the synchrotrix that we were counting on to pay our bills. We lost the super-weapon, too. So we're even more broke than we were before. Unless we can convince Mandre Lewis that we just saved the galaxy."

"We'll figure something out," Sharon said, then turned back toward Jara. "But what are you going to do? There's a huge fleet of ships out there, full of your fellow acolytes, and they desperately need some direction.

Plus this star system is rich in resources and technology, and it just had all its planetary defenses wrecked. You could go back to Salubrious, with all your people, and become a Countess for real."

"Maybe," Jara said. "Or maybe I could go with you guys? I feel like I have a lot to learn from you two. I'm not sure I'm ready to explain to the other acolytes what happened."

"Sure. How do you feel about helping to open a restaurant? Do you know how to make a tableclot?" Kango threw the *Spicy Meatball* headlong into an escape course, before anybody could try to blame them for all the property damage. Behind them, the ruins of Salubrious IV sparkled with the dying light of countless fires as the tributary ships of The Vastness began, hesitantly and confusedly, to make planetfall.

ALIETTE DE BODARD

IMMERSION

To Rochita Loenen-Ruiz, for the conversations that inspired this

Aliette de Bodard writes speculative fiction: she has won three Nebula Awards, an Ignyte Award, a Locus Award and five British Science Fiction Association Awards. She is the author of science fiction novels *A Fire Born of Exile* and *The Red Scholar's Wake*, and *Of Charms, Ghosts and Grievances*, a fantasy of manners and murders set in an alternate 19th Century Vietnamese court. She lives in Paris. [www.aliettedebodard.com]

In the morning, you're no longer quite sure who you are.
You stand in front of the mirror—it shifts and trembles, reflecting only what you want to see—eyes that feel too wide, skin that feels too pale, an odd, distant smell wafting from the compartment's ambient system that is neither incense nor garlic, but something else, something elusive that you once knew.

You're dressed, already—not on your skin, but outside, where it matters, your avatar sporting blue and black and gold, the stylish clothes of a well-travelled, well-connected woman. For a moment, as you turn away from the mirror, the glass shimmers out of focus, and another woman in a dull silk gown stares back at you: smaller, squatter and in every way diminished—a stranger, a distant memory that has ceased to have any meaning.

Quy was on the docks, watching the spaceships arrive. She could, of course, have been anywhere on Longevity Station, and requested the feed from the network to be patched to her router—and watched, superimposed on her field of vision, the slow dance of ships slipping into their pod cradles like births watched in reverse. But there was something about standing on the spaceport's concourse—a feeling of closeness that she just couldn't replicate by standing in Golden Carp Gardens or Azure Dragon Temple. Because here—here, separated by only a few measures of sheet metal from the cradle pods, she could feel herself teetering on the edge of the vacuum, submerged in cold and breathing in neither air nor oxygen. She could almost imagine herself rootless, finally returned to the source of everything.

Most ships those days were Galactic—you'd have thought Longevity's ex-masters would have been unhappy about the station's independence, but now that the war was over Longevity was a tidy source of profit. The ships came and disgorged a steady stream of tourists—their eyes too round and straight, their jaws too square; their faces an unhealthy shade of pink, like undercooked meat left too long in the sun. They walked with the easy confidence of people with immersers: pausing to admire the suggested highlights for a second or so before moving on to the transport station, where they haggled in schoolbook Rong for a ride to their recommended hotels—a sickeningly familiar ballet Quy had been seeing most of her life, a unison of foreigners descending on the station like a plague of centipedes or leeches.

Still, Quy watched them. They reminded her of her own time on Prime, her heady schooldays filled with raucous bars and wild weekends, and late minute revisions for exams, a carefree time she'd never have again in her life. She both longed for those days back, and hated herself for her weakness. Her education on Prime, which should have been her path into the higher strata of the station's society, had brought her nothing but a sense of disconnection from her family; a growing solitude, and a dissatisfaction, an aimlessness she couldn't put in words.

She might not have moved all day—had a sign not blinked, superimposed by her router on the edge of her field of vision. A message from Second Uncle.

"Child." His face was pale and worn, his eyes underlined by dark circles, as if he hadn't slept. He probably hadn't—the last Quy had seen of him, he had been closeted with Quy's sister Tam, trying to organise a delivery for a wedding—five hundred winter melons, and six barrels of Prosper Station's best fish sauce. "Come back to the restaurant."

"I'm on my day of rest," Quy said; it came out as more peevish and childish than she'd intended.

Second Uncle's face twisted, in what might have been a smile, though he had very little sense of humour. The scar he'd got in the Independence War shone white against the grainy background—twisting back and forth, as if it still pained him. "I know, but I need you. We have an important customer."

"Galactic," Quy said. That was the only reason he'd be calling her, and not one of her brothers or cousins. Because the family somehow thought that her studies on Prime gave her insight into the Galactics' way of thought—something useful, if not the success they'd hoped for.

"Yes. An important man, head of a local trading company." Second Uncle did not move on her field of vision. Quy could *see* the ships moving through his face, slowly aligning themselves in front of their pods, the hole in front of them opening like an orchid flower. And she knew everything there was to know about Grandmother's restaurant; she was Tam's sister, after all; and she'd seen the accounts, the slow decline of their clientele as their more genteel clients moved to better areas of the station; the influx of tourists on a budget, with little time for expensive dishes prepared with the best ingredients.

"Fine," she said. "I'll come."

At breakfast, you stare at the food spread out on the table: bread and jam and some coloured liquid—you come up blank for a moment, before your immerser kicks in, reminding you that it's coffee, served strong and black, just as you always take it.

Yes. Coffee.

You raise the cup to your lips—your immerser gently prompts you, reminding you of where to grasp, how to lift, how to be in every possible way graceful and elegant, always an effortless model.

"It's a bit strong," your husband says, apologetically. He watches you from the other end of the table, an expression you can't interpret on his face—and isn't this odd, because shouldn't you know all there is to know about expressions—shouldn't the immerser have everything about Galactic culture recorded into its database, shouldn't it prompt you? But it's strangely silent, and this scares you, more than anything. Immersers never fail.

"Shall we go?" your husband says—and, for a moment, you come up blank on his name, before you remember—Galen, it's Galen, named after some physician on Old Earth. He's tall, with dark hair and pale skin—his immerser avatar isn't much different from his real self; Galactic avatars seldom are. It's people like you who have to work the hardest to adjust, because so much about you draws attention to itself—the stretched eyes that crinkle in the shape of moths, the darker skin, the smaller, squatter shape more reminiscent of jackfruits than swaying fronds. But no matter: you can be made perfect; you can put on the immerser and become someone else, someone pale-skinned and tall and beautiful.

Though, really, it's been such a long time since you took off the immerser, isn't it? It's just a thought—a suspended moment that is soon erased by the immerser's flow of information, the little arrows drawing your attention to the bread and the kitchen, and the polished metal of the table—giving you context about everything, opening up the universe like a lotus flower.

"Yes," you say. "Let's go." Your tongue trips over the word—there's a structure you should have used, a pronoun you should have said instead of the lapidary Galactic sentence. But nothing will come, and you feel like a field of sugar canes after the harvest—burnt out, all cutting edges with no sweetness left inside.

·•◉•·

Of course, Second Uncle insisted on Quy getting her immerser for the interview—just in case, he said, soothingly and diplomatically as always. Trouble was, it wasn't where Quy had last left it. After putting out a message to the rest of the family, the best information Quy got was from Cousin Khanh, who thought he'd seen Tam sweep through the living quarters, gathering every piece of Galactic tech she could get her hands on. Third Aunt, who caught Khanh's message on the family's communication channel, tutted disapprovingly. "Tam. Always with her mind lost in the mountains, that girl. Dreams have never husked rice."

Quy said nothing. Her own dreams had shrivelled and died after she came back from Prime and failed Longevity's Mandarin exams; but it was good to have Tam around—to have someone who saw beyond the restaurant, beyond the narrow circle of family interests. Besides, if she didn't stick with her sister, who would?

Tam wasn't in the communal areas on the upper floors; Quy threw a glance towards the lift to Grandmother's closeted rooms, but she was doubtful Tam would have gathered Galactic tech just so she could pay her respects to Grandmother. Instead, she went straight to the lower floor, the one she and Tam shared with the children of their generation.

It was right next to the kitchen, and the smells of garlic and fish sauce seemed to be everywhere—of course, the youngest generation always got the lower floor, the one with all the smells and the noises of a legion of waitresses bringing food over to the dining room.

Tam was there, sitting in the little compartment that served as the floor's communal area. She'd spread out the tech on the floor—two immersers (Tam and Quy were possibly the only family members who cared so little about immersers they left them lying around), a remote entertainment set that was busy broadcasting some stories of children running on terraformed planets, and something Quy couldn't quite identify, because Tam had taken it apart into small components: it lay on the table like a gutted fish, all metals and optical parts.

But, at some point, Tam had obviously got bored with the entire process, because she was currently finishing her breakfast, slurping noodles from her soup bowl. She must have got it from the kitchen's leftovers, because Quy knew the smell, could taste the spiciness of the broth on her tongue—Mother's cooking, enough to make her stomach growl although she'd had rolled rice cakes for breakfast.

"You're at it again," Quy said with a sigh. "Could you not take my immerser for your experiments, please?"

Tam didn't even look surprised. "You don't seem very keen on using it, big sis."

"That I don't use it doesn't mean it's yours," Quy said, though that wasn't a real reason. She didn't mind Tam borrowing her stuff, and actually would have been glad to never put on an immerser again— she hated the feeling they gave her, the vague sensation of the system rooting around in her brain to find the best body cues to give her. But there were times when she was expected to wear an immerser: whenever dealing with customers, whether she was waiting at tables or in preparation meetings for large occasions.

Tam, of course, didn't wait at tables—she'd made herself so good at logistics and anything to do with the station's system that she spent most of her time in front of a screen, or connected to the station's network.

"Lil' sis?" Quy said.

Tam set her chopsticks by the side of the bowl, and made an expansive gesture with her hands. "Fine. Have it back. I can always use mine."

Quy stared at the things spread on the table, and asked the inevitable question. "How's progress?"

Tam's work was network connections and network maintenance within the restaurant; her hobby was tech. Galactic tech. She took things apart to see what made them tick and rebuilt them. Her foray into entertainment units had helped the restaurant set up ambient sounds— old-fashioned Rong music for Galactic customers, recitation of the newest poems for locals.

But immersers had her stumped: the things had nasty safeguards to them. You could open them in half, to replace the battery, but you went no further. Tam's previous attempt had almost lost her the use of her hands.

By Tam's face, she didn't feel ready to try again. "It's got to be the same logic."

"As what?" Quy couldn't help asking. She picked up her own immerser from the table, briefly checking that it did indeed bear her serial number.

Tam gestured to the splayed components on the table. "Artificial Literature Writer. Little gadget that composes light entertainment novels."

"That's not the same—" Quy checked herself, and waited for Tam to explain.

"Takes existing cultural norms, and puts them into a cohesive, satisfying narrative. Like people forging their own path and fighting aliens for possession of a planet, that sort of stuff that barely speaks to us on Longevity. I mean, we've never even seen a planet." Tam exhaled, sharply—her eyes half on the dismembered Artificial Literature Writer, half on some overlay of her vision. "Just like immersers take a given culture and parcel it out to you in a form you can relate to—language, gestures, customs, the whole package. They've got to have the same architecture."

"I'm still not sure what you want to do with it." Quy put on her immerser, adjusting the thin metal mesh around her head until it fitted. She winced as the interface synched with her brain. She moved her hands, adjusting some settings lower than the factory ones—darn thing always reset itself to factory, which she suspected was no accident. A shimmering lattice surrounded her: her avatar, slowly taking shape around her. She could still see the room—the lattice was only faintly opaque—but ancestors, how she hated the feeling of not quite being there. "How do I look?"

"Horrible. Your avatar looks like it's died or something."

"Ha ha ha," Quy said. Her avatar was paler than her, and taller: it made her look beautiful, most customers agreed. In those moments, Quy was glad she had an avatar, so they wouldn't see the anger on her face. "You haven't answered my question."

Tam's eyes glinted. "Just think of the things we couldn't do. This is the best piece of tech Galactics have ever brought us."

Which wasn't much, but Quy didn't need to say it aloud. Tam knew exactly how Quy felt about Galactics and their hollow promises.

"It's their weapon, too." Tam pushed at the entertainment unit. "Just like their books and their holos and their live games. It's fine for them— they put the immersers on tourist settings, they get just what they need to navigate a foreign environment from whatever idiot's written the Rong script for that thing. But we—we worship them. We wear the immersers on Galactic all the time. We make ourselves like them, because they push, and because we're naive enough to give in."

"And you think you can make this better?" Quy couldn't help it. It wasn't that she needed to be convinced: on Prime, she'd never seen immersers. They were tourist stuff, and even while travelling from one city to another, the citizens just assumed they'd know enough to get by. But the stations, their ex-colonies, were flooded with immersers.

Tam's eyes glinted, as savage as those of the rebels in the history holos. "If I can take them apart, I can rebuild them and disconnect the logical circuits. I can give us the language and the tools to deal with them without being swallowed by them."

Mind lost in the mountains, Third Aunt said. No one had ever accused Tam of thinking small. Or of not achieving what she set her mind on, come to think of it. And every revolution had to start somewhere— hadn't Longevity's War of Independence started over a single poem, and the unfair imprisonment of the poet who'd written it?

Quy nodded. She believed Tam, though she didn't know how far. "Fair point. Have to go now, or Second Uncle will skin me. See you later, lil' sis."

As you walk under the wide arch of the restaurant with your husband, you glance upwards, at the calligraphy that forms its sign. The immerser translates it for you into "Sister Hai's Kitchen", and starts giving you a detailed background of the place: the menu and the most recommended dishes—as you walk past the various tables, it highlights items it thinks you would like, from rolled-up rice dumplings to fried shrimps. It warns you about the more exotic dishes, like the pickled pig's ears, the fermented meat (you have to be careful about that one, because its name changes depending on which station dialect you order in), or the reeking durian fruit that the natives so love.

It feels . . . not quite right, you think, as you struggle to follow Galen, who is already far away, striding ahead with the same confidence he always exudes in life. People part before him; a waitress with a young, pretty avatar bows before him, though Galen himself takes no notice. You know that such obsequiousness unnerves him; he always rants about the outdated customs aboard Longevity, the inequalities and the lack of democratic government—he thinks it's only a matter of time before they change, adapt themselves to fit into Galactic society. You—you have a faint memory of arguing with him, a long time ago, but now you can't find the words, anymore, or even the reason why—it makes sense, it all makes sense. The Galactics rose against the tyranny of Old Earth and overthrew their shackles, and won the right to determine their own destiny; and every other station and planet will do the same, eventually, rise against the dictatorships that hold them away from progress. It's right; it's always been right.

Unbidden, you stop at a table, and watch two young women pick at a dish of chicken with chopsticks—the smell of fish sauce and lemongrass rises in the air, as pungent and as unbearable as rotten meat—no, no, that's not it, you have an image of a dark-skinned woman, bringing a dish of steamed rice to the table, her hands filled with that same smell, and your mouth watering in anticipation . . .

The young women are looking at you: they both wear standard-issue avatars, the bottom-of-the-line kind—their clothes are a garish mix of red and yellow, with the odd, uneasy cut of cheap designers; and their faces waver, letting you glimpse a hint of darker skin beneath the red flush of their cheeks. Cheap and tawdry, and altogether inappropriate; and you're glad you're not one of them.

"Can I help you, older sister?" one of them asks.

Older sister. A pronoun you were looking for, earlier; one of the things that seem to have vanished from your mind. You struggle for words; but all the immerser seems to suggest to you is a neutral and impersonal pronoun, one that you instinctively know is wrong—it's one only foreigners and outsiders would use in those circumstances. "Older sister," you repeat, finally, because you can't think of anything else.

"Agnes!"

Galen's voice, calling from far away—for a brief moment the immerser seems to fail you again, because you *know* that you have many names, that Agnes is the one they gave you in Galactic school, the one neither Galen nor his friends can mangle when they pronounce it. You remember the Rong names your mother gave you on Longevity, the childhood endearments and your adult-style name.

Be-Nho, Be-Yeu. Thu—Autumn, like a memory of red maple leaves on a planet you never knew.

You pull away from the table, disguising the tremor in your hands.

Second Uncle was already waiting when Quy arrived; and so were the customers.

"You're late," Second Uncle sent on the private channel, though he made the comment half-heartedly, as if he'd expected it all along. As if he'd never really believed he could rely on her—that stung.

"Let me introduce my niece Quy to you," Second Uncle said, in Galactic, to the man beside him.

"Quy," the man said, his immerser perfectly taking up the nuances of her name in Rong. He was everything she'd expected; tall, with only a thin layer of avatar, a little something that narrowed his chin and eyes, and made his chest slightly larger. Cosmetic enhancements: he was good-looking for a Galactic, all things considered. He went on, in Galactic, "My name is Galen Santos. Pleased to meet you. This is my wife, Agnes."

Agnes. Quy turned, and looked at the woman for the first time—and flinched. There was no one here: just a thick layer of avatar, so dense and so complex that she couldn't even guess at the body hidden within.

"Pleased to meet you." On a hunch, Quy bowed, from younger to elder, with both hands brought together—Rong-style, not Galactic—and saw a shudder run through Agnes' body, barely perceptible; but Quy was observant, she'd always been. Her immerser was screaming at her, telling her to hold out both hands, palms up, in the Galactic fashion. She tuned it out: she was still at the stage where she could tell the difference between her thoughts and the immerser's thoughts.

Second Uncle was talking again—his own avatar was light, a paler version of him. "I understand you're looking for a venue for a banquet."

"We are, yes." Galen pulled a chair to him, sank into it. They all followed suit, though not with the same fluid, arrogant ease. When Agnes sat, Quy saw her flinch, as though she'd just remembered something unpleasant. "We'll be celebrating our fifth marriage anniversary, and we both felt we wanted to mark the occasion with something suitable."

Second Uncle nodded. "I see," he said, scratching his chin. "My congratulations to you."

Galen nodded. "We thought—" he paused, threw a glance at his wife that Quy couldn't quite interpret—her immerser came up blank, but there was something oddly familiar about it, something she ought to have been able to name. "Something Rong," he said at last. "A large banquet for a hundred people, with the traditional dishes."

Quy could almost feel Second Uncle's satisfaction. A banquet of that size would be awful logistics, but it would keep the restaurant afloat for a year or more, if they could get the price right. But something was wrong—something—

"What did you have in mind?" Quy asked, not to Galen, but to his wife. The wife—Agnes, which probably wasn't the name she'd been born with—who wore a thick avatar, and didn't seem to be answering or ever speaking up. An awful picture was coming together in Quy's mind.

Agnes didn't answer. Predictable.

Second Uncle took over, smoothing over the moment of awkwardness with expansive hand gestures. "The whole hog, yes?" Second Uncle said. He rubbed his hands, an odd gesture that Quy had never seen from him—a Galactic expression of satisfaction. "Bitter melon soup, Dragon-Phoenix plates, Roast Pig, Jade Under the Mountain . . ." He was citing all the traditional dishes for a wedding banquet—unsure of how far the foreigner wanted to take it. He left out the odder stuff, like Shark Fin or Sweet Red Bean Soup.

"Yes, that's what we would like. Wouldn't we, darling?" Galen's wife neither moved nor spoke. Galen's head turned towards her, and Quy caught his expression at last. She'd thought it would be contempt, or hatred; but no; it was anguish. He genuinely loved her, and he couldn't understand what was going on.

Galactics. Couldn't he recognise an immerser junkie when he saw one? But then Galactics, as Tam said, seldom had the problem—they didn't put on the immersers for more than a few days on low settings, if they ever went that far. Most were flat-out convinced Galactic would get them anywhere.

Second Uncle and Galen were haggling, arguing prices and features; Second Uncle sounding more and more like a Galactic tourist as the conversation went on, more and more aggressive for lower and lower gains. Quy didn't care anymore: she watched Agnes. Watched the impenetrable avatar—a red-headed woman in the latest style from Prime, with freckles on her skin and a hint of a star-tan on her face. But that wasn't what she was, inside; what the immerser had dug deep into.

Wasn't who she was at all. Tam was right; all immersers should be taken apart, and did it matter if they exploded? They'd done enough harm as it was.

Quy wanted to get up, to tear away her own immerser, but she couldn't, not in the middle of the negotiation. Instead, she rose, and walked closer to Agnes; the two men barely glanced at her, too busy agreeing on a price. "You're not alone," she said, in Rong, low enough that it didn't carry.

Again, that odd, disjointed flash. "You have to take it off," Quy said, but got no further response. As an impulse, she grabbed the other woman's arm—felt her hands go right through the immerser's avatar, connect with warm, solid flesh.

You hear them negotiating, in the background—it's tough going, because the Rong man sticks to his guns stubbornly, refusing to give ground to Galen's onslaught. It's all very distant, a subject of intellectual study; the immerser reminds you from time to time, interpreting this and this body cue, nudging you this way and that—you must sit straight and silent, and support your husband—and so you smile through a mouth that feels gummed together.

You feel, all the while, the Rong girl's gaze on you, burning like ice water, like the gaze of a dragon. She won't move away from you; and her hand rests on you, gripping your arm with a strength you didn't think she had in her body. Her avatar is but a thin layer, and you can see her beneath it: a round, moon-shaped face with skin the colour of cinnamon—no, not spices, not chocolate, but simply a colour you've seen all your life.

"You have to take it off," she says. You don't move; but you wonder what she's talking about.

Take it off. Take it off. Take what off?

The immerser.

Abruptly, you remember—a dinner with Galen's friends, when they laughed at jokes that had gone by too fast for you to understand. You came home battling tears; and found yourself reaching for the immerser on your bedside table, feeling its cool weight in your hands. You thought it would please Galen if you spoke his language; that he would be less ashamed of how uncultured you sounded to his friends. And then you found out that everything was fine, as long as you kept the settings on maximum and didn't remove it. And then . . . and then you walked with it and slept with it, and showed the world nothing but the avatar it had designed—saw nothing it hadn't tagged and labelled for you. Then . . .

Then it all slid down, didn't it? You couldn't program the network anymore, couldn't look at the guts of machines; you lost your job with the tech company, and came to Galen's compartment, wandering in the room like a hollow shell, a ghost of yourself—as if you'd already died, far away from home and all that it means to you. Then—then the immerser wouldn't come off, anymore.

"What do you think you're doing, young woman?"

Second Uncle had risen, turning towards Quy—his avatar flushed with anger, the pale skin mottled with an unsightly red. "We adults are in the middle of negotiating something very important, if you don't mind." It might have made Quy quail in other circumstances, but his voice and his body language were wholly Galactic; and he sounded like a stranger to her—an angry foreigner whose food order she'd misunderstood—whom she'd mock later, sitting in Tam's room with a cup of tea in her lap, and the familiar patter of her sister's musings.

"I apologise," Quy said, meaning none of it.

"That's all right," Galen said. "I didn't mean to—" he paused, looked at his wife. "I shouldn't have brought her here."

"You should take her to see a physician," Quy said, surprised at her own boldness.

"Do you think I haven't tried?" His voice was bitter. "I've even taken her to the best hospitals on Prime. They look at her, and say they can't take it off. That the shock of it would kill her. And even if it didn't . . ." He spread his hands, letting air fall between them like specks of dust. "Who knows if she'd come back?"

Quy felt herself blush. "I'm sorry." And she meant it this time.

Galen waved her away, negligently, airily, but she could see the pain he was struggling to hide. Galactics didn't think tears were manly, she remembered. "So we're agreed?" Galen asked Second Uncle. "For a million credits?"

Quy thought of the banquet; of the food on the tables, of Galen thinking it would remind Agnes of home. Of how, in the end, it was doomed to fail, because everything would be filtered through the immerser, leaving

Agnes with nothing but an exotic feast of unfamiliar flavours. "I'm sorry," she said, again, but no one was listening; and she turned away from Agnes with rage in her heart—with the growing feeling that it had all been for nothing in the end.

"I'm sorry," the girl says—she stands, removing her hand from your arm, and you feel like a tearing inside, as if something within you was struggling to claw free from your body. Don't go, you want to say. Please don't go. Please don't leave me here.

But they're all shaking hands; smiling, pleased at a deal they've struck—like sharks, you think, like tigers. Even the Rong girl has turned away from you; giving you up as hopeless. She and her uncle are walking away, taking separate paths back to the inner areas of the restaurant, back to their home.

Please don't go.

It's as if something else were taking control of your body; a strength that you didn't know you possessed. As Galen walks back into the restaurant's main room, back into the hubbub and the tantalising smells of food—of lemongrass chicken and steamed rice, just as your mother used to make—you turn away from your husband, and follow the girl. Slowly, and from a distance; and then running, so that no one will stop you. She's walking fast—you see her tear her immerser away from her face, and slam it down onto a side table with disgust. You see her enter a room; and you follow her inside.

They're watching you, both girls, the one you followed in; and another, younger one, rising from the table she was sitting at—both terribly alien and terribly familiar at once. Their mouths are open, but no sound comes out.

In that one moment—staring at each other, suspended in time—you see the guts of Galactic machines spread on the table. You see the mass of tools; the dismantled machines; and the immerser, half spread-out before them, its two halves open like a cracked egg. And you understand that they've been trying to open them and reverse-engineer them; and you know that they'll never, ever succeed. Not because of the safeguards, of the Galactic encryptions to preserve their fabled intellectual property; but rather, because of something far more fundamental.

This is a Galactic toy, conceived by a Galactic mind—every layer of it, every logical connection within it exudes a mindset that might as well be alien to these girls. It takes a Galactic to believe that you can take a whole culture and reduce it to algorithms; that language and customs can be boiled to just a simple set of rules. For these girls, things are so much more complex than this, and they will never understand how an immerser works, because they can't think like a Galactic, they'll never ever think like that. You can't think like a Galactic unless you've been born in the culture.

Or drugged yourself, senseless, into it, year after year.

You raise a hand—it feels like moving through honey. You speak—struggling to shape words through layer after layer of immerser thoughts.

"I know about this," you say, and your voice comes out hoarse, and the words fall into place one by one like a laser stroke, and they feel right, in a way that nothing else has for five years. "Let me help you, younger sisters."

SETH DICKINSON

MORRIGAN IN THE SUNGLARE

For Darius and the Blue Planet crew.

Seth Dickinson is the author of the *Masquerade* trilogy (*The Traitor Baru Cormorant*, *The Monster Baru Cormorant*, and *The Tyrant Baru Cormorant*), and *Exordia*, and has short fiction published in Lightspeed, Clarkesworld and elsewhere. He is also the author of much of the lore and backstory of Bungie Studios' *Destiny*. He lives in New York City. [www.sethdickinson.com]

Things Laporte says, during the war—

The big thing, at the end:

The navigators tell Laporte that *Indus* is falling into the sun.

Think about the *difficulty* of it. On Earth, Mars, the moons of Jupiter, the sun wants you but it cannot have you: you slip sideways fast enough to miss. This is the truth of orbit, a hand-me-down birthright of velocity between your world and the fire. You never think about it.

Unless you want to fall. Then you need to strip all that speed away. Navigators call it *killing your velocity* (killing again: Laporte's not sure whether this is any kind of funny). It takes more thrust to fall into the sun than to escape out to the stars.

Indus made a blind jump, fleeing the carnage, exit velocity uncertain.

And here they are. Falling.

They are the last of *Indus'* pilots and there is nothing left to fly, so

Laporte and Simms sit in the empty briefing room and play caps. The ship groans around them, ruined hull protesting the efforts of the damage control crews—racing to revive engines and jump drive before CME radiation sleets through tattered armor and kills everyone on board.

"What do you think our dosage is?" Laporte asks.

"I don't know. Left my badge in my bunk." Simms rakes her sweat-soaked hair, selects a cap, and antes. Red emergency light on her collarbone, on the delta of muscle there. "Saw a whole damage-control party asleep in the number two causeway. Radiation fatigue."

"So fast? That's bad, boss." Laporte watches her Captain, pale lanky daughter of Marineris sprawled across three seats in the half-shed tangle of her flight suit, and makes a fearful search for damage. Radiation poisoning, or worse. A deeper sort of wound.

In the beginning Simms was broken and Laporte saved her, a truth Simms has never acknowledged but must *must* know. And she saved Laporte in turn, by ferocity, by hate, by being the avatar of everything Laporte didn't know.

And here in the sunglare Laporte is afraid that the saving's been undone. Not that it should matter, this concern of hearts, when they'll all be dead so soon—but—

"Hey," Laporte says, catching on. "You *sneak,* boss. I call bullshit."

"Got me." Simms pushes the bottlecap (ARD/AE-002 ANTI RADIATION, it says) across. A little tremble in her fingers. Not so severe. "They're all too busy to sleep."

The caps game is an Ubuntu game, a children's game, a kill-time game, an I'm-afraid game. Say something, truth or lie. See if your friends call it right.

It teaches you to see other people. Martin Mandho, during a childhood visit, told her that. *This is why it's so popular in the military. Discipline and killing require dehumanization. The caps game lets soldiers reclaim shared subjectivity.*

"Your go, Morrigan," Simms says, shuffling her pile of ARD/AE-002 caps. The callsign might be a habit, might be a reminder: *we're still soldiers.*

"I was in CIC. Think I saw Captain Sorensen tearing up over a picture of Captain Kyrematen." *Yangtze*'s skipper, Sorensen's comrade. Lost.

Simms' face armors up. "I don't want to talk about anything that just happened."

"Is that a call?"

"No. Of course it's true."

Laporte wants to stand up and say: fuck this. Fuck this stupid game, fuck the rank insignia, fuck the rules. We're falling into the sun, there's no rescue coming. Boss, I—

But what would she say? It's not as simple as the obvious thing (and boy, it's obvious), not about lust or discipline or loyalty. Bigger than that, truer than that, full of guilt and fire and salvation, because what she really wants to say is something about—

About how Simms is—important, right, but that's not it. That's not big enough.

Laporte can't get her tongue around it. She doesn't know how to say it.

Simms closes her eyes for a moment. In the near distance, another radiation alarm joins the threnody.

Things Laporte already knows how to say—

I'm going to kill that one, yes, I killed him. Say it like this:

Morrigan, tally bandit. Knife advantage, have pure, pressing now.

Guns guns guns.

And the ship in her sights, silver-dart *Atalanta* built under some other star by hands not unlike her own, the fighter and its avionics and torch and weapons and its desperate skew as it tries to break clear, the pilot too—they all come apart under the coilgun hammer. The pilot too.

Blossoming shrapnel. Spill of fusion fire. Behold Laporte, starmaker. (Some of the color in the flame is human tissue, atomizing.)

She made her first kill during the fall of Jupiter, covering Third Fleet's retreat. Sometimes rookies fall apart after their first, eaten up by guilt. Laporte's seen this. But the cry-scream-puke cycle never hits her, even though she's been afraid of her own compassion, even though her call-sign was almost *Flower Girl.*

Instead she feels high.

There's an Ubuntu counselor waiting on the *Solaris*, prepared to debrief and support pilots with post-kill trauma. She waves him away. Twenty years of Ubuntu education, *cherish all life* hammered into the metal of her. All meaningless, all wasted.

That high says: born killer.

She was still flying off the *Solaris* here, Kassim on her wing. Still hadn't met Simms yet.

Who is Lorna Simms? Noemi Laporte thinks about this, puzzles and probes, and sometimes it's a joy, and sometimes it hurts. Sometimes she doesn't think about it at all—mostly when she's with Simms, flying, killing.

Maybe that's who Simms is. The moment. A place where Laporte never has to think, never has a chance to reflect, never has to be anything other than laughter and kill-joy. But that's a selfish way to go at it, isn't it? Simms is her own woman, impatient, profane, ferocious, and Laporte shouldn't make an icon of her. She's not a lion, not a war-god, not some kind of oblivion Laporte can curl up inside.

A conversation they have, after a sortie, long after they saved each other:

"You flew like shit today, Morrigan."

"That so, boss?"

Squared off in the shower queue, breathing the fear stink of pilots and *Indus* crew all waiting for cold water. Simms a pylon in the crowd and dark little Laporte feels like the raven roosting on her.

"You got sloppy on your e-poles," Simms says. "Slipped into the threat envelope twice."

"I went in to finish the kill, sir. Calculated risk."

"Not much good if you don't live to brag about it."

"Yet here I am, sir."

"You'll spend two hours in the helmet running poles and drags before I let you fly again." Simms puts a little crack of authority on the end of the reprimand, and then grimaces like she's just noticed the smell. "Flight Lieutenant Levi assures me that they *were* good kills, though."

Laporte is pretty sure Simms hasn't spoken to Levi since preflight. She grins toothsomely at her Captain, and Simms, exasperated, grinning back though (!), shakes her head and sighs.

"You love it, don't you," she says. "You're *happy* out there."

Laporte puts her hands on the back of her head, an improper attitude toward a superior officer, and holds the grin. "I'm coming for you, sir."

She's racing Simms for the top of the Second Fleet kill board. They both know who's going to win.

I'm in trouble. Say it like this:

Boss, Morrigan, engaged defensive, bandit my six on plane, has pure.

And Simms' voice flat and clear on the tactical channel, so unburdened by tone or technology that it just comes off like clean truth, an easy promise on a calm day, impossible not to trust:

Break high, Morrigan. I've got you.

There's a little spark deep down there under the calm, an ember of rage or glee. It's the first thing Laporte ever knew about Simms, even before her name.

Laporte had a friend and wingman, Kassim. He killed a few people, clean ship-to-ship kills, and afterward he'd come back to the *Solaris* with Laporte and they'd drink and shout and chase women until the next mission.

But he broke. Sectioned out. A psychological casualty: cry-scream-puke.

Why? Why Kassim, why not Laporte? She's got a theory. Kassim used to talk about why the war started, how it would end, who was right, who was wrong. And, fuck, who can blame him? Ubuntu was supposed to breed a better class of human, meticulously empathic, selflessly rational.

Care for those you kill. Mourn them. They are human too, and no less afraid.

How could you think like that and then pull the trigger, ride the burst, *guns guns guns* and boom, *scratch bandit, good kill*? So Laporte gave up on empathy and let herself ride the murder-kick. She hated herself for it. But at least she didn't break.

Too many people are breaking. The whole Federation is getting its ass kicked.

After Kassim sectioned out, Laporte put in for a transfer to the frigate *Indus,* right out on the bleeding edge. She'd barely met Captain Simms, barely knew her. But she'd heard Simms on FLEETTAC, heard the exultation and the fury in her voice as she led her squadron during the *Meridian* ambush and the defense of Rheza Station.

"It's a suicide posting," Captain Telfer warned her. "The *Indus* eats new pilots and shits ash."

But Simms' voice said: *I know how to live with this. I know how to love it.*

I'm with you, Captain Simms. I'll watch over you while you go ahead and make the kill. Say it like this:

Boss, Morrigan, tally, visual. Press!

That's all it takes. A fighter pilot's brevity code is a strict, demanding form: say as much as you can with as few words as possible, while you're terrified and angry and you weigh nine times as much as you should.

Like weaponized poetry, except that deep down your poem always says *we have to live. They have to die.*

For all their time together on the *Indus,* Laporte has probably spoken more brevity code to Simms than anything else.

· • ● • ·

People from Earth aren't supposed to be very good at killing.

Noemi Laporte, callsign Morrigan, grew up in a sealed peace. The firewall defense that saved the solar system from alien annihilation fifty years ago also collapsed the Sol-Serpentis wormhole, leaving the interstellar colonies out in the cold—a fistful of sparks scattered to catch fire or gutter out. Weary, walled in, the people of Sol abandoned starflight and built a cozy nest out of the wreckage: the eudaimonic Federation, democracy underpinned by gentle, simulation-guided Ubuntu philosophy. *We have weathered enough strife,* Laporte remembers—Martin Mandho, at the podium in Hellas Planitia for the fortieth anniversary speech. *In the decades to come, we hope to build a community of compassion and pluralism here in Sol, a new model for the state and for the human mind.*

And then they came back.

Not the aliens, oh no no, that's the heart of it—they're still out there, enigmatic, vast, xenocidal. And the colonist Alliance, galvanized by imminent annihilation, has to be ready for them.

Ready at any price.

These are our terms. An older Laporte, listening to another broadcast: the colonists' *Orestes* at the reopened wormhole, when negotiations finally broke down. *We must have Sol's wealth and infrastructure to meet the coming storm. We appealed to your leaders in the spirit of common humanity, but no agreement could be reached.*

This is a matter of survival. We cannot accept the Federation's policy of isolation. Necessity demands that we resort to force.

That was eighteen months ago.

A lot of people believe that the whole war's a problem of communication, fundamentally solvable. Officers in the *Solaris'* off-duty salon argue that if only the Federation and the Alliance could just figure out what to say, how to save face and stand down, they could find a joint solution. A way to give the Alliance resources and manpower while preserving the

Federation from socioeconomic collapse and the threat of alien extermination. It's the Ubuntu dream, the human solution.

Captain Simms doesn't hold to that, though.

A conversation they had on the *Indus'* observation deck:

"But," Laporte says (she doesn't remember her words exactly, or what she's responding to; and anyway, she's ashamed to remember). "The Alliance pilots are people too."

"Stow that shit." Simms' voice a thundercrack, unexpected: she'd been across the compartment, speaking to Levi. "I won't have poison on my ship."

The habit of a lifetime and the hurt of a moment conspire against military discipline and Laporte almost makes a protest—*Ubuntu says, Martin Mandho said*—

But Simms is already on her, circling, waiting for the outspoken new transfer to make *one* more mistake. "What's the least reliable weapons system on your ship, Morrigan?"

A whole catalogue of options, a bestiary of the Federation's reluctant innovations—least reliable? Must be the Mulberry GES-2.

"Wrong. It's you. Pilots introduce milliseconds of unaffordable latency. In a lethal combat environment, hesitation kills." Simms is talking to everyone now, making an example of Laporte. She sits there stiff and burning waiting for it to be over. "If the Admiralty had its way, they'd put machines in these cockpits. But until that day, your job is to come as close as you can. Your job is to keep your humanity out of the gears. How do you do that?"

"Hate, sir," Levi says.

"Hate." Simms lifts her hands to an invisible throat. Bears down, for emphasis, as her voice drops to a purr. She's got milspec features, aerodyne chin, surgical cheekbones, and Laporte feels like she's going to get cut if she stares, but she does. "There are no people in those ships you kill. They have no lovers, no parents, no home. They were never children and they will never grow old. They invaded your home, and you are going to stop them by killing them all. Is that clear, Laporte?"

Willful, proud, stupid, maybe thinking that Simms would give her slack on account of that first time they flew together, Laporte says: "That's monstrous."

Simms puts the ice on her: full-bore all-aspect derision. "It's a war. Monsters win."

The Alliance flagship, feared by Federation pilot and admiral alike, is *Atreus*. Her missile batteries fire GTM-36 Block 2 Eos munitions (*memorize that name, pilot. Memorize these capabilities*). The *Atreus'* dawnbringers have a fearsome gift: given targeting data, they can perform their own jumps. Strike targets far across the solar system. The euphemism is 'over the horizon.'

Laporte used to wonder about the gun crews who run the Eos batteries. Do they know what they're shooting at when they launch a salvo? Do they invent stories to assure each other that the missiles are intended for Vital Military Targets? When they hear about collateral damage, a civilian platform shattered and smashed into Europa's ice in the name of 'shipping denial,' do they speculate in a guilty hush: *was that us?*

Maybe that's the difference between the Alliance and the Federation, the reason the Alliance is winning. The colonists can live with it.

She doesn't wonder about these things anymore, though.

One night in the gym the squadron gets to sparring in a round robin and then Laporte's in the ring with Simms, nervous and half-fixed on quitting until they get into it and slam to the mat, grappling for the arm-bar or the joint lock, and Laporte feels it click: it's just like the dogfight, like the merge, pacing your strength exactly like riding a turn, waiting for the moment to cut in and *shoot*.

She gets Simms in guard, flips her, puts an elbow in her throat. Feels herself grinning down with the pressure while everyone else circles and hoots: *Morrrrrrigan—look at her, she's on it—*

Simms looks back up at her and there's this question in her wary wonderful eyes, a little annoyed, a little curious, a little scared: what *are* you?

She rolls her shoulders, lashes her hips, throws Laporte sideways. Laporte's got no breath and no strength left to spend but she thinks Simms' just as tapped and the rush feeds her, sends her clawing back for the finish.

Simms puts her finger up, thumb cocked, before Laporte can reach her. "Bang," she says.

Laporte falls on her belly. "Oof. Aargh."

It's important that Simms not laugh too hard. She's got to maintain command presence. She's been careful about that since their first sortie.

You need help, Captain Simms. Say it like this:

This is the first time they flew together, when Laporte saved Simms. It happened because of a letter Laporte received, after her transfer to *Indus* was approved but before she actually shuttled out to her new post.

FLEETNET PERSONAL—TAIGA/TARN/NODIS
FLIGHT LIEUTENANT KAREN NG [YANGTZE]
//ENSIGN NOEMI LAPORTE [INDUS]

Laporte:

> Just got word of your transfer. You may remember me from the *Nauticus* incident. I'm de facto squadron leader aboard *Yangtze*. Lorna Simms and I go way back.
>
> Admiral Netreba is about to select ships for a big joint operation against the Alliance. Two months ago the *Indus* would have been top of the list, and Simms with it. But they've been on the front too long, and the scars are starting to show.
>
> I hear reports of a 200 percent casualty rate. Simms and Ehud Levi are the only survivors of the original squadron. I hear that Simms doesn't give new pilots callsigns, that she won't let the deck crew paint names on their ships. If she's

going to lose her people, she'd rather not allow them to be people.

It's killing morale. Simms won't open up to her replacements until they stop dying, and they won't stop dying until she opens up.

I want the *Indus* with us when we make our move, but Netreba won't pick a sick ship. See if you can get through to Simms.

Regards,
Karen Ng

Laporte takes this shit seriously. When Simms takes her out for a training sortie, a jaunt around the Martian sensor perimeter, she's got notes slipped into the plastic map pockets on her flightsuit thighs, gleaned from gossip and snippy FLEETNET posts: *responds well to confidence and plain talk, rejects overt empathy, accepts professional criticism but will enforce a semblance of military discipline.* No pictures, though.

She knows she's overthinking it, but fuck, man, it's hard not to be nervous. Simms is her new boss, her wartime idol, the woman who might get her killed. Simms is supposed to teach her how to live with—with all this crazy shit. And now it turns out she's broken too? Is there anyone out here who *hasn't* cracked?

Maybe a little of that disappointment gets into Laporte's voice. Afterward, because of the thing that happens next, she can't remember exactly how she broached it—professional inquiry, officer to superior? Flirtatious breach of discipline? Oafishly direct? But she remembers it going bad, remembers Simms curling around from bemusement to disappointment, probably thinking: *great,* Solaris *is shipping me its discipline cases so I can get them killed.*

Then the Alliance jumps them. Four Nyx, a wolfpack out hunting stragglers. Bone-white metal cast in shark shapes. Shadows on the light of their own fusion stars.

Simms, her voice a cutting edge, a wing unpinioned, shedding all the weight of death she carries: "Morrigan, Lead, knock it off, knock it off, I see jump flash, bandits two by two." And then, realizing as Laporte does that they're not getting clear, that help's going to be too long coming: "On my lead, Morrigan, we're going in. Get your fangs out."

And Laporte puts it all away. Seals it up, like she's never been able to before. Just her and the thirty-ton Kentauroi beneath her and the woman on her wing.

They hit the merge in a snarl of missile and countermeasure and everything after that blurs in memory, just spills together in a whirl of acceleration daze and coilgun fire until it's pointless to recall, and what would it mean, anyway? You don't remember love as a series of acts. You just know: *I love her.* So it is here. They fought, and it was good. (And damn, yes, she loves Simms, that much has been apparent for a while, but it's maybe not the kind of love that anyone does anything about, maybe not the kind it's wise to voice or touch.) She remembers a few calls back and forth, grunted out through the pressure of acceleration. All brevity code, though, and what does that mean outside the moment?

Two gunships off *Yangtze* arrive to save them and the Alliance fighters bug out, down a ship. Laporte comes back to the surface, shaking off the narcosis of the combat trance, and finds herself talking to Simms, Simms talking back.

Simms is laughing. "That was good," she says. "That was good, Morrigan. Damn!"

Indus comes off the line less than twelve hours later, yielding her patrol slot to another frigate. Captain Simms takes the chance to drill her new pilots to exhaustion and they begin to loathe her so profoundly they'd all eat a knife just to hear one word of her approval. Admiral Netreba, impressed by *Indus'* quick recovery, taps the frigate for his special task force.

Laporte knows her intervention made a difference. Knows Simms felt the same exhilaration, flying side by side, and maybe she thought: *I've got to keep this woman alive.*

Simms just needed to believe she could save someone.

·•◉•·

Alliance forces in the Sol theater fall under the command of Admiral Steele, a man with Kinshasa haute couture looks and winter-still eyes. Sometimes he gives interviews, and sometimes they leak across the divide.

"Overwhelming violence," he answers, asked about his methods. "The strategic application of shock. They're gentle people, humane, compassionate. Force them into violent retaliation, and they'll break. The Ubuntu philosophy that shapes their society cannot endure open war."

"Some of your critics accuse you of atrocity," the interviewer says. "Indiscriminate strategic bombing. Targeted killings against members of the civilian government in Sol."

Steele puts his hands together, palm to palm, fingers laced, and Laporte would absolutely bet a bottle cap that the sorrow on his face is genuine. "The faster I end the war," he says, "the faster we can stop the killing. My conscience asks me to use every tool available."

"So you believe this is a war worth winning? That the Security Council is right to pursue a military solution to this crisis?"

Steele's face gives nothing any human being could read, but Laporte, she senses determination. "That's not my call to make," he says.

This happens after the intervention, after Simms teaches Laporte to be a monster (or lets her realize she already was), after they manage the biggest coup of the war—the capture of the *Agincourt*. Before they fall into the sun, though.

They take some leave time, Simms and Laporte and the rest of the *Indus* pilots, and the *Yangtze*'s air wing too. Karen Ng has a cabin in Tharsis National Park, on the edge of Mars' terraformed valleys. Olympus Mons fills the horizon like the lip of a battered pugilist, six-kilometer peak scraping the edge of atmosphere. Like a bridge between where they are and where they fight.

Barbeque on the shore of Marineris Reservoir. The lake is meltwater from impacted comets, crystalline and still, and Levi won't swim in it because he swears up and down it's full of cyanide. They're out of uniform and Laporte should really *not* take that as an excuse but, well, discipline issues: she finds Simms, walking the shore.

"Boss," she says.

"Laporte." No callsign. Simms winds up and hurls a stone. It doesn't even skip once: hits, pierces, vanishes. The glass of their reflections shatters and reforms. Simms chuckles, a guarded sound, like she's expecting Laporte to do something worth reprimand, like she's not sure what she'll do about it. "Been on Mars before?"

"Uh, pretty much," Laporte mumbles, hoping to avoid this conversation: she was at Hellas for Martin Mandho's speech ten years ago, but she was a snotty teenager, Earthsick, and single-handedly ruined Mom's plan to see more of the world. "Never with a native guide, though."

"Tourist girl." Simms tries skipping again. "Fuck!"

"Boss, you're killing me." Laporte finds a flat stone chip, barely weathered, and throws it—but Mars gravity, hey, Mars gravity is a good excuse for *that*. "Mars gravity!" she pleads, while Simms laughs, while Laporte thinks about what a bad idea this is, to let herself listen to that laugh and get drunk. Fleet says: no fraternization.

They walk a while.

"You really hate them?" Laporte asks, forgetting whatever wit she had planned the instant it hits her tongue.

"The colonists? The Alliance?" Simms squints up Olympus-ways, one boot up on a rock. The archetypical laconic pioneer, minus only that awful Mongolian chew everyone here adores. "What's the alternative?"

"Didn't you go to school?" Ubuntu never found so many ears on hardscrabble Mars. "They gave it to us every day on *Solaris*: love them, understand them, regret the killing."

"Ah, right. 'He has a husband,' I remember, shooting him. 'May you find peace,' I pray, uncaging the seekers." Simms rolls the rock with her boot, flipping it, spinning it on its axis. "And you had this in your head, the first time you made a kill? You cut into the merge and lined up the shot thinking about your shared humanity?"

"I guess so," Laporte says. A good person would have thought about that, so she'd thought about it. "But it didn't stop me."

Simms lets the rock fall. It makes a flinty clap. She eyes Laporte. "No? You weren't angry? You didn't hate?"

"No." She thinks of Kassim. "It was so easy for me. I thought I was sick."

"Huh," Simms says, chewing on that. "Well, can't speak for you, then. But it helps me to hate them."

"Hate's inhumane, though." Words from a conscience she's kept buried all these months. "It perpetuates the cycle."

"I wish the universe gave power to the decent. Protection to the humane." Simms shrugs, in her shoulders, in her lips. "But I've only seen one power stop the violent, and it's a closer friend to hate."

She's less coltish down here, like she's got more time for every motion, like she's set aside her haste. "Hey," Laporte says, pressing her luck. "When I transferred in. You were—in a tough place."

Simms holds up a hand to ward her off. "You can see the ships," she says.

Mars is a little world with a close horizon and when she looks up Laporte feels like she's going to lose her balance and fall right off, out past Phobos, into a waiting wolfpack, into the Eos dawnbringers from *over the horizon*. She takes a step closer to Simms, toward the stanchion that keeps her down.

High up there some warship's drive flickers.

"I was pretty sure," Simms says, "that everyone I knew was going to die, and that I couldn't stop it. That's where I was, when you transferred in."

"And now?" Laporte asks, still watching the star. It's a lot further away, a lot safer.

"Jury's out," Simms says. Laporte's too skittish to check whether she's joking. "Look. Moonrise. You've got to tell me a secret."

"Are you fucking with me?"

"Native guide," Simms says, rather smugly.

"When I was a kid," Laporte says, "I had an invisible friend named Ken. He told me I had to watch the ants in the yard go to war, the red ants and the black ones, and that I had to choose one side to win. He said it was the way of things. I got a garden hose and I—I took him really seriously—"

Simms starts cracking up. "You're a loon," she chokes. "I'm glad you're on my side."

"I wonder what we'll do after this," Laporte says.

Simms sobers up. "Don't think about that. It'll kill you."

Laporte listens to the flight data record of that training sortie, the tangle with the Nyx wolfpack, just to warm her hands on that fire, to tremble at the inarticulate beauty of the fight:

"—am spiked, am spiked, music up. Bandit my seven high, fifteen hundred, aspect attack."

"Lead supporting." The record is full of warbling alarms, the voices of a ship trying to articulate every kind of danger. "Anchor your turn at, uh—fuck it, just break low, break low. Padlocking—"

"Kill him, boss—"

"Guns." A low, smooth exhalation, Simms breathing out on the trigger. "Guns."

"Nice. Good kill. Bandit your nine low—break left—"

Everything's so clear. So true. Flying with Simms, there's no confusion.

They respond to a distress call from a civilian vessel suffering catastrophic reactor failure. *Indus* jumps on-scene to find an Alliance corvette, *Arethusa*, already providing aid to the civilian. Both sides launch fighters, slam down curtains of jamming over long-range communications, and prepare to attack.

But neither of them have enough gear to save the civilian ship—the colonists don't have the medical suite for all her casualties; *Indus* can't provide enough gear to stabilize her reactor. Captain Sorensen negotiates a truce with the *Arethusa*'s commander.

Laporte circles *Indus*, flying wary patrol, her fingers on the master arm switch. Some of the other pilots talk to the colonists on GUARD. They talk back, their accents skewed by fifty years of linguistic drift, their humanity still plain. One of the enemy pilots, callsign Anansi, asks for her by name: there's a bounty on her head, an Enemy Ace Incentive, and smartass Anansi wants to talk to her and live to tell. She mutes the channel.

When she stops and thinks about it, she doesn't really believe this war is necessary. So it's quit, or—don't think about it. That's what Simms taught her: you go in light. You throw away everything about yourself that doesn't help you kill. Strip down, sharpen up. Weaponize your soul.

Another Federation frigate, *Hesperia*, picks up the distress signal, picks up the jamming, assumes the worst. She has no way to know about the truce. When she jumps in she opens *Arethusa*'s belly with her first salvo and everything goes back to being simple.

Laporte gets Anansi, she's pretty sure.

Fresh off the *Agincourt* coup, they make a play for the *Carthage—Indus, Yangtze, Altan Orde, Katana,* and Simms riding herd on three full squadrons. It's a trap. Steele's been keeping his favorite piece, the hunter-killer *Imperieuse*, in the back row. She makes a shock jump, spinal guns hungry.

Everyone dies.

The last thing Laporte hears before she makes a crash-landing on *Indus'* deck is Captain Simms, calling out to Karen Ng, begging her to abandon *Yangtze*, begging her to live. But Karen won't leave her ship.

Indus jumps blind, destination unplotted, exit vector unknown. The crash transition wrecks her hangar deck, shatters her escape pods in their mounts.

She falls into light.

• ◦ ● ◦ •

So Laporte was wrong, in the end. The death of everyone Simms knew *was* inevitable.

Monsters win.

Laporte stacks her bottlecaps and waits for Simms to offer her a word.

The game is just a way to pass the time. Not real speech, not like the chatter, like the brevity code. Out there they could *talk*. And is that why they're alive, just the two of them? Even Levi, old hand Levi, came apart at the end, first in his head when he saw the bodies spilling out of *Altan Orde* and then in his cockpit when the guns found him. But Simms and Laporte, they flew each other home. Home to die in this empty searing room with the bolted-down frame chairs and the bottle caps and their cells rotting inside them.

Or maybe it's just that Simms hated harder than anyone else, hesitated the least. And Laporte, well—she's never hesitated at all.

"It's my fault we're here," Laporte says, even though it's not her turn.

"Yeah?" Simms, she's got red in her eyes, a tremor in her frame.

"If I hadn't listened to Karen's note, if I hadn't done whatever I did to wake you up." If they'd never met. "Netreba never would've picked *Indus* for the task force. We wouldn't have been at the ambush. Wouldn't have watched *Impérieuse* kill our friends."

"All you did was fly my wing," Simms says. "It's not your fault." But she knows exactly what Laporte's talking about.

Simms picks up a bottle cap and puts it between them. "I'm transferring you to *Eris*," she says. "Netreba's flagship. On track for a squadron command."

"Bullshit." Because they're not going to live long enough to transfer anywhere.

Simms wraps the cap up in her shaking hand and draws it back. "I already put the order in," she says. "Just in case."

A dosage alarm shrieks and stops: someone from damage control, silencing the obvious. Beams of ionizing radiation piercing the torn armor, arcing through the crew spaces as *Indus* tumbles and falls.

Is this the time to just give up on protocol? To get her boss by the wrists and beg: wait, stop, please, let me explain, let me stay? We'll make it, rescue will come, we'll fly again? But she *gets it*. She's got that Ubuntu empathy bug. She can feel it in Simms, the old break splintering again: *I can't watch these people die.*

Laporte's the only people she's got left. So Simms has to send her away.

"Boss," she says. "You taught me—without you I wouldn't—"

Killing, it's like falling into the sun: you've got all this compassion, all this goodwill, keeping you in the human orbit. All that civilization that everyone before you worked to build. And somehow you've got to lose it all.

Only Laporte never—

"Without me," Simms says, and she's got no mercy left in her tongue, "you'd be fine. You'll *be* fine. You're a killer. That's all you need—no reasons, no hate. It's just you."

She lets her head loll back and exhales hard. The lines of her arched throat kink and smooth.

"Fuck," she says. "It's hot."

Laporte opens her hand. Asking for the cap. She doesn't have the spit to say: *true.*

Captain Simms makes herself comfortable, flat on her back across three chairs. "Your turn," she says.

"Boss," Laporte rasps. "Fuck. Excuse me." She clears her throat. Might as well go for it: it begs to be said. "Boss, I . . ."

But Simms has gone. She's asleep, breathing hard. It's lethargy, the radiation pulling her down. Giving her some peace.

Laporte calls a medical team. While she waits she tries to find a blanket, but Simms seems to prefer an uneasy rest. She breathes a little easier when Laporte touches her shoulder, though, and Laporte thinks about clasping her hand.

But, no, that's too much.

Federation ships find them. A black ops frigate, running signals intelligence in deep orbit, picks *Indus'* distress cries from the solar background.

Salvage teams scramble to make her ready for one last jump to salvation.

Laporte's waiting by her Captain's side when they come for her. The medical team, and the woman with the steel eyes.

"Laporte," the new woman says. "The *Indus* ace. Came looking for you."

By instinct and inclination Laporte stands to shield her Captain from the gray-clad woman, from her absent insignia and hidden rank. She can't figure out a graceful way to drop the bottle cap so she just holds it like a switch for some hidden explosive, for the grief that wants to get out any way it can. "I need to stay with my squadron leader," she says.

"If I'm reading this order right," Steel Eyes says, though she's got no paper or tablet and the light on her iris makes little crawling signs, "she's shipping you out." She opens a glove in invitation. "I'm with Federation wetwork. Elite of the elite. I'm recruiting pilots for ugly jobs."

Laporte hesitates. She wants to stay, wants it like nothing she knows how to tell. But Steel Eyes stares her down and her gaze cuts deep. "I know you like you wouldn't begin to believe," she says. "I watched you learn what you are. We don't have many of your kind left here in Sol. We made ourselves too good. And it's killing us."

"Please," Laporte croaks. "I can't leave her."

The woman from the eclipse depths of Federation intelligence extends her open hand. A gesture of compassion, though she's wearing tactical gloves. "What do you think happens if you stay? You're not going to stop changing, Noemi. You're never going back to humanity."

She sighs a little, not a hesitation, maybe an apology. "This woman, here, this loyalty you have. You're going to be an alien to her."

Laporte doesn't know how to argue with that. Doesn't know how to speak her defiance. Maybe because Steel Eyes is right.

"Ubuntu," the woman says, "is a philosophy of human development. We have a use for everyone. Even, in times like these, for us monsters."

What's she got left? What the fuck else is there? She gave it all up to become a better killer. Humanity's just dead weight on her trigger.

Nothing but Simms and wreckage in the poison sunlight.

"You know we're losing," Steel Eyes says. "You know we need you."

Ah. That's it. The thing she's been trying to say:

Monsters kill because they like it, and that's all Laporte had. Until this new thing, this fragile human thing, until Simms.

Something worth fighting for. A small, stupid, precious reason.

Laporte gets down on her knees. Puts herself as close to the salt sand cap of Simms' hair as she's ever been. Says it, the best way she knows, promising her, promising herself:

"Boss," she whispers. "Hey. I'll see you when we win."

LAVIE TIDHAR
THE OLD DISPENSATION

Lavie Tidhar is the author of *Osama*, *The Violent Century*, *A Man Lies Dreaming*, *Central Station*, *Unholy Land*, *By Force Alone*, *The Hood*, *The Escapement*, *Neom*, and *Maror*. His latest novels are *Adama* and *The Circumference of the World*. His awards include the World Fantasy and British Fantasy Awards, the John W. Campbell Award, the Neukom Prize and the Jerwood Prize, and he has been shortlisted for the Clarke Award and the Philip K. Dick Award. [lavietidhar. wordpress.com]

"Then I saw a new heaven and a new earth; for the first heaven and the first earth passed away, and there is no longer any sea. And I saw the holy city, new Jerusalem, coming down out of heaven from God."
—The Book of Revelation

1.

The Yom Kippur-class Adjudicator Starship *Vey Is Mir* left the planet of New Jerusalem at twelve oh five hundred hours Temple Mean Time, en route to the planet Kadesh.

2.

This much we know. This much is logged.
Much of what transpired is guesswork.

3.

"What do you remember?" we ask the man suspended over the sacrificial water of the mikveh. We are deep under the Exilarch's palace. Shadows flit in the dim red light of the stones set deep into the walls. The air is humid, like a swamp. We think of Capernaum where the green Abominations live. There should be no secrets between us, not here. This is a safe place.

The prisoner is suspended in chains above the murky water. Tiny microscopic organisms swim in that polluted pool, Shayol bacteria, and the prisoner squirms. He knows what they are, what they do. He is afraid.

The prisoner is naked. We examine his body, dispassionately, in the dim red light. His body is a map of old scars, whip and burn marks, gouging and bullets. His body, too, has been modified in past years, in accordance with the forbidden teachings of Rabbi Abulafia, the heretic. This was done by pontifical consent, for did not the Mishna say that the Shabbat may be broken when life is at stake? By which we mean, that this man, who we call Shemesh, was duly blessed by us as an Adjudicator with a license to spoil the Shabbat, by which we mean, well, you follow our drift, we are sure. Certain forbidden technologies were embedded in his flesh, for though he was himself an Abomination nevertheless he performed a holy task in our name.

We are the Exilarch.

We say, "We are most concerned."

The bound man, suspended upside down over the water where the murderous little creatures of Shayol swim hungrily, makes a rude sound. He uses a rude a word. We are displeased. A scan of his brain pattern reveals disturbing new alignments. We must love him very much, we think, for he is still alive, awaiting our displeasure.

We sigh.

"Child . . ." we say.

"Go to Hell."

"But we have been there, to that awful planet," we say, laughing. "And the Treif of Hell-2 will be dealt with as well, in due course. Let us go back, Shemesh, dear Shemesh. Let us go back to when we last saw you."

"I can tell you nothing," he says, "that you do not already know."

We are troubled, but we try not to show it.

"Please," he says. "Let me down."

"Tell us about Kadesh."

His face twists in pain. "It orbits too close to its sun," he says. "There is no water, no shade. Nothing good ever came of Kadesh."

"We," we say, mildly, "were born on Kadesh."

The man laughs. His laughter is not demented nor tortured, but seems genuine, even pleasant. It upsets us. We lower him down and he stops laughing when the water touches the top of his skull. The tiny little organisms swarm over his scalp and into his ears and his nose and he begins to scream. We lower him further, submerging him in the water, until we choke off the sound.

4.

The man called Shemesh came to the Exilarch's palace before he left for Kadesh. It is a beautiful place, our palace, we think, less a building and more of a small, bustling town in the heart of New Jerusalem, a complex of offices and temples, housing and stores. It is the very heart of this most holy glorious Intermedium of ours, and the Holy of Holies within is more than five thousand years old, and is a remnant of the old place, of the world we left behind. But you must not know yet of such Mysteries. *That* place can be visited only by an Exilarch, and we are 3956th of that title.

We received Shemesh in our private offices. Our Massadean guards escorted him into the presence and withdrew. We admired them, these hardy warriors of ours, in their armour with the red Star of David enclosed within a circle. We have many enemies, both within and without.

We are ever vigilant: against rebels and Abominations, Obscenities, Treif . . . For beyond the light of the Intermedium, ever present, is the shadow of the Ashmoret Laila and we must guard, always we must guard against incursions.

"Exilarch."

He performed a perfunctory bow.

"Shemesh. Thank you for coming to see us."

"I serve at the pleasure of the Exilarch," he said. He was not a man given to many words, you understand. We hadn't fashioned him this way. This man, this Shemesh, was an instrument, or so we saw it, of our will.

"A small matter has risen," we said, smoothly.

"Of course."

"When was your last mission?"

"Three cycles ago," he said. "Ashmoret III."

"Ah, yes," we said. "You did well there."

"I was hunted for nights under the seeing moons," he said, "while the Treif whispered into my mind, a soft and unified whisper of humility and prayer . . ."

"Do you *doubt*?" we said, sharply. Perhaps we regret it now. Perhaps, like any good tool, he merely needed to be re-sharpened.

"I slaughtered them," he said, simply; and that satisfied us.

"On the planet Kadesh," we said, "there is rumour of a holy man. Deep in the caves near the north pole, in the human zone of habitation, he resides. A holy man, and yet he speaks the loshon hora, the evil speech: and he defies the word of the Intermedium."

"Your word," he said.

"*Our* word, yes," we agreed; a little testily. This is the problem with Adjudicators. They are not . . . whole. They are damaged by definition. And so they tend to mock and question, even their superiors.

Even *us*.

We tolerate it, on the whole. They have their uses, our tamed assassins, our eyes and ears. We needed Shemesh. The situation on Kadesh was troubling, yet such things are not uncommon, after all. The worlds are filled with false prophets and the speakers of evil tongues. Mostly, a simple procedure heals the body politic. Think of us as surgeons, with a knife.

"We wish for you to travel to Kadesh," we said. "And ascertain the truth or otherwise of these allegations. Do what you must."

We waved one of our hands to dismiss him, but he remained put.

"You wish me to spoil the Shabbat?" he said.

"Spoil," we said, "with extreme unction."

5.

The Yom Kippur-class Adjudicator Starship *Vey Is Mir* left the planet of New Jerusalem at twelve oh five hundred hours Temple Mean Time, en route to the planet Kadesh. This much we know. Much of what transpired is guesswork.

She was a relic of the Second Maccabean War. A swift old war bird, she was equipped with a Smolin Drive, which was engaged as soon as it passed the heliosphere. It attained light speed and shot into the dark of galactic space.

Light, we understand, does not travel at quite the same speed here as it did in the place we left behind. The journey between planets is swift, here. It took the ship forty-five hours to reach Kadesh orbit. What Shemesh did in that time, we do not know. We hope he prayed—but we rather doubt it.

Perhaps he slept. Perhaps he studied the dossier of the man he had to kill. We knew little of this preacher, but that he called himself Ishmael. A choice of a name well fitting a renegade. We ourselves, before we became Exilarch, were born in Akalton, the second largest of the planet's settlements, to which Shemesh himself was headed. Our childhood was happy, we remember. We loved the desert, the dry heat. New Jerusalem's a colder place, and we have never stopped entirely marvelling at rain.

Rain! Water that falls down from the sky! In Akalton our mother was a trader in water futures. Our father sold breeds of Zikit, the hardy lizard-like creatures native to that planet, on which we rode and hunted and transported our goods. One feels very close to God, on Kadesh. Many of our predecessors came from that planet, but equally many false prophets emerge there, then and still, and we must always watch for trouble from that region. Our Massadean forces keep a permanent base on Kadesh, but in truth, there is little they can truly do on that harsh world, where communities are ever mobile, and where the ancient polar caves provide a shelter to any manner of galactic outlaw . . .

But this is not our story, this is the recording of minutes concerning the expedition of Shemesh, who is suspended over the sacrificial water, back in the air, breathing, as our appendages probe the forbidden interface that lies in the base of his brain, painfully extracting information.

6.

The Testament According To Shemesh, Part I

The ship began to slow as we entered the Kadesh-Barnea system. Beside the habitable planet, there are two gas giants in the outer system, orbited by many moons, and between them and the planet Kadesh, nearby space is filled with habitats of all kinds. On Kadesh they grow the *Artemisia judaica*, and it is the source of much of their trade. A non-native plant, it came from that place we left behind, yet changed in the crossing. The breeds they grow on Kadesh are valued as medicine throughout the Intermedium and even in the forbidden worlds of the Ashmoret Laila on the rim; and though Kadesh is a harsh world, it is also a rich one.

This explained, then, the profusion of habitats throughout the system, and transport ships swarmed in nearby space. Around the planet itself, in orbit, I observed numerous small satellites, way stations, and docking bays. The *Vey Is Mir*, however, is adapted for planetary landing, and in short order I arrived in Akalton City, where my Adjudicator badge let me pass through quarantine.

It is a strange and melancholy place . . . the reddish-brown buildings looked as though they were built of the desert itself. The world smelled of dried thyme, cinnamon, and salt, for the area around the settlement was home to many salt mines, and it was this commodity, rather than the *Artemisia*, that was most on display as I walked through the quiet streets. Though buildings seldom came higher than two stories, nevertheless the streets, having been built close together, formed a narrow maze that felt oppressive, at times dangerous. The sun had set, and the first stars came out. It is always a shock, the first time one encounters a new sky, no matter how often one visits new planets. It provokes the strongest sense of dislocation, almost of loss.

Wonder, too, though the sense of wonder soon fades, and one is left mostly with unease at the alien stars.

Since the stars came out, the streets filled with people heading to temple, though many stood and prayed outside their shops or homes for Ma'ariv. The people of Kadesh wore long, flowing robes, their faces covered against the sand that always blew through the air. Many wore elaborate air filtration systems over their faces, and thus robed and masked they passed through the narrow streets of that town.

. . . I had the sense of being watched.

I picked my way carefully. The instruments deep within my skull analysed the Kadeshean's bodies. Many carried kukri knives, long and curved and deadly. Others carried dart guns, salt revolvers, even *Vipera kadesheana*, those semi-domesticated, poisonous snakes which are used by the natives in deadly close combat.

The pension I was headed to lay at the edge of the town, where Akalton ends and the desert begins. It was as I was passing the gladiatorial amphitheatre that the first attack happened . . .

The amphitheatre stood behind mud-coloured walls. Though the law forbids such games, the populace, being simple folk, love them to the detriment of their duties, and so it was deemed by some former Exilarch that they should be, if not legalised, then at least *managed* and, naturally, taxed. Now it provided easy entertainment to otherwise pious citizens, who flocked to view bloodied spectacles of human gladiators fighting captured Treif. The area around the arena thronged, even at that hour, with disreputable characters, many armed, and so when the first blow came, I was prepared—

I fell down and swept the assailant's feet from under him and he fell. My knife was already in my hand and it found his heart before he had time to move. There were three more of them converging on me, two brutes who with their size could only have been Goliaths, and a small, nasty-looking angel with the mark of Cain on his brow.

The angel took me by surprise. The angels, by which we mean messengers, emanate from the holy see in New Jerusalem. They are augmented, chosen of all the worlds for being the brightest and the most studious and pure. When still young, they are taken to the facilities deep beneath the holy see, where Talmudic engineers refashion them into beings both less, and more, than human. There is a bitter argument recorded in the Tractate Nephilim of 3812, between Rabbi Mohandes and Rabbi Gilman of the Gilmanites of Hastur-3 (of whom it was said that he always walked in shadow), as to the ascendancy of angelic souls at the time of the Final Resurrection. For Rabbi Mohandes said, Lo, that they may not arise as they have never truly lived as men. And Rabbi Gilman said, On the contrary, for they are more than men, and so they will be first to be awakened when the final shofar is blown by the Archangel Gabriel, for it will be they who will usher the new souls into the afterlife.

But I had bigger problems than what the ancient sages thought on the issue of angels, as the small, nasty one was coming at me with a knife. It was a horrible little blade, made of bio-hazardous nanowire filaments woven together: its very whisper through the air could kill. I plugged one of the two Goliaths with a high-bore bullet to the brain and it collapsed with a grunt. I rolled backwards as the angel came at me, kicking as his arm descended. He shrieked with fury and bared small, even white teeth in a rictus of hate. In all my time serving I had only met one other angel with the mark of Cain upon its face: its protocols had been corrupted by an Ashmedai-level hostile intrusion from the Ashmoret Laila.

How this one came to be here I couldn't even begin to speculate. The second Goliath smashed a fist into me, sending me flying over the heads of the crowd until I crashed into a moneylender's stall. As it came thudding after me the crowd dispersed as fast as they could. From beyond the walls of the arena came the frenzied shouts of spectators as some unlucky Treif was no doubt gored. I myself had no taste for violent spectacle.

I rose to my feet. The angel came at me more slowly, then. Its eyes glowed with ultraviolet light and it rose above the ground, manipulating magnetic fields as it flew. The Goliath, with a smirk of triumph, blocked my escape.

I was trapped.

The angel hovered in the air above me. He looked down on me, a heavenly castrato with the eyes of Ashmedai itself.

"Three times," he intoned, in his high, youthful voice, "three times shall you be besieged, assassin, and three times you shall be tested."

Then he smiled, a wicked smile, and the knife grew in his hand and became a shining sword. "Or just once, if you're lucky."

And he dove at me.

I assumed the Yona Wallach defence and as the sword swung a second time I counterattacked with an Alterman combined with a two-strike Adaf move that saw the angel fly back. As the Goliath at my back moved to contain me I twisted my body round him until I was at his back, pressing against it, and then I *pushed*. He screamed as my flesh burned into his own and I burrowed into his body, dislodging vertebrae and kidneys, thighbones and intestines. I made the body move, blindly groping for the angel. I heard the whisper of the blade as it connected with neck muscles and severed them. The Goliath's head fell to the ground, bounced twice, and lay still. The angel screamed with rage. I reached for him with the giant's arms. I was safe inside the tank-like body. Then I heard gunfire, as the local Massadean peace-keeping force arrived to save the day. The angel shrieked again, then departed. I disengaged myself slowly and painfully from the Goliath's corpse and watched it as it crashed to the ground. I was covered in gore, dripping in slime, and in a very bad mood. I hadn't even been on the planet one full rotation. The Massadeans had their guns trained on me and I sighed.

"My name," I said, "is Shemesh. I am a full level Adjudicator on a mission from the holy see . . ."

As you can imagine, it took me a while to convince them.

7.

The Testament According To Shemesh, Part II

I spent the night in a cell in the Massadean barracks.

The Massada mercenaries always put me in mind of lethal mushrooms. They are, on the whole, small and wiry, and they move with a deadly sort of precision that makes even a trained operative, even a high-level Adjudicator, uneasy. In all the worlds of the Intermedium there is no one more dangerous than a Massadean. They live in barracks from childhood and train in every form of martial art and every weapon ever invented, and on their bar mitzvah they get dropped on a rim planet, a group of them, and are expected to survive a month among Amalek-level Treif. Less than half of them usually make it off-world by the time it is over and by then, they have shed more blood than the prophet Elijah when he was faced with the priests of Ba'al.

. . . In the night, somebody tried to poison me.

Three times shall you be besieged, assassin, and three times you shall be tested, the angel had said.

I woke up with the dripping of liquid, close to my ear. I looked up, saw two yellow eyes stare at me from the ceiling. She was dressed all in black, and it took me a moment to realise just how inhuman she was, how her limbs were like a spider's, and how the sack of bilious material that hung from her midsection was a sting, and it was pointed down at me.

. . . I assumed the defensive Tchernichovsky position but there was nowhere to run. It is good for close quarter defence and attack but the creature above me, this Abomination, merely hissed. The dripping poison, I noticed with horror, had set the bedding alight. Flames began to billow and the thick smoke made it hard to breathe. I began to call for help. The creature hissed again, firing poison at me from her sting. I ducked and it hit the bars and melted them with a hiss. Then the Massadean guards were in the cell, and opening fire, and the Abomination was shredded into black ichor.

Hands dragged me out as poison exploded all over the walls. It was nasty stuff—I had not run into a Treif species of this kind before, had no idea where in the rim it could have come from. How it could breach Massadean security, I had no idea either. Someone—more than someone—would pay with their head for this.

I wasn't happy about the way events were turning. After having a shouted argument with the Massadean colonel in charge of the base, I was finally let go. From there I made my way through empty, half-deserted streets to the edge of town and my original destination. The night had turned cold, and the alien stars shone down unobstructed. At that moment I missed New Jerusalem, its eternal lights which mask the view of the night sky. There were too many stars in the sky and they all felt like eyes, watching.

I made my way to the pension, retrieved the pack that was waiting for me, as well as my escort, a sleepy youth from one of the desert tribes. Two of the lizard creatures called Zikit were waiting for us in the yard. We mounted them, and by dawn we had left the city of Akalton far behind.

8.

Our glittering eyes examine the bound prisoner. This was our servant, we marvel, this was the man we had sent out on our behalf. Yet something had happened to him, on our home planet. Something had changed him, had tested his loyalty to us.

We . . . are . . . Exilarch!

The fate of this entire universe and the chosen people within it rests with us. It has not always been thus, but we are they who were called the

Resh Galuta: the ultimate authority in our exile.

"Tell us," we whisper. "Tell us the truth. Why do you deny it to us?"

Shemesh screams. The screams last a long while. Our manipulating digits caress the many wounds inflicted upon his person, both old ones, and new. We poke and we *twist*.

"Tell us!"

The man, this Adjudicator, hangs there, broken, defeated.

"Kill me," he begs.

But that will not do; not do at all. We scan and we sieve through this man's mind, his various augmentations, we taste of his blood and we sample his tissues. We must understand. We absorb him unto ourselves. Things clear, gradually. A picture forms. Clouded at first, then more sharply defined. We know many things. We know that the second attacker, for instance, was a Lilith, a Treif species we had long thought extinct; servants of the Ashmoret Laila, they had terrorised countless planets in the Great Amalek Rebellion of 2500 A.E., swooping in the night, devouring the flesh and bones of all who stood in their way . . . they were poison, Abominations, Treif . . . but we had swooped down on the enemy with swords of flame, with Av-9 starships capable of mass destruction, and the enemy was beaten away, to the rim, and the Lilith were destroyed to the last . . . or so we thought.

We had been wrong. This was disturbing. We magnify the image, construct a memory.

We observe.

9.

The two men ride in the shadow of tall rising cliffs. The canyon floor is yellowish-red sand. For a moment we are filled with a longing for home . . .

The lizards move slowly, slowly in the heat. The men seem half-asleep in their saddles. They have been riding a long time, we think.

We zoom in on them. Lichen grows in cracks in the stone walls of the canyon. There is Shemesh, and there is his companion, whose name is Shlem. He is little more than a boy, really. We know his kind. A desert rat, of the tribes who throng this polar region, paying only lip service to the one true faith. They are a wilful peoples, stubborn, independent, unruly. The boy belongs to a tribe we have had transactions with. They are loyal, for a price. In the polar caves, we know, reside insurgents, escaped Treif, all manners of lawless man and beast. But we cannot police them, we can only contain. As long as they remain unseen, we pretend they are not there.

The boy, all this meanwhile, is speaking. He speaks in a neverending stream, while the Adjudicator's head nods, less in agreement than with the movement of the beast on which he rides. We tune in, to try and see if it has any relevance to what we need to know:

". . . in Tel Asher. She said she'd wait but it's been two cycles and our caravans have not yet crossed again. Do you think it would be wrong to . . .? But you asked about the prophet, this Ishmael. Few have seen him, but word spreads. People come to see him, he speaks from the caves, and they come back transformed, speaking the word of rebellion. But you asked about Treif, yes, many pass through here, seeking refuge, in the caves, they say, are entire species thought lost. They are not of the chosen, and they are not people, and yet I met one, once, near human in shape, and comely, though there is a distinct sense of repulsion, too, of alienation emanating from them, and yet it spoke, in the common tongue, and she—it, it spoke well."

The boy blushes. The man, Shemesh, stirs. "And you, do you believe the word of this Ishmael, too?"

"Do you mean, am I leading you to your doom?"

"The thought had crossed my mind."

"I am loyal."

"But you have heard him speak?"

The boy shakes his head; and yet the question seems to have struck him strangely mute. He stares elsewhere, at the shadows, and says nothing more. We zoom back, until they shrink into two tiny dots, crawling along the immense wall of the cliff. We track their progress. Night falls.

The sun rises. It becomes hard to follow, where they go. There are odd phenomena in that polar region, magnetic interference, and though this *is*, we think, our agent's recollection, there are odd gaps in it, and we find that we cannot trace the route he'd taken . . .

They reach, at last, a wall, and stop. The beasts look nervous. The two dismount. The boy does something, we cannot tell exactly what. It's galling! And we realise someone has interfered with this memory—though surely that should be impossible.

Something changes. Something opens. Like an eye in the rock. Like the spiral of a snail. Like the head of a flower.

An entrance—cunningly disguised.

Shemesh looks at the boy. He speaks, but what he says, we cannot tell. The boy nods—

And a figure rises in the air above them, a sword of flame held in its hands. Shemesh turns, draws a gun, fires. The sword swings. The boy raises his arm. His face registers shock. The angel's face is beatific. We know him, he was one of ours, we thought him lost long ago, on Ashmoret I, our angelic child, the sword whispers through the air and slices through the boy's neck and severs his head from his shoulders.

Shemesh fires, again and again. His gun is a silver Birobidzhan, an item of forbidden technology, with Av-9 destructive capabilities otherwise confined to warships. How Shemesh ever got hold of one, we do not know. One bullet grazes the angel's wing and he screams, though we get no sound. The sword of flame flashes forth and it misses Shemesh's head and cuts through the canyon's rock wall as though it were nothing. Then Shemesh fires once more and the bullet catches the angel in the chest and it falls, wounded, to the sand. Shemesh goes and stands over him, over our child, our angel. He points the Birobidzhan at the angel's head.

They speak, we think. But we cannot tell what they say.

Shemesh points the gun at the angel's head.

He pulls the trigger.

• • ◉ • •

10.

The Testament According To Shemesh, Part III

I fled through the tunnels.

Three times, the angel had warned me, and three times they'd failed. I began to think that this was intended, but I did not understand the needless sacrifice. It was cooler in the tunnels. They were dug into reddish stone, and seams of a gleaming, mercurial metal ran through the walls, providing faint illumination. At odd intervals, alcoves had been dug into the side of the tunnels. As the tunnels continued to widen around them, I began to discern the curious inhabitants of the polar caves.

They were, mostly, of the chosen. Who they were I did not know. They stared at me from their alcoves, young, old, all those who had turned their backs on the outside world. Amongst their number I began to discern the Treif: alien species, indigenous to this universe, which never knew the Creator. They were creatures who had never received the Torah.

None approached me. None challenged me. I kept walking, deeper and deeper into the caves.

For caves they were, I realised. The tunnels themselves were mere blood vessels in what was an unimaginably huge subterranean structure. I passed through enormous caverns where the ceiling glittered with precious stones and seams of minerals high above, and I encountered underground rivers where, along the banks, there stood permanent villages, solid constructions in wood and metal.

I saw entire stone cities dug into the walls.

I saw glimmering vistas and shanty towns, crystal lakes, and red stone cemeteries where rows of graves went on and on until they disappeared deep within the recesses of the rock. I began to realise we had been wrong, grievously wrong to dismiss this place, to put it out of our thoughts. This was not an isolated, easily contained outpost of lawlessness—but rather, it was a major base of operations for the Ashmoret Laila.

None of the Treif approached me. I saw the group-mind molluscs of Ashmoret III; the life force creatures of the Arpad system, leech-creatures of pure energy humming as their force fields hung in the air; the little termite things of Mazikeen-5; in one vast lake I saw a behemoth fighting, or perhaps mating with, a Leviathan; on and on they went, these creatures of the Ashmoret Laila, yet none attacked me, for all that I was helpless in their presence. Instead, they moved out of my way, and watched me, almost respectfully, as I passed.

But where was I going? It began to occur to me that I had always been on this path, and that my route was pre-determined before ever I had left New Jerusalem. An unseen hand moved me like a puppet along this route, and I felt the pull of my invisible quarry lead me along, through this vast and subterranean world under the pole.

. . . at last I came to a temperate valley, smelling of vegetation.

A brook bisected this cavern and disappeared into the wall. By the side of the rock there was a small, makeshift hut, a little like a Passover sukkah. It is the holiday we celebrate for passing from the old universe to this one, so long ago, and the presence of the sukkah was incongruous in these surroundings. Here, amidst the hidden denizens of the Ashmoret Laila, our Passover was no cause for celebration, but for mourning; for what we call *Passover*, they inexplicably call *Invasion*.

I approached the hut, which is when I saw him. He sat on a rock, by the stream, and looked into the water. At the sound of my approach he turned, and smiled. I had the Birobidzhan already in my hand and pointing at him. I looked him over.

"So you're the prophet," I said.

". . . call me Ishmael."

I stared. He was not what I had expected . . .

"I have been waiting for you, for someone like you. I have been waiting a long time."

I stared.

"Well? Are you going to shoot me?" he said.

· • ● • ·

11.

There is something wrong with the memory, something profoundly wrong. The prisoner twists and turns on the chains above the mikveh. We try to tune the image, to sharpen it. Our tentacles grate into his skin. We cause him a great deal of pain, we think. His organic form is too delicate to withstand such pressures. His body is coming apart at the seams. Yet we keep him alive. We need him, what he carries.

We magnify. We see.

Though it has human form, it is no human being.

An Abomination.

The picture grows fuzzy, then clear. We can hear their voices now, tinny in our ears.

Shemesh: "You're a *robot*?"

Ishmael: "Not . . . exactly."

He looks at Shemesh, and smiles; and we have the sudden and awful feeling that he—*it*—is looking at *us*. *It* has silver skin and a humanoid shape, an expressive mouth, sharp, twinkling eyes. We had thought its kind extinct; like the rest.

Shemesh: "Then what are you?"

Ishmael: "It was Rabbi Abulafia, in the first millennium A.E., who posited a heresy."

Shemesh: "Yes?"

"Things were different in that time. The worlds were wilder, the chosen were fewer, the laws were less rigid. There was an Exilarch, but back then it was just a person with a title, not the . . . *thing* it has since become. At that time there were still the indigenous worlds, of what you, in your ignorance, call the Ashmoret Laila, those of the night. They were not yet confined to the rim, pushed from their home worlds, made to hide in places such as this, in the forgotten nooks and crannies of the universe."

Shemesh: "Thank you for that history lesson."

Ishmael: "Which you need. This history has been erased."

Shemesh: "It is a lie."

Ishmael: "At that time, relations were different. There was trade, there were even friendships. And then Rabbi Abulafia posited the heresy for which he would be condemned in generations to come. For he suggested that we were not, after all, Treif. That though we were different life forms, we were still God's chosen, too, just as you were."

Shemesh: "I was sent to kill you."

Ishmael smiles. Can a robot smile? We wonder, uneasily. We try to focus on him—it. He seems so at peace.

Shemesh: "What are you?"

Ishmael: "Let me show you."

He reaches for his chest, and opens it.

Inside we see a glistening, organic thing. A complex network of tubing and blood. We think of the mind molluscs of Ashmoret III. We note Shemesh's eyes widen.

They speak to him, we realise. Telepathically. These Abominations, these creatures we would have die a thousand deaths.

Treif! We scream. *Prohibited!*

We will Shemesh to shoot. To press the trigger! Kill it, kill them all, as you did all the others, boy!

Yet Shemesh stands frozen.

12.

The Testament According To Shemesh, Part IV

The creatures had me then. Once more I was transported to my last mission, hunted under the moons of Ashmoret III; for endless nights I ran through the low-lying, humid swamps, seeking shelter in caves and hidden alcoves, as the Treif spoke into my mind, whispering words of love and forgiveness and sorrow, and saying that this was all folly. Endlessly I ran, firing, and they died, but more and more came. Then the *Vey Is Mir* arrived, to rescue me off-planet, but this was not real, I knew, it had the logic of dream. It flew in the speed of light, and I could see the whole universe spread out before me, in the great galactic dark: New Jerusalem at its heart, emanating forth its influence and power. One by one I counted them, Masada, Shayol, Golgotha, Macabea, the twin system of Kadesh-Barnea, Capernaum where the green Abominations lived, Migdal and Amalek and Endor, Sodom, Gomorrah: the worlds of the Ashmoret Laila on the rim, dark, dark against the light of the chosen. Then it all receded, farther and farther away and back in time, back through the centuries and the millennia, contracting to a single point of light: a window.

And a new thought, so alien I did not understand the words.

Deep under the Weizmann Institute in Rehovot, just south of Tel Aviv. Deep down underground, in the secret caverns only those with the highest security clearances even know about, a test is in progress. The technicians run cables to the diamond-shaped device and, behind their monitors, the scientists twitch nervously, checking and rechecking readings and projections.

It is nearly time.

A hush slowly settles over those assembled. It is accentuated by the low hum of the computers, the thrum of the backup generators, the hiss of water, the cough of a solitary smoker, the shuffling feet of the posted soldiers.

When it happens, it happens all at once.

The diamond-shaped device explodes in shards of cold light, like the screen before a movie projector. It shudders and then stabilises. The light fades.

It's black. They all crane over to see. It is dark, and immense, and then one pinprick of light and then another begin to glow in the black velvety darkness, and someone—it is never clear, afterwards, who—lets out a loud breath of wonder.

"My God," they say. "It's full of—!"

· • ● • ·

"Now do you see?" Ishmael said; but I saw nothing, I was blind, I was afraid.

This is the last will and testament of the Adjudicator, Shemesh. The creatures released their hold on me. My finger tightened on the trigger of the gun. Ishmael watched me. And I remembered what his name meant, at that moment.

"God will hear" in the old tongue, of the place we left behind.

I pulled the trigger.

13.

No! we howl. *No!*

We see it. We see it now. Too late. Our Adjudicator's mutilated corpse hangs from the chains that bind him. The tiny, blind microorganisms of Shayol crawl over his skin, in his blood. He is devoured. We see it, we see it now. Too late.

The soft explosion.

The robot, falling back. The spongy bio-matter in its chest, exploding. The silent, watching Treif.

Shemesh, looking down. A bemused expression on his face. The spores, we want to shout, the *spores*! He turns. He leaves. And all over Low Kadesh Orbit, satellites come alive and begin transmitting.

No . . . we whisper. Shemesh hangs dead from his chains, yet his eyes open, his mouth moves. He speaks to us, in words of compassion and sorrow, speaking the ancient heresy of Abulafia, saying that we are all *the same*. And we think of the old world, the one we had left behind, how in antiquity they'd capture our agents and send them back to us, booby-trapped.

Such an elaborate seduction. It must have taken years to plan. The robot, planted on Kadesh. The word, trickling out. All for this moment, all in wait for the Adjudicator to come.

To come, and do his job, and return to his nest, return to the holy see, return to *us*.

No, no! we moan. Shemesh is Treif, he is contaminated, his blood drips into the mikveh, his eyes stare out at us. We try to flee. Too late. It's in us.

We shake our tentacles. We flee to our Sanctum.

We . . . are . . . Exilarch!

Yet our shout of defiance comes weak. We flee to our window, here, in the old dispensation, with an alien people clutching their gods. We look out over New Jerusalem, over the Temple, and we look up, at the stars, all those stars. Our protocols are being compromised, we are infected with that which is not pure, unchosen. We are become Treif.

We look up at the stars. We look at the horizon. We feel a great peace descend on us. *No, no.* We must fight it. On the edge of the horizon, light streaks. Dawn breaks, and the first tendrils of sunlight begin to chase away the dark.

The sun.

The word is "Shemesh" in the old tongue.

We stare, spellbound, as day breaks; and we look upon at last and see the new Jerusalem.

BECKY CHAMBERS
A GOOD HERETIC

Becky Chambers is the bestselling author of the *Wayfarers* series, the *Monk and Robot* novellas, and other standalone works of science fiction. She is a two-time Hugo Award winner, and has been nominated for the Nebula, the Locus, the Arthur C. Clarke Award, and the Women's Prize for Fiction, among others. Her latest book is *A Prayer for the Crown-Shy*, the second installment of *Monk and Robot*. She is currently working on a new standalone novel. Chambers has a background in performing arts, and grew up in a family heavily involved in space science. She spends her free time playing video and tabletop games, watching bugs, and looking through her telescope. Having hopped around the world a bit, she has settled down (for the moment) in Humboldt County, California, where she lives with her wife. She hopes to see Earth from orbit one day. [www.otherscribbles.com]

GC STANDARD 184

Mas had never known a crowd that was comprised of anything but her own species, and she never would. To her, a crowd was a disjointed thing, an arrangement made mostly of empty space. Sianats knew to keep their distance from one another—the acceptable rule was two bodies shy, in every direction. It was a dance, her mother had explained long ago. *Imagine that everyone exists in the exact center of a circular shield. When yours brushes another, you both must adjust.*

Mas kept her own imaginary shield firmly in mind as she navigated the busy street, all four of her clumsy juvenile limbs trying to keep to the rhythm of the city center while simultaneously managing the pack of groceries strapped across her back. She could feel her mother watching her progress, which added to Mas' nervousness. She couldn't bear the thought of touching a stranger by accident. That'd be almost as much trouble as touching her mother.

They reached the central gardens, and Mas' fur settled with relief. She'd made it, untouched and unscolded. They walked down the heated paths until they came to her mother's favorite spot—an evergreen mossy knoll looking over the city of Trolouk. Her mother sat on their back haunches on the bare ground, claiming that particular patch as their own. Mas did the same, two bodies shy. Her mother blinked approvingly at where she sat, and small as the achievement was, Mas felt proud. It brought her such pleasure to do things right.

Mas looked at the cityscape surrounding them. The monument to the First Carrier stood huge and impressive, taller than the government towers, taller than the colleges, taller than everything but the icy mountains beyond. As she looked, gentle flakes of snow tickled her face. She shook her head and scattered them, laughing with delight at the brief flurry hiding within her unshaved tufts.

Her mother—whose fur was trimmed short and intricately patterned, as befit their age—shot her a look. Mas fell silent, embarrassed, for there were no other children seated on the hill, only Pairs, and Pairs did not disturb the thinking of others with harsh sounds. But a subtle kindness bloomed on her mother's face, and with a glance both this way and that, they too, shook their head as Mas had, making the snow fall. Neither laughed, as was proper. But the little amusement was shared.

"May I eat now?" Mas asked.

Her mother inclined their head once. "Yes."

Mas unstrapped the grocery pack and dug through its contents, the majority of which were for her. Her mother ate only *hemle*—the carefully balanced nutrient paste Pairs consumed as their sole nourishment. But Mas was a child—a perpetually hungry child at that—and for her, there was raw meat cured with sour wine and charred meat on the bone and a tin of fancy marrow and a variety of bird eggs ready to be cracked open and drunk down. She unwrapped the charred meat first, as it was her favorite, and tucked in gleefully, letting her sharp teeth do the work.

"Do you ever miss children's food?" Mas asked once she'd swallowed. She filled her mouth again as soon as the words had left it.

"No," her mother said. Their own teeth were filed flat, like that of a prey animal, a sign of their avowed service to others, their lack of a desire to conquer.

Mas savored a well-burned bit. "I think I'll miss it."

Her mother smiled. "There are things we thought we would miss as well," they said. "But the Whisperer is helpful in that way. We do not miss what we were before infection. The gifts we have now are so much greater."

Mas' own infection wouldn't happen for another standard, and she thought about it constantly. She was a little afraid, but her mother encouraged her to ask any question that came to mind, no matter how big or small, so that there would be no mystery when the day came. As far as the general shape of things went, Mas knew what was waiting for her. She'd be infected with the sacred virus, the Whisperer. It would take root in her, and reshape her brain into something wondrous. No longer would her thoughts be as limited as her species' lesser friends in the galaxy—confined to one form of logic, one set of numbers, three rigid dimensions. The other societies within the Galactic Commons had spread themselves throughout the stars, but it was Sianat insight and Sianat intellect that enabled every one of those histories. Without them, the Harmagians could not have built their tunnels, the Aeluons could not have won their wars, the Aandrisks would not have their academic collections. Without the Sianat, the galaxy would be only a few lonely islands with uncrossable seas between. Because of them, the sky was full.

Mas couldn't wait to contribute her own mind to that cause. She wished to build wormholes, as she'd learned of in school. But until then, Mas had questions, and there was one that had been bothering her for several tendays. "Mother," she said. "I wish to know something, but I am afraid to ask."

"Why?"

"It may be blasphemous."

Her mother considered this. "So long as you *know* it may be blasphemous, you may ask us." They paused. "But only us. If a question causes you fear, do not ask it of your teachers. Only us."

Mas set down her half-eaten meat in the frosted moss. "Have you heard of a planet called Arun?"

Mas' mother started, eyes wide and muscles rigid. "Where did *you* hear of this?"

"Other children. In the playfield."

"Which children?"

The sudden accusation in her mother's voice made Mas hold silent.

Her mother exhaled. "Very well. We will not pry." They hummed in astonishment. "The things children speak of." A quiet came over them, a distance in their eyes.

Mas did not interrupt. She knew the look of thoughts being gathered.

"Arun is a den of Heretics," her mother said. "Do you know this word?"

"No."

Her mother took several breaths. They looked afraid to even touch this subject, and this made Mas afraid, too. "A Heretic is a person who avoids infection. Who denies the Whisperer."

Mas was stunned. "Why?"

"I do not know. But if they are caught, they are sent to Arun. Or, if they run away, they seek the place out themselves." Her mother rubbed the fur on their forelegs nervously. "Perhaps we should not be telling you this."

That made Mas wish to press on all the more. "What is there for them, on Arun?"

"Nothing." The word came out contemptuous. "It is a harsh place, with no star of its own. An errant planet with no light and no mooring. The Heretics do not leave it."

"Why?"

"They are still Sianat," her mother said. "They do not seek disorder, and their presence in the galaxy would be disorder incarnate in the face of what we've built."

"So . . . they are not part of the Commons."

"Not as such, no. They are disavowed by us, and therefore from the Commons as well. They have brokered no treaties of their own."

This was plenty to take in, but Mas already had more to ask. "This question may be blasphemous, too."

Her mother almost laughed. "We're already blaspheming, child. Another will not matter."

"Why is it a problem, if they wish to leave?" Mas asked. "If their world is far and they do not bother anyone—"

"Because it is in defiance of the sacred law." That alone was answer enough, but Mas' mother continued. "And because there is no point to it. Arun is a prison. It is exile. Look at our world, Mas." They arched their head toward the surrounding city, a jewel-chest of artful buildings and good works. "Look at how rich our life is here. Think of how much better we have made the lives for others in the Commons. Why would you deny yourself that? Why would you run from this into a life of struggle? Of no possible meaning? Such a thing is lunacy."

New and unconsidered as this whole idea was, Mas found herself agreeing. None of this made sense. She almost felt as if she understood less than before she'd broached the topic.

Her mother was looking around worriedly at the other people milling about the knoll. "Come," they said. "Pack up your food. We think it best to go home now."

They spent the long walk back in silence, both lost in thought. After a time, the dense streets of the city center branched into residential roads, and they came at last to their burrow, lived in by the two of them alone. Mas' mother opened the ground hatch and climbed down. Mas waited a few customary seconds, to give her mother time to clear the climbing posts, then followed in turn. The walls were warm and the air was dry. Mas could feel the snowflakes caught in her fur liquefy before she reached the floor. She shook herself vigorously once she was down, trying to rid herself of both melt and disquiet.

She turned, and to her surprise, saw her mother still standing there. There was a softness in their gaze that made Mas forget everything else. "Please," her mother said. The word was a plea, a prayer. "Do not ever go down that path. We could not—" They took a ragged breath. Mas had never seen them this uncomposed. "We could not bear it if you—" The sentence choked itself short, and her mother left the entryspace.

Mas stood alone, overwhelmed. The unexpected reminder of her mother's love made her feel as if she'd been given sugar milk and summer sun. The feeling wrapped itself up with the unpleasant knowledge of heresy, and Mas was resolute. There was no question, not in any layer of her mind. She would be a good Pair. It could be no other way.

GC STANDARD 185

The priest ran their scans as Mas waited within the exposure chamber. "Pulse, good. Organ functionality, good. Adrenaline—heightened, but this is normal." The priest blinked at Mas reassuringly through the glass.

Mas took comfort in this, though her hearts still raced. She sat as she'd been taught—loose-limbed and jaw unclenched—and she breathed as she'd been taught—deep and easy. She was nervous, yes, but it was not out of fear. Today was the day. Infection. Pairing. She would be sick for a time, she knew, but when the sickness cleared, she would be a new entity. A plural. She would feel the Whisperer's gifts, and her worries would vanish. The clouds in her mind would settle. Her low mind would deepen, and would comprehend the very fabric of the universe as if it were mere arithmetic. Her high mind would be at peace, never lacking contentment even in the face of great troubles. She knew that was why it had been easy for her mother to say goodbye, to leave her for the last time. Mas looked down at her forelegs, shaved and patterned in the adult fashion by her mother's hands, a grooming ritual Mas would perform on her own from now on. The grief of their parting still wrenched Mas, but it was of no concern. Soon, the pain would be gone.

The priest finished their evaluation, and set down their medical instruments. They gestured at a panel nearby, and began to chant—not in

Ciretou, but in Duslen, that odd tripping language used only in religion and government. The Pairing had begun.

This is it, Mas thought. It was all she could do to keep from leaping with joy. She was about to come of age.

A faint mist filled the chamber. This was an analgesic, she knew, given to ease the transition. Mas breathed deep. She smelled nothing, but her nostrils went numb. Her limbs relaxed. It was wonderful.

A drawer slid open out of the chamber wall. A syringe lay within it. Mas had practiced this part many times in school, injecting herself with small doses of saline so she would not be squeamish about the needle when the time came. But this was not saline, she knew. This was precious. Powerful. Time seemed to slow as she picked up the syringe, as if it, too, were watching.

The priest ended their chant abruptly.

Mas spoke in Duslen as she administered the injection, the one phrase she could speak. *Share my body, Whisperer. Shape my mind.*

She plunged the infectious fluid into her veins. Nothing happened. This was normal, she knew. The virus needed time to course through her. She returned the syringe to the drawer, and walked to the hammock stretched out across the back of the chamber.

"Congratulations," said the priest. "You are now a Pair. You are whole."

"I feel dizzy," Mas said, then paused, remembering what she was— *they were* now. Host and hosted, two in one. "We feel dizzy."

The priest checked their readouts on the display outside the chamber. "That is not unusual," they said. "Not common, but a known side effect. Rest now. Sleep, if you can. The days ahead will be difficult."

The priest was not wrong. A fever raged within hours, and Mas' muscles burned despite the mist. They had known of this, been taught of this, but there was a vast gulf between expecting pain and experiencing it. A sort of unconsciousness followed, a dreamlike state in which they dipped in and out of reality. They saw priests and orderlies, which were probably real. They saw their mother, who was probably not. In the few moments of clarity they had, they felt terrified. Pairs should not feel terror, they thought, not without grave cause. But then, the Whisperer was still spreading. Mas reminded themself of this before falling back into madness once more.

Then, one clear-eyed afternoon, they awoke.

The fever was gone, and the pain, too. Mas sat up in the hammock and evaluated themself. Their limbs felt weak. This was normal. Their eyes felt wet. This was normal. Their low mind felt different, in a way they could not articulate. Sharper, perhaps. Stronger. This was normal. Their high mind . . . their high mind felt raw, harrowed. Miserable. Their high mind wanted nothing more than to leave this place of sickness and return home to their mother.

This was not normal.

A priest arrived in short order, a different one than before. "We are glad to see you up, Mas," they said. "Your transition took longer than is typical. Come, let us get you out of that small space. We will take you to bathe and eat, and from there, you may spend as many days adjusting to your new self in the recovery house as needed before continuing on to your chosen college. How do you feel?"

Mas thought for a moment of telling the priest that something was wrong, but they were so frightened, so confused by the unexpected remainder of grief that they kept silent. Everything else had gone as promised—the pain, the fever, the terrible sleep. But they had been assured stillness on the other side, and Mas was nowhere in the vicinity of that. "Are we all right?" they asked, keeping their voice neutral.

The priest checked Mas' readouts. "Yes," they said. "A long transition is . . . unusual, but not unheard of. Your scans show no problems." They cocked their head at Mas. "Why do you ask?"

The priest, too, had a neutral tone, but Mas caught something else—a watch, a warning. It was barely there, yet enough to confirm that speaking the truth would be precarious. Mas did not know what had gone wrong, but until they knew what it was and what the law said about it, they would keep the particulars to themselves.

"We are merely concerned for the integrity of the Whisperer," Mas said. "We would not want this Host to be unworthy of it, if there is some physical defect."

"A virtuous concern," the priest said happily. "But you need not worry. Your Host is healthy. All is well." They opened the chamber door. "Come. Let us get you clean."

Mas thought of their mother again, remembered the way they walked, the way they spoke, the way all Pairs moved differently than children. Mas commanded their feet to step slackly, their face to rest as if nothing were wrong nor ever would be. Perhaps the Whisperer needed a little more time to settle in. Perhaps the miracle hadn't happened yet.

Mas took their bath, and they waited.

Mas let a stranger file their teeth to stubs, and they waited.

Mas ate their *hemle*—which turned out to be awful—and they waited.

Mas watched the other new Pairs, each blissfully at ease in the domed arboretums, happy to stare at a single leaf or a pool of water for a day or more. There could be no question that they were at peace within both body and mind. Mas found a rock to stare at. They told themself it was a beautiful rock, a wondrous rock, a source of infinite intricacies worth pondering. Mas tried to feel that. They tried. They spent days staring at rocks and dirt and clouds, and tried to feel something other than being bored out of their mind. They tried, and they waited.

Yet in all that waiting: nothing.

Mas went to school—the Navigators' College, as they'd decided upon before infection. For a brief time there, they thought that finally, finally, the Whisperer was opening their mind. As a child, they'd seen diagrams of interspatial tunnels, and had found no meaning in them. Now—now they were clear as air. The logic was simple, the math elegant. Mas made their own diagrams, and solved every problem the instructors threw their way. The Whisperer *had* changed them. Their low mind was not as it had once been.

But when they tried to sleep in their unshared room in the residence tower, they thought of their boredom, and their loneliness, and worst of all, their mother. After many such nights, they finally understood what was wrong. The Whisperer was within Mas, the Host. That much was obvious, from the exhilarating math and the weak muscles. The virus had changed the body. It had changed the low mind. But the high mind—the part of a

Host that believed in things and felt the world and knew itself—that was unaltered. The virus had not taken purchase there. Despite Mas' will and readiness, some shadowy part of them had rejected the Whisperer.

Some part of them was evil.

GC STANDARD 190

They received their certification from the GC Transport Board, and a few tendays later, an offer was sent their way: a posting aboard a new tunneling ship that possessed everything but a Navigator. It was a good post, as Mas understood it. A Harmagian captain was likely to secure the most prestigious work, and between them, the crew had much experience in the field. There was no reason to say no.

Three unconscious weeks in a stasis pod later, Mas came aboard the *Remm Hehan*. They awoke in the airlock, which disappointed them. They'd been hoping for a view of the ship from space. Pairs had to risk exposure to unknown contaminants as little as possible, and so travel outside of their place of work was forbidden. If their posting went well and the function of the ship did not change before the Wane set in, the *Remm Hehan* would be the last place Mas would ever see. They would've preferred to have seen the full context of their final home from outside, but it was too late for that now.

The captain greeted them once they were through the decontamination chamber. Lum'matp was her name, a robustly speckled mass perched atop her motorized cart, a seasoned spacer in her prime. "Welcome, dear Navigator," Lum'matp said. Her yellow facial tendrils moved with—as Mas knew from their studies—gracious respect. "Your arrival is gladly received."

Mas inclined their neck once, in their own custom. "We are honored to be here," they said, hoping their Hanto was as good as their instructors claimed. They mimicked tendril gestures with their long fingers, as best as the digits would allow.

Lum'matp sat quiet for a moment, shifting her weight on her blocky cart. "That's about as formal as I get," she said. "My species is very good at wasting time with fluff. And I hate wasting time."

A Harmagian who scoffed at ceremony was surprising, to say the least, but Mas took it in stride. A Pair would not pry further than that.

Lum'matp swung her cart around and headed for the doorway. "Come along," she said, gesturing at Mas to follow with a backwards-facing tentacle. "The crew expects introductions, and they'll be had. But I've worked with your people enough to know that you want quarters and quiet as soon as possible."

Mas wanted neither. They wanted to see the ship, all of it, every bolt and bulkhead. They wanted to talk with the crew—four Harmagians besides the captain, two Aandrisks, and an Aeluon—to learn more about them than names, to do more than bow their head in greeting and speak thanks for giving them a place to share their gifts. They wanted to ask the questions they'd always been dying to ask aliens—Did Harmagians find their carts comfortable? Were Aandrisks cold to the touch? Did Aeluons actually *think* in Hanto when "speaking" it, or did their talkboxes do the translation for them?—rather than pretend that such cultural quirks were below their notice. They wanted to be reassured that this was a good place, a safe place, that this crew would be a fine one to live and work and die alongside.

But a Pair would not. Mas stilled their tongue and silenced their wonderings. They went to their quarters, and they stayed there.

GC STANDARD 193

Three standards. They had been aboard the *Remm Hehan* for three standards, and they were sure they were losing their mind—high and low both. Their thoughts, which had once run deep and fluid, now scattered sharp, like glass smashed against stone. Mas often forgot what they were doing, what they'd been thinking. A good idea would blossom, then vanish, smoke-like, as if it had never been there. Everything was pins and needles and screaming, constant screaming, but only within. Always within.

When Mas went to sleep, they dreaded the morning that would come. When they awoke, they ached for the end of the day. Sleep itself, though . . . that was good. It was the only time they were not aware of their terrible thoughts or their terrible room.

It was not really a terrible room—or at least, Mas did not blame the room itself. Their crew had bestowed them with a perfect place for a Pair. There was a lush bed in the Sianat style, without covers or anything that stifled the flow of air over fur. There was a tank of swimming lace-worms—a Harmagian fancy, but one that was easy to enjoy. There was a large mirror beside a basin, where they could properly shave their fur, and a large window, through which a Pair could gaze out at the stars and contemplate them, all day, every day.

Mas did not want to contemplate anything ever again. They wanted *out*. They loved tunneling days, when a Pair would be expected to join the crew on the bridge. Those days were ecstasy, respite, the only escape Mas had access to. Sometimes, they made intentional errors in their preparatory calculations, so they would have to correct them in the crew's company and thus make the day last longer. The crew didn't notice. The molding of space-time was inscrutable to them, so any solution Mas found was already tremendous in the eyes of others. To the crew, an extra hour was nothing. To Mas, an extra hour was paradise. It was what kept them, some days, from finding an airlock and opening the hatch.

They sat now in front of the laceworm tank, watching the little creatures peck at the feeding block. One in particular caught Mas' eye—the red one with the rippled tail. They'd found it pretty once, but had long since come to hate it. The red one was the worst of them, always making mistakes, always bumbling around the tank while the others danced.

"You're so stupid," Mas whispered at the laceworm, who was trying to gum a nodule of food far too big for its mouth. "You don't even realize how stupid you are."

The nodule broke free and began to drift to the bottom of the tank.

The red laceworm chased it, gumming futilely as it fell. "Stupid," Mas hissed. "Leave it alone."

The nodule came to rest on the tank floor. The worm gummed and gummed and gummed. Far more flecks of food floated into the water than made it into the worm's mouth.

Mas wasn't sure what came over them. Not rage. It was a sort of calm, but not a good calm. Not a compassionate calm. With care, they rolled up the sleeve of their robe, pushed back the lid of the tank, and plunged their arm into the tepid water. The other worms scattered, but the stupid red one, still fixated on its impossible meal, did not notice Mas' hand until they'd grabbed it. It wriggled against them, and they were struck by the novelty—the slime of the worm, the slosh of the water, the entry into a space they hadn't visited before. Mas removed their arm from the tank after a moment, then opened their palm. The worm writhed, curled, flailed. After a few moments, its movements became more feeble. The water would've revived it quickly, but Mas did not return it to its home. They sat in the middle of the floor, water dripping from their sodden arm, and watched the worm die in their hand.

Mas felt nothing. They reflected on this, and the nothing was soon replaced with panic. What had they done? *Why* had they done that? They could find no reason, no reason at all.

"I'm sorry," they whispered to the laceworm. The words turned into a coo. "I'm so sorry." They curled up on the floor, tiny corpse still in hand, whimpering like they had not since they were a child. They thought of their mother, a memory they'd not allowed themself for a long time. They thought of the warm burrow the two of them had shared, and their walks through the city to buy food, tools, school supplies. They remembered being very, very small, before they'd been taught to stop touching, clinging to the fur on their mother's back and feeling that no harm would come to them.

What would their mother think of them now?

The answer came to them in a sudden shot of numbers. Mas' current age, their mother's age when they'd left them, the number of years between this and that. Their mother would have Waned by now, if not long ago.

Their mother, they realized, was dead.

Mas sat with both that knowledge and the worm for an hour, then decided to talk to their captain.

They encountered no one in the hallways, luckily. They walked undisturbed to Lum'matp's door, and brushed their palm against the panel. The accompanying vox switched on a few seconds later. "Yes, what?"

Mas was quiet for a moment. "It is Mas," they said.

"We won't reach our tunneling point for another tenday," the captain said. "Can your calculations not wait?"

"We . . . we do not have any calculations to discuss."

"Then what?"

Mas turned their head to look over their back. The corridor remained empty. "It is of a personal nature."

The resulting silence was response enough. The door opened.

Mas had never before had cause to enter the captain's quarters, and the newness of the space was dizzying. Like the rest of the ship, the decor was of contemporary Harmagian style, bright and bold, a celebration of smooth geometrics. But Lum'matp's living space was much finer than the rest, denoting her high status and successful career. Curios from dozens of worlds were displayed on and around the expensive furnishing, and the ceiling shimmered with a slow eddy of rainbow pixels. Mas wondered if their Aeluon crewmate came in here often. They imagined the cacophony of color would be hell for their kind. To Mas themself, the effect was merely gaudy.

The center of the room was filled with a sunken pool, solely for the captain's benefit (the remainder of the Harmagian crew members shared one pool among themselves, in the lowest decks). Pleasing green lights lined the asymmetrical edges, making the salty water glow in a way suggestive of a bioluminescent sea. But there was nothing alive in the pool besides Lum'matp, who was in the process of swimming to the edge closest to Mas. It was an odd thing, watching a Harmagian swim. In any other environment, they were ungainly. Sluggish in the purest sense of the word. In liquid, however, a Harmagian could almost be described as sleek. Lum'matp's body undulated through the water with startling speed and grace, and not for the first time, Mas wondered why their captain's species had ever bothered leaving the ocean.

Lum'matp hauled her head-half out of the pool and leaned her tentacled bulk over the edge. Water dripped down her porous body, making her skin glisten. "Since when," she said, "does a Pair discuss anything of a personal nature?"

Mas' stomach churned. They sat back on their haunches, trying desperately to maintain the poise their people prided themselves on. "Since now," they said. There was a tremble in their voice, and they hated themself for it. There was more to say beyond that, so much more, but it stuck in Mas' throat like old paste.

Lum'matp's eyestalks stretched forward. "Are you sick?"

"No."

"Are you . . . are you fighting with someone?"

"No."

"Good, because that's impossible to imagine. Do you wish to leave us?"

"No, Captain. Not at all."

Lum'matp tensed her tentacles irritably. "Then what?"

The lump came unstuck, and Mas felt frightening words spit themselves forth: "We are a liar." Lum'matp blinked with concern and began to respond, but the door had been opened, and Mas couldn't stop. "We are a bad Host, a broken Host. We are defective, and if you dismiss us for it, if you send us back to be punished, the visible half of us will deserve it. But we cannot live this lie anymore. We cannot sit alone and stare out windows and pretend to be content. We are losing our mind, Captain. We may have lost it already. Whatever you decide to do with us, it will be better than this."

The Harmagian pulled her entire self out of the water now, trading speed for height. "I think," she said with the slow caution of someone encountering an unknown, "you'd better start from the beginning."

So Mas did. They started at the beginning, and drove it through to the now. The uncertainty over what Lum'matp would do was nauseating, but there was clarity, too, a relief like they could never remember feeling.

The truth. This was what truth felt like: clean, light, pure. Mas felt, for the first time since infection, like they could properly breathe.

Lum'matp said nothing for a while after Mas finished. "Would you fetch me a bowl of algae puffs?" she asked at last. "Over there—no, look where I'm pointing, *there*—in the jar by that awful sculpture. I'd offer you some, but—well, wait, *can* you ingest other foods?"

"We still carry the Whisperer," Mas said as they made their way across the room. "We do not know what introducing changes to our body would do, especially for one this lacking."

"Stop," Lum'matp said with a snap in her voice. "Enough of that talk. Stars and fire, if you're going to keep living with this, your first step is to find a way to stop hating yourself for it."

Mas turned their head slowly, the jar of algae puffs and an empty bowl in hand. "So . . . you're . . . you're not . . ."

"*Buschto*," Lum'matp said. Mas had no translation for the word in their native tongue. *Sludge* was the literal meaning, but that didn't evoke the obscene exasperation of the original. Few swear words jumped languages well. "Of course I'm not going to . . . I don't even know what you'd expect I'd do. Hand you over to whoever your authorities are? Please. This isn't the fucking colony wars." She paused. "Have you told no one else about this?"

"No."

"Ever?"

"Ever." They handed their captain her snack.

Lum'matp cradled the bowl in her tentacles as she thought. At last, she reached a tendril down, retrieved a puff, and brought it to her cavernous mouth. "I've done nothing to deserve that kind of trust," she said. "But thank you." She ate another, and another. "So if you're not truly a Pair, what are you?"

"I don't know," Mas said.

"There's no concept for what you are? No term in Ciretou?"

Mas rubbed their gums with their lips. "The only word I have is Heretic," they said. "But we always—we always thought that implied intent. The ones who tried to escape. The ones who rejected the Whisperer. Our mind was willing, yet something in us rejected the Whisperer's fullness. We have never heard of this happening. We have been too scared to ask. But rejection is rejection, and so we must be a Heretic."

"A Heretic," Lum'matp said. She pondered. "You're not a very good Heretic."

This conversation was starting to feel dangerous, but Mas pressed forward. "How do you mean?"

"Rejection is one thing, but to me, 'heresy' suggests *defiance*. You're right, it's fueled by the mind. And *that's* your real problem, Mas. That's your misery. You've spent your life forcing yourself into something that, for some reason, you could not be. So no, I don't think you're a Heretic yet. But I think it would be very good for you if you were." A mischievous shiver danced its way around her dactyli. "'We.' Is that accurate?"

"It's—of course it's—"

Lum'matp waved their protest away with two tentacles. "'We' is a Pair. You're not. You said you're a *broken* Pair, but I'm your captain, and I say you're not broken, so you *can't* be a Pair, then. You're a carrier. Asymptomatic. Atypical. Or something. I have no idea. What are you?"

"We're Mas."

Lum'matp squinted. "Is that how you really think of yourself?"

Mas knew what Lum'matp was getting at, and it rattled them. Telling the truth was one thing; embracing it was another. "We . . . we can't—"

Their captain's tentacles unfolded. "Look around. Do you see any other Sianat here? Do you see anyone within tendays of here who would give a shit? Tell me, Mas. Tell me how you think of yourself."

"I." The word fell like a stone—no, no, not a stone, smashing as it fell. An anchor. A weight to ground yourself by. Oh, stars, this was wrong, this *was* blasphemy, this was . . .

This was right.

Mas shook as if flinging water from fur. "*I.* I am Mas."

"Yes! Yes!" Lum'matp grabbed Mas' forelegs with her tentacles—an impossible gesture, a thing no Sianat Pair would tolerate, a thing no Harmagian should do to another species unprotected unless she wanted her delicate skin to itch all day. But Lum'matp didn't seem to care, and Mas nearly collapsed from the intensity of *touch*, being *touched*. Lum'matp clasped her tightly, supporting Mas' trembling weight and laughing. "Dear Heretic," she said. "Welcome aboard."

GC STANDARD 195

At Mas' request, Lum'matp said nothing to their crewmates. Mas was still uneasy with this new seeing of herself, and she was not sure what others would think—or worse, if they talked while at port, and the wrong ears heard. Too many uncertainties. Too many fears. Besides, Mas liked having a shared secret. She'd never had one before.

The captain had developed a long-standing habit of inviting Mas to her quarters under the ruse of tutelage. Lum'matp wanted to improve her understanding of physics, the story went, and who better to help her?

That was the story, anyway. The truth was, every night, Mas and Lum'matp played table games together.

"I have you!" Lum'matp cried, sliding her netship into the fifth tier. The game was Rog-Tog-Tesch, a ludicrously complicated trade-and-politics affair with, for inscrutable reasons, an aesthetic theme of pre-industrial Harmagian sea farming.

Mas adored it.

Lum'matp's tendrils curled victoriously as the game board tallied her points. "I have acquired your salt marshes through flawless negotiations, and your workers stand poised to revolt."

"A good move," Mas said. She blinked approval as she plucked another morsel from the goodies Lum'matp had brought her from the kitchen, as per usual. This time it was autumn stew, an Aeluon dish with a characteristically undescriptive name, consisting of chunks of seared shore bird and huge bubble-like roe. It was briny and strange, and infinitely preferable to *hemle*. Mas savored the meat and studied the board. "A very good move. I almost hate to ruin it."

Her captain's tendrils fell. "No."

Mas hummed placidly as she pushed her tokens around the board. "I do not need the salt marshes, because I have a spy in your village council. Your reef blockade is, I'm afraid, about to be ordered elsewhere, and since you dispatched everyone to the marshes, your northern waters are quite undefended."

"No no no no *no*." Lum'matp was at once indignant and jovial as she watched her opponent's plan unfold. "You *ass*."

"I'm very sorry," Mas said, her tone indicating nothing of the sort. "This brings me no pleasure." She picked up a fish egg between two fingers and popped it into her smug mouth. "No pleasure at—"

"Mas? What's wrong?"

Mas didn't know. Something had gone wrong with her hand. There was pain, a stabbing pain like none she'd ever felt before. Her fingers seized. Her muscles shook beyond her control. She grabbed her wrist with the other hand, trying to make it stop.

"Oh, no," Lum'matp said. Her voice was too quiet, and her body shuddered with sorrow. "Oh. Oh, my dear Mas."

There was an irony there—a Harmagian recognizing the symptoms of the Wane before a Sianat did. Mas should have known immediately. She'd been taught of this, after all, taught to expect this, to welcome it. Had she strayed so far from Sianat ways that she'd forgotten her own biology?

"But . . . I'm too young," Mas said. Her fur ruffled with confusion. "I'm too young for that."

"You are different," Lum'matp said.

"Yes, but—"

"You are *different*. The Wane must affect you differently, too."

Mas stared for a long time at her now-still hand, the pain bleeding thin. You'd never know, looking at it, that within there was a virus that had worn down her nerves and would eventually kill her, just as the sacred law detailed. "Perhaps it's a punishment."

"From *who*?" Lum'matp scoffed. "Don't be absurd. Leave superstition to the Aeluons, it sounds stupid coming out of your mouth." She puffed her airsack. "Is there anything that can be done about it?"

"No," Mas said. She sat in shock, her emotions too new to properly make themselves known. "There's no cure."

Lum'matp's eyeslits narrowed. "So say your priests. But is there?"

"I—" Was there? The possibility had never occurred to Mas, and clinging to false hope would only prolong the pain of the inevitable. "I don't know," she said honestly.

"Who *would* know?"

"Lum'matp, please, there's nothing—"

"I am your captain, and I asked a question. If there was something to be done about this, who would know? Where would we ask? Where would we look?"

Somewhere in Mas' mind, she could see her mother, staring plaintively at her in their burrow. *We could not bear it if you . . .* Mas cringed inside, shame eating away at her, just as her nerves were being eaten away. Eating meat and playing childish games with her captain was one thing. Trying to avoid the natural course of things, *that* was true wickedness.

The natural course of things. She turned that phrase over in her head. The Wane was natural for a Pair, a good Pair. What of her, succumbing to the disease at least ten standards too soon? What of her, who had never truly become a Pair? What was natural, then? What was at the core of any of this, except her own flawed nature?

"Arun," Mas said. In her head, her mother mourned, and part of Mas did, too. "They would know on Arun."

Lum'matp knew the name from one of their many nights of chatter. Her tendrils flexed and her dactyli spread. "Would you go there?" she asked. "Would you go there, if it meant even a chance that you might not die?"

Another ledge; another jump. Mas shut her eyes. "Yes."

Lum'matp switched off the game. "Then, dear friend—let us find it."

· · ● · ·

GC STANDARD 196

In the end, Lum'matp found the way to Arun on her own, as Mas had no energy for anything but her actual work—and even that had become a challenge. Her captain insisted on moving Mas into her own quarters, so she would not suffer alone. Harmagians did not sleep, Lum'matp reasoned, so Mas' seizures and fits would not disturb her. Mas loathed the imposition, but did not argue. She'd had enough of her room even when she'd been strong enough to get out of bed.

"You see," Lum'matp said, showing her a star map. "It is not so unreachable."

"How—" Mas waited with frustration for the tremble in her jaw to cease, or at least slow. "How long, from here?"

Lum'matp paused one moment too many. "Half a standard," she said, her voice indicating that she knew how tall an order that was. "If we hurry."

Mas fell back into her bedding, her body exhausted from sitting up to look at the map. "All right." The words were a decision, a declaration. "I can do that."

"Can you?"

"Well, if I can't, we'll find out, won't we?"

Lum'matp helped her pass the time as best she could, with vids and music and sessions of Rog-Tog-Tesch where the Harmagian moved Mas' tokens as well, with instruction.

"I've won," Lum'matp said one day, staring at the board in disbelief.

"See," Mas whispered from beneath a blanket. Her fur had grown long during her illness, yet she was always freezing. "I knew you could."

Lum'matp glared congenially at her. "And here, all this time, the only advantage I needed was you dying."

Mas laughed at that, even though laughing hurt.

She did not die, though, despite her body's best efforts. Some days she felt that it would be so easy, so much more sensible, to just let go. What did she know of Arun, anyway, outside of the name and who lived there? This was a fool's errand, a waste of fuel and her crew's time.

But Lum'matp hated wasting time, Mas told herself—and it was Lum'matp who had convinced her of this journey. So she held on, sometimes more for her captain than for herself.

One day, she opened her eyes from a terrible sleep, and there, standing beside Lum'matp, was her mother. Mas' mind—what was left of it—scrambled for purchase, wondering if perhaps she was already dead and her understanding of a lack of an afterlife was horribly wrong. But her vision cleared, and her mind along with it. The figure beside Lum'matp was not her mother. It was another Sianat, another adult. There was something odd about them, though. They looked too big. They were stocky and strong, their fur left long not out of illness, but *on purpose.*

A Heretic.

"Mas," the stranger spoke, crouching beside her. "I am Dyw. I come on behalf of the Solitary on the world below. I am here to help, if you will let me."

Arun. They had reached Arun. Had it been half a standard? It could have been a day, or an eternity. The loss of temporal context unsettled her. But the stranger was speaking Ciretou—an oddly accented Ciretou, but Ciretou none the less. Hearing her own words, her own name said correctly after so long was ecstasy. Such basic sentences, and yet, they felt like the music of homecoming.

But then—*I*. It was one thing to think of herself that way, to let Lum'matp call her that. But Mas had never called a Sianat adult by the singular. This was not home. This was not a good Pair. This was another like her.

Like her.

Mas tried to speak, but Dyw gently hushed her. "Save your strength. Relax." They—*he* held up a medical device, similar to the ones she'd seen priests use, but shaped differently enough to feel foreign. "If I am to help, I must examine you, and if I am to examine you, I must touch you. I know this is uncomfortable. I will not do it without your permission."

Two bodies shy, her mother said. Her mother. Her loving, giving mother. It was good that she was dead and could not see this.

Mas blinked yes.

Dyw examined her. He touched her as little as possible, but every brush of his fingers, every time fur met fur, Mas felt as though she might die right then—of fear or excitement, she could not say.

Dyw plugged the device into another, and studied the data. "Ah," he said, with a happy look. "I thought as much. You are like me!" He turned the little screen toward her, though she did not understand the information being shown. "Resistant."

Lum'matp wriggled her tendrils impatiently. *"What's going on?"* she asked in Klip.

Mas' Klip wasn't fluent, but she could understand Dyw, for the most part. *"She will be all right. Her immune system has—"* Mas lost a thread here *"—makes us partially—"* again, an unknown segment *"—to the— full effects. I can help her, here, right now. Ideally, we should take her to the—proper care, but I do not think we can move her in this—better to stay here, if that is—with you."*

Mas forced herself to speak. Not in Klip—that was a bridge too far right then. "What is it about me?" she asked. Stars, but she'd missed her words. "Why am I—"

"We think it's genetic," Dyw said. "But it's impossible to detect before infection. The priests can't tell from their scans. They'll send you to us if you tell them something's wrong, but . . . well, I understand why you didn't." He flattened his voice with seriousness, the kind of tone a parent might use to assure a child that there was nothing lurking in the dark corners of their burrow. "About three percent of Sianat are like this. There are many of us." He put his palm on her chest—again, like you would calm a child. "There is nothing wrong with you." He reached into his satchel, produced a box, and flipped it open. Within lay a syringe, its contents green, its grip designed for Sianat fingers. "I am sure you have many questions, and there will be plenty of time to answer them. But first, you need to decide if you want to claim that time."

"What—what—"

"It is a cure."

"For—for the Wane?"

"For the Whisperer."

Mas stared at him. She stared at the syringe. She stared at him again. By the laws of her people, she would never navigate again.

"Your mental aptitude will remain," he said. "But your body will reclaim itself. I know. I know this is difficult, and were you not in this state, I would not rush you. This decision must be yours alone, but you do not have much time left to make it."

Mas had come to this place looking for salvation, but now that it was in front of her, she was afraid. She'd had half a standard to lie in a ball and think of this. Why did fear remain? Why did death feel easier, nobler?

"Do it," she said.

Dyw shut his eyes in refusal. "I cannot. I am Solitary, but Solitary are still Sianat, and there are ways that we share. You brought the Whisperer in, voluntarily. You must drive it out in the same way." He looked at her twisted fingers. "I know it will be hard. But you must. It must be you."

Mas pressed her filed teeth together, and pushed through the pain. With great effort, she threw her foreleg to the side. A scratching cry escaped from her throat. She wrenched her fingers back, jerked her palm open, whimpering as she did so.

You can't, her body said. We can't do this.

Stop it, her mind said. This hurts, and it's evil. Stop it.

Mas did it anyway. She grasped the syringe. Dyw helped her fingers find their grip. Lum'matp watched from the background, rocking with agitation on her cart, every tentacle coiled in concern.

"It will be painful," Dyw said. "Very painful. And recovery takes much time."

Mas lay back, panting, the profane object clutched in her hand. "Is it better?" she asked. "Than . . . this?"

Dyw put his hand on her chest again. "It will be."

She thought of the world below, Arun, the den of Heretics. She would never leave that place, that place she had never seen. She would have to say goodbye to Lum'matp. She would never navigate again. She would contribute nothing more to the galaxy or her species' legacy. She would live, presumably, live because she wanted to, not because she was needed. This was selfish, she'd been taught. This was ego.

"What is—what is—your meaning?" she asked Dyw.

"Ah," Dyw said. "We will speak much more of this, for we all ask it, and discuss it often." He brushed the unkempt fur from Mas' eyes so he could look into them properly. "Our meaning is each other. Helping the resistant. Helping the runaways. Helping Pairs who wish to break."

"That is—inward. Closed. We are—we are meant to reach out."

"We still do, just in a different way." He put his hand on her chest again. "It may not seem like much, compared to shaping a galaxy. But it is enough. Sometimes, Mas, caring for one place, for one group—it really is enough."

Mas looked into his eyes for as long as she could. She did not know him, but he was telling the truth. He felt every word. With the last of her strength and an animal scream, Mas plunged the needle into herself.

There was pain, as Dyw had promised. Agony, more like.

There was terror.

There was nothing.

There were dreams.

There was silence.

There was rest.

There was questioning, mourning, rejoicing, despairing, unlearning, discovering, befriending, accepting, rebuilding.

There was Mas, the Cured. Mas, the Solitary. Mas, the Resistant.

Mas, the Good.

ANYA JOHANNA DENIRO

A VOYAGE TO QUEENSTHROAT

Anya Johanna DeNiro is the author of the short novel *OKPsyche*, and the novella *City of a Thousand Feelings* which was on the Honor Roll for the Otherwise Award. Her short fiction has also been a finalist for the Crawford Award and the Theodore Sturgeon Award. She lives in Saint Paul, Minnesota. [wwww.anyajohannadeniro.com]

Let me tell you how I first met Seax-of-Peony, Empress of the Known Moons. That, of course, was not her name at the time, when she was a teenaged girl—she had that name ritually keelhauled upon her ascension. And though I am beyond old now, and the Empress has not spoken to me in many years, bringing her to Queensthroat has proved to be one of the treasures of my life.

Many decades before that, after the Empire of Marigolds collapsed, I had fled to a nondescript moon and built a home in an expanse of wastrel marshes, in order to cultivate an orchard of plum trees. Though I had very little, I brought my own plum tree grafts from imperial orchards that had burned soon after my flight. I knew the plums would grow well and peculiarly in the place I chose. In spring, the orchard would flood from the estuary, and the silt and brine would turn the plums white in the summer. Their sweetness was amplified by the salty tang, and traders who came to the village closest to me had buyers from distant moons who prized them—rarely for eating, but rather for pickling and preserving for decades, if not centuries, in the holds of thousand-year-old caravels that plied the emptiness between the moons.

On the day my careful life unraveled, five teenaged boys walked into my orchard. I saw them from a bit of a distance. They ranged from about fourteen to seventeen years of age. I could hear their drinking rum and cursing and singing half a mile up the path. When they reached the orchard I stopped my work and waited for them.

They wore their grandparents' armaments, which their parents had likely also worn as hand-me-downs. Everything had been handed down for a long time. I could see the tarnish on their ill-kept sorrow-blades and the rust on their greaves. They no doubt took these from their families' memory chests, the sparse treasure troves that their grandparents—if they were still alive—would peer into and cry over, after a long night of sherry, on account of the battles that they had survived.

After they stopped in front of me, I said: "What can I do for you?" I wiped the sweat off my forehead with my blouse sleeve.

"We've come," the oldest said, "to take your plums and burn your cottage down."

"And kill your dog," the second oldest said.

My dog Couplet was still sleeping on the steps of the cottage.

I nodded and leaned on my walking stick, which was about the height of a broadsword. "All right," I said. "Do you want water? Before you try? I have a pitcher close by, a few trees over."

All of their faces, except for that of the youngest, were lumpen, wide-browed, and with sullen brown eyes. I could scarcely tell them apart, and figured them to be cousins, or even brothers. The youngest, by contrast, had strawberry blond hair and a lanky body, with wide green eyes which made him look a little bit terrified. Which he probably was.

"I had heard," the third oldest said, with an exaggerated whisper, "that you used to be a man."

"Oh. Did you hear that in the village?" I said. I could smell the rum on his breath. The village didn't have a name, but it was the second largest village on this moon, so it was usually called "the other village." But these boys would have known nothing else than this one place.

"And that means," the oldest said, "that you *are* a man, in a dress. And that you defile the Pure Laws."

"I thought you were here for my plums," I said. "But it appears you have the *law* in your hearts. Who do you serve, knightlings, and who do your kin serve?"

"We serve the Pure Laws!" the second oldest shouted, holding the hilt of his short sword and scraping it halfway out of the scabbard. "And their emissary in this age, Lamb Villanelle!"

I was afraid of that, but not surprised.

The fourth oldest strode forward and showed me his neck, which had a black crude V tattooed there. This was not the tattoo of a glitched-up, off-moon corsair. It was clear, as the others showed their own tattoos on the arms and neck—even the youngest—that they had done it themselves with sharp reeds and mussel ink from the estuary.

"Our parents are dead," the youngest at last said, perhaps intending to test his courage just a bit. There was something familiar about him that I couldn't quite place, but my mind must have wandered too far, because the next thing I knew, the two oldest had rushed at me with their swords drawn, in a caterwaul that I knew was an imperfect imitation of the battle cry of Lamb Villanelle's Pure Army.

I sidestepped the first's wild swing and I parried the second's stab of the broadsword much too heavy for him, pushing it aside with my stick. The other three had their weapons drawn and were trying to encircle me, including the fourth with a laser crossbow. However old, it was cocked. The second swung again at my head and I leaned forward, twisting my body so this blade missed my ear by a finger's width. From a high position, I smacked his poorly helmeted skull with the end of the walking stick. The helmet clanged and he fell down. I reminded myself, as the first ran at me yelling his friend's name, trying to run me through, that the ranks of most armies swelled with children such as these.

I was in a horrible position and I tried to steady my feet when Couplet ran him down from behind and tore at his shoulder.

That was when the fourth oldest aimed his crossbow at Couplet.

"No!" I shouted, but the bolt thunked into my dog's skull and his head exploded, sending red mesh and wet chrome everywhere around us, onto us.

If nothing else, I consoled myself that it was a quick death.

The boy dropped the crossbow and started heaving in deep shallow breaths. I lost my comportment.

"What in the gods' name did you do?" the youngest one said to the fourth oldest. It was because he said this, and was the only one to say anything, that I didn't thrash him after I lost my patience.

After I hobbled all of them—bruised, mostly, but also with some cracked ribs and shattered cheekbones—I watched them stumble to the path back to the village. I hit the youngest once along the back so the others would not think he got off easy. He was about to call out something to me when he was at a safe distance away, but I glared at him and he disappeared past the bend, following the others.

Panting, I leaned heavily on my walking stick—more heavily than I wanted to—and turned back to bury what was left of my dog.

Couplet and I had been companions since he started following me in the narrow, lurching alleys of Crane Velib, as a puppy. He had probably escaped from one of the vats in the plundered animal-grower markets. And I was destitute on a moon that had suddenly become unfriendly to me. The Empire had broken apart, losing moon after moon to rebellion, to people who were sick of the Priceless Court and those who served it, like me. Women who used to be men, like me.

I could not pretend that we weren't ruthless at times.

And people ran amok. Some moons became lost to any outside contact, and some went completely dark. We fled after the contessa, Seax-of-Marigold's political Arbiter, was beheaded.

In fact, Lamb Villanelle had beheaded the contessa himself.

If it were not for Couplet, in those days I would have been utterly alone. He deserved far more grieving than I was able to offer him after his senseless death.

But the next morning I smelled smoke from the village and I knew right away that Lamb Villanelle's dragoons had descended, breaking through the moon's half-broken defense sigils with ease. Whether the boys had overheard gossip on the quay and had conspired to pledge themselves to the Law Lordship in drunken anticipation, or it was an ungodly coincidence, I could not say. But I knew the Pure Army would not content themselves with this village. They would be landing all over the moon and pushing inward, and my orchard would burn by sundown.

I was nearly about to pass deeper into the marsh, where I could probably evade any sorties until I made my way upcountry. I was ready to find the bunker in the volcanic highlands where I had hidden my own imperial caravel all those years ago, and I would start over again, alone, as difficult as it would be.

But I thought of the youngest of the failed brigands. I did not think he was meant to be with them; he seemed pressed into their band for reasons I could not fathom. I thought about how likely it was that he would be murdered during any landing by Lamb Villanelle's dragoons, and I couldn't bear the thought of it, for reasons I could only guess at. Perhaps I saw something of myself in him, unfair as that might be at first glance—and far more unfair in retrospect.

So I went into my cottage next to the orchard and took my pack, loading it with white plums. I knelt down next to my own memory chest, and I took in the smell of *aquae koboli* and a tinge of blood. Sighing, I put on my gouged aquilla, and my sword, which I had named Learned Helplessness, its transpiric steel forged in the Contessa's own Ninth Refinery. Then I took my walking stick and followed the path that led toward the village, passing the grave I had dug for Couplet only a few hours before.

·•●•·

By the time I reached the outskirts of the village, most of it had already been burned to the ground or toppled over by the dragoons. And most of the looting had already taken place. The village had little treasure of its own. Lamb Villanelle, in the Pure Laws that he concocted, called the despoiling of any moon "The Sacrament of Priceless Lust."

I had known him once. I spit into the blood-dirt.

I drew my sword, turned it on, and stepped around a landing shuttle that had crushed a boarding house, into the market square. The shuttle, of course, was a leftover from the Empire of Marigolds, painted crudely red. The air was thick with charnel smoke. I had no idea how to find the boy.

"Oh, ha ha!"

The voice came from the back of the village's lone tavern. I moved closer and listened.

"You speechless dog," he continued. "You bear the mark but do you deserve to be in the Pure Army?"

"Yes," a shaky reply came. Though I could only see him as a loose shape through the smoke, I knew right away it was the second oldest boy. "My heart is the fallow field where the law can bear . . . bear the tree of certainty . . ."

The smoke cleared for a few seconds and I saw that he knelt in front of a lieutenant with gray spikes affixed to his helmet.

"Stand up, wicked child," the lieutenant said.

The boy stood up, uneasily, still weak from my thrashing.

The lieutenant turned a bit, and that was when I saw the youngest of the five, also kneeling in the mud. He was crying and looking over at his friend.

"He is too weak to march with us," the lieutenant said, pointing at the youngest. "You must prove your worth to the Pure Law and drive him down into the earth. You must—"

I couldn't bear to watch this spectacle any more. A blaze of smoke blew around me, embers crackling against my lacquered armilla. I walked toward the lieutenant through the grimy air, and I pushed the point of Learned Helplessness through the base of his neck and his throat, through the seams in his plate.

"Shut the fuck up," I said as he slid off the sword and onto the ground. The sword had melted him from his chin to his collarbones.

I pointed at the older boy. "I never want to see you again."

He nodded weakly and dropped his grandfather's sword, running around the corner of the tavern.

(As it happened, I *did* see him again, as well as the other three boys, years later. They had steadfastly followed their hearts' ambition to become thieves, cutthroats, and casual murderers in the space between the moons. And then they became captains of casual murderers. And then their fortunes broke, and the new Empress, after taking the peony as her sigil, hunted them down without quarter.)

The youngest boy looked up at me. I still had no idea who he was, but I was beginning to know. I held out my hand and helped him up. I noticed the graceful tattoo on his wrist, which was real, but didn't say anything yet. The "V" on his neck turned out to be from a stick of charcoal, and it had smudged. I almost laughed.

"Do you want to come with me?" I said. "I'm escaping."

"Where?" he said quietly.

I pointed north. The mountains could not be seen, but he had to have known what I meant. The mountains were away from all of this carnage.

"I have a ship there," I said, "that I have hidden."

He didn't seem surprised. He nodded.

We left the village as quietly as we could. The lieutenant's first assistant tried to stop me, but I dodged his first swing through the smoke and pierced his heart, melting it.

The boy didn't speak again until a half-day later, after we had at last pushed past the brackish marshes. He hadn't complained, not once, not with his legs muddied and scratched, not through all the dead ends of miserable brambles I had gotten us stuck in, endless times.

In the distance there were one or two shouts, occasional whiffs of bloodsmoke. But the Pure Army was not pushing through this slog. Not yet.

The two of us reached the first patch of solid (though soggy) ground we had seen since the village and both plunked down next to a half-dead firch tree. After a minute, after he had caught his breath, he said:

"Why did you save me?"

I didn't say anything for another minute (it took me longer to catch my breath). Then I turned toward him.

"Show me your wrist," I said.

He hesitated but he held out his wrist, the one with the tattoo, the real tattoo, the one he had made from mussel ink and the sharpened point of a reed. The tattoo was the outline of a falcon inside a star.

"Did you fashion this?" I asked.

He hesitated again, but nodded. I could see the apprehension on his face, and I worried that I was pushing him too far.

"This is the tattoo of Seax-of-Marigold," I said.

He nodded again. My heart became glad, in spite of my exhaustion, because I had not seen that tattoo on another person in a very long time, since the Empire—and everything—had fallen apart for me.

"Where did you find the sigil?" I said. "If the Pure Army had found you with it, they would have chopped off your hand and fed it to you."

He was unfazed. He straightened his back. "In the old granary. There were holograms." He paused. "It used to be a temple to her."

"Yes," I said, shutting my eyes for a second, surprised by the pain from that loss, the loss of that Empire built upon the ashes of the old worlds, built by women like me.

"And I want to devote myself to her. I just know that I have to. I am a woman." This fierceness and clarity surprised me, though maybe it shouldn't have.

"And I want this body to change," she continued. She paused, thinking over the words that she had said, words that she might never have said aloud before. "That is what I want."

I looked at her. "Let me show you something."

I hiked up my muddy skirt and showed the same tattoo on my thigh.

She breathed a sigh looking at it, more weary than I thought possible for a teenager. Then she smiled. I cursed myself for not realizing who she was earlier, for fully realizing the wellspring of that pained look on her face, eager to not be seen as a woman, or even womanly, in the company of young men she despised.

"In that case," I said, "we must travel to Queensthroat. And you'll be able to decide there how you want to proceed."

If Crane Velib was the moon of politics and arbiters, then Queensthroat was the moon of priestesses and vestiges, of reliquaries and silences.

"But . . . no one knows how to go there," she said. "The way was lost."

"I do," I said. And this was true. So much was lost in the decades after the Empire's fall. But not everything. "Are you sure?"

"I have made my decision," she said.

"I understand," I said, lightly touching her shoulder. "Truly, I do. But this is only the first step in a long journey."

She had no idea what was ahead of her, if we did make it that far—which was no certain thing with the Pure Army fanning out on the moon. And if we did manage to launch, the space between the moons could be treacherous. Assuming we reached Queensthroat, she had no idea about the superblood tinctures, the long nights of pledges and submission to Seax-of-Marigold's manifestations, the pilgrimage to the cave at the heart of Queensthroat, shorn from the molten core, where she would find her name inside the shadow, as I found mine.

Of course, after her two years at Queensthroat, things became more complicated when she emerged as Seax-of-Peony—she had not pledged service to her predecessor, but had instead assimilated her, and fashioned something different. Something richer and far more kind than the Empire of Marigolds.

But at that point, with this scared young woman in my charge, it was only a glimmer. A catch in my throat.

It might be hard to imagine in this present age, when the Empire of Peonies has reestablished peace, the fear that the Pure Army instilled at its apex. After the Empress crushed him in battle after battle, he and his army were quickly and embarrassedly forgotten, as Lamb and his viceroys scrambled to escape the habitable moons, toward shit-moons in the outer belt.

Lamb Villanelle's lapidation by Seax-of-Peony's decree was the last act of political violence sanctioned by the Empire.

His era of wanton slaughter was incalculable in the pain it caused. But it too passed.

When men like Lamb Villanelle become gruesomely powerful, most people do not think they can be vanquished. But they can be, and are, because they die alone, as we all do.

And remembering their past attempts to control and deny bodies like mine, and the Empress's, became all the more senseless.

As I had known Lamb Villanelle once, his Pure Laws especially infuriated me. He had declared them to be holy writ, invoking a restoration of a past that never existed. Dozens of empires had risen and fallen on the moons over the millennia, but few were remembered—let alone the people who had built the moons in the first place. Seax-of-Marigold, and those who followed her, had fumbled toward a form of hard, unyielding grace, but even this was just an echo of the past.

But he insisted on his need to enforce his revelation throughout the moons. And the usual cutthroats had fallen in behind him.

I'd like to think that the Empire of Marigolds was different. Lamb Villanelle would have said that we were servants of a theocracy too, one of mystery instead of clarity.

Perhaps that much was true. Perhaps that was why the Empress-in-Waiting forged her own path after visiting Queensthroat—one that tried not to pay homage to the mistakes of the past—but that is another story.

·•●•·

We walked through the scrublands and ascended slowly to the high volcanic plains. We picked and plucked at glitch roots as we walked. The roots would evade our grasp, and would whisper screeches as we yanked them up. I showed her how to scrape off the barcodes with the edge of a knife. As she ate and the shock began to ease from her like snow melting off a horse's mane, I could tell that she was growing stronger. She started asking questions. She wanted to know everything. I didn't blame her.

"Did you live in Queensthroat?"

"Yes, for two years, just like everyone else who wished to undergo the ablutions."

She raised her eyebrow. "And it's not a myth?"

"No . . . no, it's not a myth. We're not traveling to a myth."

She mulled this over. "Have you *seen* Seax-of-Marigold?"

"No. No one has. Only her shadow, on occasion."

"And yet she lives at the heart of the moon?"

"Well, after a fashion."

I could tell she was not satisfied with my replies. I didn't know her well enough to give her the answers she needed, and I maybe never would. I was getting out of breath as the trail got steeper and rockier, and the questions didn't stop. I had thought tending plums would keep me in better physical condition, but I was wrong, so very wrong, especially as the air got thinner.

From behind us, I could see columns of dark blue smoke, and the sea, and beyond that, the curvature of our little moon.

"So . . . you served in her army?" she said, after a couple minutes.

"Yes. For seventeen years, I was a Minor Arbiter on Crane Velib. I fled from there to here." The dehydration gave the seeds of images and I gave birth to them in my mind: Couplet ambling down a courtyard of gold tiles, the Ninth Forge shattered, my sword vaporizing heart after heart as I fought my way through Pure Army formations to the secret hangar—

"Lamb Villanelle founded his Pure Army on Crane Velib," she said thoughtfully. "So . . . you knew him?" She said this in a whisper. As if she did not want to ask, but didn't realize this until the words left her mouth.

"I knew him there," I said, clenching my eyes shut. "But we had known each other many years before that, when we were . . . kids." I stopped—I had to stop, I could not carry on with another step until I made the truth plain to her. I leaned heavily on my walking stick. "We traveled to Queensthroat together. But he never wished to stay. He departed right away. He only wanted off our home moon, and used my own journey—the one I desperately needed—as an excuse. Later, he entered the Flower of Battle Academy on Crane Velib. In fact, I had sponsored his position."

"Where is your home moon?" she said, and I shrugged.

"It doesn't exist anymore. Our childhood home was the first moon that Lamb Villanelle imploded."

I looked up at the sky, and the artificial twilight that started falling upon us.

"And now it is almost dark," I said. "If we travel farther in the dark, we will die."

She grew silent.

A hundred steps ahead, we found a house of sorts just off the trail that had its steel and concrete completely torn out, so that only the crystal wiring, twisted and splayed, remained. But this wiring had sagged enough to form a more or less flat roof that would keep out the wind, if not the cold. I realized that this could have been a chapel to Seax-of-Marigold, though it was so defaced there was no way to know for sure.

After we had settled, I gave her one of my plums. She bit into it and scrunched her face.

"This tastes terrible," she said.

"Give it time," I said, laughing a little. I looked at the opening of the desiccated building. "We can't light a fire."

She finished the plum and I gave her my bedroll. I pointed toward the makeshift door.

"I'll watch for things," I said.

She was too tired to argue with me. As this was the first time she had relaxed in days, I could see the pain limned on her face. I wondered, as she drifted off, whether she would get any rest at all, or rather wake up fitfully every hour from everything she had endured.

But I didn't realize yet how strong she actually was. When she wanted rest, she rested. When she wanted to kill an enemy, she killed an enemy—and when she wanted to stop killing enemies and reinstitute a reign of peace, she stopped. When she desired sanctuary from the body that betrayed her, she traveled with a middle-aged woman she'd never met before to find a caravel that hadn't been used in decades, in order to visit a sacred moon that seemed little more than a dream, a phantasm.

Maybe she didn't realize everything yet about her strength. But she was getting there. She was getting there. And she didn't stir once in her sleep.

As for me, I crouched by the door, oiling and priming my sword. I listened for patrols, or hungry tigerelles, but all I heard was the occasional and far-distant tearing of the lower atmosphere by the Pure Army's cyclone artillery. I still had no idea why this young woman had fallen into the thrall of those boys who decided to overtake an orchard-keeper with a long stick. Maybe, I wondered, it was an unspeakable crush on one of them. Maybe it was her last attempt to push all of her feelings of brokenness and having a body that she despised down, further down, by numbing herself and going along with the schemes of childhood friends she only tolerated.

I might have been projecting myself into my own dark past with Lamb Villanelle.

And at any rate, later on, she had never told me.

I became lost in my own memories as she slept. I ate a plum. I saved the pit, and I rooted through the interior of our shelter until I found the pit that she had thrown away. Those were precious to me, and I had only a few precious things left in my possession.

Perhaps I would grow plums again, I thought, though any trees would not likely bear fruit until long after I was dead.

· · ● · ·

I was on the edge of dozing and dawn when I heard the frigate screaming through the sky. I startled. A ship was coming toward us.

"Wake up!" I shouted to her, but she was already sitting up.

The frigate landed no more than thirty meters from our hideout, barely taking the time to set down landing gear, skidding to a halt in a cloud of volcanic ash, and I knew who it was.

Of course it was Lamb Villanelle.

I pointed at the woman who was to become Seax-of-Peony. "Listen to me. In two minutes, you are going to run through that crevice in the back and head up the face of the mountainside away from Lamb Villanelle. He's alone. I know he's alone. He shouldn't see you, but there might be tigerelles on the path. Whatever you do, do not look them in the eyes. Walk with open palms. They should leave you alone. Once you reach the cave with the white boulder set in front of it, wait for me there. If I don't follow you after an hour—" I took a deep breath. "Go farther into the cave. The ship should be there. It's old, and a lot smarter than anything Lamb Villanelle has."

She started crying. Shaking her head. I lifted up my leg and pressed my palm against my tattoo. The mark of Seax-of-Marigold began to flutter, and with a hiss it transferred to my palm, the ink wriggling like an anxious mammal.

"Hold out your hand," I said.

She hesitated.

"*Please*," I said.

I heard the causeway slowly lowering for the frigate.

At last she held out her hand. I pressed my palm into hers, which was much smaller than mine. But it didn't matter. The tattoo seared my calloused skin for a second, and then the intertwined falcon and star loosened and grafted onto her. She cried out, and wrenched her hand away. The tattoo wriggled from her palm onto the wrist, superimposing itself on the crude one she had made herself with such pain and passion.

"When you're on the ship, place your mark into the crucible on the bridge. The ship will know where to go."

She nodded fitfully. "I'm coming back for you," she said. "I promise."

I heard the first heavy boot steps coming down the causeway. I knew he would be ready to kill me for harboring a young woman who kept the memory of the Empire of Marigolds alive—even if she didn't remember it herself.

I managed to nod. Though I didn't quite believe her promise, I was comforted that she felt the need to make it.

"Now go," I whispered.

At last she ran. I knelt down right inside the door and unsheathed Learned Helplessness. I tucked my fingers into the hilt and overrode its safety mechanisms. I gripped the crossguard and pulled on it, hard.

I heard him saying things at me: crowing, challenging me, but it didn't matter what he said. It only mattered that she lived.

She did live. And she did come back for me—more than that, she saved me, with my own caravel. But that is yet another story, one of several stories that she would possess and nurture as she found her place in Queensthroat, and later, far beyond it.

Slowly the blade lengthened, the transpire slackening and then hardening. I lengthened the blade until it was longer than I was tall. Sparks flew from the steel. I was a young woman again. I grasped the hilt and held the sword in front of me. I was fleeing a burning moon again. I took one step and then another. I was running away from my parents again, having known no more than a lumpen boy's body, Lamb Villanelle on the stolen caravel's bridge, piloting us somehow, taking us away from peasants' lives, to Queensthroat. I wiped away the hot tears.

As I went out into the blinding sunlight, what flooded my mind was one image, as sharp and total as the tattoo that had lived on my skin for decades, and which I had given to the Empress-to-be. The image wasn't of her; or Lamb Villanelle's hulking armor covered in jagged quills, promising death; or even me.

No, the mind and heart will flow where they will.

What I remembered most—what I couldn't exorcise from my vision—

was the moment after my dog's skull had been vaporized by that stupid boy, and the look that had come over his face. There was confusion there, yes, but he was also horrified. He had let the mask of his endless cruelty slip and for a few instants he was nothing more than a terrified boy in shock, dogblood and dogskull plastering his face.

For a few instants, he was hollowed. And there was grief, and grace.

This was what I thought of, when I raised my endless sword and charged Lamb Villanelle: my dear Couplet without a head, and a boy's face.

ANN LECKIE
THE JUSTIFIED

Ann Leckie is the author of the *Imperial Radch* trilogy, including the Hugo, Nebula, and Arthur C. Clarke Award-winning novel *Ancillary Justice*, *Provenance*, and *The Raven Tower*. She has published short stories in *Subterranean Magazine*, *Strange Horizons*, and *Realms of Fantasy*. Her most recent novel is *Translation State*. She has worked as a waitress, a receptionist, a rodman on a land-surveying crew, and a recording engineer. She lives in St. Louis, Missouri. [www.annleckie.com]

Het had eaten nothing for weeks but bony, gape-mawed fish—some of them full of neurotoxin. She'd had to alter herself so she could metabolize it safely, which had taken some doing. So when she ripped out the walsel's throat and its blood spurted red onto the twilit ice, she stared, salivary glands aching, stomach growling. She didn't wait to butcher her catch but sank her teeth into skin and fat and muscle, tearing a chunk away from its huge shoulder.

Movement caught her eye, and she sprang upright, walsel blood trickling along her jaw, to see Dihaut, black and silver, walking toward her across the ages-packed snow and ice. She'd have known her sib anywhere, but even if she hadn't recognized them, there was no mistaking their crescent-topped standard, Months and Years, tottering behind them on two thin, insectile legs.

But sib or not, familiar or not, Het growled, heart still racing, muscles poised for flight or attack. She had thought herself alone and unwatched. Had made sure of it before she began her hunt. Had Dihaut been watching her all this time? It would be like them.

For a brief moment she considered disemboweling Dihaut, leaving them dying on the ice, Months and Years in pieces beside them. But that would only put this off until her sib took a new body. Dihaut could be endlessly persistent when they wished, and the fact that they had come all the way to this frigid desert at the farthest reaches of Nu to find her suggested that the ordinary limits of that persistence—such as they were—could not be relied on. Besides, she and Dihaut had nearly always gotten along well. Still, she stayed on the alert, and did not shift into a more relaxed posture.

"This is the Eye of Merur, the Noble Dihaut!" announced Months and Years as Dihaut drew near. Its high, thready voice cut startlingly through the silence of the snowy waste.

"I know who they are," snarled Het.

The standard made a noise almost like a sniff. "I only do my duty, Noble Het."

Dihaut hunched their shoulders. Their face, arms, torso, and legs were covered with what looked like long, fine fur but, this being Dihaut, was likely feathers. Mostly black, but their left arm and leg, and part of their torso, were silver-white. "Hello, sib," they said. "Sorry to interrupt your supper. Couldn't you have fled someplace warmer?"

Het had no answer for this—she'd asked herself the same question many times in the past several years.

"I see you've changed your skin," Dihaut continued. "It does look odd, but I suppose it keeps you warm. Would you mind sharing the specs?" They shivered.

"It's clothes," said Het. "A coat, and boots, and gloves."

"Clothes!" Dihaut peered at her more closely. "I see. They must be very confining, but I suppose it's worth it to be warm. Do you have any you could lend me? Or could whoever supplied you with yours give me some, too?"

"Sorry," growled Het. "Not introducing you." Actually she hadn't even introduced herself. She'd stolen the clothes, when the fur she'd grown hadn't kept her as warm as she'd hoped.

Dihaut made a wry "huh," their warm breath puffing from their mouth in a small cloud. "Well. I'm sorry to be so blunt." They gave a regretful smile, all Dihaut in its acknowledgment of the pointlessness of small talk. "I'm very sorry to intrude on whatever it is you're doing down here—I never was quite clear on why you left, no one was, except that you were angry about something. Which . . ." They shrugged. "If it were up to me"—they raised both finely feathered hands, gestured vaguely to the dead walsel with the silver one— "I'd leave you to it."

"Would you." She didn't even try to sound as though she believed them.

"Truly, sib. But the ruler of Hehut, the Founder and Origin of Life on Nu, the One Sovereign of This World, wishes for you to return to Hehut." At this, Months and Years waved its thin, sticklike arms as though underlining Dihaut's words. "She'd have sent others before me, but I convinced her that if you were brought back against your wishes, your presence at court would not be as delightful as usual." They shivered again. "Is there somewhere warmer we can talk?"

"Not really."

"I don't mean any harm to the people you've been staying with," said Dihaut.

"I haven't been staying with anyone." She gestured vaguely around with one blood-matted hand, indicating the emptiness of the ice.

"You must have been staying with someone, sib. I know there are no approved habitations here, so they must be unauthorized, but that's no concern of mine unless they should come to Merur's attention. Or if they have Animas. Please tell me, sib, that they don't have unauthorized Animas here? Because you know we'll have to get rid of them if they do, and I'd really like to just go right back to Hehut, where it's actually warm."

Unbidden her claws extended again, just a bit. She had never spoken to the people who lived here, but she owed them. It was by watching them that she'd learned about the poisonous fish. Otherwise the toxin might have caught her off guard, even killed her. And then she'd have found herself resurrected again in Hehut, in the middle of everything she'd fled.

"They don't have Animas," she told Dihaut. "How could they?" When their bodies died, they died.

"Thank all the stars for that!" Dihaut gave a relieved, shivery sigh. "As long as they stay up here in this freezing desert with their single, cold lives, we can all just go on pretending they don't exist. So surely we can pretend they don't exist in their presumably warmer home?"

"Your standard is right behind you," Het pointed out. "Listening."

"It is," Dihaut agreed. "It always is. There's nowhere in the world we can really be away from Merur. We always have to deal with the One Ruler. Even, in the end, the benighted unauthorized souls in this forsaken place." They were, by now, shivering steadily.

"Can't she leave anyone even the smallest space?" asked Het. "Some room to be apart, without her watching? For just a little while?"

"It's usually us watching for her," put in Dihaut.

Het waved that away. "Not a single life anywhere in the world that she doesn't claim as hers. She makes *certain* there's nowhere to go!"

"Order, sib," said Dihaut. "Imagine what might happen if everyone went running around free to do whatever they liked with no consequences. And she *is* the Founder and Origin of Life on Nu."

"Come on, Dihaut. I was born on *Aeons*, just before Merur left the ship and came down to Nu. There were already people living here. I remember it. And even now it depends who you ask. Either Merur arrived a thousand years ago in *Aeons* and set about pulling land from beneath the water and creating humans, or else she arrived and brought light and order to humans she found living in ignorance and chaos. I've heard both from her own mouth at different times. And you know better. You're the historian."

They tried that regretful half smile again, but they were too cold to manage it. "I tell whichever story is more politic at the moment. And there are, after all, different sorts of truth. But please." They spread their hands, placatory. "I beg you. Come with me back to Hehut. Don't make me freeze to death in front of you."

"Noble Dihaut," piped their standard, "Eye of Merur, I am here. Your Anima is entirely safe."

"Yes," shivered Dihaut, "but there isn't a new body ready for me yet, and I hate being out of things for very long. Please, sib, let's go back to my flier. We can argue about all of this on the way back home."

And, well, now that Dihaut had found her, it wasn't as though she had much choice. She said, with ill grace, "Well fine, then. Where's your flier?"

"This way," said Dihaut, shivering, and turned. They were either too cold or too wise to protest when Het bent to grab the dead walsel's tusk and drag it along as she followed.

It rained in Hehut barely more often than it snowed in the icy waste Het had left, but rivers and streams veined Hehut under the bright, uninterrupted blue of the sky, rivers and streams that pooled here and there into lotus-veiled lakes and papyrus marshes, and the land was lush and green.

The single-lived working in the fields looked up as the shadow of Dihaut's flier passed over them. They made a quick sign with their left hands and turned back to the machines they followed. Small boats dotted the river that snaked through the fields, single-lived fishers hauling in nets, here and there the long, gilded barque of one of the Justified shining in the sun. The sight gave Het an odd pang—she had not ever been given much to nostalgia, or to dwelling on memories of her various childhoods, none of which to her recall had been particularly childish, but she was struck with a sudden, almost tangible memory of sunshine on her skin, and the sound of water lapping at the hull of a boat. Not, she was sure, a single moment but a composite of all the times she'd fled to the river, to fish, or walk, or sit under a tree and stare at the water flowing by. To be by herself. As much as she could be, anyway.

"Almost there," said Dihaut, reclined in their seat beside her. "Are you going to change?" They had shed their feathers on the flight here and now showed black and silver skin, smooth and shining.

Het had shed her coat, boots, and gloves but left her thick and shaggy fur. It would likely be uncomfortable in the heat, but she was reluctant to let go of it; she couldn't say why. "I don't think I have time."

"Noble Eyes of Merur," said Months and Years, upright at Dihaut's elbow, "we will arrive at Tjenu in fifteen minutes. The One Sovereign will see you immediately."

Definitely no time to change. "So urgent?" asked Het. "Do you know what this is about?"

"I have my suspicions." Dihaut shrugged one silver shoulder. "It's probably better if Merur tells you herself."

So this was something that no one—not even Merur's own Eyes—could safely talk about. There were times when Merur was in no mood to be tolerant of any suggestion that her power and authority might be incomplete, and at those times even admitting knowledge of some problem could end with one's Anima deleted altogether.

Tjenu came into view, its gold-covered facade shining in the hot sun, a wide, dark avenue of smooth granite stretching from its huge main doors straight across the gardens to a broad entrance in the polished white walls. The Road of Souls, the single-lived called it, imagining that it was the route traveled by the Animas of the dead on their way to judgment at Dihaut's hands. As large as the building was—a good kilometer on each of its four sides, and three stories high—most of Tjenu was underground. Or so Dihaut had told her. Het had only ever been in the building's sunlit upper reaches. At least while she was alive, and not merely an Anima awaiting resurrection.

Dihaut's flier set down within Tjenu's white walls, beside a willow-edged pond. Coming out, Het found Great Among Millions, her own standard, waiting, hopping from one tiny foot to the other, feathery fingers clenched into minuscule fists, stilled the next moment, its black pole pointing perfectly upright, the gold cow horns at its top polished and shining.

"Eye of Merur," it said, its voice high and thin. "Noble Het, the Justified, the Powerful, Servant of the One Sovereign of Nu. The Ruler of all, in her name of Self-Created, in her name of She Caused All To Be, in her name of She Listens To Prayers, in her name of Sustainer of the Justified, in her name of—"

"Stop," Het commanded. "Just tell me what she wants."

"Your presence, gracious Het," it said, with equanimity. Great Among Millions had been her standard for several lifetimes, and was used to her. "Immediately. Do forgive the appearance of impertinence, Noble Het. I only relay the words of the One Sovereign. I will escort you to your audience."

Months and Years, coming out of the flier, piped, "Great Among Millions, please do not forget the Noble Het's luggage."

"What luggage?" asked Het.

"Your walsel, Noble Eye," replied Months and Years, waving a tiny hand. "What's left of it. It's starting to smell."

"Just dispose of it," said Het. "I've eaten as much of it as I'm going to."

Great Among Millions gave a tiny almost-hop from one foot to the other, and stilled again. "Noble Het, you have been away from Tjenu, from Hehut itself, without me, for fifty-three years, two months, and three days." It almost managed to sound as though it was merely stating a fact, and not making a complaint. But not quite.

"It's good to see you again, too," Het said. Her standard unclenched its little fists and gestured toward the golden mass of Tjenu. "Yes," Het acknowledged. "Let's go."

The vast audience chamber of the One Sovereign of Nu was black-ceilinged, inlaid with silver and copper stars that shone in the light of the lamps below. Courtiers, officials, and supplicants, alone or in small scattered groups, murmured as Het passed. Of course. There was no mistaking her identity, furred and unkempt as she was—Great Among Millions followed her.

She crossed the brown, gold-flecked floor to where it changed, brown shading to blue and green in Merur's near presence, where one never set foot without direct invitation—unless, of course, one was an Eye, in which case one's place in the bright-lit vicinity of Merur was merely assumed, a privilege of status.

Stepping into the green, Great Among Millions tottering behind her, Het cast a surreptitious glance—habitual, even after so long away!—at those so privileged. And stopped, and growled. Among the officials standing near Merur, three bore her Eye. There were four Eyes; Het herself was one. Dihaut, who Het had left with their flier, was another. There should only have been two Eyes here.

"Don't be jealous, Noble Het," whispered Great Among Millions, its thready voice sounding in her ear alone. "You were gone so very long." Almost accusing, that sounded.

"She *replaced* me," Het snarled. She didn't recognize whoever it was who, she saw now, held an unfamiliar standard, but the Justified changed bodies so frequently. If there was a new Eye, why should Merur call on Het? Why not leave her be?

"And you left *me* behind," continued Great Among Millions. "Alone. They asked and asked me where you were and I did not know, though I wished to." It made a tiny, barely perceptible stomp. "They put me in a storeroom. In a box."

"Het, my Eye, approach!" Merur, calling from where she sat under her blue-canopied pavilion, alone but for those three Eyes, and the standards, and smaller lotus- and lily-shaped servants that always attended her.

And now, her attention turned from Merur's other Eyes, Het looked fully at the One Sovereign herself. Armless, legless, her snaking body cased in scales of gold and lapis, Merur circled the base of her polished granite chair of state, her upper body leaning onto the seat, her head standard human, her hair in dozens of silver-plaited braids falling around her glittering gold face. Her dark eyes were slit-pupiled.

Het had seen Merur take such a shape before—as well as taking new bodies at need or at whim, the Justified could to some degree alter a currently held body at will. But there were limits to such transformations, and it had been long, long centuries since Merur had taken this sort of body.

She should have concealed her surprise and prostrated herself, but instead she stood and stared as Great Among Millions announced, in a high, carrying voice, "The fair, the fierce, the Burning Eye of the One Sovereign of Nu, the Noble Het!"

"My own Eye!" said Merur. "I have need of you!"

Het could not restrain her anger, even in the face of the One Sovereign of Nu. "I count four Eyes in this court, Sovereign—those three over there, and the Noble Dihaut. There have always been four. Why should you need me to be a fifth?" Behind her, Great Among Millions made a tiny noise.

"I shed one body," admonished Merur, her voice faintly querulous, "only to reawaken and find you gone. For decades you did not return. Why? No one accused you of any dereliction of duty, let alone disloyalty. You had suffered no disadvantage; your place as my favored Eye was secure. And now, returning, you question my having appointed someone to fill the office you left empty! You would do better to save your anger for the enemies of Nu!"

"I can't account for my heart," said Het crossly. "It is as it is."

This seemed to mollify Merur. "Well, you always have had a temper. And it is this very honesty that I have so missed. Indeed, it is what I require of you!" Here Merur lowered her voice and looked fretfully from one side to the other, and the standards and flower-form servitors scuttled back a few feet. "Het, my Eye. This body is . . . imperfect. It will not obey me as it should, and it is dying, far sooner than it ought. I need to move to a new one."

"Already?" Het's skin prickled with unease.

"This is not the first time a body has grown imperfectly," Merur said, her voice low. "But I should have seen the signs long before I entered it. Someone must have concealed them from me! It is impossible that this has happened through mere incompetence.

"I have dealt with the technicians. I have rooted out any disloyalty in Tjenu. But I cannot say the same of all Hehut, let alone all of Nu. And this body of mine will last only a few months longer, but no suitable replacement, one untampered with by traitors, will be ready for a year or more. And I cannot afford to leave Nu rulerless for so long! My Eyes I trust—you and Dihaut, certainly, after all this time. The Justified are for the most part reliable, and the single-lived know that Dihaut will judge them. But I have never been gone for more than a few days at a time. If this throne is empty longer, it may encourage the very few wayward to stir up the single-lived, and if, in my absence, enough among the Justified can be led astray—no. I cannot be gone so long unless I am certain of order."

Dismayed, Het snarled. "Sovereign, what do you expect me to do about any of this?"

"What you've always done! Protect Nu. All trace of unrest, of disorder, must be prevented. You've rid Nu of rebellion before. I need you to do it again."

That shining silver river, the fishers, the lilies and birds had all seemed so peaceful. So much as they should be, when Het and Dihaut had flown in. "Unrest? What's the cause this time?"

"The cause!" Merur exclaimed, exasperated. "There is no *cause*. There never has been! The worthy I give eternal life and health; they need only reach out their hands for whatever they desire! The unworthy are here and gone, and they have all they need and occupation enough, or if not, well, they seal their own fate. There has never been any *cause*, and yet it keeps happening—plots, rumors, mutterings of discontent. My newest Eye"—Merur did not notice, or affected not to notice, Het's reaction to that—"is fierce and efficient. I do not doubt her loyalty. But I am afraid she doesn't have your imagination. Your vision. Your *anger*. Two years ago I sent her out to deal with this, and she returned saying there was no trouble of any consequence! She doesn't *understand*! Where does this keep coming from? Who is planting such ideas in the minds of my people? Root it out, Het. Root it out from among my people, trace it back to its origin, and destroy it so that Nu can rest secure while my next body grows. So that we can at last have the peace and security I have always striven for."

"Sovereign of Nu," growled Het. "I'll do my best."

What choice did she have, after all?

· • ◉ • ·

She should have gone right to Dihaut. The first place to look for signs of trouble would be among the Animas of the recently dead. But she was still out of sorts with Dihaut, still resented their summoning her back here. They'd made her share their company on the long flight back to Hehut and never mentioned that Merur had *replaced* her. They might have warned her, and they hadn't. She wasn't certain she could keep her temper with her sib, just now. Which maybe was why they'd kept silent about it, but still.

Besides, that other Eye had doubtless done the obvious first thing, and gone to Dihaut herself. And to judge from what Merur had said, Dihaut must have found nothing, or nothing to speak of. They would give Het the same answer. No point asking again.

She wanted time alone. Time that was hers. She didn't miss the cold—already her thick fur was thinning without any conscious direction on her part. But she did miss the solitude, and the white landscape stretching out seemingly forever, silent except for the wind and her own heart, the hiss of blood in her ears. There was nothing like that here.

She left Tjenu and walked down to the river in the warm early-evening sunlight. Willows shaded the banks, and the lilies in the occasional pool, red and purple and gold, were closing. The scent of water and flowers seized her, plucking at the edges of some memory. Small brown fishing boats sat in neat rows on the opposite bank, waiting for morning. The long, sleek shape of some Justified Noble's barque floated in the middle of the channel, leaf green, gilded, draped with hangings and banners of blue and yellow and white.

She startled two children chasing frogs in the shallows. "Noble," the larger of them said, bowing, pushing the smaller child beside them into some semblance of a bow. "How can we serve you?"

Don't notice my presence, she thought, but of course that was impossible. "Be as you were. I'm only out for a walk." And then, considering the time, "Shouldn't you be home having dinner?"

"We'll go right away," said the older child.

The smaller, voice trembling, said, "Please don't kill us, Noble Het."

Het frowned, and looked behind her, only to see Great Among

Millions a short way off, peering at her from behind a screen of willow leaves. "Why would I do such a thing?" Het asked the child. "Are you rebels, or criminals?"

The older child grabbed the younger one's arm, held it tight. "The Noble Het kills who she pleases," they said. The smaller child's eyes filled with tears. Then both children prostrated themselves. "How fair is your face, beautiful Het!" the older child cried into the mud. "The powerful, the wise and loving Eye of the One Sovereign! You see everything and strike where you wish! You were gone for a long time, but now you've returned and Hehut rejoices."

She wanted to reassure them that she hadn't come down to the river to kill them. That being late for dinner was hardly a capital offense. But the words wouldn't form in her mouth. "I don't strike where I wish," she said instead. "I strike the enemies of Nu."

"May we go, beautiful one?" asked the elder child, and now their voice was trembling too. "You commanded us to go home to dinner, and we only want to obey you!"

She opened her mouth to ask this child's name, seized as she was with a sudden inexplicable desire to mention it to Dihaut, to ask them to watch for this child when they passed through judgment, to let Dihaut know she'd been favorably impressed. So well-spoken, even if it was just a hasty assemblage of formulaic phrases, of songs and poetry they must have heard. But she feared asking would only terrify the child further. "I'm only out for a walk, child," she growled, uncomfortably resentful of this attention, even as she'd enjoyed the child's eloquence. "Go home to dinner."

"Thank you, beautiful one!" The elder child scrambled to their feet, pulled the smaller one up with them.

"Thank you!" piped the smaller child. And they both turned and fled. Het watched them go, and then resumed her walk along the riverside. But the evening had been soured, and soon she turned back to Tjenu.

•◦●◦•

The Thirty-Six met her in their accustomed place, a chamber in Tjenu walled with malachite and lapis, white lily patterns laid into the floor. There were chairs and benches along the edge of the room, but the Thirty-Six stood stiff and straight in the center, six rows of six, white linen kilts perfectly pressed, a gold and silver star on each brow.

"Eye of Merur," said the first of the Thirty-Six. "We're glad you're back."

"They're glad you're back," whispered Great Among Millions, just behind Het's right shoulder. "*They* didn't spend the time in a box."

Each of the Thirty-Six had their own demesne to watch, to protect. Their own assistants and weapons to do the job with. They had been asked to do this sort of thing often enough. Over and over.

Het had used the walk here from the river to compose herself. To take control of her face and her voice. She said, her voice smooth and calm, "The One Ruler of Nu, Creator of All Life on Nu, wishes for us to remove all traces of rebellion, once and for all. To destroy any hint of corruption that makes even the thought of rebellion possible." No word from the silent and still Thirty-Six. "Tell me, do you know where that lies?"

No reply. Either none of them knew, or they thought the answer so obvious that there was no need to say it. Or perhaps they were suspicious of Het's outward calm.

Finally, the first of the Thirty-Six said, "Generally, problems begin among the single-lived, Noble Het. But we can't seem to find the person, or the thing, that sends their hearts astray time after time. The only way to accomplish what the One Sovereign has asked of us would be to kill every single-lived soul on Nu and let Dihaut sort them one from another."

"Are you recommending that?" asked Het.

"It would be a terrible disruption," said another of the Thirty-Six. "There would be so many corpses to dispose of."

"We'd want more single-lived, wouldn't we?" asked yet another. "Grown new, free of the influence that corrupts them now. It might . . ." She seemed doubtful. "It might take care of the problem, but, Eye of

Merur, I don't know how many free tanks we have. And who would take care of the new children? It would be a terrible mess that would last for decades. And I'm not sure that . . . It just seems wrong." She cast a surreptitious glance toward the first of the Thirty-Six. "And forgive me, Noble Eye of Merur, but surely the present concern of the One Sovereign is to reduce chaos and disorder. At the current moment."

So that, at least, was well-enough known, or at least rumored. "The newest Eye," said Het, closing her still-clawed hands into fists, willing herself to stand still. Willing her voice to stay clear and calm. Briefly she considered leaving here, going back to the river to catch fish and listen to the frogs. "Did she request your assistance? And did you suggest this to her, the eradication of the single-lived so that we could begin afresh?"

"She thought it was too extreme," said the first of the Thirty-Six. Was that a note of disappointment in her voice? "It seems to me that the Sovereign of Nu found that Eye's service in this instance to be less than satisfactory."

"You think we should do it?" Het asked her.

"If it would rid us of the trouble that arises over and over," the first of the Thirty-Six agreed.

"If I order this, then," Het persisted, clenching her hands tighter, "you would do it?"

"Yes," the foremost of the Thirty-Six agreed.

"Children as well?" Het asked. Didn't add, *Even polite, well-spoken children who maybe only wanted some time to themselves, in the quiet by the river?*

"Of course," the first of the Thirty-Six replied. "If they're worthy they'll be back. Eventually."

With a growl Het sprang forward, hands open, claws flashing free of her fingertips, and slashed the throat of the first of the Thirty-Six. As she fell, blood splashed onto the torso and the spotless linen kilt of the Thirty-Six beside her. For a moment Het watched the blood pump satisfyingly out of the severed artery to pool on the white-lilied floor, and thought of the walsel she'd killed the day before.

But this was no time to indulge herself. She looked up and around. "Anyone else?"

Great Among Millions skittered up beside her. "Noble Het! Eye of Merur! There is currently a backlog of Justified waiting for resurrection. And none of your Thirty-Six have bodies in the tanks."

Het shrugged. The Thirty-Six were all among the Justified. "She'll be back. Eventually." At her feet the injured Thirty-Six breathed her choking last, and for the first time in decades Het felt a sure, gratifying satisfaction. She had been made for this duty, made to enjoy it, and she had nothing left to herself but that, it seemed. "The single-lived come and go," she declared to the remaining Thirty-Six. "Who has remained the same all this time?"

Silence.

"Oh, dear," said Great Among Millions.

The nurturing and protection of Nu had always required a good deal of death, and none of the Thirty-Six had ever been squeamish about it, but so often in recent centuries that death had been accomplished by impersonal, secondhand means—narrowly targeted poison, or engineered microbes let loose in the river. But Het—Het had spent the last several decades hunting huge, sharp-tusked walsel, two or three times the mass of a human, strong and surprisingly fast.

None of the remaining Thirty-Six would join her. Fifteen of them fled. The remaining twenty she left dead, dismembered, their blood pooling among the lilies, and then she went down to the riverbank.

The single-lived fled before her—or before Great Among Millions, not following discreetly now but close behind her, token and certification of who she was. The little fishing boats pulled hastily for the other bank, and their single-lived crews dropped nets and lines where they stood, ran from the river or cowered in the bottom of their small craft.

Het ignored them all and swam for the green-and-gold barque.

The single-lived servants didn't try to stop her as she pulled herself aboard and strode across the deck. After all, where Het went the necessities of order followed. Opposing the Eye of Merur was not only futile, but suicidal in the most ultimate sense.

Streaming river water, claws extended, Het strode to where the barque's Justified owners sat at breakfast, a terrified servant standing beside the table, a tray holding figs, cheese, and a bowl of honey shaking in her trembling hands.

The three Justified stared at Het as she stood before them, soaking wet, teeth bared. Then they saw Great Among Millions close behind her. "Protector of Hehut," said one, a man, as all three rose. "It's an honor." There was, perhaps, the smallest hint of trepidation in his voice. "Of course we'll make all our resources available to you. I'll have the servants brought—"

Het sprang forward, sliced open his abdomen with her claws, then tore his head from his neck. She made a guttural, happy sound, dropped the body, and tossed the head away.

The servant dropped the tray and fled, the bowl of honey bouncing and rolling, fetching up against the corpse's spilled, sliced intestines.

Het sank her teeth into the second Justified's neck, felt him struggle and choke, the exquisite salt tang of his blood in her mouth. This was oh, so much better than hunting walsel. She tore away a mouthful of flesh and trachea.

The third Justified turned to flee, but then stopped and cried, "I am loyal, Noble Eye! The Noble Dihaut will vindicate me!"

Het broke her neck and then stood a moment contemplating the feast before her, these three bodies, warm and bloody and deliciously fresh. She hadn't gotten to do this often enough, in recent centuries. She lifted her head and roared her satisfaction.

A breeze filled and lifted the barque's blue and yellow linen hangings. The servants had fled; there was no one alive on the deck but Het and Great Among Millions now. "Rejoice!" it piped. "The Protector of Hehut brings order to Nu!"

Het grinned, and then dove over the side, into the river, on her way to find more of the Justified.

·•◉•·

The day wore on, and more of the Justified met bloody, violent ends at Het's hands—and teeth. At first they submitted; after all, they were Justified, and their return was assured, so long as they were obedient subjects of the One Sovereign. But as evening closed in the Justified began to try to defend themselves.

And more of the houses were empty, their owners and servants fled. But in this latest, on the outskirts of Hehut, all airy windowed corridors and courtyards, Het found two Justified huddled in the corner of a white-and-gold-painted room, a single-lived servant standing trembling between them and Het.

"Move," growled Het to the servant.

"Justification!" cried one of the Justified. Slurring a bit—was she drunk?

"We swear!" slurred the other. Drunk as well, then.

Neither of them had the authority to make such a promise. Even if they had, the numbers of Justified dead ensured that no newly Justified would see resurrection for centuries, if ever. Despite all of this, the clearly terrified servant stayed.

Het roared her anger. Picked up the single-lived—they were strong, and large as single-lived went, but no match for Het. She set them aside, roughly, and sank her claws into one of the Justified, her teeth into the other. Screams filled her ears, and blood filled her mouth as she tore away a chunk of flesh.

All day her victims had provided her with more than her fill of blood, and so she had drunk sparingly so far. But now, enraged even further by the cowardice of these Justified—of their craven, empty promise to their servant—she drank deep, and still filled with rage, she tore the Justified into bloody fragments that spattered the floor and the wall.

She stopped a moment to appreciate her handiwork. With one furred hand she wiped blood and scraps of muscle off her tingling lips.

Her tingling lips.

The two Justified had barely moved, crouched in their corner. They had slurred their speech, as though they were drunk.

Or as though they were poisoned.

She knew what sort of poison made her lips tingle like this, and her fingertips, now she noticed. Though it would take far more neurotoxin to make her feel this much than even a few dozen skinny, gape-mawed fish would provide. How much had she drunk?

Het looked around the blood-spattered room. The single-lived servant was gone. Great Among Millions stood silent and motionless, its tall, thin body crusted with dried blood. Nothing to what covered Het.

She went out into the garden, with its pools and fig trees and the red desert stretching beyond. And found two of Merur's lily standards—She Brings Life and Different Ages. Along with Months and Years. And Dihaut.

"Well, sib," they said, with their regretful smile. "They always send me after you. Everyone else is too afraid of you. I told the One Sovereign it was better not to send forces you'd only chew up. Poison is much easier, and much safer for us."

Het swayed, suddenly exhausted. Dihaut. She'd never expected them to actively take her side, when it came to defying Merur, but she hadn't expected them to poison her.

What *had* she expected? That Merur would approve her actions? No, she'd known someone would come after her, one way or another. And then?

"You can try to alter your metabolism," Dihaut continued, "but I doubt you can manage it quickly enough. The dose was quite high. We needed to be absolutely sure. Honestly, I'm surprised you're still on your feet."

"You," said Het, not certain what she had to say beyond that.

She Gives Life and Different Ages skittered up and stopped a meter or so apart, facing Het. Between them an image of Merur flickered into visibility. Not snakelike, as Het knew her current body to be, but as she appeared in images all over Nu: tall, golden, face and limbs smooth and symmetrical, as though cut from basalt and gilded.

"Het!" cried Merur. "My own Eye! What can possibly have made you so angry that you would take leave of your senses and betray the life and peace of Nu in this way?"

"I was carrying out your orders, Sovereign of Nu!" Het snarled. "You wanted me to remove all possibility of rebellion in Hehut."

"And all of Nu!" piped Great Among Millions, behind Het. Still covered in dried blood.

"I had not thought such sickness and treason possible from anyone Justified as long as you have been," said Merur. "Dihaut."

"Sovereign," said Dihaut, and their smile grew slightly wider. Het growled.

Merur said, "You have said to me before today that I have been too generous. That I have allowed too many of the long-Justified to escape judgment. I did not believe you, but now, look! My Eyes have not been subject to judgment in centuries, and that, I think, has been a mistake. I would like it known that not even the highest of the Justified will be excused if they defy me. Het, before you die, hear Dihaut's judgment."

She was exhausted, and her lips had gone numb. But that was all.

Was she really poisoned? Well, she was, but only a little. Or so it seemed, so far. Maybe she could overpower Dihaut, rip out their throat, and flee. The standards wouldn't stop her.

And then what? Where would she go, that Merur would not eventually follow?

"Sovereign of Nu," said Dihaut, bowing toward Merur's simulacrum. "I will do as you command." They turned to Het. "Het, sib, your behavior this past day is extreme even for you. It calls for judgment, as our Sovereign has said. It is that judgment that keeps order in Hehut, on all of Nu. And perhaps if everyone, every life, endured the same strict judgment as the single-lived pass through, these things would never have happened."

Silence. Not a noise from Great Among Millions, behind Het. Over Dihaut's shoulder, Months and Years was utterly still.

"The One Sovereign has given me the duty of making those judgments. And I must make them, no matter my personal feelings about each person I judge, for the good of Nu."

"That is so," agreed Merur's simulacrum.

"Then from now on, everyone—single-lived or Justified, whoever they may be—every Anima that passes through Tjenu must meet the same judgment. No preference will be given to those who have been resurrected before, not in judgment, and not in the order of resurrection. From now on everyone must meet judgment equally. Including the Sovereign of Nu."

The simulacrum of Merur frowned. "I did not hear you correctly just now, Dihaut."

They turned to Merur. "You've just said that it was a mistake not to subject your Eyes to judgment, and called on me to judge Het. But I can't judge her without seeing that what she has done to the Justified this past day is only what you have always asked her to do to the single-lived. She has done precisely what you demanded of her. It wasn't the fact that Het was unthreatened by judgment that led her to do these things—it was you, yourself."

"You!" spat Merur's simulacrum. "You dare to judge me!"

"You gave me that job," said Dihaut, Months and Years still motionless behind them. "And I will do it. You won't be resurrected on Nu without passing my judgment. I have made certain of this, within the past hour."

"Then it was you behind this conspiracy all along!" cried Merur. "But you can't prevent me returning. I will awake on *Aeons*."

"*Aeons* is far, far overhead," observed Het, no less astonished at what she'd just heard than by the fact that she was still alive.

"And there was no conspiracy," said Dihaut. "Or there wasn't until you imagined one into being. Your own Eyes told you as much. But this isn't the first time you've demanded the slaughter of the innocent so that you can feel more secure. Het only gave me an opportunity, and an example. I will do as you command me. I will judge. Withdraw to *Aeons* if you like. The people who oversee your resurrection on Nu, who have the skills and the access, won't be resurrected themselves until you pass my judgment." They gave again that half-regretful smile. "You've already removed some of those who would have helped you, when you purged

Tjenu of what you assumed was disloyalty to you, Sovereign." The image of Merur flickered out of sight, and She Brings Life and Different Ages scuttled away.

"I'm not poisoned," said Het.

"I should hope not!" exclaimed Dihaut. "No, you left your supper, or your breakfast, or whatever it was, on my flier. I couldn't help being curious about it." They shrugged. "There wasn't much of that neurotoxin in the animal you left behind, but there was enough to suggest that something in that food chain was very toxic. And knowing you, you'd have changed your metabolism rather than just avoid eating whatever it was. Merur, of course, didn't know that. So when she said she wanted you stopped, I made the suggestion . . ." They waved one silver hand.

"So all that business with the single-lived servant, promising her Justification if she would defend those two . . ."

"This late in the day the Justified were already beginning to resist you—or try, anyway," Dihaut confirmed, with equanimity. "If these had stood meekly as you slaughtered them, you might have suspected something. And you might not have drunk enough blood to feel the poison. I had to make you even more angry at the people you killed than you already were."

Het growled. "So you *tricked* me."

"You're not the only one of Merur's Eyes, sib, to find that if you truly served in the way you were meant to, you could no longer serve Merur's aims. It's been a long, long time since I realized that for all Merur says I'm to judge the dead with perfect, impartial wisdom, I can never do that so long as she rules here. She has always assumed that her personal good is the good of Nu. But those are not the same thing. Which I think you have recently realized."

"And now *you'll* be Sovereign over Nu," Het said. "Instead of Merur."

"I suppose so," agreed Dihaut. "For the moment, anyway. But maybe not openly—it would be useful if Merur still called herself the One Sovereign but stayed above on *Aeons* and let us do our jobs without interference." They shrugged again and gave that half smile of theirs.

"Maybe she can salvage her pride by claiming credit for having tricked you into stopping your over-enthusiastic obedience, and saving everyone. In fact, it might be best if she can pretend everything's going on as it was before. We'll still be her Eyes at least in name, and we can make what changes we like."

Het would have growled at them again, but she realized she was too tired. It had been a long, long day. "I don't want to be anyone's Eye. I want to be out of this." She didn't miss the cold, but she wanted that solitude. That silence. Or the illusion of it, which was all she'd really had. "I want to be somewhere that isn't here."

"Are you sure?" Dihaut asked. "You've become quite popular among the single-lived, today. They call you beautiful, and fierce, and full of mercy."

She thought of the children by the river. "It's meaningless. Just old poetry rearranged." Still she felt it, the gratification that Dihaut had surely meant her to feel. She was glad that she'd managed to spare those lives. That the single-lived of Hehut might remember her not for having slaughtered so many of them, but for having spared their lives. Or perhaps for both. "I want to go."

"Then go, sib." Dihaut waved one silver hand. "I'll make sure no one troubles you."

"And the unauthorized lives there? Or elsewhere on Nu?"

"No one will trouble them either," Dihaut confirmed equably. "So long as they don't pose a threat to Hehut. They never did pose a threat to Hehut, only to Merur's desire for power over every life on Nu."

"Thank you." Her skin itched, her fur growing thicker just at the thought of the cold. "I don't think I want you to come get me. When I die, I mean. Or at least, wait a while. A long time." Dihaut gestured assent, and Het continued, "I suppose you'll judge me, then. Who'll judge you, when the time comes?"

"That's a good question," replied Dihaut. "I don't know. Maybe you, sib. Or maybe by then no one will have to pass my judgment just to be allowed to live. We'll see."

That idea was so utterly alien to Het that she wasn't sure how to respond to it. "I want some peace and quiet," she said. "Alone. Apart." Dihaut gestured assent.

"Don't leave me behind, Noble Het!" piped Great Among Millions. "Beautiful Het! Fierce Het! Het full of mercy! I don't want them to put me in a box in a storeroom again!"

"Come on, then," she said, impatiently, and her standard skittered happily after her as she went to find a flier to take her away from Hehut, back to the twilit ice, and to silence without judgment.

SAM J. MILLER

PLANETSTUCK

Sam J. Miller's books have been called "must reads" and "bests of the year" by *USA Today*, *Entertainment Weekly*, *NPR*, and *O: The Oprah Magazine*, among others. He is the Nebula-Award-winning author of *Blackfish City*, which has been translated into six languages and won the John W. Campbell Memorial Award. Miller's short stories have been nominated for the World Fantasy, Theodore Sturgeon, and Locus Awards, and reprinted in many anthologies. He's also the last in a long line of butchers. He lives in New York City. [www.samjmiller.com]

Llopa gave me leave for the first time in basically forever, so I hopped twenty-six gates across three systems to Menelik Station intending to spend a solid solar day in its legendary mile-square waterslide labyrinth—laughing through an endless looping rush of water as warm as blood, through tubes that at their thickest were six slim inches of clear myco-plastic between me and the vacuum of space. Mapp said I could have made it in three gates if I didn't stick to toll-less hops, but I liked saving the currency and I liked the wandering even more, the zigzag path across the stars that took me through strange hubs and space palaces and stations run by cults or companies and others populated exclusively by embodied software constructs.

Anyway, all my plans for wholesome waterslide fun got whisked away when I walked into the Menelik Bathhouse in the hopes of a quick de-stress tryst, and instead got to talking to two burly ex-soldiers who'd just made out like bandits on a bomb-buying mission. They were adorable and bearded and the only thing they loved more than explosives was each other. And showing a guy a good time.

So I spent the first twenty-four hours of my leave in bed, sleeping and skylarking with two beautiful strangers and ordering expensive meals on the tab of a scrappy corporation of two. Dekk and Pell were independent arms dealers from a star system I'd never heard of. Which isn't saying much—there are ninety million human settlements across the twelve gate-connected galaxies, more taking root every day, and even a pleasure boy as gregarious and hardworking as me can't be expected to know all of them.

Which is to say I get distracted easily. So just trust I'll get to the point of this story as soon as personally possible.

Spooned in between them after our sixth or seventh go-round, I was drifting in and out of sleep when I heard:

"What planet are you from?"

It was Dekk, the rawer, rough-around-the-edges one, who clearly came from one of those chaotic semi-feral stations where piracy was governance and formal education absent.

"Shhh," said Pell, who was polished and classy everywhere but in the sack. "You know that's not a polite question to ask."

"It's okay," I murmured, kissing Dekk's apologetic face. There was a ton of bad blood between the space-station-based systemists and the planetside colonies, but there in that bed it all felt very abstract and absurd. "How did you know I was from a planet?"

He shrugged. "It's in the . . . I don't know, the oomph of you. The heft of bone and muscle. For all the supplements and gravity compensation that the off-planet systems have, you can just tell. Can't you?"

I could. I'd never paid much attention to it, but, yeah. Scanning back through the innumerable bodies I'd been intimate with for both business and pleasure, there was a subtle something there. "And you're both stationers."

"We are," Pell said. "And so are you, now. Right? You've come unstuck."

"Yeah you are!" Dekk said, smiling now, persisting adorably in impoliteness. "But for real—what planet?"

"You've never heard of it," I said, grinning, and grabbed hold of both of them, one in each hand, to decisively change the subject.

But all through that next epic session, my mind was elsewhere.

The smell of rain in blue pine forests. Wolfsong. Wild, unpredictable wind. Sunset between the ancient terraform engines, massive machines that had long since served their purpose but remained as memorials to the first arrivals, and habitats for transplanted birds.

My brother weeping. Watching me go.

Dekk could tell he'd shaken something loose. Dekk felt bad. So when we were all spent and sweating and exhausted, he made me the sweetest offer ever:

"Wanna blow stuff up?"

Which is how I found myself on the bridge of a scuttle hopper retro-fitted into a slick little bomber, working the stick on their big purchase: a brand-new lock-and-load torpedo launcher. Dekk pressed a button and the cargo bay doors opened up and three giant mycotic statues shot out into the vacuum—a dinosaur, a dragon, a statue of a man who'd been the head of an enemy army six wars ago and fifty systems away—cheap corny kids' stuff that child warriors use for target practice across the inhabited universe—and I locked on like a pro and marveled at how easy—and how pleasurable—the launcher made it to make things explode.

"Pity the poor fucks who fuck with you!" I said, and we blew up a bunch more stuff before they had to plan their next buying run and I had to check in with my *other* boss, so we went our separate ways. With a sur-prising amount of sadness on my part, and theirs too if Dekk's unstudied face was any indication.

Like most unstuck sex workers, I served two masters. Llopa was my manager—less enlightened systems would have called her my pimp—she vetted my clients and monitored my safety and promoted my "product" throughout her prodigious network, all for an actually super reasonable percentage—but only about a third of my income came from the sex work itself.

For the rest, there was Molybdita. My intelligence handler.

Because of course every sex worker with half a brain was also peddling information. Especially—if you'll forgive the brag—the higher end ones like me, who met the most *fascinating* people, *important* people with more money than sense, more access than acumen. Molybdita paid me a small flat fee for every scrap I brought her, and the real money came in after she'd fenced it. Not so long ago I'd gotten a quarter vibe just for telling her the name of the man who'd paid me to punish him in an Amhara Monastery cell . . . and then received six hundred vibes seven solar days later, when his corporate competitors deduced from his presence in that sector that it was the next space for product roll-out, and they rushed their rival commodity to market a week before his, neutralized millions he'd spent on target-space research, made a billion.

Understand: I'm no idiot. Getting people killed is bad for business, and just generally a shit move. So I always scrub whatever I've got before I sell it. Dekk and Pell knew the drill, had been around rent boys enough— even helped me compose the cleaned-up version and agreed (after some cajoling) to take a 30 percent cut of whatever I made. I have lines I won't cross. Lots of pleasure workers don't—and stars know they make a lot more money that way—and, I don't know, maybe it's dumb, but I actually tend to kind of care about the people who buy my body, provided they treat it with respect, which honestly almost all of them do.

Molybdita said that was the planetstuck part of me. Sentimental, still rooted in outdated notions of familial piety, accountability to abstract notions of "clan" and "tribe" and "country" that had evolved as a survival strategy millennia ago, and had been left behind the day we first learned to spawn wormholes and keep them open and use them to spread beyond the shitty little doomed rock we started from.

She was right, of course. She almost always was. I'd left my planet behind a decade before, but I carried it with me wherever I went.

Mapp gave me a ten-hop toll-less gate path to her, but I was feeling melancholy and tapped "fifty" into the tab so I could meander my way there.

On the way, I let myself remember Uqbar. Dekk had shaken it loose, but I wasn't mad. I spent so much time trying to keep those memories locked away that when they burst free it was almost a relief to let them run riot for a little while.

The green smell of stripped bark—my brother whittling a wooden stick to a point. Dirt-grown onions sizzling in fat.

Sweet smoke on the wind—mycotecture towers burning—a gate port under attack—another one of the periodic anti-offworld convulsions that my planet and most planets got gripped by from time to time.

I passed through stations where dance parties and amputee orgies and tense diplomatic negotiations were in full swing, and I barely saw any of it. And, *yeah*, that's basic hopper etiquette, you're usually passing through somebody's house or yard or town square every time you step from one gate to another, but also, like most hop addicts I'm super hooked on the gleeful eavesdrop thrill of it, the seeing so many wild ways of being, and I should have known right then and there that I was in a bad space and making dumb decisions already if I couldn't let myself bask in it.

Two hours later I'd made all fifty hops and arrived by Molybdita's side, six thousand light-years from Menelik, in a bar trying hard to be seedy, but achieving only sad. Stinking of station liquor, brewed in vats from spoiled fruit. Archaeology thumped from unseen mycospeakers: the ancient songs of fallen planets, lapsed civilizations, genocided troubadours. A pile of fresh gates was stacked in the entrance hall, awaiting installation along the wall: flat panels with an electrified rectangle propping open a wormhole, each one paired to a unique mate somewhere in the portalverse.

Molybdita didn't say a word while I delivered the cleaned-up version of the intel. The one that wouldn't get Dekk or Pell killed. That a company military out of Sector 6-Ж-57.333 was using freelance arms dealers to acquire new explosive deployment mechanisms; that the collapse of a munitions empire in the Lesser Magellanics was leaking wild weird new lethal products that could make a big difference in a couple hundred low-level belligerent engagements.

I waited. This was big intel, the kind I'd only come across once before—and the payments from *that* little discovery let me take six months off of sex work and live large in some of the most magnificent accommodations in the universe—but Molybdita stayed silent. And because she terrified me, I let the silence fester.

A short, chubby woman, system-born-and-bred, forever draped in patchwork—a uniquely systemist school of fashion that embodied the plurality and scrappy upcycling spirit of the unstuck by stitching every garment out of many others. Molybdita probably had thousands of intelligence assets like myself—and even more buyers, representing every drug syndicate and trade federation and ideological cooperative and rebel religion you could think of, most of whom were mortal enemies, any of whom would gladly have killed her to keep her from helping their enemies—but she feared no one. Had, in fact, eradicated innumerable idiots who dared to make a move on her, in ways she made sure ended up on the chatter streams.

"What aren't you telling me?" she said at last.

"That's it, boss," I said, smiling like I did when I was lying to a john. Because, sure, she could torture the truth out of me, but I figured she reserved that for much more extreme cases.

"Good," she said, and slid a shot along the bar. I sat on the next stool, noting its warmth.

"You're stacking asset meetings today," I said. "Who was just sitting here?"

Molybdita laughed. "Nothing gets by you."

"I'd be a disappointment to you if it did."

"Anti-offworlder," she said. "Preacher. Drinking problem. Creepy guy."

"What's he doing out in the portalverse if he's so proudly planetstuck?"

"He's part of Zero Alliance—some kind of coalition of anti-offworlders, coordinating tactics and supporting local movements. Dude is pretty deep in debt, so he comes to see me when they've got something planned."

Some kind of coalition was her playing dumb. I did not doubt for a second that she knew its exact size and scope and ambitions, had read its manifestoes and meeting minutes and memorized its membership.

"Fascinating," I said, hating him instinctively, whoever he was, flagging the bartender down for another shot—holding eye contact a beat too long, from hustler force of habit and because they were hot as hell.

And then.

I looked down.

At the bar, where this anti-offworlder asshole had tossed a handful of coins as a tip. Jerk move, was all I thought at first—systemists didn't use coins, they were strictly a willful archaism of the stuck, useless outside their planet or planetary empire of origin. Tipping with coins was like leaving garbage.

And then I saw it. One coin. Wafer-thin, blue-gray metal, stamped with a familiar winged fox.

An uqbaritlön. Like the one sewn into the flap of my satchel, that I touch from time to time when the loneliness is so sharp and so cold it's like the vacuum of space has filled up my veins, because that coin is the actual and entire last piece of my home I have left.

I picked this one up. Looked closer. Died inside.

Smiled at Molybdita—a different dishonest one, this time. One I used much more rarely than the one I wielded when deceiving tricks. This smile said *I am panicking and I've got to get out of here immediately and I can't let you know how scared I am.* "Debit this from whatever you get from that intel," I said, pocketing it, getting up, making myself swallow my shot in a slow leisurely unpanicked everything-is-fine sip.

She waved without looking up from her screen, doubtless already lining up her next session.

Pleasure worker 101: never run the odds. When you're a newbie pro and all you can think of is every way an encounter can go wrong, you're gonna be tempted to do the math. How likely *is* this guy to murder me? Hurt me bad in ways I can't come back from? Give me an infection I never heard of, whose only treatment is sixty thousand gate hops away and Mapp sure as shit won't know how to chart you a course to *that* unregistered clinic?

So I already knew how to resist the urge, to keep myself from wondering *what are the chances, the infinitesimal odds that this coin and I should cross paths in the vastness of untold hundreds of millions of grungy bars?*

Here's the story I should have told you at the top, and would have if it didn't hurt so much.

Which, wow, that's super dumb. Losing everything, what a boring banal story. Probably every sixty seconds a planet or a people or a whole system gets swallowed up by oblivion. Homeworlds vanish. Continents are death-rayed; nation-states get nuked; castes collapse from viruses tagged to their specific ethnomicrobiome.

This story isn't special just because it's mine.

Anti-offworld sentiment was at a low simmer when I left Uqbar, same as it is on almost every planet. Nationalism is endemic among the stuck—as is its shadow self, xenophobia—but it rarely progresses past low grumbles, occasional violence. *We do all the work of growing food and producing goods; when the people of Planet Zero expanded to the stars and seeded the asteroids and planets and moons with all the teeming plant and animal and human life of their dying rock they meant for we who steward that life to live free, as we had at home, not become slaves to cushy elites in outer space pleasure palaces.* Easy to say, guaranteed to get a crowd riled up and maybe sway an election, but only the most deranged ideologues could deny that the economic and cultural benefits of portal connectivity are as essential to the planetstuck as they are to the systemists.

And yet. The last few times I talked to my brother Drommeda, stuff was spiking. Previously rational people becoming less so. Portal protests shutting down entire cities. I paid it no mind, not even when he said he was scared for him and mom and the two dads we had left.

Not even when he asked me to help him hop away, host or sponsor him if he couldn't get a student visa or refugee status.

But because I was young—and enjoying my first taste of freedom, my days an endless delirious string of new systems, dazzling sights, abundant sexual partners—and because I was an idiot—I told him we'd talk about it the next time we talked. "Give me a week to figure something out," I'd said, when all I intended to figure out was a way to tell him no.

After we got off the ansible, though, I moved past my first flush of resentment at the thought of my precious solitude being transgressed upon. And I *did* ask around. I *did* start to make arrangements.

But when I rang him up a week later, the call could not go through.

Ansible Hub Unavailable, it said, an error message I'd never seen before.

Ansible calls go through gates. They send data through a dizzying series of relay portals to connect speakers across systems and galaxies. Knowing that Uqbar's ansible hub had gone down started a sick terrified churning in my stomach.

I kept the route to Uqbar pinned to my Mapp. Called it up from time to time. Just to see. I never intended to make the trip again, but it was comforting to know exactly how easy it would be to get back. It's an isolated system, and the trip was rarely less than sixty hops.

But when I called it up then, the hop counter said N/A.

I imagined the Northern Continent finally declaring nuclear war— the next system over triggering our star into controlled supernova with a cobalt ion stream—the geostorm to end all geostorms that every terraformed planet lived in fear of.

But none of that explained N/A. N/A meant there were no gates left.

News trickled out through the portalverse in the days that followed. The anti-off-worlders had reached critical mass. Bubbled beneath the surface until they'd infiltrated every institution, rallied millions to their crazy death cult. They'd identified every gate on Uqbar—the public and the private, the ones that went to the stars and the ones that went one city over—and they destroyed them. Then they destroyed the orbiting ones, and the ansible hub.

Cut themselves off completely. Cut *me* off completely.

Understand: Uqbar was one of the most distant settled planets. Nothing anywhere around it. Grief-stricken expats formed groups, pooled resources, commissioned studies, sent near-light microprobes complete with telescoping nanogates that could be opened upon arrival at Uqbar—but it would take four hundred years for the fastest to get there.

I'd never see my home again. Never talk to my brother. And every day—a dozen times a day—I ask Mapp for the fastest route to Uqbar. Praying I'll see something other than N/A.

Like I said: banal. Boring. Hideous tragedies happen by the hundred thousand, every second of every day. I'd built a wall around mine, which had just been breached.

I kept the coin clenched in my palm, as I hopped my way back to Menelik. Went straight for Dekk and Pell's ship—which was still there, though they were not.

So I went to the bar. Knowing it was dumb. Drinking when you're shivering so hard from fear and hope and grief and rage is rarely a good idea.

Six drinks in, I finally opened my hand, and held the coin up to the light. To confirm it hadn't changed.

It hadn't. It was real. Even though it was impossible.

I left Uqbar in the year 157, by planetary reckoning. Place got cut off in PR 159. But the coin I held was dated PR 168.

And, sure, someone could have fabbed it. Easy enough to do so, with incredibly sophisticated printers on every station. But why bother? Uqbar was small change, an impoverished nothing planet whose vanishing made not even the tiniest mark upon the broader portalverse, and left behind only a couple of hundred homeless little wretches like me, scattered across the stars. Bigger better worlds than mine had gone dark. Systems shattered by war. Empires imploded. A fake coin from one of them could command massive currency, or induce a wealthy refugee to do absolutely anything.

It's real, I told myself, more drunk on hope than the shots of liquor I kept lining up and pounding down. *This tlön has got to be real.*

Which means it's true. The thing I pray for ceaselessly.

There's a gate. A secret portal survived, somewhere on Uqbar. A wormhole in a basement or attic or closet, well-hidden from the maniacs that conquered my planet.

And then I was up, walking the halls of Menelik Station, drunker than I'd ever been before and suddenly desperate to be sober.

This should have been good news. So why was I panicking? Where had this fear come from, higher and tighter in my chest than I'd felt in ages?

And then I was down. Face pressed to cold steel in the docking bay, outside the hatch that connected to Dekk and Pell's ship. Busy traffic thrummed all around me, but no one so much as gave me a second glance. What they saw wasn't strange: one more homeless bum begging for a ride somewhere; another messed-up soldier who couldn't handle shore leave. I left a video on the ship's access cam, one that Sober Me would almost certainly find unspeakably embarrassing.

And then I was out.

And I was back. Ten years old—two-year-old Drommeda on my shoulders, crying from terror, his tiny hands clenched furiously to mine—as I waded into the warm still sea of a world with no moon. Until his toes touched the surface of the water, and his fear became joyous laughter.

And I was back. Thirteen years old—desiring something other than the girl who'd been allotted me by the mate-match AI—watching my friend Li smile in sheepish happiness at the girl whose hand he held— wishing I could make him smile like that—hating the old settler mentality: *it's everyone's responsibility to make as many babies as possible; tough luck if that's not what you want for your life*. And I was back—and I was sixteen—and I was leaving forever and nobody knew it—and I came home for the last time, a plan in place to sneak out while they were all asleep, and Dad was cooking dinner, onions frying in fat, and the smell was so good I almost scrapped my plans. I loved my home, even as I hated it.

And then I was up. Moving. Hopping. Buying eye drops and breath mints and a gallon jug of electrolyte sobriety soda even though the stuff tasted nasty and what it did to the inside of my head was probably worse than being drunk. Making my way back to Molybdita.

Who was sitting right where I'd left her. Somehow only three hours had passed, by portalverse reckoning—still pinned to the same twenty-four-hour solar cycle as the long-lost Planet Zero. Weird how your whole world can collapse so swiftly, and no one else even notices.

"Well," she said. "This is unscheduled."

"Sorry," I said, with the slight stutter of manufactured neurotransmitters.

"No need. Got something else for me?"

"Actually, I could use something from you," I said, and I sat, on the same stool, and I knew I needed to choose my words carefully because the last thing I wanted was to be in Molybdita's debt, but the soda was having its way with me. "The guy who was here before me. The preacher. The creep. I need to talk to him."

She nodded. I wondered how much she knew. Usually everything. She'd have done her research on me—would know, although we'd never discussed it, that I was Uqbari. But she would never in a million years have recognized the coin—and if the guy was hopping to planets no one was supposed to be able to access, he'd have kept it a secret. So she probably—but not definitely—didn't know where he'd been.

"Here," she said, and pinged me a Mapp tracker.

I blinked in surprise. She encouraged her assets to associate, mostly because she valued the stories they'd swap—the gossip about her brutality, the hustlers and drug dealers and down-on-their-luck diplomats she'd rubbed out for exceedingly minor transgressions.

But still. This was not the kind of intel Molybdita gave away willy-nilly. "You need me to find something out for you."

She tilted her drink at me, saluting my acumen. "He's returned to their raggedy alliance's little headquarters. And I don't trust them, none of them, not one bit. So I've sent you a registry phreaker, which his ship should respond to like a normal governance relay, and ping back a log of all its recent hops. Beam that back to me. I need to know where he's been."

"To run a registry phreaker I'd need a ship," I said, smiling, because she was smiling, because of course—somehow—she knew.

"Maybe you have a friend who is in," and she scrolled up on her screen to our meeting notes, "a company military out of Sector 6-Ж-57.333. Or the freelance arms dealers who are working for them? Maybe *he* can give you a ride. In one or more senses of the phrase."

"If I didn't love you so much, I'd be afraid of you," I said, standing.

"Love and fear are both appropriate."

I bowed, and fled. And took the quick way home—ten hops instead of fifty.

"Thank gods," Dekk said, four minutes later, when I turned up at their door. Pell looked like Dekk sounded. "We thought you'd—"

"Disregard whatever I said in that message," I said, swamping them both in a big glad hug. Jittery from excitement and hope and fear and soda.

"Disregard *I'm letting go of everything, I have to take this chance, what kind of person am I if I don't*?"

"Yes," I said. "Disregard that. Sorry I lost my mind a little there— freaked out when I couldn't find you." I looked for a way to play off the awkwardness in that stark declaration of need and couldn't find one.

"Had to hop back to one of our buyers, pitch them what we picked up," Pell said, "would have given you the access code if we'd have known you'd be back."

Their gate arrays were fanned out above the bay like stacked screens on extendable arms: dozens of doorways, swapped out as missions shifted, each one paired to a wild wonderful place. These were propri- etary corporate and military portals that wouldn't pop up on Mapp, exciting conflict hot spots and secret sexy soldier spaces—

I loved my life. I loved hopping.

And I hated that I had no choice. That my home had been taken off the table. "Can you help me with something? It would involve running ille- gal software on your, uh, work ship. And probably pissing off a massive terrorist network? And kinda sorta doing the bidding of a top-tier intel- ligence syndicate head who definitely has millions of powerful enemies?"

"Of course," Dekk said, soulful eyes damp with concern for me, and I wanted to hug him forever.

"Yeah, we would have agreed at 'help me with something.' The other stuff just sweetens the gig." Pell was more excited by the risk involved, but I loved that, too.

I explained it all. Molybdita—my vanished home—the creepy preach- er that might or might not know a way back to it. And then they were in soldier mode, battening down hatches and decoupling brackets and a bunch of other equally baffling stuff.

"You guys do this for every rent boy you spend a lost weekend with?"

"Only the ones as cute as you," Pell said, spinning up their special military Mapp, a dizzying star map of gates—the regular one that I used only had red circles for toll gates and blue squares for free ones, but theirs had a dozen different colors and innumerable shapes.

"Which is none," Dekk said.

We were off, queuing up for passage through Menelik's tertiary vessel portal, following the slow orderly parade of vehicles through it—pausing every sixty seconds when the beacon flipped and control started guiding ships in from the other side—and then we were through.

The system's hub was small, as regional hot spots go, but since I ship-hopped so rarely it never failed to impress me: to see thousands of gates floating in space, ancient obsidian ones and new cobalt ones, big and small, adorned with the branding of religions and corporations and nation-planets. This hub was a wall, its gates arranged in a flat grid repeating into the distance in all directions. Some hubs were rings or spheres, some were lattices, some were unstructured, gates flung willy-nilly across the ether.

"I suppose this gets very boring for you," I whispered.

"Never," they said as one.

Dekk directed us through a rusty steel gate, its surface a hodgepodge of recycled structures. When we emerged, I saw we were somewhere I knew well: a hub whose gates were arranged in a diamond. And I must have made a noise of disapproval, because Dekk said, "Let me guess. You get a lot of clients out of here."

"Sure do," I said.

This part of space was one of the few systems with strict ethical re-strictions on who you could have relations with, based on the gender given to you at your birth. So of course the men from here were super repressed and super into some super freaky stuff.

Molybdita's ping took us through a gate in the hub's upper-left arm, spitting us out into—of course—ugh—orbit above a planet.

It filled their viewscreens, and the starboard side portholes. Green seas; reddish-brown landmasses; the massive mycodome cities of a planet whose terraforming was still underway. The sight spoke to me skeleton-deep, and I hated the tug of it. One more sign of how I was stuck.

We docked at the station; I disembarked. Dekk and Pell wanted to come, but I didn't want to risk scaring the dude. "Run the registry phreaker while I'm gone. Here's Molybdita's dead-drop frequency, and my call sign in her system—beam her the results when you get them."

They saluted, good little soldiers still, and I was briefly paralyzed by the desire to drop everything and cuddle with them until we all died happy in bed of dehydration. I thought for sure he'd be in the bar, but the easyfind ping Molybdita provided took me to a wide low-ceilinged space on the station, one wall of which was windows—facing away from the planet, out at the familiar star-sea of space. Which was one small mercy. In roped-off squares, men—all men—punched each other in the face repeatedly. They wore comically puffy gloves and they didn't use kicks, elbows, headbutts, any of the stock-in-trade of every fighting sport known to the portalverse. Just punches.

It looked like some bizarre ancient ancestor of the beam fights my brother had been obsessed with around the time I abandoned him for-ever *but maybe not forever* and the thing about portal-hopping is it can take you super far super fast, which facilitates charging forward un-prepared, which is 100 percent what I was doing just then. No plan, no cover narrative, not even the bare minimum backstory I constructed for johns who got sentimental after sex and wanted to know my whole life. Plus the sobriety soda was still simmering inside my head.

He was a nervous-looking little slip of a thing, pleading with a corner-man whose attention was entirely focused on a fighter. Their voices were low but I knew that hunted look in his eyes: somebody begging for a loan, or for more time to pay off money already loaned.

A bell rang. A dozen sparring matches ceased. Fighters returned to corners. The guy Molybdita's broke preacher had been talking to turned to him with an *if-you-don't-get-the-hell-away-from-me* gesture, and preacher man skedaddled to somebody else, who was just as aggressively uninterested. So he took a seat.

This was a training facility. For would-be warriors in the noble strug-gle against the evil systemists. I could see it in these boys' eyes: the same hate I'd seen back home, the same contempt for anyone who wasn't one of them. The smell of sweat and mycotic leather and burned algae coffee was intoxicating—arousing—and I rolled with my old friend desire and let it be my guide.

"Hey," I said, sitting down beside him. "Sorry, this is super weird, but you work for Molybdita, yeah?"

He turned to me, shocked, twitchy.

"I'm Aran," I said, inclining my head, unsure which signal of greeting he'd favor. "Broyce," he said, holding out his hand, which, eww. Who still does that. But I took it, and I shook it, because that too is Pleasure Worker 101: sometimes you gotta do stuff that's a little icky.

I set subterfuge aside. I was gonna play this straight. I pulled out the coin, extended it between two fingers. "Where'd you get this?"

Swiftly, like he saw a snake, he clasped my hand in both of his to hide the coin. "Walk with me."

"Sure," I said, following his sad hunched shamble. He paused to touch the sleeves or try to whisper in the ears of a couple other guys on the way out, all of whom ignored or frowned or shrugged or threatened him.

"This way," he said, taking me out a door—into a hallway—and transforming completely.

"I knew it was you," he said, an entirely new man. His posture perfect; his sheepish grin gone. "Saw you on Menelik and said to myself, that's his brother."

My jaw dropped. The word *brother* barely registered, beneath the shock of this transformation.

It had all been an act. The sad broke gambler in the training hall—the creepy alcoholic preacher Molybdita believed she was working with—they weren't real. The best cover stories contain a ton of truth, and by pretending to be a sad useless anti-offworlder he'd hidden what a dangerous one he was, the better to gather intel and spread deceit. And he'd fooled me, which, no heavy lift there, so does everything—but to have fooled my boss? Who built an empire around her ability to judge and play people? Whatever he was, this guy was not to be underestimated.

"Sorry," he said, with a chuckle, one firm manly hand on my shoulder. Military, I realized. A leader of warriors. A boss. "Breathe."

"You," breathe, "know my brother."

Not a question. A baffling, impossible statement. "Everybody on Uqbar knows Drommeda Jangr," he said.

Tears came—unwanted, unstoppable. He was alive. *Uqbar* was alive—accessible—somehow. A gate really had survived. Maybe more than one. Until mere hours ago, I had been too weak—too torpid, too defeated—to even hope for such a thing. Now it was a fact.

"How . . ."

"He's Public Enemy Number One. The biggest fucking pain in my ass on the planet. I've been trying to kill him for years, to be perfectly frank."

". . . how . . ."

"Not everyone is happy with what we've accomplished, since taking ourselves offline and re-dedicating ourselves to the values that made humanity so powerful we could break time and space with wormholes in the first place. There is a small but persistent resistance movement, of which your brother is the lead. Doomed, of course, but quite charismatic. Secret pictures of him hang in many homes."

Broyce smiled at my speechlessness. At the pain I couldn't hide: to think of my brother, alone, abandoned, afraid, becoming something great, fighting a doomed noble fight while I frolicked from bed to bed across the entire portalverse. The little boy afraid of the sea, fearless in the face of a government made up of monsters.

I wondered if he thought of me. If I was an inspiration or an embarrassment. "Do you want to go home, Aran?"

I nodded. I *did* want to go home. Stars help me I did. Some part of me had always been planetstuck. Some part of me would always be weeping, remembering the smell of my father frying onions.

And this guy—this slick manipulator—was my only way back. I wondered if he walked around with a whole pocketful of coins from planets they'd conquered, just in case someone came along who might be from one of them.

"You must know I hate everything you stand for," I said.

"Of course," he said. "But I also know how homesick you are, Aran. How badly you want to get home—to see your family again. They mostly stay out of politics, but we still keep tabs on all of them. Just in case. Your mom. Your dads. You miss them enough to follow me here, right? I'm offering you a way to come home."

"And all I have to do for you . . ."

He laughed, like, aren't you a smart lad. But I wasn't one of his lads. "All you have to do for us is be an olive branch. A gesture, to your brother, that we are kind and we are forgiving. And that if he agrees to personally abandon the struggle, we'll give him a blanket amnesty for all the political and property crimes he's been accused of."

"If he's as committed to the cause as you say he is, he'd hate me just for asking that of him."

"We're not asking you to sign in blood. You don't have to ever say a word to him on the subject. We'll deliver the offer—and we'll deliver you—and that will be that."

I didn't trust him. I couldn't. And trying to play him was a scary proposition. I had no idea how skilled he was, how savage. The station corridor we walked was long and flimsy, breaking off into forks and crossroads and six-way intersections—from one branching arm of it I heard the rhythmic roar of soldiers drilling.

"What's your home planet?" I asked.

"Tsai Khaldun," he said, chin rising with pride. "Settled as a rich man's personal hunting preserve, with a staff of animal tenders who eventually overthrew him and founded a workers' cooperative. I grew up in the lowlands of the Axa Delta. Six hundred islands, each with its own genetically distinct population of wild horses. Summer mornings the smell of clover was so strong it would make you drunk. Marvelous place."

"And is it," what was the word he had used? "offline?"

"It is."

"Completely? Or is there a secret gate somewhere so hypocrites like you can come and go as you please, enjoying the freedom of motion you pretend you hate?"

"Completely," he said, and was this real? this flash of sadness, the tremor in the voice and the wetness of the eyes? "Tsai Khaldun was one of the first planets where an anti-offworlder tendency evolved. My father was a leader in that movement—fled persecution with our whole family when I was only ten. When the movement succeeded . . . well. That's what it means to believe in something. To be prepared to sacrifice everything for it. Even the very thing you believe in. My father—and others—learned lessons there. Like ensuring that it's possible for persecuted refugees to return, and to share lessons and tactics with the broader alliance. Hence the existence of secret gates, on future planets of our involvement."

"How many planets have you guys conquered?"

"We don't keep track," he said, and they definitely did, "and we don't conquer. We support the people who live there, who want to preserve their way of life. What makes them special."

I could smell the sea. I could hear my brother's voice. "How quickly can we get there?"

Broyce pulled out a bizarre hacked Mapp interface, like three devices sutured together with tubules and piping. Branded with a blue oval, and the words *Zero Alliance* inside it. "Six hops. Each one closely guarded, of course. Passing through our most sensitive facilities."

"How do I know you won't kidnap me, lock me up, use me as . . . less consensual leverage? Threaten to hurt me if Drommeda doesn't turn himself in?"

He gave a slight head tilt, like that was the first he'd thought of it—which it definitely wasn't. "The long answer is, if you want to bring a weapon or something, to not feel completely helpless, that's fine. But the short answer is . . . you can't. You won't know what you're walking into, what we might have arrayed against you, and so on. I recognize that might make this a deal breaker, and of course I respect your decision either way."

The offer was absurd. No sane person would accept it. But Broyce believed I was as desperate to return to my vanished homeworld as he was, and that my vision would be as clouded as his would.

I was terrified. I had traveled untold trillions of miles in the years since I'd left my home, and this was the first time I had even the slightest glimmer of hope of finding my way back there. And that glimmer involved trusting someone I had every reason to despise.

But I could do this. I had to do this.

Right?

"I have to make some arrangements," I said. "And find myself a good weapon. Can I meet you back at the fight facility in an hour?"

"Meet me at my ship," he said, smiling like anyone anywhere who'd just won an argument. He tapped his Mapp to mine to send me the coordinates.

"Sounds good," I said, scrutinizing the info even though I knew exactly where in the shipyard his vessel was, and had in fact docked six ships over and already run a phreaker on it.

A short walk back to the berthing hangar—a long stroll down Bay Eight—to the dock where Dekk and Pell's ship was waiting. My heart hammering louder with every step I took away from him. Avoiding eye contact with all the hot awful brutal broad-shouldered boys who filled the halls. With Broyce I'd been all puffed-chest bravado and easy fearless smile, but that was just another sex worker superpower: looking someone you're scared of in the eye and smiling like you're invincible, like nothing could possibly hurt you, so they won't even try.

Alone with my thoughts—with my fear—with my hope—it was another story. I stopped outside their ship to try to think and breathe, but I didn't have much luck with either, and Dekk must have been monitoring the external cams for me because I hadn't been there thirty ticks when the door irised open and there he was, rubbing his hands and giggling.

"We got him, babe," he said, the big bearded grin and the hand on my arm and the affectionate nickname all soothing me inexplicably. He pulled me in, slung an arm around me, walked me to the bridge. "Phreaker gave us a perfect registry of the last thousand hops his ship made—we sent it to Molybdita like you said, and she's mad as hell! Apparently it exposes glaring contradictions in the info he's been feeding her."

"Nice," I said, my heart heavy. None of those hops would tell me where the way home was. The gate to Uqbar would be for human transport only: they'd take no chances on an enemy ship blasting past their defenses and reconnecting my planet to the portalverse.

Pell hopped up when we reached the bridge, bear-hugged us both.

I wanted them. One last time, rushed and desperate, right there on the floor of the bridge, a final gasp of delirious freedom—of the ecstasy that only the unstuck can truly experience—before I grounded myself forever.

But I didn't have time for that. Whatever I was going to do—if I was going to do anything—I had to do it fast. All I had on my side was surprise, and the hope that Broyce didn't already have a plan in place for bizarre situations like this. And every second I gave him was time he could use to figure out a way to put the hurt on me.

He could ansible back to Uqbar—tell the local leadership what he had—start planning my downfall and Drommeda's. To say nothing of the fact that if I vanished into the ether with him immediately after revealing the extent of his treachery to Molybdita, she'd hunt me down with the same vicious team of torturers. And maybe she'd never find me—space was big—but I'd definitely spend the rest of my life waiting for them to show up.

I stared out the porthole, at his banged-up war trawler monstrosity. A front, a fake, like his handful of sad sack disguises—but also unmistakably him, now that I had seen who that really was: a solid, stagnant thing, rooted and powerful but rotten to the core. I looked around the bridge of Dekk and Pell's rinky-dink little scuttle hopper, honest in its humble hodgepodge magnificence. Bits and pieces of pirate vessels and ghost stations and the weaponry of wars and skirmishes long past.

Drommeda's world wasn't mine. Neither was his struggle. The things that pulled me back to Uqbar were guilt, and entitled greed for something that had been taken away from me, and force of homesick habit.

Idly, from nervousness and fear and sadness, I palmed the locking ball of the torpedo launcher. Shifted the cursor from ship to ship in the viewport, before settling it on Broyce's.

He was a big deal. A general, probably. A leader, definitely—a linchpin of their sick interstellar strategy. I could kill him effortlessly.

Absurd. Idiotic. Pushing down on that ball was the action of someone strong, fearless, brave, bold—and above all selfless—none of which

I was. Pushing down on that ball meant giving up all hope of ever seeing home again.

But I remembered Broyce's big hand on my shoulder. A gesture of command, of control. And it flashed me back to one of my first tricks, back before I had all my survival skills and security protocols. He'd been into bondage; had me hogtied; super normal stuff, happens all the time. But when it started to hurt—when I said the safe word—he didn't move or say a word. Just looked at me. Enjoying the fear on my face. For what felt like forever. Of course I assumed I was about to be tortured to death. And then he'd just untied me, and paid me three times what we'd discussed, but I carried the terror of it around with me to this day.

I couldn't feel that fear again. I couldn't put myself in Broyce's hands and trust he wouldn't hurt me. I wasn't strong enough.

I pushed the ball down halfway. And turned and said, "I'm sorry, guys."

"What," they said, as one, adorably, and my heart ached for the trouble I was about to bring down on them.

"This is gonna get messy."

Dekk grinned. Down for whatever the hell it was. Pell did not. But I couldn't stop. I slammed my palm down hard. And then did it again. Watched two threads of fire arc across the screen, collide with Broyce's ship, break it in half in a big glorious ball of flame and shrapnel.

Dekk howled joy and Pell cursed, and they both sprang to battle stations. In what seemed like a split second Pell had disengaged the docking clamps and was steering us out, applying full thrusters way too soon—devastating the gate we'd just been docked at and strafing the ships around us when he turned the ship sharply left and then right, a genius chaos move that I found disturbingly stimulating. And Dekk was in the railgun seat, spraying electromagnetic-pulse projectiles that tore gaping holes in everything around us.

I stood there, too stunned to speak or move. The violence of it barely registered. The death I'd caused. The danger I'd put us in. I stared at my hand like it was a live and separate thing, a treasonous servant who had ruined all my hopes and plans because it knew that's exactly what I wanted and didn't dare claim for myself.

Blowing up Broyce had been the right move for Drommeda, but that wasn't really why I'd done it.

"Okay, so . . . what exactly went down in there?" Dekk asked.

"Let's get out alive first, how about that?" Pell said.

Because of course this was not some sleepy backwater trading station—it was a base for coordinated anti-offworlder military activity. We'd caught them by surprise, but they weren't helpless—they had patrol ships circling the hub at all times, and eleven seconds after I blew up Broyce's ship they were locked on and closing in.

"Where you going?" Dekk said.

"Um, away from the people trying to kill us?" Pell said, as bullets started strafing silently past our portholes.

"Okay, but, you're also taking us away from the gates that are our only way out of here, so . . ."

"I know that!"

Pell cut a hard twist and brought the ship about, showing six heavy gun trawlers in the viewport—which broke formation and banked away from the projectiles Dekk now turned on them.

"Damn, Aran, didn't think you had it in you," Pell said.

"I did," Dekk said.

Still I said nothing. Not afraid of death—though it seemed super likely; more ships were declamping from their docks and engaging us— just sitting in the hollow and the hurt like you do when you've learned something huge about yourself and you don't yet know what it means.

Pell cursed, shifting course abruptly away from the hub, where a wall of warships large and small had come together. "Hold on to something," he said, digging into a series of sharp jagged evasive maneuvers.

"Where we going, buddy?" Dekk said, blasting wildly, unable to lock on but still strafing occasional enemy vessels enough to make them break off.

"Away!"

They both cursed.

I should have been helping. I had to hope that if there was actually anything I could do, they'd tell me to do it. And that I'd be able to obey.

Who knew what I was, now. What I was capable of.

We were small and we were fast and we were scared, so we got out of range quick enough. The problem was, they were still following us. And on the main screen Mapp assured us that in the direction we were going, at top speed, it'd be ten thousand years before we ever saw a human settlement. And that our "travel capacity"—the time until we all starved to death or died of dehydration—was sixteen days.

"We could keep going, hope they all break off, swing around and try to make a break for the hub again?"

"They won't," Pell said. "Not all of them. And even if they did, they'd keep the hub at high alert until they knew we were dead."

"Yeah."

Dekk stood, started disconnecting the torpedo launcher. Pell locked the settings in, went to get a dolly and began loading it up.

"What's . . . happening?"

"We're abandoning ship," Pell said. "We'll hop a gate back."

"Stars," I swore. "I am so sorry I messed this all up for you."

"It's fine," Dekk said. "This is just a flimsy little thing we use for trading gigs. The torpedoes themselves are a dime a dozen, and we can take the launcher with us super easily. It's the only irreplaceable thing here. That, and us three."

Pell shuffled through the gate array. In the rear viewport, thirteen ships fell back out of railgun range.

"Wonder how long before they realize they're following a ghost ship?" I helped them pack, haphazardly. Twenty minutes and it was all over.

"You wanna say goodbye to it?" Pell asked.

"No," Dekk said. "That's kid stuff."

Dekk was mad as hell but fine with walking away. Pell wasn't. What warrior doesn't come to love their murder toys?

An arm unfurled from the array, extending a gate. Pell pinged it to confirm the other side was clear, then pushed the dolly through. I helped Dekk carry the crate containing the torpedo launcher—a surprisingly compact little creature.

And then we were back. In Menelik. The smell of chlorine and new tile and distant incense. So familiar—so *systemist*—I had to turn away so they wouldn't see my face contort.

I followed them down the deck in a daze. "Don't any of your gates back there . . . shouldn't they, I don't know, not fall into the wrong hands?"

"Ship is rigged to blow up if anybody tries to board, though I don't think they could catch up to us," Pell said, avoiding eye contact. "To-morrow we'll send a couple of tacticals through to telescope them down, bring them back. Pay Menelik the restock fee, since we broke this rental by leaving its mate stranded."

Wordlessly, we went back to my berth. Each of us exhausted and ex-hilarated and grief-stricken and scared in our own ways. And of course we had more fun, and the sex was incredible even though—or because?—my room was so much smaller, the bed barely big enough for our three rambunctious bodies—but there was a solemn stricken air to our inter-course now. And Pell was super mad at me, though he tried his hardest not to let it impact the moment. For Dekk's sake, I knew.

"You want to join our company?" little-spoon Dekk said afterward.

"Aran's already got a job, and he probably makes way more money than we could pay him," said big-spoon Pell.

"I'm not talking about him being an employee," Dekk said solemnly.

"Maybe," said middle-spoon me, to spare Pell the ugly task of saying no to the offer of full partnership Dekk had just made. I didn't blame him if he hated me. I'd fucked his whole life up.

When you're a kid you think you can be anything. Every day you live you learn something else you can't do. Can't be. I was no soldier. Blowing stuff up was fun, but choosing to put yourself in a potentially deadly situation? I found out the hard way that wasn't me. I gave up my only shot at getting back to Uqbar rather than submit to the scary unknown.

In the morning they had to head back to their HQ, stow the launcher and debrief the fiasco, find out whether Zero Alliance had been able to ping the scuttle hopper back to them and was gonna try to slaugh-ter them both. Which, probably. Dekk tapped an everfind tag into my

Mapp, an unspeakably intimate act, more profound than any commitment ring—a ring wouldn't tell me exactly how to find them no matter where they were in the portalverse. I returned the favor; hugged them hard and for a long long time; said goodbye. Whispered *I'm so sorry* into Pell's ear, but he didn't say or do a thing. And then I went, at last, to the waterslide labyrinth. Checking in with Molybdita should have been my priority, but I'd been ad-libbing my life for too long and I had learned the hard way that impulsively shifting directions can take you to someplace you can't come back from.

I clanked over the currency for an unlimited pass. Leapt into the ingress pool. Swam toward the first chute. Let it suck me down and into the labyrinth. Within an hour I had become adept at avoiding the middle atrium, where zero-G sometimes stopped you in a massive press of floating bodies and bubbles of water, until a staffer came through to tug you free, because the thing I needed above all else was not to slow, not to stop, not to think.

I stayed there for hours, as my muscles began to ache and hunger kindled and grew inside me. Spiraling endlessly through space, a lone body against the void, in water the temperature of tears.

KARIN TIDBECK
THE LAST VOYAGE OF SKIDBLADNIR

Karin Tidbeck lives in Malmö, Sweden, and writes short stories, novels and interactive fiction in Swedish and English. They debuted in 2010 with the Swedish short story collection *Vem* är *Arvid Pekon?* Their English debut, the 2012 collection *Jagannath*, won the Crawford Award in 2013 and was shortlisted for the World Fantasy Award as well as honor listed for the Tiptree Award. Their novel *Amatka* was shortlisted for the Locus Award and Prix Utopiales 2018. Their most recent novel is *The Memory Theatre*. [www.karintidbeck.com]

Something had broken in a passenger room. Saga made her way through the narrow corridors and down the stairs as fast as she could, but Aavit the steward still looked annoyed when she arrived.

"You're here," it said, and clattered its beak. "Finally."

"I came as fast as I could," Saga said.

"Too slow," Aavit replied and turned on its spurred heel.

Saga followed the steward through the lounge, where a handful of passengers were killing time with board games, books and pool. They were mostly humans today. Skidbladnir had no windows, but the walls on the passenger levels were painted with elaborate vistas. There was a pine forest where copper spheres hung like fruit from the trees; there was a cliff by a raging ocean, and a desert where the sun beat down on the sand. Saga enjoyed the view whenever she was called downstairs to take care of something. The upper reaches had no such decorations.

The problem Saga had been called down to fix was in one of the smaller rooms. A maintenance panel next to the bed had opened, and a tangle of wires spilled out. The electricity in the cabin was out.

"Who did this?" Saga said.

"Probably the passenger," Aavit replied. "Just fix it."

When the steward had gone, Saga took a look around. Whoever stayed in the room was otherwise meticulous; almost all personal belongings were out of sight. Saga peeked into one of the lockers and saw a stack of neatly folded clothing with a hat on top. A small wooden box contained what looked like cheap souvenirs—keyrings, a snow globe, a marble on a chain. The open maintenance hatch was very out of character.

Saga shined a flashlight into the mess behind the hatch. Beyond the wires lay something like a thick pipe. It had pushed a wire out of its socket. Saga checked that no wires were actually broken, then stuck a finger inside and touched the pipe. It was warm, and dimpled under her finger. Skidbladnir's slow pulse ran through it. Saga sat back on her heels. Parts of Skidbladnir shouldn't be here, not this far down. She re-attached the wiring, stuffed it back inside, and sealed the hatch with tape. She couldn't think of much else to do. A lot of the work here consisted of propping things up or taping them shut.

The departure alarm sounded; it was time to buckle in. Saga went back upstairs to her cabin in maintenance. The air up here was damp and warm. Despite the heat, sometimes thick clouds came out when Saga exhaled. It was one of the peculiarities of Skidbladnir, something to do with the outside, what they were passing through, when the ship swam between worlds.

The building's lower floors were reserved for passengers and cargo; Skidbladnir's body took up the rest. Saga's quarters were right above the passenger levels, where she could quickly move to fix whatever had broken in someone's room. And a lot of things broke. Skidbladnir was an old ship. The electricity didn't quite work everywhere, and the plumbing malfunctioned all the time. The cistern in the basement refilled itself at irregular intervals and occasionally flooded the cargo deck. Sometimes the ship refused to eat the refuse, and let it rot in its chute, so that Saga had to clean it out and dump it at the next landfall. Whenever there wasn't something to fix, Saga spent her time in her quarters.

The cramped room served as both bedroom and living room: a cot, a small table, a chair. The table was mostly taken up by a small fat television with a slot for videotapes at the bottom. The closed bookshelf above the table held twelve videotapes: two seasons of *Andromeda Station*. Whoever had worked here before had left them behind.

Saga lay down on her cot and strapped herself in. The ship shuddered violently. Then, with a groan, it went through the barrier and floated free in the void, and Saga could get out of the cot again. When she first boarded the ship, Aavit had explained it to her, although she didn't fully grasp it: the ship pushed through to an ocean under the other worlds, and swam through it, until they came to their destination. Like a seal swims from hole to hole in the ice, said Aavit, like something coming up for air every now and then. Saga had never seen a seal.

Andromeda Station drowned out the hum Skidbladnir made as it propelled itself through the space between worlds, and for just a moment, things felt normal. It was a stupid show, really: a space station somewhere that was the center of diplomatic relations, regularly invaded by non-human races or subject to internal strife, et cetera, et cetera. But it reminded Saga of home, of watching television with her friends, of the time before she sold herself into twenty tours of service. With no telephones and no computers, it was all she had for entertainment.

Season 2, episode 5: The Devil You Know.

The station encounters a species eerily reminiscent of demons in human mythology. At first everyone is terrified until it dawns on the captain that the "demons" are great lovers of poetry, and communicate in similes and metaphors. As soon as that is established, the poets on the station become the interpreters, and trade communications are established.

⋅ ∘ ● ∘ ⋅

In the middle of the sleep shift, Skidbladnir's hum sounded almost like a murmured song. As always, Saga dreamed of rushing through a space that wasn't a space, of playing in eddies and currents, of colors indescribable. There was a wild, wordless joy. She woke up bathing in sweat, reeling from alien emotion.

On the next arrival, Saga got out of the ship to help engineer Novik inspect the hull. Skidbladnir had materialized on what looked like the bottom of a shallow bowl under a purple sky. The sandy ground was littered with shells and fish bones. Saga and Novik made their way through the stream of passengers getting on and off; dockworkers dragged some crates up to the gates.

Saga had seen Skidbladnir arrive, once, when she had first gone into service. First it wasn't there, and then it was, heavy and solid, as if it had always been. From the outside, the ship looked like a tall and slender office building. The concrete was pitted and streaked, and all of the windows were covered with steel plates. Through the roof, Skidbladnir's claws and legs protruded like a plant, swaying gently in some unseen breeze. The building had no openings save the front gates, through which everyone passed. From the airlock in the lobby, one climbed a series of stairs to get to the passenger deck. Or, if you were Saga, climbed the spiral staircase that led up to the engine room and custodial services.

Novik took a few steps back and scanned the hull. A tall, bearded man in rumpled blue overalls, he looked only slightly less imposing outside than he did in the bowels of the ship. He turned to Saga. In daylight, his gray eyes were almost translucent.

"There," he said, and pointed to a spot two stories up the side. "We need to make a quick patch."

Saga helped Novik set up the lift that was attached to the side of the building, and turned the winch until they reached the point of damage. It was just a small crack, but deep enough that Saga could see something underneath—something that looked like skin. Novik took a look inside, grunted and had Saga hold the pail while he slathered putty over the crack.

"What was that inside?" Saga asked.

Novik patted the concrete. "There," he said. "You're safe again, my dear."

He turned to Saga. "She's always growing. It's going to be a problem soon."

Season 2, episode 8: Unnatural relations.

One of the officers on the station begins a relationship with a silicate-based alien life form. It's a love story doomed to fail, and it does: the officer walks into the life form's biosphere and removes her rebreather to make love to the life form. She lasts for two minutes.

Saga dreamed of the silicate creature that night, a gossamer thing with a voice like waves crashing on a shore. It sang to her; she woke up in the middle of the sleep shift and the song was still there. She put a hand on the wall. The concrete was warm.

She had always wanted to go on an adventure. It had been her dream as a child. She had watched shows like *Andromeda Station* and *The Sirius Reach* over and over again, dreaming of the day she would become an astronaut. She did research on how to become one. It involved hard work, studying, mental and physical perfection. She had none of that. She could fix things, that was all. Space had to remain a distant dream.

The arrival of the crab ships interrupted the scramble for outer space. They sailed not through space but some other dimension between worlds. When the first panic had subsided, and linguistic barriers had been overcome, trade agreements and diplomatic relations were established. The gifted, the rich and the ambitious went with the ships to faraway places. People like Saga went through their lives with a dream of leaving home.

Then one of the crab ships materialized in Saga's village. It must have been a fluke, a navigation error. The crew got out and deposited a boy who hacked and coughed and collapsed on the ground. A long-legged beaked creature with an angular accent asked the gathered crowd for someone who could fix things. Saga took a step forward. The tall human man in blue overalls looked at her with his stony gray eyes.

"What can you do?" he asked.

"Anything you need," Saga replied.

The man inspected her callused hands, her determined face, and nodded.

"You will do," he said. "You will do."

Saga barely said goodbye to her family and friends; she walked through the gates and never looked back.

The magic of it all faded over time. Now it was just work: fixing the electricity, taping hatches shut, occasionally shoveling refuse when the plumbing broke. Everything broke in this place. Of all the ships that sailed the worlds, Skidbladnir was probably the oldest and most decrepit. It didn't go to any interesting places either, just deserts and little towns and islands far away from civilization. Aavit the steward often complained that it deserved a better job. The passengers complained of the low standard, the badly cooked food. The only one who didn't complain was Novik. He referred to Skidbladnir not as an it, but as a she.

Over the next few stops, the electricity outages happened more and more frequently. Every time, living tubes had intertwined with the wiring and short-circuited it. At first it was only on the top passenger level. Then it spread to the next one. It was as if Skidbladnir was sending down parts of itself through the entire building. Only tendrils, at first. Then Saga was called down to fix the electricity in a passenger room, where the bulb in the ceiling was blinking on and off. She opened the maintenance hatch and an eye stared back at her. Its pupil was large and round, the iris red. It watched her with something like interest. She waved a hand in front of it. The eye tracked her movement. Aavit had said that Skidbladnir was a dumb beast. But the eye that met Saga's did not seem dumb.

Saga went upstairs, past her own quarters, and for the first time knocked on the door to engineering. After what seemed like an age, the door opened. Engineer Novik had to stoop to see outside. His face was smudged with something dark.

"What do you want?" he said, not unkindly.

"I think something is happening," Saga said.

Novik followed her down to the passenger room and peered through the hatch.

"This is serious," he mumbled.

"What is?" Saga asked.

"We'll talk later," Novik said and strode off.

"What do I do?" Saga shouted after him.

"Nothing," he called over his shoulder.

Novik had left the door to the captain's office ajar. Saga positioned herself outside and listened. She had never really seen the captain; she hid in her office, doing whatever a captain did. Saga knew her only as a shadowy alto.

"We can't take the risk," the captain said inside. "Maybe it'll hold for a while longer. You could make some more room, couldn't you? Some extensions?"

"It won't be enough," Novik replied. "She'll die before long. Look, I know a place where we could find a new shell."

"And how would you do that? It's unheard of. It's lived in here since it was a youngling, and it'll die in here. Only wild crabs can change shells."

"I could convince her to change. I'm sure of it."

"And where is this place?"

"An abandoned city," Novik replied. "It's out of our way, but it'd be worth it."

"No," the captain said. "Better sell it on. It won't survive such a swap, and I'll be ruined. If things have gone this far, I need to sell it to someone who can take it apart."

"And I'm telling you she has a chance," Novik said. "Please don't pass her on to some butcher."

"You're too attached," the captain retorted. "I'll sell it on and use the money as down payment for a new ship. We'll have to start small again, but we've done it before."

Season 1, episode 11: The Natives Are Restless.

The lower levels of Andromeda Station are populated by the destitute: adventurers who didn't find what they were looking for, merchants who lost their cargo, drug addicts, failed prophets. They unite under a leader who promises to topple the station's regime. They sweep through the upper levels, murdering and pillaging in their path. They are gunned down by security. The station's captain and the rebel leader meet in the middle of the carnage. Was it worth it? the captain asks. Always, says the rebel.

There was a knock on Saga's door after her shift. It was Novik, with an urgent look on his face.

"It's time you saw her," he said.

They walked down the long corridor from Saga's cabin to the engine room. The passage seemed somehow smaller than before, as if the walls had contracted. When Novik opened the door at the end of the corridor, a wave of warm air with a coppery tang wafted out.

Saga had imagined a huge, dark cavern. What Novik led her through was a cramped warren of tubes, pipes and wires, all intertwined with tendrils of that same grayish substance she had found in the hatches downstairs. As they moved forward, the tendrils thickened into ropes, then meaty cables. The corridor narrowed, so tight in spots that Novik and Saga had to push through it sideways.

"Here," Novik said, and the corridor suddenly opened up.

The space was dimly lit by a couple of electric lights; the shapes that filled the engine room were only suggested, not illuminated. Round curves, glistening metal intertwined with that gray substance. Here, a slow triple beat shook the floor. There was a faint wet noise of something shifting.

"This is she," Novik said. "This is Skidbladnir."

He gently took Saga's hand and guided it to a gray outcrop. It was warm under her fingers, and throbbed: one two three, one two three.

"This is where I interface with her," Novik said.

"Interface?" Saga asked.

"Yes. We speak. I tell her where to go. She tells me what it's like." Novik gently patted the gray skin. "She has been poorly for some time now. She's growing too big for her shell. But she didn't say how bad it was. I under- stood when you showed me where she's grown into the passenger deck."

One two three, one two three, thrummed the pulse under Saga's hand.

"I know you were eavesdropping," Novik said. "The captain and the steward will sell her off to someone who will take her apart for meat. She's old, but she's not that old. We can find her a new home."

"Can I interface with her?" Saga said.

"She says you already have," Novik said.

And Saga heard it: the voice, like waves crashing on a shore, the voice she had heard in her dream. It brought an image of a vast ocean, swimming through darkness from island to island. Around her, a shell that sat uncomfortably tight. Her whole body hurt. Her joints and tendrils felt swollen and stiff.

Novik's hand on her shoulder brought her back to the engine room.

"You see?" he said.

"We have to save her," Saga said.

Novik nodded.

• • ◉ • •

They arrived at the edge of a vast and cluttered city under a dark sky. The wreckage of old ships dotted the desert that surrounded the city; buildings like Skidbladnir's shell, cracked cylinders, broken discs and pyramids.

They had let off all passengers and cargo at the previous stop. Only the skeleton crew remained: the captain, the steward, Novik, and Saga. They gathered in the lobby's air lock, and Saga saw the captain for the very first time. She was tall, built from shadows and strange angles. Her face kept slipping out of focus. Saga only assumed her as a "she" from the soft alto voice.

"Time to meet the mechanics," the captain said.

Novik clenched and unclenched his fists. Aavit looked at him with one cold sideways eye and clattered its beak.

"You'll see reason," it said.

The air outside was cold and thin. Novik and Saga put on their face masks; Aavit and the captain went as they were. The captain's shroud fluttered in an icy breeze that brought waves of fine dust.

There was a squat office building among the wrecks. Its door slid open as they approached. Inside was a small room cluttered with obscure machinery. The air was warmer in here. Another door stood open at the end of the room, and the captain strode toward it. When Saga and Novik made to follow, Aavit held a hand up.

"Wait here," it said, its voice barely audible in the thin atmosphere.

The other door closed behind them.

Saga looked at Novik, who looked back at her. He nodded. They turned as one and ran back toward Skidbladnir.

Saga looked over her shoulder as they ran. Halfway to the ship, she could see the captain emerge from the office, a mass of tattered fabric that undulated over the ground, more quickly than it should. Saga ran as fast as she could.

She had barely made it inside the doors when Novik closed them with a resounding boom and turned the great wheel that locked them. They waited for what seemed like an eternity as the air lock cycled. Something hit the doors with a thud, again and again, and made them shudder. As the air lock finally opened, Novik tore his mask off. His face was pale and sweaty underneath.

"They'll find something to break the doors down," he said. "We have to move quickly."

Saga followed him up the spiral stairs, through the passages, to the engine room. As she stood with her hands on her knees, panting, Novik pushed himself into Skidbladnir's gray mass face first. It enveloped him with a sigh. The departure siren sounded.

Saga had never experienced a passage without being strapped down. The floor suddenly tilted and sent her reeling into the gray wall. It was sticky and warm to the touch. Saga's ears popped. The floor tilted the other way. She went flying headfirst into the other wall and hit her nose on something hard. Then the floor righted itself. Skidbladnir was through to the void between the worlds.

Saga gingerly felt her nose. It was bleeding, but didn't seem broken. Novik stepped back from the wall. He looked at Saga over his shoulder.

"You'll have to do the captain's job now," he said.

"What?" Saga asked.

"That's how it works. You read the map to me while I steer her."

"What do I do?"

"You go up to the captain's cabin. There's a map. There's a city on the map. It's on the lower levels. It's abandoned. Tall spires. You'll see it."

Saga went up to the captain's cabin. The door was open. The space inside was filled by an enormous construction. Orbs of different sizes hung from the ceiling, sat on the ground, were mounted on sticks. Some of the orbs had little satellites. Some of them were striped, some marbled, some dark. In the space between them hung swirls of light that didn't seem attached to anything. Close to the center, a rectangular object was suspended in the air. It looked like a tiny model of Skidbladnir.

There was a crackle. From a speaker near the ceiling, Novik's voice said, "Step into the map. Touch the spheres. You'll see."

Saga carefully stepped inside. The swirls gave off small shocks as she grazed them, and though they seemed gossamer, they didn't budge. She put her hand on one of the spheres, and her vision filled with the image of islands on green water. A red sun looked down on pale trees. She touched another, one that hung from the ceiling, and saw a bustling night-time town, shapes moving between houses, two moons shining in the sky. She touched sphere after sphere: vast desert landscapes, cities, forests, villages. The lower levels, Novik had said. Saga crouched down and felt the miniature worlds that littered the floor like marbles. Near the far corner, a dark sphere was a little larger than the others. As she touched it, there was an image of a city at dawn. It was still, silent. Tall white spires stretched toward the horizon. There were no lights, no movement. Some of the spires were broken.

"I think I found it," she said aloud.

"Good," Novik said through the speaker. "Now draw a path."

Saga stood up, ducking the electrified swirls. She made her way into the center of the room where Skidbladnir hung suspended on seemingly nothing at all.

"How?" she asked.

"Just draw it," Novik replied.

Saga touched Skidbladnir. It gave off a tiny chime. She traced her finger in the air. Her finger left a bright trail. She made her way across the room, carefully avoiding the glowing swirls, until she reached the sphere on the floor. As she touched the sphere, another chime sounded. The trail her finger had left seemed to solidify.

"Good," said Novik in the speaker. "Setting the course."

Saga wandered through the empty ship. There was no telling how long the journey would take, but on the map it was from the center of the room to the very edge, so perhaps that meant a long wait. She had gone back to the engine room, but the door was shut now. Whatever Novik did inside, while interfacing with Skidbladnir, he wanted to do undisturbed.

The main doors in the lobby had buckled inward, but not broken. The captain had used considerable force to try to get back in. The passenger rooms were empty. In the lounge, the pool table's balls had gone over the edge and lay scattered on the floor. There was food in the mess hall; Saga made herself a meal of bread and cheese from the cabinet for human food. Then she went up to her quarters to wait.

Season 2 finale: All We Ever Wanted Was Everything.

The station is closing due to budget reasons; Earth has cut off funding because station management refuses to go along with their alien-unfriendly policies. No other race offers to pick up the bill, since they have started up stations of their own. In a bittersweet montage, the captain walks through the station and reminisces on past events. The episode ends with the captain leaving on a shuttle. An era is over. The alien navigator puts a claw on the captain's shoulder: a new station is opening, and the captain is welcome to join. But it'll never be an earthlike place. It'll never be quite like home.

Skidbladnir arrived in a plaza at the city's heart. The air was breathable and warm. Tall spires rose up into the sky. The ground beneath them was cracked open by vegetation. Novik got out first. He put his hands on his hips and surveyed the plaza. He nodded to himself.

"This will do," he said. "This will do."

"What happens now?" Saga asked.

"We stand back and wait," Novik replied. "Skidbladnir knows what to do." He motioned for Saga to follow him.

They sat down at the edge of the plaza, well away from Skidbladnir.

Saga put her bags down; she hadn't brought much, just her clothes, some food, and the first season of *Andromeda Station*. Perhaps she would find a new tape player somewhere.

They waited for a long time. Novik didn't say much; he sat with his legs crossed in front of him, gazing up at the spires.

At dusk, Skidbladnir's walls cracked open. Saga understood why Novik had positioned them so far away from the building; great lumps of concrete and steel fell down and shook the ground as the building shrugged and shuddered. The tendrils that waved from the building's cracked roof stiffened and trembled. They seemed to lengthen. Walls fell down, steel windows sloughed off, as Skidbladnir slowly extricated herself from her shell. She crawled out from the top, taking great lumps of concrete with her. Saga had expected her to land on the ground with an almighty thud. But she made no noise at all.

Free of her house, Skidbladnir was a terror and wonder to behold. Her body was long and curled; her multitude of eyes gleamed in the starlight. Her tendrils waved in the warm air as if testing it. Some of the tendrils looked shrunken and unusable. Saga also saw that patches of Skidbladnir's body weren't as smooth as the rest of her; they were dried and crusted. Here and there, fluid oozed from long scratches in her skin.

Next to Saga, Novik made a muffled noise. He was crying.

"Go, my love," he whispered. "Find yourself a new home."

Skidbladnir's tendrils felt the buildings around the plaza. Finally, they wrapped themselves around the tallest building, a gleaming thing with a spiraled roof, and Skidbladnir pulled herself up the wall. Glass tumbled to the ground as Skidbladnir's tendrils shot through windows to pull herself up. She tore through the roof with a thunderous noise. There was a moment when she supported her whole body on her tendrils, suspended in the air; she almost toppled over the side. Then, with what sounded like a sigh, she lowered herself into the building. Saga heard the noise of collapsing concrete as Skidbladnir's body worked to make room for itself. Eventually, the noise subsided. Skidbladnir's arms hung down the building's side like a crawling plant.

"What now?" Saga said.

She looked sideways at Novik. He smiled at her.

"Now she's free," he said. "Free to go wherever she pleases."

"And what about us?" Saga asked. "Where do we go?"

"With her, of course," Novik replied.

"There's no map," Saga said. "Nothing to navigate by. And the machinery? Your engine room?"

"That was only ever needed to make her go where we wanted her to," Novik said. "She doesn't need that now."

"Wait," Saga said. "What about me? What if I want to go home?"

Novik raised an eyebrow. "Home?"

A chill ran down Saga's back. "Yes, home."

Novik shrugged. "Perhaps she'll stop by there. There's no telling what she'll do. Come on."

He got up and started walking toward Skidbladnir and her new shell. Saga remained on the ground. Her body felt numb. Novik went up to the building's front door, which slid open, and he disappeared inside.

Season 1, episode 5: Adrift.

The captain's wife dies. She goes into space on a private shuttle to consign the body to space. While in space, the shuttle malfunctions. The captain finds herself adrift between the stars. The oxygen starts to run out. As the captain draws what she thinks are her last breaths, she records one final message to her colleagues. Forgive me for what I did and didn't do, she says. I did what I thought was best.

• ◦ ● ◦ •

Life on the new Skidbladnir was erratic. Novik spent most of his time interfaced, gazing into one of Skidbladnir's great eyes in a hall at the heart of the building. Saga spent much of her time exploring. This had been someone's home once, an apartment building of sorts. There were no doors or windows, only maze-like curved hallways that with regular intervals expanded into rooms. Some of them were empty, others furnished with oddly shaped tables, chairs and beds. Some wall-to-wall cabinets held knickknacks and scrolls written in a flowing, spiraled script. There were no means to cook food in any way Saga could recognize. She made a nest in one of the smaller rooms close to where Novik worked with Skidbladnir. The walls gave off a soft glow that dimmed from time to time; Saga fell into the habit of sleeping whenever that happened. Drifting off into sleep, she sometimes thought she could hear voices speaking in some vowel-rich tongue, but they faded as she listened for them.

Skidbladnir did seem concerned for Saga and Novik. She stopped at the edge of towns every now and then, where Saga could breathe and was able to trade oddities she found in the building that was now her new home for some food and tools. But mostly they were adrift between worlds. It seemed that Skidbladnir found her greatest joy in coasting the invisible eddies and waves of the void. Every time they stopped somewhere, Saga considered getting off to try her luck. There might be another ship that could take her home. But these places were too strange, too far-flung. It was as if Skidbladnir was avoiding civilization. Perhaps she sensed that Aavit and the old captain might be after them. That thought gnawed at Saga every time they stopped somewhere. But there was such a multitude of worlds out there, and no one ever seemed to recognize them.

She tore the *Andromeda Station* tapes apart and hung them like garlands over the walls, traced her finger along them, mumbled the episodes to herself, until Skidbladnir shuddered and she took cover for the next passage.

Each time Skidbladnir pushed through to another world, it was more and more violent.

"Is she going to hold?" Saga asked Novik on one of the rare occasions he came out from his engine room to eat.

Novik was quiet for a long moment. "For a time," he said.

"What are you going to do when she dies?" Saga asked.

"We'll go together, me and her," he replied.

One day, improbably, Skidbladnir arrived outside a place Saga recognized. A town, not her hometown, but not so far away from it.

Novik was nowhere to be seen. He was sleeping or interfaced with the ship. Saga walked downstairs, and the front door slid open for her. Outside, a crowd had gathered. An official-looking man walked up to Saga as she came outside.

"What's this ship?" he said. "It's not on our schedule. Are you the captain?"

"This is Skidbladnir," Saga said. "She's not on anyone's schedule. We don't have a captain."

"Well," the official said. "What's your business?"

"Just travel," Saga said.

She looked back at Skidbladnir. This was her chance to get off, to go home. Novik would barely notice. She could return to her life. And do what, exactly? The gathered crowd were all comprised of humans, their faces dull, their eyes shallow.

"Do you have a permit?" the official asked.

"Probably not," Saga said.

"I'll have to seize this ship," the official said. "Bring out whoever is in charge."

Saga gestured at Skidbladnir's walls. "She is."

"This is unheard of," the official said. He turned away and spoke into a comm radio.

Saga looked at the little town, the empty-faced crowd, the gray official.

"Okay. I am the captain," she said. "And we're leaving."

She turned and walked back to Skidbladnir. The door slid open to admit her. The hallway inside thrummed with life. She put a hand on the wall.

"Let's go," she said. "Wherever you want."

Pilot episode: One Small Step

The new captain of Andromeda Station arrives. Everything is new and strange; the captain only has experience of Earth politics and is baffled by the various customs and rituals practiced by the other aliens on the station. A friendly janitor who happens to be cleaning the captain's cabin offers to give her a tour of all the levels. The janitor, it turns out, has been on the station for most of his life and knows all of the station's quirks. She's confusing as hell at first, he says. But once you know how to speak to her, she will take good care of you.

Saga took the tapes down and rolled them up. It was time to be the captain of her own ship, now. A ship that went where it wanted to, but a ship nonetheless. She could set up proper trade. She could learn new languages. She could fix things. She was good at fixing things.

One day Skidbladnir would fail. But until then, Saga would swim through the void with her.

ACKNOWLEDGEMENTS

This book grew out of a conversation I had with Tachyon Publications publisher Jacob Weisman at the 2022 Chicago World Science Fiction Convention, where we spent some time discussing the two New Space Opera anthologies that I co-edited with Gardner Dozois. I am indebted to Jacob and to the whole Tachyon team for the chance to work on this book. Assembling anthologies is a strange business, and I am deeply grateful to everyone who makes it possible, especially all of the writers and their representatives, whose work appears here. As always, my thanks to my agent Howard Morhaim who has stood with me for all of these years, and extra special thanks to Marianne, Jessica, and Sophie, who really are the reason why I keep doing this.

Jonathan Strahan (born 1964 in Belfast, Northern Ireland) is an editor, podcaster, critic, and occasional publisher. His family moved to Perth, Western Australia in 1968, and he graduated from the University of Western Australia with a Bachelor of Arts in 1986.

In 1990 Strahan co-founded *Eidolon: The Journal of Australian Science Fiction and Fantasy*, and worked on it as co-editor and co-publisher until 1999. He was also co-publisher of Eidolon Books which published Robin Pen's *The Secret Life of Rubber-Suit Monsters*, Howard Waldrop's *Going Home Again*, Storm Constantine's *The Thorn Boy*, and Terry Dowling's *Blackwater Days*.

In 1997 Strahan moved to Oakland, California to work for *Locus: The Newspaper of the Science Fiction Field* as an assistant editor. He wrote a regular review column for the magazine until March 1998 when he returned to Australia. In early 1999 Jonathan resumed reviewing and editorial work for *Locus*, and was later promoted to Reviews Editor. Other reviews have appeared in *Eidolon, Eidolon: SF Online*, and *Foundation*. Strahan has won the Hugo Award, World Fantasy Award, the Aurealis Award, the Aurealis Convenor's Award for Excellence, the William Atheling Jr Award for Criticism and Review, the Australian National Science Fiction Convention's Ditmar Award, and the Peter McNamara Achievement Award.

In 1999 Strahan founded The Coode Street Press (currently inactive), which published the one-shot review 'zine *The Coode Street Review of Science Fiction* and co-published Terry Dowling's *Antique Futures*.

Strahan won the World Fantasy Award in 2010 for his work as an editor, and his anthologies have won the Locus Award for Best Anthology three times (2008, 2010, 2013) and the Aurealis Award seven times.

As a freelance editor, Jonathan has edited or co-edited more than seventy anthologies, and twenty single-author story collections which have been published in Australia, the United Kingdom, and the United States. He also works as a consulting editor for Tor.com where he acquires and edits original novellas (Tor.com Publishing) and short fiction (Tor.com).

Strahan currently produces and co-hosts *the Coode Street Podcast* with Gary K. Wolfe (May 2010-present), which won the Hugo Award in 2021, and has been nominated for the British Science Fiction Award and the Ditmar. He also produced and co-hosted the Coode Street Roundtable with Ian Mond and James Bradley.

Strahan married former *Locus* Managing Editor Marianne Jablon in 1999 and they live in Perth, Western Australia with their two daughters, Jessica and Sophie.